THE MOON BEYOND THE FIRE

JAYCEE ANDERSON

THE MOON BEYOND THE FIRE

JAYCEE ANDERSON

CRYSTAL UNITY SERIES: BOOK 2

CONTENTS

PROLOGUE – THE SOUL CONTRACT SESSION

Flipping the pages of a docket, the secretary for the Shepherds of Soul Contracts entered the vestibule. "Morgan, Morgan, Kenton, and Reeves, please stand by to present yourself to the magistrate. I am Secretary Three, and I will be delivering you to Shepherd One."

The room was circular with bronze panels so perfectly lined up that one could not tell where one door started and the other ended. Three panels of equal distance opened up.

An older, statuesque woman with a long, white braid hanging over her shoulder stepped over the threshold. She wrapped her coral patchwork cardigan tighter around her floral dress as she looked around to orient herself. Vague memories of being there before started to emerge.

"Mozelle Reeves. Is that correct?" the young, bald man confirmed.

"Yes, sir," she said, rubbing her arms to warm herself. She gave a slight bow.

He placed a checkmark on his clipboard. "Please follow me. The rest of you, please wait until I come to get you."

He grabbed his yellow robe and turned on his heel. She

followed him down a long dark hall, but their path lit up as they made their way to the next room. He guided her to a pitch-black room except for a single light that hung over a long folding table in the center.

"Please stand here," he directed, positioning her in an area the light didn't reach. "I'll be back with another one," he explained and walked out of the room.

He lifted his clipboard as he reentered the vestibule. "You," he said dryly, as he pointed to a man with tapered brown hair, brown eyes, tan skin, and an average build. The man, wearing a dark blue suit, stepped forward. His jaw was set.

"Chris Morgan?"

"Yes, sir," he said, puffing out his chest a bit as if to prove he wasn't scared.

Secretary Three made a checkmark and brought Chris to the same room as Mozelle, placing him near her, but not near enough for them to see each other. He explained he would be back one more time before the session was to begin.

He made his way back and stood in front of a panel with a man and woman standing inside. Their hands, wrists, and fore-arms were bound together with red, green, blue, and white cords. "The two of you."

The thirty-something-year-old man with soft green eyes and short, honey-blond hair grabbed the beautiful woman's hand and guided her through the door. Her lush brown hair flowed behind her as she moved.

"Mr. Wade Kenton and Mrs. Robin Morgan?"

Giddy, the two of them looked at each other and smiled. "Yes, sir," they said together.

"Something amusing?"

They stopped gazing into each other's eyes, then stood tall as if waiting for further instruction. "No, sir. We apologize."

"Lovers are the worst," Secretary Three complained. "Please come with me," he said, annoyed.

Once the four were in position, Secretary Three advised Shepherd One that the session could begin.

"Step forward into the light, please," Secretary Three commanded.

All four moved into view. They looked each other up and down with judgment and anger.

A man wearing a blue velvet hooded robe took a seat at the table. The single light shone from up above and created an even deeper shadow over the man's hooded face. "I am Shepherd One."

Secretary Three laid out four manila files, some thicker than others, and moved them about as if deciding on the order to present them.

Shepherd One drew a deep sigh and cleared his throat. "According to the document I have before me, you all died in a fire when Chris," the shadowy figure pointed to Chris, "barged in and interrupted a soul preparation ceremony that led to him getting hit with the bifurcating lightning strike that Mozelle had harnessed with her wand. Half of the strike struck him in the shoulder, and the other strike hit the mirror behind him, ricocheting, then striking Mozelle in her shoulder. He then fell forward onto the altar with candles and oils burning, setting the room ablaze."

Chris looked around as if wondering if he should be the one to speak up. "Yes, sir," Chris said.

"And Mozelle," the figure now pointed to her. "You are an oracle and used said wand to, for lack of a better term, brand Robin and Wade as part of a ritual to help them find each other in their next life. This was also performed while Robin was still married to Chris."

"That's correct," Mozelle said.

"And you felt that Robin and Wade," he stretched his arm in their direction as they stood together, the cords binding arms and wrists, "are a mated pair."

"I do."

"And you performed three different rituals at that time with the guidance of your grandmother's journals that she gifted to you."

"Yes, that's correct."

"The first involved encasing their love and memories in a twinned crystal, assuring that if they come into close proximity of the crystal, it will playback how and why they fell in love. The second was a handfasting ceremony that spiritually married them, hence the ribbons. And the final was the branding portion of the ritual, which required you to place an eight-sided star on their chests so the scars would show up in their next lives as birthmarks and become beacons or homing devices of sorts."

"Yes, that's correct."

"And it was during the last ritual that this all happened."

"Yes."

"And the reason you chose to do this ritual now, even while Robin here was still married to Chris, is because Robin was dying from a cancerous brain tumor."

"That's right."

"Mozelle, you seem to be the most senior person here. Please fill me in on anything I'm missing," the shadowy figure encouraged.

"This is all my fault," she began, splaying her fingers across her chest.

"No! It's *their* fault!" Chris spoke up and pointed to Robin and Wade, who stood holding hands, wide-eyed.

"I'm the one who performed the ritual," Mozelle redirected.

"Maybe if Chris wasn't such a raging asshole alcoholic, I wouldn't have fallen for Wade," Robin cut in.

"Well, I wouldn't say that's necessarily true," Mozelle corrected. "You guys *are* a mated pair, probably since we were here last time," she said, then realized they didn't understand what she was saying. "You know, prior to the life we just left. If you're unaware, meeting with the Shepherds of Soul Contracts happens every time your soul leaves your earthly vessel. As far as we know, you might have been a mated pair for over several lifetimes."

"Give me a break with all your mystic crap," Chris said.

"Says the man standing in front of the Shepherds of Soul Contracts," Wade finally chimed in.

"You can go to Hell," Chris snapped.

"You and Robin should have never married." Wade pointed at Chris. He wasn't going to hold back. "You were wrong for each other from the beginning, and you know it. You let your controlling parents get the better of you, and if anyone here is to blame, it's you."

"I take all the responsibility," Robin said. "I, too, knew we should have never gotten married, but at the same time, if we hadn't, then Lyndsey wouldn't have been born. I was the one who opened my heart to Wade. But when we're together," she said, turning to him and gazing into his eyes, "it's like this powerful force can't be resisted."

Wade looked her over and brushed her hair behind her ear. He placed his hand under her chin and lifted as if allowing himself passage to bask in her captivating eyes. "Look at you. You're healthy and radiant," he said.

"I think I'm going to be sick," Chris spat.

Shepherd One stood up. He was a commanding figure, so everyone fell silent.

He walked into the light. He was an older man with deep wrinkles, a Grecian nose, and stood well over six feet. "That's enough! There is nothing you can do to change things. Now, there is one more thing I need to do, and that's check your marks." He walked over to Robin and Wade. They lowered their shirts, prompting him to lean down and take a closer look. "Uh-huh, okay."

He then turned to Mozelle. "Let me see where you were struck. And the same goes for you, Chris."

Mozelle removed her cardigan.

"Okay, interesting. When you were struck by lightning, it resulted in a branching pattern," he observed, then moved over to Chris, who had already removed his coat and unbuttoned his dress shirt. "Looks like Mozelle's, but reversed. Probably because hers was reflected off the mirror."

He moved back to his seat behind the table. "I've concluded the intake process, and I have made my decision. You will all reincarnate in the same year—looks like that will be 2002, when Farrah gets pregnant—"

"Farrah gets pregnant? Aww, I'm so happy for her!" Mozelle said with excitement in her voice.

"Mozelle, you are interrupting, but yes, your request for your infertile niece has been granted," he said through his lashes. "Where were we?"

"2002, sir," Secretary Three said from within the darkness.

"Right. So write that down—2002. You will be in close proximity to your daughter, Lyndsey, and you can go from there. I'm not here to tell you your future, and we will not be discussing any modifications. I need you to sign here. After you walk through those doors, you will have no memory of this, or your past life."

One by one, each signed their contract, and walked out the door.

1

THE HOURGLASS

SUMMER 2004

Even though the merciless flames that had taken her parents and her mother's caretakers had now been extinguished for over five years, Lyndsey's anger remained stoked. Now eighteen, she stood before the floor-length mirror in her bedroom situated in an isolated part of the estate owned by her grandparents, Alastair and Elizabeth Morgan, an area she referred to as The Repository. The name was consistent with how they treated her—like an item they possessed but didn't know what to do with, or where to put it. She knew they tried their best, but they were older and didn't understand the needs of a millennial, let alone a marred one.

Her desire to hide in plain sight followed a tedious daily routine of applying stage foundation on her neck to cover the disfiguring burn scars that stretched from her jaw, along her neck, down her shoulder blade, and eventually ceasing in the middle of her back. This entire process was an attempt to stay under the radar of double takes and rude comments at school. She stepped closer to the mirror, pulled her long brown hair aside, and gently moved her fingers along the fresh mask to judge the integrity of the façade. No discoloration would allow her to move to the next phase—the choosing of the turtleneck. She had a spectrum of colors to choose from, each responsible for matching her mood and the season.

She moved about her closet, dragging her hand along the hangers that held the day's status. She deferred to her self-image scale, which ranged from *visceral disgust* to *nasty* to *yuck* and at the very top—*meh*. On this day, she felt pretty good, so *meh* usually translated to brighter colors. It was July, so a bright blue turtleneck would be the winner.

As the fabric passed over her turbulent skin, she winced at the nerves firing off mixed signals of prickly and numb. She wondered if the sensation would ever cease. After another trip to the mirror, she smirked in satisfaction as she swiveled. A breeze that flowed through her window changed everything, however.

Her curtains undulated, and sunlight spilled in, illuminating the pristine twin crystal she had found just after the fire. It shimmered as it bathed in the rays, and she couldn't help but stare at it, even though it triggered her to remember that haunting day—five years, one month, and two days prior.

Transfixed, she brushed her fingers over her scar as the memory of the pain she felt when the burning banister crashed down onto her back, resurfaced. She recalled trying to reach her parents, who were in Mozelle's room, even as flames stretched along the ceiling. She had been rendered powerless after being struck, forcing her to abandon her parents as she ran out of the house—on fire.

But it was the events that led up to the fire that made her question which pain was worse. She clenched her teeth as she recalled each holler that escaped her mouth during those morphine-ladened days filled with torturous baths where they abraded her scabs and agonizingly redressed her wounds—all, she realized later, because her mother had fallen in love with a man who was not her father.

I live every damned day of my life with physical reminders of the choices you made over a stupid crush. We had all made our peace with you dying when you were unconscious for two days. But then you rally back and confess your love? She scoffed, then walked over to the window to close it, halting the breeze. *Action and reaction —it's all over a chain of events.*

Had Mom not confessed to Wade, Mozelle would not have performed what I later discovered was a lover's reincarnation ritual. Had their behavior seemed normal, I wouldn't have called Dad, urging him to come home. He wouldn't have arrived in a panic.

She pressed the window's latch closed, adding far more pressure than needed.

He wouldn't have walked in on them, becoming so shocked over what Mozelle was doing with Robin and Wade, that he fell onto the candle and oil-filled altar. Action and reaction.

She shoved herself away from the windowsill.

I wouldn't have found the journal and that damn crystal that miraculously survived the fire because there would have been no need for it.

She sighed deeply and grasped the top of her hair, exasperated.

Dad, who is as much a victim in all this as I am, would still be alive, and we would have been a normal family who would've missed her terribly. Instead, I'm left here all alone to live out a life that had been full of potential, beauty, and love, but is now a life of pervasive darkness, depression, dread, and unimaginable loneliness.

Flashes of her falling to her knees, screaming and tearing at her hair when she discovered four body bags on the front lawn, assaulted her mind.

Her desire to get answers had become overwhelming, as Mozelle's journal had remained unread for so long. After a year of working up the courage, she'd gone back to her old home, now ruins, and opened up the journal. She'd discovered things she wished she hadn't. The purpose of the crystal, why her mom and Wade's arms were bound with cords, and the reason behind it all—to find each other in their next life and boldly continue their love affair.

Seething, she grabbed the pristine crystal. *This encases the memories of their love, which will come back if they touch it.* She raised the crystal to watch the sunlight scatter through its facets. *How can something so beautiful be such the opposite? If I didn't have other plans for you, I would obliterate you with a hammer, crushing all the memories infused in this thing.* She slammed the crystal back down.

Now miserable, her self-image ranking plummeted from *meh* to *visceral disgust*, and she stormed back to her closet. A black turtleneck would now be the presiding champion.

She searched her closet, then remembered she had worn the last of her black turtlenecks a couple of days prior. She headed to the laundry room. Finding the shirt was something the staff could have easily done, but she never let them handle her belongings or go into her room.

She walked through corridors of the estate that presented itself like a museum, minus the velvet ropes and stuffy, white-gloved tour guides. The Repository was just that—the area where priceless artifacts and artwork from all over the world were placed to be forgotten. But even in The Repository, every item had its place, just in case someone happened to venture off and turn up there.

She supposed that was why she'd ended up in the more isolated part of the house. Perhaps they'd thought they were doing her a favor, and over time, she believed that to be true as well. It gave her the space to research more of Mozelle's beliefs and craft. Once she read the journal and thought back on the events of that fateful night, she became a believer herself. And the time spent in seclusion offered her the ideal setting to contrive a plan against mother and that lover of hers when they inevitably reincarnate.

She rummaged through the dryer, tossing out the brightly colored turtlenecks and collecting the dark ones. She grabbed one of the black ones, wincing as she exchanged blue for black, and left to go back to her room.

As she hurried down the hallway, she stopped. She turned on her heel and tilted her head, raising her eyebrow. Several items had been rearranged as if strategically hiding the one artifact that intrigued her most—an ornate hourglass.

She recalled the first time she saw the hourglass. It was shortly after she and Alastair had revisited the burn site. Elizabeth had been yelling at Alastair over decorative choices.

It was a sunny afternoon when the two of them returned. The sound of her grandmother's heels clicking against the white porcelain floor in rapid secession echoed in the dormant hallway of The Repository.

"This has no place over there. It needs to be put in the hallway over here," Elizabeth argued.

She cracked open her bedroom door at the unusual sound of sadness in Elizabeth's voice. Her eyes grew big as Elizabeth walked by with an hourglass caught in her white-knuckled grip. Her short gray hair fell forward as she firmly arranged the items in such a way that the hourglass faded into anonymity.

Alastair stood tall behind her with one arm crossed, the other rubbing the back of his neck. "Really? Here?" he asked, removing the hand from his neck to point at the piece. "This gift is very meaningful to me, from a time before you and I even met. You know that."

She rested her hands on her hips just below her blue and white pinstriped blouse. "Which is my point. We're not getting rid of it, but it's like, what? A gift from forty years ago? It's like I'm competing with a ghost," she snapped, raising her arms in frustration.

"I don't know why you feel there's a competition," Alastair said, reaching toward her shoulders as if to reassure her.

She shoved his hands away from her. "Gee," she said, putting her finger to her lips, "I don't know—because you need still need trinkets like this to keep her memory alive? When heaven knows there are daily reminders of her."

"Elizabeth!" Alastair growled in warning. He gritted his teeth as he mumbled something to her, Lyndsey couldn't make out.

Lyndsey's eyes darted about as she tried to figure out who they were talking about.

He swept his hands through his collar-length salt-and-pepper hair. "The hourglass is more than just about her. It's about what happened on that trip and the events that followed. It was life changing. Which, by the way, includes you, and I think you know that. So, let's compromise. We can keep it in this part of the house, but I want it here," he said as he placed it in the forefront.

"Whatever," Elizabeth said, throwing up her arms and walking away.

As soon as they went their separate directions, Lyndsey opened her door, cleared the path, and walked up to it. Her mouth dropped in surprise, and a chill ran down her spine. The hourglass was the same exact one depicted on the cover of Mozelle's journal. She shook her head. What the hell? Am I seeing this right? How can this be?

Later that day, Lyndsey went to Alastair to see if he could shed some light on her discovery. His response was short, but he did explain that he had acquired it from some nomadic group that lived along the Amazon. He'd been told it was special but had forgotten why he got it. She could believe it was from Brazil, but she knew that everything else he said was a lie.

Now, as she stood in the hallway, she dropped her shirts onto the floor, reached behind the collection of misfit relics, and pulled the hourglass from its new placement. She grasped the foot-tall artifact by one of four outer supports made of pewter. She had never actually handled it before. It was heavier than she'd expected. Her thumb glided along its deep engravings. The detail was so extraordinary that she couldn't help but wonder if its creation was of the same realm of transcendence as the journal. She blew the dust off the top, revealing a sun engraved on it, with a ribbon of the planets around the circumference. She inspected the bottom—the moon was engraved there, with a ribbon of stars encircling it. Under the top was a band divided into twelve sections, each representing a zodiac sign. The base had four sections depicting each of the four seasons. The posts that supported it were all different, too, and looked to represent the four main elements. One post was a waterfall landing on rocks. Another post was a hand fan, followed by a lantern, and lastly, a tree. The glass that held the pure white sand was so pristine and brilliant as it imprisoned colors like that of abalone.

Why does it feel like the Universe is telling me the time is now *to do the thing I've wanted to do since this whole nightmare started? It's time that I learn the ways of witchcraft. Because as much as I've read Mozelle's journal, it's not enough. Reading a spellbook is not like reading a cookbook.* She was going to have to seek help.

But it was the hourglass that was calling out to her more than anything. *Brazil? What's of such significance that this artifact is in my grandparents' home and on Mozelle's journal?* She recalled learning about Brazil in her social studies class right around the time of the fire, specifically, an article written by a professor from Stanford University. That, she decided, would be her starting point.

That afternoon, she reached out to the anthropology department to check on their summer hours. A phone interview wasn't going to do it for her. She wanted to speak with someone in person and see where it would take her.

August Cariso left the meeting with his department head and made his way toward his office. He huffed. "Can this day get any worse?" he asked aloud to no one in particular, shoving his hand through his hair and pursing his lips. "Through adversity comes growth. I have to keep remembering that," he said, disappointed the meeting had not gone the way he'd been expecting.

He pulled out his cell to vent to his former colleague and friend, Shani, but got her voicemail instead. Clenching his teeth, he flipped his phone shut. "Damn it!"

LYNDSEY WALKED into the reception area of the anthropology department and was greeted by a frumpy older woman with short orange hair—she probably thought it looked red—and thick reading glasses. Her resting bitch face came as a warning to Lyndsey that the woman was the gatekeeper, and if she were caught lying, she'd be made an example of.

"Who are you here to see?" Frumpy asked, looking Lyndsey up and down.

"Hi! I'm from *The Stanford Daily*, and we're doing a feature in the summer edition on the department's research on iconology," Lyndsey said, proud to be a daughter of an attorney who knew how to hold herself with confidence, even though on the inside, her stomach felt like it was twisting in knots.

"Hmmm. I didn't get any notices about this. Do you know which professor you're supposed to be seeing?" the woman asked as she stared at her computer. Her reading glasses reflected her scrolling through hundreds of emails.

Shit! Lyndsey thought. "Um, I'm not sure. I'm just a contributing writer. They just tell me where to go. Um, let me see if I can get a hold of them," she said, trying to remember the name of the professor who was in her social studies book all those years ago. She hadn't prepared for a gatekeeper. She just figured she could walk through the halls of the professors' offices and figure out his name that way.

"Okay. Why don't you take a seat and let me find out who you're supposed to interview?"

Concerned she might have hit a dead end, she decided to see how this would play out. Plus, she had too much pride to run away scared. She walked about the room and browsed the many books published by the professors in the department. One book that caught her eye was titled *Trees Through the Forest: An Examination of Myths and Folklore of the Amazon*, by August Cariso.

That's it. That's the book and author I read about.

She picked it up and hurried back to Frumpy, but she was on the phone. Never looking up at Lyndsey, she waved her thick, intimidating finger to stop Lyndsey's approach. Lyndsey tried pointing to the book, but that only provoked Frumpy to wave her hand and deepen her frown.

Lyndsey walked back over to the table where she'd found the book and took a seat on the accompanying couch. She studied the book, flipping it over. On the back of the jacket, there was a photo of him. He was a surprisingly young man, with medium-length dark hair, olive skin, and intense dark brown eyes. *He would be the perfect person to talk to about this.*

THE WALK from the department head's office was the breather August needed. Otherwise, he'd been liable to bite someone's head off. He stopped at the entrance to the department reception area and glared at a female student wearing a black turtleneck in the middle of summer as she thumbed through his book. He looked over at the wide-eyed receptionist, who shook her head and shrugged her shoulders.

"Is she here for me?" he mouthed to the receptionist. He stared at the student. *Is she one of my former students? I don't recognize her from my summer session.*

The receptionist shrugged her shoulders again and beckoned him over. "She said she's from the school paper but doesn't know who she's supposed to interview. I'm on the phone with the paper right now, but I'm on hold," she explained.

He looked over at her again, then pulled down on his collar. Her long hair and thick collar made her look like she was ready to build a snowman while it was ninety-five degrees outside. He felt sweat trickle down the back of his neck.

I'm so not in the mood for this. He walked over to her, looking over her shoulder. *No, she's never been in my class before. So why the interest in my book?*

He took a deep breath. "Can I help you?"

SHE JUMPED at the closeness of a bold male voice, his breath blowing across her scar. She twisted her neck to look up at him and met the same large brown eyes as the guy on the book. She stepped aside, startled. His glare freaked her out a bit.

"Oh, yeah, umm, I'm here from *The Stanford Daily,* and I was wondering if I could interview you on the book you wrote … about Brazil," she said, holding the book up to prove that was why she was there, then glancing over to Frumpy to make sure she didn't catch the lie. She seemed to have moved on.

His leather bracelets slid down his arms as he crossed them over his olive-green button-down shirt, which showcased more jewelry. "I'm the author of that book. I wasn't called beforehand," he said as if questioning the validity of her assignment.

"I'm a contributing writer. I'm not sure what they do beforehand. They just tell me where to go," she said, reducing herself to a cute shrug, a trait her mother used to use when she wanted something. She gritted her teeth at the thought of that, but mentally shook it off. *Please take the bait.* She held her breath, waiting to see if he believed her.

"What's your name again?" He was still looking at her with squinted, accusatory eyes.

"Lyndsey. Lyndsey Morgan," she said, reaching her hand out.

Still looking out the side of his eyes, August reached out and shook her hand. "My office is over here," he said and blew out a long breath as if already regretting his decision.

She followed him into a tiny, dark office. Her jaw dropped as she looked around. The room barely fit his desk, two chairs, and a file cabinet, all because the hundreds of books stacked from floor to ceiling took up most of the space. *He's a book hoarder.*

"Wow! Do you have a life?" A twisted grin emerged as she realized her statement hadn't come out of her mouth the way it had sounded in her head.

"Excuse me?" Frowning as if insulted, he swiftly moved his chair back and took a seat.

"I'm sorry, I didn't mean it like that. I meant that you're, what, thirtyish, and you've read all these books? You're probably more well-read than anyone, like, ever in the history of the world. I've never seen anything like it." She took a seat in the wooden chair next to his desk. Her eyes continued to scan the room, bewildered over his collection of books.

"I'm twenty-eight, and you need to quit while you're ahead," he said, perturbed, then sat back.

"Right. So…" She took out her notebook, crossed her leg, and straightened up as she played up her idea of how a journalist should act. "Why did you write the book?"

He scoffed. "That information is on the jacket of my book. Next question," he said, his chair squeaking as he rocked impatiently.

"Yes, um, do you consider yourself an expert on folklore in Brazil?" She needed to know if she was wasting her time.

"I'll use your words. I am 'probably more well-read than anyone, like ever in the history of the world.'" He leaned forward against his desk and clasped his hands. He pursed his lips as if he was getting bored. She feared he still questioned if this was a legit interview.

She straightened up again. "Good to know. Do you believe in reincarnation?" she asked, immediately regretting her question. She had a feeling that was the wrong move. She didn't know if that topic was even discussed in his book.

He tilted his head to the side in frustration. "Come on, Ms. Morgan, are you *really* from the school paper? Something's off."

She gave a deep sigh and surrendered. She reached for something in her purse, pulled out a photo of the hourglass, and gave it to him.

He took it while looking at her, then looked at the photo. He rubbed under his chin that had far more stubble than his book photo had. He remained emotionless, then looked up at her again. Something in his eyes was different. "Where did you get this?"

"Okay. I'm not from the paper. I'm not even a student, but I need help. I came here not knowing who to talk to, but when I saw that you wrote a book on Brazil, I thought, 'What luck?'" she said rapidly, and cutely shrugged her shoulders again.

There was a long pause.

———

"Uh-huh." Another long pause. He set his jaw, uncertain if he should kick her out for the ruse she'd pulled or do his own interview and question her about the photo in his hand. He certainly wasn't bored anymore. He swallowed, resetting his emotions. "This artifact is priceless and sacred. In fact, it really doesn't belong in someone's home. It belongs to the people who've been missing it for the last forty years and who rely on its time-measuring capabilities. But more so than that, on its energy." He was losing his grip as his calm demeanor splintered. "How did you get a photo of this?" he demanded. "Under no uncertain terms, this needs to be brought back to the people it belongs to. So tell me—who has this artifact?"

Her eyes grew wide. "I don't know," she said, then looked away like she was hiding something.

"You don't know?" he asked angrily, gripping the photo tighter.

"I'm not giving you any information until I get what *I'm* looking for," she said as she lifted her chin and raised her eyebrows.

August stood up and towered over her. He held the photo up and pointed to the sun engraved on the top of the hourglass. "See this? These people believe the souls of their relatives who have passed have been in limbo because they don't have the hourglass. That is *years* of people dying and believing that their loved ones have been unable to pass on. Some believe that they have been sought after by these souls because they're angry and have become twisted. They live in *fear* of these hauntings. So I'll ask again. Where is the fucking hourglass?"

<hr>

LYNDSEY BIT the inside of her cheek. *I'm not getting anywhere with him. There must be other anthropologists who can help.* She stood up and started for the door. Dodging around his desk, August shoved the door closed and kept his arm against it, preventing her escape. She turned around, breathing heavily. She looked up into his eyes to see if he was going to hurt her. He, too, was breathing heavily.

"Open the fucking door, or I'll scream!" she warned. Her nostrils flared. She was seething.

He lowered his head to speak into her ear. "Tell me where this is," he said in a low voice, still holding the door closed, then put his other hand on the door, thoroughly trapping her and calling her bluff.

She sucked in air to belt out a scream.

His hand flew up to cover her mouth. "Okay … Alright.

Listen, we got off on the wrong foot. I can see that," August said in resignation.

She searched his eyes for sincerity.

"Okay?" he repeated.

She nodded her head.

"Great! Let's go back to the desk and start over, shall we?"

She nodded her head again.

"If you promise not to scream, I'll let go."

"I promise," she said under his hand, barely audible.

"What was that?" he asked and slowly removed his hand.

"I promise," she repeated, and he let go completely. "Asshole!"

"Riiight," he said, nodding. "You're a feisty one. Now take a seat … Please." He was patronizing her. "Okay. My name is August Cariso. What can I do for you today?" he asked, trying his hardest to be patient.

"I was wondering …" she started.

"What? You're not going to state your name?"

She raised her eyebrows. "Okaaay. I'm Lyndsey Morgan. I was wondering if you could help me. And in exchange, tell you what you want to know," she said, glad they were starting over.

"Now tell me where the hourglass is," he said with a smile.

She stood up to leave again, and he grabbed her wrist. A charge shot through both of them, and they looked into each other's eyes. They quickly disengaged, not understanding what that was.

"I was joking," he said. "Please have a seat. It was just a joke."

"Well, it's a long story, and the details aren't important, but I acquired a journal of sorts, and the hourglass is embossed on the journal," she explained.

"What kind of journal?"

She paused and took a deep breath, looking him in the eye to judge if she could trust him. She clasped her hands together and took the risk. "A casting journal focusing on reincarnation," she admitted.

He leaned back in his seat. "Okay. Go on."

"I believe that a ritual was performed on someone that will be reincarnated, but they'll be reincarnated with a curse," she lied to elicit sympathy. "I want to learn how to recognize this person when they reincarnate, and I want to learn how to remove the curse," she said, still looking into his eyes for assurance that he believed her.

"Who is this person?"

"That's part of the long story that I'm not ready to go into. So can you help me or not? I'm just looking to be pointed in the right direction to someone who can teach me, um ..." She looked down in embarrassment.

"Witchcraft," he stated for her. He sat back up and rested his arms on his desk. "I can point you in the right direction. If ..."

"I know ... If I tell you where the hourglass is," she finished for him.

"Right."

"I can get it to you, but understand that it'll take time to get it. It belongs to ..."

"Belongs?" he challenged.

"Sorry, it's in the possession of someone I know, and I have to take it when they aren't looking. To be honest, I'm not sure if giving it to you is the best idea. How do I know you're not going to do something bad with it? Maybe you're the 'wrong hands.'" She rubbed her forehead as she contemplated the thought of that.

"Well, how do I know whether you'll learn witchcraft for good or for bad?"

"I see your point. We will have to trust each other," Lyndsey conceded.

"Yes, says the girl who lied to get herself in here," he announced as if she'd won a prize. "Of course, you can always deliver the hourglass yourself, but good luck figuring out how to find these people. So, do you have a passport? You'll also need to get a Visa—we're taking a trip to Brazil."

Her jaw dropped. "Wait, what? You want me to jump on a plane to a foreign country with you. You? The guy who just trapped me at the door?"

"Well, the way I see it, your choices are quite limited. The missing hourglass story is well documented in my book. I can present it to the police and tell them who stole it. Perhaps whoever has it has other stolen artifacts. Either way, I *will* get that hourglass back. So Brazil or jail. You decide," he said, leaning back with a smirk on his face.

"Can I think about it? This is way too much information for me to process. I really don't know what to do. I mean, you only know my name. There are a lot of Lyndsey Morgans," She pointed out.

He leaned toward her and, with a low voice, said, "Yes, but how many have a nasty burn scar on their neck?" he said, thrusting the perpetually embedded machete deeper into her chest.

She shuttered at his remark. No one ever said anything to her about her scar. Most people were scared even to admit that they saw it for fear it would hurt her feelings. They were right, she thought. She was hurt. All she heard was "nasty." She heard *him* call her "nasty." She quickly stood up and turned away so he wouldn't know how much his words pulverized her. He had reduced her to nothing but a scandalous story of a disfigured, lonesome girl. "Fine! Don't you have a class to teach?"

"Don't worry about me. I can easily work that out. Oh, and by the way, a turtleneck might work even on summer mornings here, but that won't work in Brazil," he cautioned conde-scendingly.

"Don't worry about me. I can work that out," she echoed. "Give me a couple days."

"What's your phone number?"

"Google it. 'Lyndsey Morgan, nasty burn scar.'" Her voice wavered ever so slightly.

"I wasn't saying—" he began, but she had already opened the door and walked out.

2

BRAZIL

Forty-eight hours almost to the minute from when she walked out of August's office, Lyndsey's phone rang. She was still in bed even though it was the middle of the day. His remark continued to torment her. 'Nasty,' he'd said.

He's now Googled me and probably read everything that happened.

She closed her eyes and grasped her hair on top of her head. She knew he was on the other end of that call, and she wasn't ready to hear any explanation or apology—or worse, nothing at all. She put the phone down, ignoring the voicemail notification, and turned on her side. It took her three hours to work up the courage to call him back.

"Ms. Morgan, I—" he started.

"Stop right there. I just want to tell you that I assume you know everything. And yes, that was the long story, and yes, one of those people—my mother to be exact—is to be reincarnated, cursed."

August began speaking before she could continue. "I'm sorry about the other day—all of it. I was a jerk, and it had nothing to do with you. I had no idea that you were involved in that horrible fire. I feel terrible," August said wholeheartedly.

"It's okay. I'm sure you saw the leaked images of how extensive the scarring is. It's disgusting, I know. Are you totally grossed out by it? Because I'm letting you know ahead of time that I will not be wearing anything that makes it easy for people to notice. I refuse," she promised.

"Wow! So, you've made up your mind to come with me?" he asked. She heard his chair squeak like he was leaning back and rocking. "I think you're doing the right thing. They'll be so appreciative to get their sacred hourglass back."

She let out a deep sigh. "Someone else will need to join us. Another woman, since you're a man I don't know, and I don't have friends. Maybe someone from your department?" Even when she had friends, she didn't have guy friends, and the thought of traveling outside the country with a man she didn't know made her uncomfortable.

No friends? How scarred is she? "I have a partner I can bring along with us. She's in my department, and we've gone on several research trips together. And even though this isn't about research, I think I can get her to go. We won't be there for more than a week or ten days at the most. Let's plan to leave in two weeks."

"Okay. Let me work it out with my grandfather. When do you want me to bring the hourglass?"

"Wait, are you telling me that your grandfather has it?"

"It's better if you don't know. Maybe this is one of those times when it's best to be left in the dark, so if anyone asks, you won't be lying."

"You're very calculating and smart. I like that," he complimented. "Hold on to it until we leave."

Lyndsey stood at the gate, waiting for August and his companion to arrive. She held tightly to her carry-on that harbored the hourglass. She thought about how clever she was, taking the actual hourglass and leaving one that was far inferior and, at best, only slightly resembled the sacred one. She figured if her grandfather ever confronted her, she would explain that it was stolen property. And he was too much of a do-gooder to insist she bring it back to him. He might even be proud of her. Her stomach churned as flashes of her grandparents fighting over it popped into her mind, but she was now beyond the point of no return.

After a short time, August showed up with a beautiful, tall African woman wearing a 35mm camera around her neck. She was the epitome of a model working the runway in Paris in her floral maxi dress, buzzed hair, and not even a stitch of makeup. Actually, they both looked like models, like August, with the perfect amount of facial stubble, wore a short-sleeved cream shirt with large brown buttons and cotton pants with sandals. The shirt had a couple more buttons opened than the last shirt she'd seen him in. He wore several necklaces, both beaded and leather, that draped over the olive skin of his exposed chest.

She smiled politely.

They were both out of breath. She supposed they'd rushed in excitement to see the hourglass. Lyndsey diverted her eyes away from his chest that flaunted his breathlessness.

"Lyndsey, this is Shani. She's worked with me throughout the years, and she speaks multiple languages, including Brazilian Portuguese," he introduced, then let out a long breath as he was still trying to catch his breath.

Of course, she does. She maintained her smile and put her hand out.

"This is Lyndsey. She has the hourglass and wants to learn about the Incorporealist culture."

She shook Shani's hand.

"It's such a pleasure," Shani said sincerely with a British accent. "But didn't August tell you what to wear, love? You'll be very hot."

Lyndsey felt a pang in her gut. It was rare for her people to speak to her with such care in their voice.

August put his hands on his hips and shook his head, looking at Shani. "Don't even bother with that. I did tell her. She's a stubborn one who needs to learn things the hard way."

Lyndsey's mouth dropped open. "You don't even—"

He lifted his hand to stop her. "Let's not do this dance again. If anything, that's a compliment," he said, then placed his hand on his chest. "I mean that."

She nodded, dropping the argument. "What is Incorporeal culture?" Lyndsey asked.

"We'll explain on the way," he said, then pointed to the small suitcase Lyndsey was holding onto. "Is that it?" He beamed.

Straight teeth. So what? I had braces too. "Oh, right, yes," she said with excitement—or at least working hard to change her attitude.

"Can I get a peek of it?"

Lyndsey sat down, unzipped the suitcase, and invited him to take it from there. She snorted as images of her being in the middle of a spy movie entered her mind. He lifted the top enough for him to know it was the real thing.

There were tears in his eyes when he looked back up at her. "You have no idea the immense feeling of gratitude we all have for you in bringing the hourglass back to its rightful owners," he said genuinely. "Shani, come take a look."

Her eyes filled quickly with tears, too, as she stared in awe at it. She turned, leaned down, and gave Lyndsey a big hug.

Lyndsey contorted her face to counter her wince.

"Thank you," Shani whispered.

Lyndsey calmed as she refocused her reaction and surrendered to Shani's display of appreciation.

The suitcase zipped once more, and they took seats near each other in the terminal as they waited to be called. Business-class was called first, and August and Shani stood up. Lyndsey stood too.

"Yeah, um, so, we're in business. You're in coach. It's nothing personal. Shani and I racked up points over years of traveling together to earn an upgrade."

"Oh," Lyndsey said and pretended to look at her ticket to hide her embarrassment. "Whatever. That's fine," she commented and plopped back into her seat.

When she finally got on board, the line halted just feet from where August and Shani were sitting. The two of them were drinking champagne, looking at each other, and laughing. She could feel herself peering at August as his deep laugh beguiled her. He didn't seem the type to laugh very often, but when he did, it was like it came from the deep within his belly, completely authentic.

Her teeth clenched. They were too involved to notice or care that she was standing right in front of them as she waited for some annoying passenger who was trying to fit something the size of a circus tent into the overhead compartment. She rolled her eyes. *I'm not sure who's more annoying—Mr. Circus Tent or 'Mr. and Mrs. Look at us sipping champagne and laughing because we travel the world and have stupid mileage points.' So what?*

During the flight, August got up, his book in hand, and approached Lyndsey. He knelt down and spoke in a low voice. "Hey, I know we were going to talk, but it looks like it'll have to wait until we get to the hotel. Here's my book," he said, handing it to her. "I marked the pages to read. This will introduce you to the people, culture, beliefs, and environment."

Lyndsey took the book and thanked him.

She skimmed through most of August's book until she got to the part that spoke of a nomadic group of people who lived along the Amazon and called themselves Incorporealists. They were described as peripatetic nomads, meaning they were prone to moving around but lived in or around populated areas. They supported themselves by offering goods and services, like jewelry, art, pottery, tarot readings, and even tours of their camp and lifestyle.

She learned they practiced an earth religion called Incorporealism. It was a practice similar to Spiritism, but Incorporealists didn't believe in mediumship—the act of being temporarily possessed by those who have moved on or channeling a foreign spirit that allowed the medium to speak/write in another language or tongue. They also didn't believe that spirits could direct their thoughts, actions, or choices. The primary belief system was understanding first and foremost that the most omniscient being was supreme. They believed that souls not only existed in living things, but to some extent, nonliving things. Therefore, love and respect for their environment were essential to the advancement of the spirit.

They lived to learn so that they could take that knowledge into the next life. Many of the rituals they performed demonstrated appreciation for the legacy of wisdom the passing souls left behind. This was why the hourglass was so sacred. They hadn't been able to perform some of these ceremonies without it and feared the souls were still waiting for closure and permission to move on.

And lastly, because it was more of an earth religion, they practiced some witchcraft through the use of crystals, oils, herbs, and candles.

She closed the book, exhausted from information overload. She was fascinated by what she was learning, but at the same time, could not figure out how her grandfather had stumbled upon the group, only to then end up with the hourglass they could barely manage without. Those would just have to remain questions for another time.

After three flights and twenty hours of traveling through the most beautiful, green, lush, and enchanting landscape she had ever seen, they finally arrived at their hotel in Manaus.

August and Shani moved ahead to get the room keys. Lyndsey lagged behind. It was hot and humid, and she was uncomfortable. She stopped to wipe the sweat from the healthy skin of her neck. The scarred area lacked sweat glands, so she sweltered under her suffocating turtleneck. *I just need a day or so to acclimate. I'm not giving up on how I choose to dress. Stupid August —he won't win.*

She straightened herself up and moved behind August and Shani as they checked in. Her eyes darted between them, studying how they interacted with each other. She was under the impression that they might be *together* together, but she wasn't sure. It struck her that August seemed very gentle and caring with Shani, hanging on to every word she spoke.

When it was their turn to check in, he encouraged Shani to move forward by placing his hand on the small of her back and guiding her two steps forward.

Lyndsey finally snapped. "Oh, please! Get a room. Oh wait, you are."

Her snarky remark was returned with belittling laughter as August looked over his shoulder. "Oh, are you tired? Do you need a nap?" he shot back.

"Come on now. I think we're all a bit tired," Shani reffed as she rubbed August's back.

Lyndsey looked away, annoyed. It was a glaring reminder that she longed for someone to be like that with her. Her stomach sank, knowing that would never happen. She was too nasty. All thanks to her selfish mother.

"Hello? Are you in there?" August asked, waving his hand in

front of her face and breaking her out of her perseverating thoughts.

"Sorry. What?" she asked.

"I said that we have adjoining rooms. Are you okay with that? Not that you have a choice."

"Um, yeah, that's fine. I prefer to have my own room anyway." She was never one for sharing.

"No, silly, you two in one room and me in the other room. I don't know what you're thinking, but Shani and I don't have that kind of relationship," he asserted, clearly irritated. "Geez, Lyndsey, you're not going to make this experience miserable for us, are you?" He yanked the carry-on suitcase that held the hourglass from her and looked her in the eye. "After all, I have what I need."

Lyndsey drew a heavy breath and swallowed. "I guess Shani's right. I must be tired," she retreated.

"You look like you're going to pass out. Your face is red like a tomato, and you're sweating profusely. I told you, you will not survive here in a turtleneck."

"Whatevs," was all she could say, looking away from him. She could still feel his gawking. After a moment, she looked up just as he shook his head, turned around, and walked toward the elevator.

"Lyndsey, hun," Shani said, putting her arm around her shoulders. Lyndsey immediately recoiled, and Shani raised her hands. "I was just going to say it'll be okay," she said sweetly. Her approach was reminiscent of Mozelle back when Lyndsey liked her.

"I just want to go to the room," she said, pursing her lips. *Annoying August—making me constantly defend myself is distracting me from my mission. Why do I allow him to get to me so much?*

Lyndsey followed Shani to the room. When she entered the room and caught sight of the two beds tucked into the small room, her bag slipped from her hand. She stood there for a moment, holding her breath as her heart began to race. The last time she'd shared a room with another person was in junior high when she spent the night at Claudine Remington's house. That had resulted in Lyndsey promising she would never spend the night at someone's house ever again.

Shani spoke up. "You can sleep in the bed next to the window and take a shower first, if you'd like."

Lyndsey finally released her breath. She was thankful for Shani's graciousness as she pretended not to notice her mini panic attack.

"Okay. Thank you, Shani. I'm sorry I'm being difficult, especially since the only reason you're here is that I didn't want to be alone with August," she admitted. "I really don't know what set me off. I don't even know him, but the couple times we've spoken, ugh. He infuriates me," she said, balling her fist.

"Well, love, you'll need to swallow your pride, because starting tomorrow, you'll be spending a lot of time together. A lot," Shani warned.

"What? Why? He's just going to give them the hourglass. All I need from him is a ride," she groaned.

"Well, not everyone in the group speaks English. That's first, but second, August *is* an Incorporealist."

"He is?" Lyndsey asked, bewildered. *Well, that explains why he's so passionate about this whole thing.*

"Yes, and not only that, but the group holds him in high regard. They view him as one of the main leaders," she continued. "This means August is going to be your mentor."

Lyndsey reached behind her ear and grasped her hair. "I don't know what to say." She paused, trying to comprehend the new information. "Really? I would never take him to be the patient, non-judgmental, love thy neighbor, crystal-praying, herb-growing, journal-keeping kind of guy."

"I do have to admit, the way he acted toward you earlier –

I've never seen him like that before. You're both spirited people. You come across like a Scorpio, right?"

Lyndsey tilted her head, impressed, and nodded. "Scorpio."

"He's a Leo, hence his name," she said with kindness in her voice. "That means fireworks in love and in hate."

Lyndsey could feel a flush emerge. *Love? Never. I hope she doesn't think I like him. Ew!* "Hate in this instance, but I see what you mean." She smiled. "You are very kind and patient. Thank you for explaining. This is a whole new experience for me, and sometimes I just don't know how to act," she explained. She wanted to move on because she was dangerously close to making a friend, which was the last thing she wanted. "I'm going to take a shower. This might take a while." She left it at that. She didn't want to detail the ritual of bathing with burn scars. And then there were the compression garments which no longer served a purpose, but she wasn't ready to let go of yet. The same went for her exercise regimen. She sighed, wishing she was alone.

"No problem. I'll probably hang out in August's room for now."

Lyndsey watched Shani leave to join August. As soon as the door latched, Lyndsey closed her eyes, and her shoulders slumped as the tension left her body.

A COUPLE OF HOURS PASSED, and Lyndsey was finishing her exercises when there was a knock at the adjoining door. It was August.

"Hold on!" She scrambled to put her turtleneck on.

After a few minutes, August knocked again, louder than before. "Lyndsey, I just want to go over the itinerary. Jesus, is this about your scars? I really couldn't care less about your damn scars."

After another short pause, Lyndsey sprung open the door just as August was about to pound on it. "Hey!" she said, winded as she adjusted her collar.

August scoffed and rolled his eyes. "Tomorrow, we leave to travel further into the Amazon. You will need to douse yourself with bug spray as if you're trying for a radioactive glow. I've also secured rubber boots and a walking stick for you to use as we trench through some of the swampy areas."

She nodded her head as she looked down, listening.

He moved his head into her field of vision. "I really need you to listen," he urged, locking his eyes on hers. She raised her eyebrows in impatience. "I need you to remain quiet and only speak when spoken to. It won't always be that way, but for the first day and maybe the next, I will be the one who does all the talking. Not that you could anyway, but there are areas that we will pass through where women are the property of the men. Some of these groups are welcoming, but some are hostile, and some are even deadly, especially if you're white. Do you understand?"

"If you insist," she forfeited.

August growled. "I insist," he said through gritted teeth.

"Okaaay, good night," she said as she began to close the door.

August stopped the door with his hand and drew a deep breath. "We're leaving tomorrow at five a.m."

"Okay," she responded condescendingly, then closed the door.

They traveled through tropical forests rich in animal and plant life that looked like they were from another more beautiful planet. Often, they were the only humans on the small rivers for miles. The water served as a mirror that magnified the beauty, taking up their entire field of vision. Sometimes they could see the riverbanks on both sides, while other times, they paddled through small streams. They cowered as if requesting permission to pass from the majestic but intimidating, moss- and vine-laden trees that stood tall in the middle of the streams.

The splendor caused Lyndsey momentary lapses in self-awareness as she felt a state of peace she was not familiar with. She closed her eyes when the symphony of the forest became deafening with sounds of songbirds singing, frogs croaking, water lapping, cicadas whining, and occasional thunder rolling.

After a couple hours, they came across an isolated dock. August tied a rope to secure their rowboat and climbed out first. "Shani," he called, stretching his arm out to help her up. "You okay?"

"Of course," Shani replied, then took a few steps forward and snapped a couple photos of the scenery.

He then turned to Lyndsey and held his hand out.

Lyndsey looked into his eyes. Her heart raced, and she wasn't sure if it was the heat or how August looked with his arm out, wanting to help her. *He looks like Aladdin when he asks Jasmine if she trusts him. But he's not Aladdin. He's not.* Her gaze lasted too long, and his expression was growing confused. Looking away, she grabbed his hand. Another charge hit them, and he overestimated his strength in hoisting her up, causing her to fall into him.

"Sorry," he said, breathing hard. "You're lighter than I was expecting. Either your thick clothing covers your small body, or you've lost too much water from sweating." He carefully moved her away from his body, dusting himself off awkwardly.

"Or maybe you're just trying to show off." *Redirect, redirect, redirect.*

"Okay," August said, his hands on his hips as his upper lip succumbed to the suction of his lower lip. He smacked. "Shall we?" He turned and walked off the dock into the forest.

After twenty minutes of trudging through muddy pathways,

August stopped, took a swig from his water pouch, and turned to Lyndsey. "We're coming to a friendly village, but please, remember what I told you yesterday," August pleaded.

Lyndsey mimed locking her mouth and throwing away the key.

August scoffed, turned around, and shook his head. "You kill me," he said, then looked to Shani as if wondering if she was as irritated as he was.

Lyndsey rolled her eyes.

Shani compassionately tilted her head, holding the sides of her camera that hung around her neck. "Come on now, you two. We're a team here, right?"

After a pause of consideration, they both reluctantly nodded their heads.

A small, flat, open area with several huts on stilts came into view as they passed a massive tree with towering gnarly roots. Lyndsey was awestruck. Her eyes darted about while taking in the entirety of what laid before her: thatched-roofed huts made of bamboo and wood, stacked boats with peeling paint along the perimeter, children running and laughing while trying to scare each other, women sitting on bamboo porches watching the kids, all while smoke billowed from the largest hut as it carried the smell of a hearty fish stew. She was captivated.

A shirtless man with red and black markings on his face came to them with a big smile on his face.

She watched August as he greeted the village leader in Portuguese. He squatted down, reached into his backpack, and pulled out a pouch. He handed it to the man like he was giving him a gift. *He's so respectful.* The village leader turned and called out. A woman and two teenage girls came over, with bright smiles on their faces and dreaminess in their eyes. As he spoke with them, August's smile and charm made her want to roll her eyes. *His demeanor with them is different from how he really is, right? What am I missing?*

August thrust his hand out in Lyndsey's direction while speaking to the villagers as if he was telling them about her. His tone was pleasant. *I mean, why can't he be like that with me? Oh, right, because I'm nasty.*

He turned around and looked at her. Heat shot up her body, and she quickly averted her gaze. *That look he just gave me—okay, so sometimes he can be good-looking. Nope ... nope. That's the heat getting to you. Get a grip!*

The man smiled and said some words in her direction that sounded like he was impressed with her. The women who surrounded him nodded in agreeance. After another round of pleasant exchanges, the man walked them through his camp and directed August where to go from there.

The next village was the same as the previous one. Lyndsey avoided looking at him altogether so she could cool down and become rational again. She needed to pull herself together.

She remained quiet as they passed through a third village. The only sound that came from her was the occasional *thwack* of her walking stick hitting a rock. August and Shani walked silently, never once hitting a rock. *What am I doing wrong?* She scoffed at the thought.

But it was one rock in particular that she hit as they walked through an isolated area that set off a sequence of events she didn't expect. A scantily clad man with blue, black, and white paint on his face and a bow across his back called out to Lyndsey in a way that was not friendly. He moved quickly toward her.

Adrenaline blasted through her, and she let out a small scream. Like a flash, August yanked her behind him. He, too, was breathing heavily. He began to speak calmly as if letting this man know they were just passing through. The man wasn't having it and pointed to Lyndsey. August let go of her but held his hand up for her to stay still. He out-muscled and out statured the man. He jutted out his chin and puffed out his chest as he towered over the other man. He stepped into the man's personal space, pushing him backward, repeating the same phrase. The words no longer sounded Latin in nature, and when he trapped the man against a tree, August took a crystal from one of his pockets. Still in August's hand, it began to glow. The man fell to his knees and placed his head on the forest floor. Lyndsey wasn't sure if it was out of fear or if he was apologizing. After a moment, the man stood up, grabbed his bow, and took off, never looking back.

August immediately spun toward Lyndsey. There was a protective fierceness in his eyes. His chest was still heaving over the encounter. *Jesus, he's hot. I'm jealous of the woman who gets to have him, who'll be able to throw her arms around his broad shoulders to assure him he did right by her and calm the protectiveness that rages within him. What I would do to be the one ... Holy shit, I'm attracted to him. No! Fuck me!*

He moved to her quickly. "Are you okay? Did he hurt you?"

She shook her head. "I-I'm okay." Frustrated at the wavering of her voice, a deep frown emerged, and tears sprang up, betraying her attempt to look unaffected.

He took a deep breath. "You're fine, Lyndsey. You did nothing wrong. That rock you hit might have been a boundary for them, but it's not your fault," he reassured.

I wish he would stop talking in that tone to me—all caring and shit. And now I'm crying. This is humiliating. She just nodded.

They rested for a bit, then began hiking again.

Despite her attempts to stop looking at August, she failed. He continued to impress her with his skill in communicating with each diverse community they came across. The same sweetness he showed Shani was bestowed upon all the people of the various villages they passed through. He continued to be generous with his gifts to the village leaders and their families. She had to admit to herself that she was becoming very enamored with him.

After thirteen hours, they finally set up camp about a mile from where the Incorporealist tribe was.

"Okay, so let's set up here. I'm going to leave on my own tomorrow and speak with the group leader, Magnus, and let him know why we're visiting. I'm sure he'll be overcome with joy. I'm going to be the one to present the hourglass and, um, I'm going to fabricate some of the details of how we got it to keep you safe, Lyndsey."

There he goes with that caring bullshit. I wish he would stop. He's going to end up hurting me. The more he's like this, the greater the pain, she thought to herself as heat traveled through her body and to her face. She was thankful that she was already red and sweaty so he wouldn't notice her blush.

They began to set up their respective tents. Lyndsey just stood there, stakes in her hands as she surveyed all the tools needed to pitch the tent. *What the hell am I supposed to do with a hammer, ropes, poles, plastic stakes, metal stakes, and a tarp?* She turned her head ever so slightly in August and Shani's direction, hoping they wouldn't catch her looking like an idiot, as she tried to get a glimpse at what they were doing. *Okay, lay the tarp down. Easy enough.* She got down on her knees and spread the tarp out like it was a bedsheet. Taking another peek at the two of them, her lips twisted. Their tarps were so much smaller than hers. *I guess I wasn't supposed to unfold it this much. Just continue, like I meant to do this.* She started stretching the tarp to get all the wrinkles out and then folded it into a perfect, wrinkle-free square. *Ha, mine probably is better than theirs.* Glancing at them again, her mouth dropped. They were done.

Shit! What am I supposed to do next? Forget the stupid tarp and deal with the tent. She unfurled the tent. It was much longer than the tarp it laid on. *Forget it! I'm not starting over. I can do this. I don't need anyone's help. It's just one uncomfortable night. Heaven knows I've had my share.*

She picked up the hammer and a stake. *Just nail these near the corners of the tent.* After nailing the metal stakes into the ground, she fed the flexible pole through the straps. Satisfied with herself, she lifted the tent. It hung there like a dirty sheet on a clothesline before it slumped over. She gripped the inside of her hair and pursed her lips as she held in a scream. *I hate myself right now.*

She began yanking out one of the poles from the loops when a hand reached from behind her and grabbed hold of the pole, startling her.

"Sorry. I didn't mean to scare you," August said, slowly taking the pole out of her grasp.

"Well, what do you expect, sneaking up on someone like that," she said. "And you don't have to do that. I can figure it out myself. I'm not a damsel in distress, you know."

"You are definitely not that. But night is falling," he said as he continued to reverse engineer all her work.

"Fine. It's just that I've never been camping before."

"Really, Lyndsey. It's okay," he said with kindness in his voice.

She found herself staring at August as he continued setting up her tent for her. His grip on the hammer and his corded muscles as they strained against the fabric of his shirt with every strike —*I can't not look.* She'd never allowed herself to crush on anyone, but this was totally out of her control. The more she thought about it, the more depressed she felt. *No one will ever love a repulsive, nasty freak like me,* she thought to herself over and over and over again.

Within a few minutes, her tent was up, and she and August walked over to where Shani had started a fire. They sat there for a moment in silence, August between them on the short log that served as a bench. She could practically feel his body heat. Uncomfortable, Lyndsey leaned away from him.

"How are you holding up?" he asked like he actually wanted to know.

"I'm fine. Just tired," Lyndsey said, mirroring his tone and planting her hand off to the side to allow more distance between them.

"Yeah, I think we all are, but tomorrow, the two of you can sleep in. You'll be here for a large part of the day until I come and get you," he said, looking at Lyndsey oddly. "Are you sure you're okay? You seem different. Your vibe is different," he said, moving his hand in a circular motion.

Lyndsey quickly looked away. "I'm fine," she said, then faked a yawn. "I'm going to bed." She got up. "Good night." She hustled to her tent, determined to get away from *him*. She despised that she was so attracted to him. It was a rude awakening—forcing her to learn that this was the life of an adult outside the safety of the museum she called home. The museum she hid in. The museum that understood her and protected her from these kinds of things happening to her. She wasn't sure how much more of the real world she could take.

<hr>

AUGUST AND SHANI remained by the campfire talking. They reminisced about the last time they were there and how they'd gotten themselves in and out of precarious situations. They talked about school, upcoming research projects, and even their personal lives. Shani shared about her long-term relationship with a professor from the engineering department. August shared how his work, his writing, and his books were his lovers. They had a good time, but the moment Shani brought Lyndsey up, the energy shifted.

"What are your thoughts about her?" she whispered, pointing her head in the direction of Lyndsey's tent.

"I think she's annoying. She's stubborn, bitchy, strong, determined. It's hard to be around someone who hates themselves so much. I find that much more repelling than her scars," he admitted. "But I think that learning how to manipulate her environment, and maybe saving her mom, will help her recognize her good qualities and love herself again."

"Oh, August, you're such a rescuer," Shani said and playfully shoved him. "But did you notice how much her behavior changed as the day progressed?"

He smiled and looked down. "I did. I was surprised that she did as I asked."

"August, hun, I think she saw you in action and has developed a crush on you," Shani pointed out.

"Really? I don't see that." He shook his head in denial, but then considered what she was saying. "But then again, I guess that explains a change in her energy. It's been a while since she threw one of her usual snarky remarks at me, and she's been rather subdued. Well, if that's true, then I could use that to work in my favor. I won't lead her on, but if I put on the charm, maybe she'll be a better listener. One thing's for sure—I'll get her to take off those damn turtlenecks. It's painful just looking at her."

"A girl lost, isn't she?" Shani asked as if permitting August to seize the opportunity so that Lyndsey could heal and become her best self.

3

OVERHEATED

The following day, August returned from his visit with the Incorporealists in the late afternoon. He was sweaty, and his T-shirt was soaked through. He was curious if Lyndsey noticed. He smiled inwardly when he caught her looking at him. A zing traveled up his spine and into his head. *Yeah, I could see how a guy might find her cute, that is until they realize how annoying she can be.* She averted her gaze, confirming his effect on her, and he decided to play with his newfound discovery.

"Lyndsey, are you ready to go?" August asked kindly.

"Um, well, do you see anything that would suggest otherwise?" Lyndsey was being insolent.

August looked at Shani, smirked, and winked. "Let's go. They're very excited to see you, but you'll need to take off the turtleneck."

"You'll do anything to get me out of this shirt, won't you?" *That's it. I'll get him to stop asking me about my damn shirts by embarrassing him and confronting him as if he likes me.* But that belief was short-lived, as she hadn't anticipated setting herself up for greater pain.

"Ummm, no," he retorted with a chuckle.

Like knives in the chest, that hurt her a lot.

"Then stop asking!" She hoped she could get *something* out of this painful exchange.

"Have it your way. It's about a fifty-minute hike. Let's get going," he said.

She could have sworn he turned and rolled his eyes.

The hike proved to be more difficult than she was expecting. She felt like she was overheating, but then a brief rainstorm would make her feel better until it dried up and the heat overtook everything again.

She exhaled in relief when a clearing came into view. As they entered the clearing, relief became awe. The three of them stood at the camp's perimeter, behind a large amphitheater with an open stage, large fire pit, and ample log benches to accommodate everyone in the camp.

As they waited to be greeted by the leader, Lyndsey's eyes widened as she scanned her surroundings. This village was full of whimsy and beauty and love. It was lively and enchanting. There were yurts of different sizes throughout that served many purposes, but it still felt vast. String lights and colorful translucent fabrics wrapped around the poles and accented the whole camp.

Just beyond the amphitheater, people of all kinds of ethnicities, nationalities, and ages were enjoying an afternoon ritual of some sort. Their fluid movements resembled tai chi but with twirls and short leaps. They raised their hands toward the sun as if giving thanks to a beautiful day.

Shani snapped a few photos, then leaned over. "This is a blessing ritual they perform every mid-afternoon. It's to give thanks for the abundance of resources they've grown dependent on. They are especially grateful when the sun acknowledges their prayers by allowing the sky to be clear enough to see a rich Brazilian sunset," Shani explained. She, too, had the intonation of a college professor, which put Lyndsey at ease. She had made the right decision to have August bring someone else along.

The ritual only lasted another minute before they bowed and moved on with their day. Lyndsey watched, captivated, as the people continued to dance about and sing to themselves, just going along with their typical day. They seemed to be a very happy group of people.

To the left of the amphitheater was a yurt with the word *Enfermaria* engraved in a wooden sign over the opening. It was there that the camp leader exited and bound over to August. He was wearing the traditional garb that men wore—cotton pants that ended mid-calf and an open, printed, button-down shirt with rolled-up sleeves that proudly displayed his chest and rows of beaded necklaces.

"Augusto!" the leader called out, running toward August with his arms open for a big hug. "*Stefon me pediu para esperar você!*" He greeted them in a language only August and Shani understood.

August approached the man with open arms as well. "Magnus!" The two men embraced.

"*Estou tão feliz por você ter feito isso! Desculpe ter perdido você antes, mas caramba, como senti sua falta!*"

August replied in the same language. "*Eu também senti sua falta!*" he said as he stepped back. "*Você se lembra da Shani?*"

"*Claro que eu me lembro,*" Magnus said, taking Shani's hand and kissing it. He cupped his other hand over hers as he looked at Lyndsey. "*E quem é essa linda mulher?*"

"*Essa é a Lyndsey. É ela que tem o dom. Tenha cuidado. Ela é agressiva,*" he said, and they all laughed—except Lyndsey, who had no idea what they were talking about. She scowled.

"I guess we should speak in English," August suggested.

"Lyndsey, I am Magnus. It is a pleasure to meet you," the man said, greeting her as he had Shani. Lyndsey responded with a bright smile but did not speak as she'd been instructed.

"So ladies, you can settle into your yurts," he said and pulled out a map from a visitor information box that hung on one of the nearby posts. "You won't really need this—it's pretty easy to figure out the layout of the village—but for now, you can use this to orient yourself. You're right here at the stage on the south end of the camp. To the left, you have the yoga or meditation yurt. Next to that is the medical yurt. That's where I just was. Across the way, you have the arts and crafts yurt, where we make artisan items to sell to visitors or in the marketplace. Straight ahead is the kitchen and dining area. The yurts where everyone sleeps are behind the building with the kitchen. Okay?" He waited for understanding. "Bethany will show you to your yurts. August, it would be a pleasure if you stayed with me in my yurt," he said, then clasped his hand and gave a slight bow. "Go ahead and get settled, then come to the fire pit for the welcome presentation and other festivities," Magnus said as he beckoned Bethany over.

Lyndsey and Shani's yurt had two twin beds with accompanying end tables, a sitting area, and large windows. There wasn't a bathroom, but there were private dressing areas. Lyndsey chugged her water and laid down for a bit to regain her energy. After a few minutes, she got up and changed into another turtleneck. When she was finished, she saw that Shani had been waiting for her.

"I wasn't expecting you to wait for me," Lyndsey said, surprised that someone would do that for her.

"Of course, hun. Ready?" she asked. She was wearing what all the female villagers were wearing—a colorful skirt and a light fabric tube top wrapped around her torso. A crystal was worn around her neck, and a pouch full of herbs, crystals, or vials of oil lay against her side. Shani looked so beautiful.

Lyndsey looked down in envy as she wished she could wear the same thing. She wanted to look beautiful too.

After some time, the two women left the yurt and followed the lit torches that led them to the amphitheater. People from the village scurried all around them.

"No camera tonight?" Lyndsey asked Shani.

"Not during sacred gatherings. They feel that taking pictures might shy away good and helpful spirits. Plus, some moments are meant to be experienced, not memorialized."

"Oh. Okay," Lyndsey said, looking around. "I wonder if it's like this every night?" Lyndsey asked as two young girls with flowers in their hair whizzed by them, carrying a couple of chairs to the stage.

"This is for the return of the hourglass, love," Shani said. "That altar between the stage and the fire pit was created for this momentous event."

"But we just arrived," Lyndsey said, confused.

"It's like they've been preparing for this all along. It's impressive, but they did have some time to put this all together because August came here earlier. That being said, love, they are very intuitive. Perhaps they knew were coming," Shani said with a wink.

Lyndsey nodded in agreement. "I wonder where August is," Lyndsey inquired, looking around as the two of them took a seat on the log bench in the last row.

Shani looked at Lyndsey and gave her a smile that looked like she knew Lyndsey's secret. "He's preparing the presentation."

Lyndsey nodded and continued to observe like a child going to a fair for the first time. The sights were overwhelming. Along with the twinkle lights, and pastel-colored paper lanterns that lit up the place, ribbons and flowers lined the central aisle. A white canvas tarp served as a canopy, waving in the gentle breeze that blew through the camp.

A woman came by and offered a flower wreath to each of them to wear in their hair. They agreed, and when she reached out to hand them their flower crowns, Lyndsey noticed the woman had a brand on her wrist in the shape of a crescent moon. Lyndsey wondered if this was similar to what her mom had branded on her chest.

"Wow. That's really pretty," Lyndsey complimented, enticing the woman to open up about it.

She smiled as she looked at it. "Thank you," she replied with a French accent. "I got this with my husband and soulmate over there," she pointed to a man working with electrical cables near the stage. As if he knew she was talking about him, he turned to her and winked. "This was done during our handfasting ceremony about one year ago, and it will help us find each other in our next lives," she continued with a sparkle in her eyes.

Mixed feelings surged through Lyndsey's veins, and she fought the urge to roll her eyes. *How could my mother use such a sacred ritual for a fling?* She was triggered as she tried to draw differences between this woman who was really in love and her mother. *Clearly, this woman and a real soulmate used the ritual respectfully,* she assumed. At the same time, there was a sense of relief knowing she was in the right place.

"That's so nice," Lyndsey replied, hoping she didn't sound patronizing.

People took their seats along the long wooden benches. The evening gathering began with a ceremonial dance performed by the women in of the camp. This was followed by a small group of men who moved about the stage with segmented rings of fire. Shortly after their sacred offerings, Magnus came out onto the stage with August. They then lit the candles on the four corners of the altar. The glowing candlelight enriched an energizing vibe that erupted around them. It was an intoxicating, hopeful, peaceful feeling that flowed, and no one was immune to it.

Lyndsey couldn't look away from August, who wore his shirt wide open, exposing his chest and several necklaces made of beads, leather, and shells. His hair was half up in a ponytail. He hadn't shaved, either, so more stubble covered his face than usual—the contrasting shades brightening his eyes. She took a deep breath as her nerves began to hum through her whole body.

After some welcoming words in Portuguese, Magnus called Shani and Lyndsey up onto the stage. August stood in front of the fire, ready to greet them as they made their way down the aisle.

Lyndsey walked behind Shani. Jealousy flamed within her as August extended his arm to Shani. *This is what it looks like when the groom takes the bride's hand, and together they walk to the altar to seal their love.* She suddenly felt like a child and a voyeur. *Maybe I should be walking in front of them—tossing rose petals before their feet so they can ooze all over each other in the floral wake of ever-lasting love.* She rolled her eyes and shook her head at the thought. *Get it together,* she thought and refocused her attention.

All four of them stood at the end of the aisle. Magnus introduced them and then requested that August and Lyndsey come to the stage. After a few words, August spoke in English. He used kind words to describe Lyndsey and how she had done an amazing thing in finding and recovering the hourglass.

As he continued, Shani came up behind them with a decorative, velvet, cinched bag and presented it to Magnus, who bowed in appreciation for the gift, then brought it over to the altar. He untied the cinch bag and stretched it open. He peeked inside, then stepped back against the stage as the bag unfurled, exposing the hourglass that was enshrouded within it. Gasps, mumbles, and cries resonated throughout the amphitheater. The children who didn't know what was happening tugged on their parents' clothes for an explanation. Magnus held his hands in front of his chest, pressed palm to palm, and was overwhelmed with emotion. He buried his face into them and shook as he cried.

"I can't believe this," he said many times. After several minutes of disbelief, Magnus got up onto the stage and hugged August, then Shani.

Lyndsey's breath quickened, her palms began to sweat, and she stiffened at the thought that Magnus was going to hug her too. She was just going to have to endure it. And so she did. He hugged her with tremendous strength. Pain shot through her. She wasn't sure if it was physical pain or emotional, but she forced herself to suffer through the discomfort. She lightly reciprocated and then looked at August. At first, he seemed happy for her, but then his expression changed. She wondered if he saw her wincing in pain.

Magnus held on to her longer than he had the others. "I'm so deeply grateful," he whispered in her ear.

She dropped her arms as a cue for him to follow suit, but then he started swaying. She squeezed her eyes closed. When he finally released his embrace, he bodily turned her so they were both facing the audience but kept his hand on her shoulder. Her head started hurting. Her smile began to quiver over the discomfort, but she did everything she could to continue hiding her pain.

Magnus finally let go and faced her. He expressed over and over what an amazing thing she had done for the village and that before she left, they would find a way to repay her kindness. He invited them to stay on stage for the rest of the ceremony, but they decided to take a seat to be less of a distraction.

When they sat down, August immediately turned to Lyndsey. "Are you okay? Is there anything I can do for you? Do you need to lay down?" he fired off.

She was taken aback by his sincere concern. The day before had been different with the tribesman because he'd been a threat to all three of them. A twinge in her gut reminded her that his kindness meant more to her than to him. "I'll survive," she told him. "Whether I want to or not," she added under her breath.

The ceremony lasted a couple hours, but it was engaging. She never felt bored, even though most of it was in a different language. At the end of the ceremony, everyone stood up as the girls in the camp passed a drink out to everyone. It was non-alcoholic, August explained, but it did include some herbs that aided in relaxation. However, in the right conditions and the right dosage, it could cause hallucinations. They called the drink Olhos das Nuvens—Eyes of the Clouds.

August stood close to Lyndsey and held the small wooden cup shoulder level. "They have this every night before bed. It's fine to drink. It'll help relax you and give you sweet dreams." His mouth turned up on one side while raising an eyebrow, then downed the shot.

"I could definitely use something to calm me down," Lyndsey said, then took the shot just as August had. It was slightly thicker than she was expecting and tasted how she imagined nectar would taste. She closed her eyes and placed her hand on her chest as the fluid filled and warmed her chest. She opened her eyes to find August's fixation on her, dropping her empty wooden cup. "Geez, August, what's with the stare?"

He leaned down to pick up the cup. "Sorry. It's a rite of passage. I just wanted to see your expression."

Frowning, she snatched the cup from him. "Why do you care?" she said quietly and turned away from him.

When the festivities were finally over, they walked back to their yurts and began to discuss what the next few days were going to look like. "Magnus wants us to gather some items for a ceremony that he hopes will allow the wandering souls to move on. The first item on tomorrow's schedule will be to take a forty-minute hike to Caverna da Visão, a sacred cave that possesses some of the world's rarest herbs. This cave is one of the reasons the group has stayed so long despite being considered nomadic," August explained in his professor voice. "It's also where they will keep the hourglass."

"Oh, okay." Her mouth lifted on one side. "So is that what it sounds like when you lecture your students? All smart and shit?" She smiled, swaying as she leaned against one of the posts to her yurt.

He chuckled. "Ms. Morgan, are you disrupting the class with an irrelevant question?"

"Oh, you have no idea." She snickered as memories of some of the darker moments of her childhood mischief came flooding back.

"Really?"

"Yeah. Let's not go there." Her face dropped.

"Well, now you have me curious." He raised an eyebrow.

"Another time, August."

"Okay, I'll back off," he said, then put his hands on his hips. "So you've been a feisty one from the get-go?"

"Yes, August. So you should know when to back off." She pushed herself away from the post.

He raised his hands in surrender. "Sorry," he said and looked down. "Lyndsey, I really want to thank you again for all you've done. The joy you've brought back to this group is immeasurable, and I don't know if any repayment will be enough."

She nodded and relaxed back into the post again. His demeanor was sweet, and the interaction was pleasant enough. Desperate to keep *this* August in front of her, she did what she could to keep him there longer. She was genuinely enjoying the moment. She asked him about his schedule and what his life was like as a professor. She wasn't sure if this was a side effect of the drink, but she liked it and wasn't going to ruin the fun by questioning it.

When she ran out of questions, she wished him good night and went to bed. There, she stared at the ceiling, wondering if their time together would be a lot better now that they'd had this great night. She fell asleep with a smile on her face.

SHE WOKE up feeling refreshed and excited about their hike. She tried to get through her morning routine quickly. She rushed out just as she finished pulling on her turtleneck and saw Shani and August waiting for her. August shook his head in disappointment. Lyndsey's heart sank as his attitude was a complete departure from the night before.

August crossed his arms. "I know you've asked me to stop saying anything, but haven't you learned to trust us by now? Seriously, you will roast out there," he warned, then took a step forward. "We. Don't. Care. About. Your. Scars," he asserted, as though if stated slowly and with force, she might cave.

"I. Won't. Do. It," she bit back through gritted teeth.

"Yet," he finished. "I thought that we connected last night and that you've started trusting that we aren't bothered by your damn scars. Do you know, being that we're anthropologists, the things we've seen?" he asked and waited to see if she could come up with an answer. "We've seen things that would make even the most reckless, self-mutilating, tattoo-wannabe cry home to their mom and promise to be good."

"That's the part that *you* don't understand," she accused, pointing to his chest. "It's not about what *you* think. I get that you've seen a lot, and maybe I'm not as *nasty*—and yes, I'm throwing your word back at you—as I might think you think, but it's *my* choice. *My* consequence," she thundered, pointing back at herself.

"Fine! Have it your way!" He tossed her a backpack, turned on his heel, and walked out of camp.

"Lyndsey, love," Shani started. Her head tilted in concern. "We just want to make sure you're safe. That's all. We won't look if that's what you want."

"Thank you for your concern, but I'll be fine."

"I can't stop you, but know that I'm not comfortable with this," she said, then turned and caught up to August fifteen steps ahead.

August led the way while Shani walked just behind him. It was hard to tell who was leading—they were so close to each other. August pointed out the wildlife and spoke more about the village.

Ten minutes into the hike, Lyndsey felt proud of her ability to keep up with them—that was until the sun peeked over the mountain tops.

She began to struggle under the sun's inescapable blazing rays, and she began trailing behind. Jealousy raged through her as she watched Shani and August make their way through the thick underbrush with the ease of an eel gliding its way through a marsh. She became tired, sweaty, and before she knew it, she was out of water. She hated that August was right, but pride got the best of her, and she soldiered on. But each step became more brutal than the last. She was overheated. She needed to stop, and she needed water. She tried yelling out to them to stop, but they were too far ahead, and they couldn't hear her over the lively, wild jungle noises. She took one step at a time and tried to call out, but it was to no avail. Her stomach clenched as nausea rolled over her. She looked down and saw fresh cuttings where they'd hacked a trail. *All I need to do is rest, and then I can just follow these cuttings. I'll only be a few minutes behind.*

She took her backpack off and sat for a moment, but the nausea didn't let up. She was going to vomit. She knelt on all fours and wretched. August's voice warning her that she would roast ran on loop in her head, and she yelled out in anger because he was right. She hit the forest floor with her fist and laid back down. She started crying, but no tears came out. Tunnel vision crept in, and she was determined to fight it by trying to get back up, but she was too weak. She collapsed as she slipped into unconsciousness.

<hr>

She was inside a yurt when she opened her eyes, hooked up to an IV. She felt a lot better. She wasn't sweaty or nauseous. She felt the coolest she'd felt since the day they arrived. At first, she allowed herself to luxuriate in the feeling, but then she questioned it. As she sat up to figure out where she was, the sheet that covered her slid down. She gasped when she looked down to see that she was wearing a tube top. "Where the fuck are my clothes? Hello?"

"And she's up," Lyndsey heard August say begrudgingly.

"Get me my clothes! This is *not* okay! Hello? Can anyone hear me?"

August's hand cracked open the flap to the yurt.

"You*!* Get the fuck out of here. I'm not asking for *you* unless you bring me my damn shirt, you fucker!" she yelled. She was hyperventilating and losing her mind.

"Cover up, Lyndsey. I'm coming in," he announced.

She fully wrapped herself in the sheet that she'd woken up in, but had no intention of inviting him in. Instead, she began looking around for her clothes.

<hr>

She didn't answer.

"Lyndsey?" He waited another beat. "I'm not waiting anymore." He threw open the flap and was met with a shoe flying past his head. He walked in and met her rage head-on. "You need to calm down," he said, his hands up.

"What is *wrong* with you? You know what this means to me! How could you?" she yelled, tears in her eyes. She was armed with another shoe. "You set this whole thing up, didn't you?"

August took another step forward. "I need you to stay calm and just listen to me. Can you do that?"

"Do I look like I'm in the mood for a chit-chat? Fuck *you!*" she yelled through streaming tears.

He took another step forward, intending to trap her so he could explain. She threw the other shoe, and he ran to her, wrapping his arms around her. When she started screaming, he covered her mouth.

She yelled through his hand, "Don't touch me!"

"I'll let go if you let me explain," he promised.

She nodded her head.

He dropped his hand.

"Touching me is way, *way* over the line! I'll listen to you, but don't fucking touch me again. *Ever! Okay?*"

He immediately let go. "You're right. I'm sorry," he said, taking a deep, calming breath. She did the same. He looked down and moved his hand through his hair. One hand remained on his hip as he began to explain. "It took us a minute before we realized that you were trailing behind. We called out for you, and when we didn't hear anything, we trailed back and found you lying on your side. You were obviously dehydrated," he explained, then waved his hand. "No. It was beyond that. You were so dehydrated – your organs were on the verge of shutting down. Shani took care of cooling you down, and fortunately, we were still close to camp—I mean, really, you didn't even last a

50

hundred meters. So Shani brought you here and saved your life. I know you wish your clothes were your new skin ..."

"You don't understand. Don't tell me what I wish or think," she spat.

"You're right. I apologize again," he said, both hands up. He stood there for a moment with his hand over his mouth as he planned his next statement. "Listen, I'm just going to get to the point. Those turtlenecks of yours have come to an end. It's one thing if you want to endure heat and everything that comes with dressing inappropriately for the weather, but when that creates a safety hazard or health risk to others, that's something else entirely. So from here on out, you either dress appropriately—like the top they put you in—or you'll have to leave. I'm done. Seeing you lying on the ground like that was traumatizing. I honestly thought you'd died. I won't go through that again!" He paused to read her reaction. "So here's what you're going to do. I'm going to leave for twenty minutes. When I come back, you'll either be in the top that they put you in, or you can go over to the corner there and put your other shirt on, and that will tell me how the rest of this trip will go." He stayed in place for another minute to gauge her reaction.

She just stood there as he turned and left.

SHE CLOSED her eyes to release the rest of her tears, knowing she was going to have to surrender at some point. She dreaded being subjected to whispers, comments, snickering, pity, questions, or even being ignored. She wasn't ready to let go of what had protected her from judgment and rejection all these years. To shed her shield, her protection, her skin, sooner than she was ready, and be naked and vulnerable? That would be pain that could completely crush her. And to be that way in front of the person—the *only* person—she'd ever had a crush on was a heartbreak she wasn't sure she could endure. She could thank him for his time and head home and be safe and figure everything else out on her own. There was no question that he had power over her, but she didn't know which side would tip the scale.

<hr>

After twenty minutes, August spoke from outside the entrance to the yurt. "Are you ready?"

"You can come in," she invited.

He was surprised to see her standing there in her turtleneck. His chest tightened in disappointment and sadness, but he'd drawn the line and had to stand by it. He rubbed a hand down his face and drew a deep breath before placing it on his hip. "Okay. We'll head back in the morning," he said, looking down. He lifted his hand. "I gotta be honest. I'm shocked, and quite frankly, I'm deeply disappointed." He began to turn around.

"Wait!" she ordered.

He turned back around. "What?" he asked, still looking down.

"I need you to look at me," she pleaded.

He looked up at her. He was breathing heavily.

"I'm so fearful of letting go, but I fear *you* the most, August. I'm afraid of *your* reaction to my nastiness." Tears teetered at the brim of her eyes.

"I never meant it like that," he bit through gritted teeth.

"Well, I still believe it to be true. But I know, and really, *really* hate the fact that you're right," she admitted, tears beginning to fall. "I need you to be here when I shed my skin. I *do* trust you, but I also know that you'll look at me differently from now on, and that hurts." Her chin quivered as she placed her fist over her heart.

He started to say something but stopped when she looked

directly into his eyes and slowly lifted her top. He couldn't move an inch. He could barely breathe. In his nearly twenty years of seeing some of the most awe-inspiring things the world had to offer, he was captivated at that moment like never before. She turned just before she raised her top over her breast to reveal her back. He swallowed hard and shifted himself when she wasn't looking.

She removed her shirt completely, then held the shirt in front of her bare chest to cover herself. She stood in place, looking over her shoulder at him. August took a step closer. He was compelled to touch her, and she didn't seem to want to stop him. He lightly touched the scar and slowly moved his hands up her back, feeling a sadness that grew more profound the further he followed the trail of a spirit decimated, a light extinguished, and a soul sentenced to isolation. Thick, tough patches transitioned to thin translucent whorls. He couldn't imagine how anyone would have been able to withstand the pain. They weren't nasty, or horrific, or unpleasant for him to look at. They held so much pain for her, but all he saw was her strength, her resilience, her determination to keep moving forward in a life that had tried to slow her down.

"I'm so, so sorry, Lyndsey," he said in a low voice.

"Stop! I don't want your pity."

"It's not pity. It's an apology."

"Because now you understand why I must cover up."

"I don't think that in the slightest. I just mean that in no way did I try to understand your emotional scars. Those scars run much deeper than your physical ones, and I didn't understand, and for that, I'm sincerely sorry."

A deep frown emerged as if his words touched her. She looked away as tears streamed down her cheeks. "Thank you. I guess that's what I was looking for. Just to be heard," she said, then paused.

"Are you going to be okay? Do you want time alone?"

She nodded, and a sob escaped.

"Lyndsey," he whispered and hesitantly reached his hand out. He wanted to pull her into his arms and comfort her.

She lowered her head. "Um, well, I need to get dressed."

"Right. Yes." He dropped his hand. "I'll be out there." He turned to walk out, then stopped and looked over his shoulder again. "Thank you, Lyndsey, for including me in something so deeply personal to you. It opened my eyes to the fact that I thought I knew more than I did. I hope in some way I was able to do the same for you."

He left without waiting to hear a reply.

LYNDSEY CLOSED her eyes as she recalled his touch. In places, she could still feel his fingertips—the sensation sending shivers down her spine that awakened her nerves. She replayed hearing his shaky breath escape him as he touched her. She wasn't sure if it was shock over seeing her scars in real life or something more than that. Her heart began to fill with hope that maybe, one day, someone would actually love her, scars and all.

She exited the yurt in a scarf top that wrapped around her chest, down to her midsection, and tied in the back. She had never felt so exposed and indecent. But as she made her way out to find August, all the women in the village came to her and gave her beautiful, long silk scarves to wear, designing for her a whole wardrobe. She loved each and every scarf she was handed, and for the first time since the fire, she felt loved and accepted, and allowed herself to not only own her scars, but exert power over them.

AUGUST STOOD in front of his window, staring at Lyndsey as she exited the med yurt. Her smile lit up the entire camp as the women and girls gifted her with the clothing they'd made.

She probably doesn't realize how she radiates. She was right—I'll never see her the same way again. But not how she thought. She's not that annoying girl anymore. She's so much more than that. She's a breathtaking woman who—

He turned away from the window.

"Shit," he whispered, shaking his head over his discovery.

She's a breathtaking woman who is driving me nuts. What the hell? You need to stop where you're going with this, August, or you'll destroy her.

4

OLHAS DA NUVENS

The next morning, Lyndsey got up and dressed herself in a blue tube top and a long, floral skirt. When she stepped out of the changing area, Shani stood there with a proud look on her face.

"You are so beautiful, Lyndsey. I hope you see that now," she said with prayer hands.

Lyndsey pulled at a strand of her hair and smiled sheepishly. "It'll take time getting used to this. I feel naked, like everyone is staring. It makes me uncomfortable, but at the same time, it's not as bad as I thought it would be. Like I didn't realize my own strength. When I showed August my scars, I don't know, I suddenly realized that these scars are something I have, not something I *am*," she said nervously, rubbing her hands down her skirt.

"You're an amazing young woman," Shani said. "Come here. Let me put some flowers in those lovely locks of yours."

Lyndsey sat on the bed and allowed Shani to braid colorful flowers into her hair. As Shani placed the last flower, August called for them from outside their yurt.

"Hold on, August, love," Shani called to August. She turned

to Lyndsey. "I know you've been avoiding my camera, but may I take a photograph of how beautiful you look?"

Lyndsey hesitated. It had been so long since she'd had a photo taken of her, and even longer for the purpose of showing how beautiful she was. *You can do this,* she thought, then nodded. She remained on the bed, looking out the window, sliding her hand down the length of the braid to feel the smooth twists of her hair, while Shani grabbed her camera.

Click. Click.

"Sorry. You just looked so lovely looking out the window like that."

"It's okay," Lyndsey said.

"I'll make sure August gets these photos to you. I won't be able to get them developed until we get back."

"Um. Okay," she said. She'd never considered what it would be like with August once they got home. *Will we remain friends after this? I want to, but I don't know if he does.*

August called out again.

Lyndsey turned to Shani. "I need a minute," Lyndsey pleaded in a whisper to Shani.

"Take your time. I'll see what he needs," she said, then took her camera and left.

Lyndsey looked at herself in the mirror. She didn't recognize the woman reflecting back at her. The traditional dress she wore accentuated the curves of her midriff and hips. Staring at herself, a sense of shame came over her for liking what she saw. The belief of thinking she was attractive had gone away with the fire. She had forgotten how it felt to have a favorable notion about herself. It was all that she had known.

She glanced over to the turtleneck she'd left on the chair, pursing her lips as she resisted going over there and putting it back on. Hearing August's voice just on the other side of the canvas that lined the yurt, along with the memory of his pride in her, strengthened her resolve. She stood tall, turned on her heel, and left the yurt.

August was talking to Shani when Lyndsey stepped out. He looked at Lyndsey and stopped mid-sentence.

Lyndsey tilted her head down in embarrassment.

"What a difference. I've got to say, it's nice to be able to look at you and not feel heat exhaustion," August said, hands on his hips.

Lyndsey's knee-jerk reaction was to make a snarky remark, but instead, she just nodded.

"Are you ready for me to teach you some of our ways? I know that you want to learn how to reverse your mom's curse, but it's not as effective if you don't understand the roots and methodology of the process," August explained.

"Makes sense. I'm ready," she said with a smile.

"Before you go, can I take a photo of the two of you?" Shani asked.

Lyndsey looked at August to gauge if he was uncomfortable with Shani's request. He shrugged his shoulders, then took a step towards her.

"Um," he said and hovered his hand around her back, not knowing where he could place it.

"Here." Lyndsey grabbed his hand and placed it around her waist. She thought she heard him catch his breath and step out of his hold. "Sorry."

"No, there's nothing to be sorry for," he said. His eyes were wide. "I just wasn't expecting that from you."

"We're just taking a picture. Isn't that what people do?"

"Right. Yes," he said and slid his hand around her waist again. A shiver moved down her spine at the warmth of his soft hand that rested over her hip. His breath seemed uneven, but she wasn't sure why.

She threw her hand around his waist and looked at the camera.

Click.

Lyndsey's arm immediately dropped to her side. Then August's did. She looked at him and saw that he had been looking at her. Deep down, it was a big moment for her. Not only had she encouraged someone to touch her, but she had allowed herself to take pleasure in it. And even if August was uncomfortable, she knew it wasn't because he thought she was nasty. *He probably thinks I took it to mean that he was making a move on me.* "Easy peasy," Lyndsey said with a shrug, trying to convince August it was no big deal and that she hadn't taken it the wrong way.

"Oh, that is going to look so lovely," Shani said.

"Thanks, Shani," he said and turned to Lyndsey. "Shall we?" he asked as if he wanted to get beyond the camera thing just as quickly as she did.

"We shall," she said and stepped aside for him to take the lead.

They walked together into the forest along the camp's perimeter and went to the herb garden.

He crouched down by a rosemary bush, his back to Lyndsey. "I came here as an undergrad and saw things I didn't think were possible." He took out the same crystal he'd had when he'd confronted that man on the way to the village. "Don't be afraid."

"Wait, what?" she asked. She could hear panic in her voice.

By then, it was too late. He turned around.

She gasped. She didn't recognize the man standing before her. He had a flat nose, beady, intimidating black eyes, and crooked teeth. "Where's August?" she demanded. "August? Aug—"

"Lyndsey, it's me," he said and took a couple of steps toward her.

"No, no, you're not August," she said as her flight response kicked in. She took a few steps backward and backed up to a tree. She let out a scream.

August leapt toward her. "Shhh. Look at me. It's called a glamour," he explained as he opened his other hand, exposing a green crystal. She covered her mouth in horror as his facial features seemed to slide down his face like it was melting before he was back to looking like himself again.

She shoved him. "Asshole! You scared me."

"Silly, I told you not to be afraid," he said and looked her deep in her eyes. "You're safe with me—haven't you learned that by now?"

She looked away. "Yeah, whatever," she said. "So, is that what you did to that guy who charged me?"

He nodded. "It's something that's rarely used because there's rarely a reason to deceive people like that, but I wanted to let you know that this is the real thing and that I'm a believer."

"Does it hurt? I was horrified watching you change back."

"Not at all. It just looks weird." He snapped his fingers. "I should have screamed out in agony just to mess with you." His mouth turned up on one side.

"Like you haven't done that enough already?"

<hr>

THAT DAY, and in the days that followed, August taught her the Incorporeal belief systems and practices. It didn't take long for Lyndsey to realize that this wasn't just something he knew about and haphazardly practiced. It was his identity. He was animated and passionate about his beliefs, but he didn't come across as preachy. With the use of crystals and other natural materials, he demonstrated how to create and cast spells to bring positivity to the lives of others, as well as herself. He taught her how to meditate, shift her vibrations, and visualize to attract good things in her life.

His excitement energized her, and she looked forward to learning more. The principles and purposes practiced were far more significant than just finding and punishing her mother. Her dedication to understanding the tenets began taking on a life of its own. It now meant so much more than that.

———

ONE NIGHT, August didn't show up to dinner. Magnus explained to Lyndsey that he was in the middle of a project and that he'd head over to her yurt in the morning.

Lyndsey awoke the next morning to August calling for her from outside. "Are you ready for some real fun today?" August asked. There was something mischievous in his tone.

"Always. I'll be out in ten minutes."

They hiked all the way to the cave they'd tried to get to the day she overheated.

She dropped her backpack and walked inside. Her mouth dropped at the beauty of the glowing crystals and gems. Every color brilliantly glistened in the sunlight that poured through small openings in the cave's ceiling. Its breathtaking beauty humbled her, and how she was of only a few people who'd ever seen this world wonder.

"I've never seen anything like this," Lyndsey said as she reached down to touch a glowing blue crystal.

"This cave is protected by an enchantment that prevents miners from ever discovering it," August said as he stood at the entrance behind her. He crouched down and reached inside his backpack. "I gotta say, I'm glad you were able to finally see this. It was nice that you made it all the way here with no problems," he continued and pulled a carved stick from one of the inner pockets of his pack. "This was what I was working on last night. It's a wand," he presented. "I made it for you."

She could feel her eyes grow wide with surprise. She had never been given a gift from a guy before. "Wow. I don't know what to say. Um, thank you," she said as he placed the wand in her hands.

"It's made from the Walking Palm. That's the tree with those really tall roots we've seen on our hike to the camp. It grows new roots to replace old ones, but some say the new roots allow for the tree to move a few centimeters, hence the name," he explained.

She stared at the wand and glided her fingers along the engraved details. On the hilt of the wand had a silhouette of a woman walking with a lion. The stem was contoured to look as if it was twisted, and the top was a flame that made the entire piece resemble a torch.

She blinked a few times as tears pricked her eyes. He moved near her, provoking her to turn her head so he wouldn't catch her reaction. His fingers were close to hers as he explained the meaning behind his work. "The woman and the lion is from the tarot card for Strength. It's about your courage and bravery. These engraved swirls are traditional markings the villagers do when they paint their faces. The flame at the top has multiple meanings. Aside from the fact that you're fiery to your core—" he chuckled, "—it's also a symbol of you exerting power and control over what defeated you in the past," he said, smiling as he looked into her eyes.

"August," she whispered, shaking her head, causing tears to tumble down.

He reached out to put his arms around her shoulders, but stopped.

Lyndsey moved closer to him, resting her head on his shoulder.

He gently put his arm around her. "Is this okay?"

She nodded, and a sob escaped. "Sorry."

His touch warmed her body, and she wanted to stay in that cave and never leave. This was going to be a moment she would forever reflect upon as one of her greatest.

"Now," he said, letting go and leaving her bereft. "Pick any of these crystals that speak to you, and I'll place it in the wand." He took out a pick and a hammer. "You were admiring that blue one. Maybe that should be the one."

"Um, sure," she said, taking the tools from him. She kneeled down, glanced between the tools and the crystal, uncertain what to do.

August knelt beside her. His close proximity would normally make her stiffen up, but not this time. "Just place the pick alongside the crystal," he said and placed his finger beside the crystal, encouraging her to start there. "The stone walls are not that thick, so you shouldn't have a problem."

She smiled and nodded, and after a few light strikes, the crystal was liberated.

"Good job," he praised.

She placed the tools on the ground and stared at the crystal cradled in her hand. "It's so beautiful."

"Just wait til it gets polished." He gleamed like he was impressed with the crystal as well. "I'm going to remove one over here," he said and took the tools back.

She tried to stay focused on her treasure, but when he began to strike the pick, her eyes drifted to his backside. Staring, she imagined his back was as robust as his arms and chest. Each strike of the pin was more forceful than the previous. *He's driving me crazy.* He grunted while working the crystal, sending a shockwave of desire through her body.

"Come on," he uttered as he continued to pry the orange crystal from the wall.

She turned away to discreetly wipe the perspiration from her forehead.

"Err," he grunted again. "Yes," he said aloud as it was released. "Whoo, that took some work," he chuckled.

You have no idea. "That's a pretty one too," she complimented.

Still a bit breathless, August placed the crystal in his backpack. "A wand can be very powerful, but it takes time to cure it," he explained.

"The woman who was my mom's caretaker, Mozelle, who cast the curse. I remember her telling me that spirits leave signatures on wands. Is that what you mean by cure?"

"Yes, but we're talking master-level classes when it comes to demonstrating the power a wand wields. In short, it's used to channel your vibrations when casting spells or using magic. People usually start by pointing at a photo of someone they want to send positive vibes to. But as you advance, you will start appealing for help from positive spirits so that you can perform more involved castings. A true master can communicate their thoughts to the wand and move objects or create instant enchantments—a power most try to avoid because abusing its power can become enslaving." He paused for fear he had gone total professor on her. "Anyway, the actual application of that power will be a lesson for another time." A slanted grin emerged. "Until then, let's head back."

She put her pack on and left the cave, clutching the gift she would treasure for the rest of her life.

OVER THE NEXT COUPLE DAYS, Lyndsey's belief in the Incorporealist's principles continued to flourish. She was thankful that August was the one to be her guide. Her attachment to him grew more intense with each encounter.

Gazing at August while he demonstrated the use of his wand, crystals, and spell casting did nothing to slow the runaway train that was her feelings. Sometimes, he would illustrate something that required him to be near her, and, like the day in the cave, she didn't resist. She liked how he continued to respect her boundaries and avoided touching her back or shoulders. On occasions that he did need to touch her, he would stand in front of her and guide her while holding her arms or hands. One time when he stood behind her, even though he was a safe distance from her, she had been able to feel his heat and hear his breath, and she found herself fantasizing that he would come closer to her and do more than just touch her arms. He stirred something inside her, and those feelings of disgust were becoming a distant memory.

On a walk back to the village one night, Lyndsey stopped. "We're friends, right?" Lyndsey asked, absently pulling a leaf from a plant they'd stopped in front of.

He walked over and faced her. "I like to think so," he said, tilting his head as if not knowing where she was going with such a question.

She looked into his eyes to gauge his trust. His serious look assured her that it was safe to be honest about her past. "When I was younger, I had a hard time with other kids. I did mean things—like really mean things," she began. Then looked down. "I cut some girl's hair, I pushed another kid down some steps, and I got expelled a couple times, all before I even left elementary school. My parents brought me to psychologists and the whole thing."

His mouth lifted to one side as he took a step closer to her. "You have a strength about you, Lyndsey, that is beyond your ability to handle. What I mean is that you have been given a gift that, as a child, you didn't know what to do with, but now that you're aware—" he shook his head, "—you can use that gift to move mountains."

She held his gaze. *You're the only one who can save me, aren't you?* She blinked and looked away to keep her emotions in check, but a single tear slipped out, betraying her.

August reached out to wipe her tear. She moved to swat his hand away, but he grabbed her wrist with his other hand. "Don't fight me, Lyndsey," he said. He looked down at her mouth, breathing rapidly. His jaw was set, but she couldn't tell if he was angry or not.

Thunder rolled in the distance, yanking them back to their senses. August looked up and loosened his grip as his expression turned playful. "Let's go back to camp," he said, giving her a slight tug.

Within a few steps, the sparse raindrops turned into a downpour. She found herself smiling as he pulled her quickly along the trees. *Was that a moment? Was he going to kiss me? Does he like me like that?* Her heart raced as she imagined him leaning down and sweeping his lips across hers. *I would be the happiest person in the world. Could this be my fate? Action—reaction.*

He took his shirt off to shield her from the downpour until they got to her yurt.

"This will pass shortly. I'll see you in a little bit," he told her. He took his drenched shirt and threw it over his shoulder, leaving her alone in her doorway.

She stared at his muscled back as he walked away, pulling back his long, wet hair with both hands. The rain was still coming down hard. She closed her eyes as she replayed the moment they'd just shared. She wanted to run up to him, turn him toward her, and kiss him as the rain poured down on them. She snorted at the thought and turned back into her yurt.

Once inside, she saw Shani sitting before her altar, meditating. In front of her was a newly carved wand with an orange crystal embedded at the top. Her smile dropped, and her heart splintered into a million pieces. She wasn't so special after all.

She grasped and yanked at the hair behind her ears. Heat rattled from within as betrayal and humiliation settled into every one of her nerve endings. She looked up to stop the tears from flowing. She spun around, hitting her hand on the post that divided the yurt's entry flaps. "Fuck!" She grabbed her hand and ran out.

August was several feet away helping a young woman get to

her yurt by shielding her from the rain, just as he had with Lyndsey barely two minutes prior.

She ran through the rain and into the forest, yelling at herself, relieved that the pounding rain was loud enough to drown out her cries. "What was I thinking? Did I think there was a chance with him? Did I really think that the day I bared my scar and my soul to him, or the day in the cave, was as special to him as it was to me? I could just kick myself." She looked up toward the sky. "Damn you, *Beauty and the Beast*, for being the farce that you are!"

Anger radiated throughout her body, and it recharged her mission. She picked up a rock and threw it, then clutched her hand when pain struck her. She hadn't realized how hard she'd slammed it when she ran out. "Fuck!"

<hr>

August quickly helped the young woman back to her yurt and ran back to Lyndsey and Shani's yurt. "What happened? Why did Lyndsey run out of here like she was upset?" he asked, not caring that he'd broken Shani out of her meditative state.

Shani turned around. "I didn't hear her."

He saw Shani's wand, and his gut sank. "I bet you she saw your wand." He closed his eyes. She was jealous. "Shit!"

"You didn't mention that you made wands for both of us?"

He bit his upper lip and shook his head. He raked his hand through his hair, taking a deep breath. "Screw it. Make her forget."

She stood up and faced him. "I won't do that." She lifted her finger at him, emphasizing that he was overstepping, then crossed her arms. "Why are you so stressed about it? Putting on the charm to get her to be more amenable is one thing, August, but you don't want to lead her on, do you?"

He wiped his hands down his face and sighed.

Shani tilted her head. "August?" she asked with accusation in her voice.

"I'm outta here." He swiftly turned, left the yurt, and headed the same direction he'd seen Lyndsey go.

Shani's right. What the hell am I doing? This is my opportunity to put things back in place. I got the hourglass. I just have to fulfill my obligation to teach her how to find her mom. The rest is straight-up bullshit. Right? He shook his head as he trudged through the undergrowth. *Just find her. Let her know she only has herself to blame for letting her attraction get out of hand. It's not like I gave her an engagement ring.*

He stopped when he spotted her sitting on a log. She was cradling herself, shivering with cold in the pouring rain. He looked away in shame over his previous thoughts. She always came across as strong. When she hated herself most, or when she'd revealed her scar to him—even then, in her greatest moment of vulnerability—she was strong. But sitting there with her head down, holding herself because no one else would, she appeared defenseless, wounded, and fragile. He resisted how badly he wanted to run to her and throw his arms around her, to protect her from any more hurt. He closed his eyes at the thought that he was the source of her pain.

"Please go away, August," she said, looking over her shoulder. Her hair was plastered in a zigzag pattern across her face.

He marched over to her. "I need you to tell me what has you so upset," he demanded. He guessed it was over the wand, but he wanted to hear it from her.

"Nothing. I'm frustrated that we're losing time, and I still don't know how to help my mom."

"Really? Is that the real reason you're so upset? Or is it something else?"

"What? You think I'm upset over something *you* did?" She scoffed. "Don't flatter yourself," she said and took a breath. "And now that we've established that it's not all about you, please leave me the hell alone."

"Damn it, Lyndsey! You can be so infuriating," he yelled, walking around the log to face her. He put one leg up on the log. "Listen, I was going to tell you about the wand I made for Shani," he explained.

Lyndsey turned her body away from him as if to hide her emotions. "I hadn't even noticed," she said weakly.

He waved his hand to brush away her lie. "But when I saw how moved you were, I didn't want to ruin the moment by making you feel like it was meaningless, because it wasn't."

"I don't care about the wand," she mumbled.

"The hell you don't!"

She shot him a look.

"I *did* make yours special. Hers doesn't have the symbolic engravings that yours does."

She stood up. "Oh yeah? And why is that, August? Why did you make mine special?"

His mouth was agape as he struggled to find the words. "I just—"

"You just what?" she asked. Then cocked her head as if trying to make eye contact.

"I just wanted to reward you for all the progress you've made," he fibbed. He had a hard enough time admitting to himself that his motivation was more than that, let alone confessing anything to her.

"Well, thank you, *professor*, for my progress report. I think it's only appropriate for me to grade *you* now," she said, raising her eyebrows.

August pursed his lips while waiting for her to go off on him. His eyes followed her as she paced. He watched as her breath quickened, then she licked her full lips while she considered her next statement. Her long, wet hair and the fire in her eyes stirred something in him. Taking a step closer, he wanted to cover her mouth with his just to stop her from saying another word and reel her back in.

"The grade I … I give you …" She stopped, looking him in the eye. "What are you doing?"

He took another step closer.

"What grade are you going to give me?" he asked, taking yet another step. He was close enough that he could feel the heat from her body.

She placed her hand on his chest, and her eyes dropped from his eyes to his mouth. "I … I give you an 'A' for being an assho—"

He reached behind her head and pulled her in. "Yeah?"

They were both panting. "Yeah, and an 'A' for angering the holy hell—"

He grabbed her hand that rested on his chest. She gasped, yanking her hand back.

"Shit. Did I hurt you? What is it?" he asked, wanting to comfort her but not knowing what to do with his hands as she cowered away from him.

"I hurt my hand running out of the yurt. Shit. This hurts."

"Let me see."

"No. It's fine."

"Lyndsey, damn it! I'm not playing. Let me see your hand."

She scoffed and flung her hand at him.

He gently took her hand to examine it. He could feel her tense up as he brushed his thumb over her smooth palm. He looked up at her and saw she was staring at him.

"You were going to kiss me," she accused.

"I was going to shut you up."

"By kissing me."

"By whatever means necessary," he said, looking down to study her hand again.

She yanked her hand away. "Why can't you admit that you might have feelings for me?"

He put his hands on his hips and bit his lower lip. "To be honest, I don't know what I feel. You get me all riled up, and I act impulsively. I'm sorry. I shouldn't have done that," he said, placing his hand on his chest.

She looked down at her hand as she continued to rub it. "Well, if you haven't guessed…" She paused to prepare herself for the big rejection. "I like you. I don't know what happened because you've maintained an 'A' in assholerly from the beginning." She chuckled nervously and looked back up at him. "But you can also be so tender, attentive, and kind. That's on top of having so much passion, and you're so damn hot that when you're being protective, it makes me crazy," she said with wide eyes.

He shook his head in shame. "Obviously, there's something here, but you're not the only one who has fears."

"Like what?"

"Relationships are complicated, time-consuming, and I know I would lose myself in you. I'm like you in that sense—I'm not a half-in kind of guy—and I don't think I want that in my life right now."

"I'm not worth it. I get it," she said, rubbing along her scar and rolling her eyes like she was sick and tired of surrendering to her fate.

He could feel his nostrils flare in frustration, and he took another step toward her. "That—" he pointed at her sternly, "—right there is the reason why this wouldn't work," he snapped through gritted teeth. He began pacing. "I see the strides you've made to overcome all the horror you've endured, but I hate how insecure you are." He shook his head. His resistance against confessing was fracturing. "I didn't realize how beautiful you were until I saw you leave the yurt the day you revealed your scar to me. You were radiant." He shook his head again in disbelief. "And then there's this fierceness about you too. And *that* is what inspired me to make the wand." He swept his hand through his hair. "What I'm saying is that you're worth it, Lynd-sey, but I have work to do, and right now, I will only disappoint you. If this were ever to happen, it will happen when I know *I'm* worthy of *you*. That's it—that's how I feel." He put his hands on his hips and breathed out a long breath.

Lyndsey stood there, blinking as if in shock. "I don't know what to say."

"There's nothing left to say. We know where we stand. Now let's get that hand looked at," he advised, and they walked back to camp in silence.

THE NEXT DAY, Lyndsey waited outside her yurt for August to finish his conversation with a young woman in the camp. She twisted the hair behind her ear in frustration as August inter-acted with the woman with the gentleness and attentiveness that she wanted just to herself. He'd confessed his true feelings for her, but he'd also followed through with his promise to *not* move the relationship forward. After he'd been a no-show at dinner the night before, she believed he was avoiding her. *Is it because he's weak around me? Or because he thinks I'm weak around him and he doesn't want to hurt me?*

He finally turned and walked toward her, looking around camp and waving to fellow group members. It felt strategic like he was trying to convey that she wasn't as important as she might think.

He finally stopped in front of her. "How's your hand?" he asked like he was obligated.

"It's fine. That herbal salve they gave me helped. Anyway, we need to address the reason I came here—you know, aside from the hourglass," she said, looking him in the eye and rubbing it in that he'd gotten what he needed, so now it was her turn. "So are you going to teach me how to find my mom or not?" she grumbled.

He cleared his throat. "Um, right."

"Yeah. Great. Tell me more about reincarnation."

"Let's take a walk," he said, and she followed him into the forest to a stream she hadn't seen before. He stopped on the stream bank and looked thoughtfully at the ground on the other side. "Reincarnation is an extraordinary gift, but it's also complicated. The belief is that you return to a corporeal being to address all kinds of problems. Everything you learn from the experiences in one life is carried with you to your next life, but you have no memory of it. You continue the cycle until you eventually reach such a level of wisdom and love that reincarnation is no longer warranted. But even then, a soul will cycle over and over to help guide others through their challenges."

He crouched down and put his hand in the stream. "There is a thing called a soul contract. It's something that is done in-between lives. When you die, you meet with the Shepherd of Soul Contracts. They review your life and might even go over how you died. They make a recommendation, and sometimes they will negotiate—but typically not, because they can see the overall plan, like a college advisor in a sense." He chuckled. "It's all for the purpose of personal growth by way of trials."

Lyndsey sat down next to him. "How do you know so much? Do you have any memory of meeting with the Shepherd?"

"I don't. Trying to remember is considered disrespecting the process, and Incorporealists feel that it's bad luck to try. However, it's different than trying to remember your past life. That can be a helpful tool, but it's also not encouraged because it can become a total mind fuck," he said, rolling his eyes at the thought of it.

He got up and sat on a nearby log. "It's actually fascinating when it comes to the Shepherds. They can get pretty creative. For example, some soul contracts allow for soul walk-ins." He realized he was lecturing the same way he taught his classes. He smiled at how closely she was paying attention and hoped this was reeling her back in.

"Soul walk-ins?"

"Yes," he said, and in hoping to maintain her attention, he put on the charm and leaned in closer to explain. "Some souls can reincarnate into someone already living. This is not the same as possession. They do this because they want to bypass all the trauma of childhood and adolescence. They either made a soul contract to share a body with another soul beforehand, or they enter a body that is in bad shape, maybe in a coma, or a drug addict living on the street, strung out and hopeless. That sort of thing. They're easy to spot, too, because they're the ones you hear about making a miraculous recovery."

"Wow. Well, that complicates things even more. My mother could be anyone, anywhere, anytime."

He crossed his leg. "Tell me more about what you know. How did you find out that your mom is going to reincarnate and be cursed?"

"Well," she started, then paused for a second so she would get the lie right. "When my mom was alive, she had a friend named Mozelle, who considered herself an oracle. My mother was dying of cancer. At some point, Mozelle told my mom she could help her find my dad in the next life. I don't know. I guess she had an axe to grind because she twisted the ritual so that they would *never* be able to be together. Something will always get in the way, and they will live many lives of heartbreak. I know this because I found her casting journal in the ashes after the fire.

Fortunately, it had been protected, so I was able to salvage it. Anyway, I read the pages she had earmarked, and that's when I learned what she had been up to. Right now, the only thing that can help me find my mom is that Mozelle branded my mom with a star on her chest so she'd reincarnate with a star birthmark."

"Ah, the birthmark thing is common. I'm not sure if you noticed that most married villagers have branding marks or birthmarks."

"I did notice. I saw a woman with a crescent moon branded on her wrist, and she pointed out who her soulmate was, but I didn't see his brand."

"That's Eunice, and her mate is Audi," he said with a smile.

"So would that mean that Mozelle was an Incorporealist?"

"I doubt it. We don't use our skills with malevolent intentions."

"Right. That makes sense," she said, looking away. *I guess I'll never be like him. Why does that make me sad?*

"Well, this is my take. Your mom will probably reincarnate soon, and close to where you live, for a couple of reasons. First, since you're still living, they may reincarnate just to be near you, which is very common. And second, Mozelle probably planned it that way so that she could be there to witness and take pleasure in your mother's misery." He shook his head. "It's terrible, and I'm sorry that happened."

"I guess it was all for naught because Mozelle died in that fire too."

"I definitely can help you with some basic curse-reversal spells, and I can speak with the camp leaders to see if they can get a read on what they feel the future holds for you. But without the spellbook or other items, that's about the most I can do. When we get back home, please come by with the casting journal and anything else that might help me help you. I'm sorry. I wish I could do more."

"Okay. I guess I don't have much of a choice."

Over the next couple days, they worked on curse reversals, as well as really tuning into spiritual guides and learning what to listen for. He taught her about the use of crystals, candles, oils, and herbs. It was a lot to take in, but she was a quick study and felt energy changes occurring within her body. She began to embrace the idea of visualization—harnessing energy and vibrations to manipulate her environment.

ON THEIR LAST NIGHT THERE, the villagers put on a grand party that served as a ceremony to celebrate the passage of souls moving to their next stage and a farewell party for August, Lyndsey, and Shani. The night included emotive blessings, inspiring speeches, and dances that were beautiful and poignant. They presented them with handmade gifts, including a replica hourglass. Magnus stood on the stage with citrine and red jasper crystals around his neck to manifest prosperity, virility, and anything one desired. Along with the villagers, he wore thick, black eyeliner and gold chokers in addition to the standard jewelry. They enjoyed a bean and pineapple soup, as well as multiple shots of Olhas da Nuvens, which turned their gathering into an all-out party.

The light from the torches that lined the perimeter flickered as people moved to live music. Seduction stirred through the air like a storm. The beat of the drums was like the slink of a jaguar, and people were entranced. The more people joined in, the more the temperature surged. Women raised their arms, sliding their hands along the skin of their forearms as they slowly spun around. Others moved their hands along their bodies, their hips swaying side to side. Some men peeled off their shirts to cool themselves.

Breathless, Lyndsey's eyes widened at the complete abandonment of restraint around her. The drink, the rhythm of the music, even the feel of the fabric as it caressed her skin impassioned her, and all her inhibitions evaporated.

Driven to test who was weaker, her or August, she scanned the crowd looking for him. When she spotted him, his eyes were already on her. She began dancing with Shani. She glided her hands down the length of her neck, along the sides of her breast, and over her undulating hips. She looked back at August. There was a stern look in his eyes and his arms were crossed. He jutted his jaw and looked away from her like, before turning and walking away.

What does that mean? Well, shit! I guess I'm the weaker one. She left the make-shift dance floor and walked in the direction she'd seen him head. As she came around back, lust pulsated the second she saw him leaning against a post, his shirt wide open. Enraptured, she strode toward him as she watched him watch her.

***

RELIEVED SHE CAME AFTER HIM, August couldn't take his eyes off her as she sauntered closer. Lust continued to radiate from her just as it had while she was dancing. Ever since he'd acknowledged his feelings for her, he'd wanted her with an intensity he had never experienced. His breathing quickened as she neared, and before words could escape her mouth, he grabbed her, crushing his mouth onto hers. He kissed her deeply and with the same passion as their heated exchanges. She was right there with him. He wrapped his arm around her waist and pressed her against him as she held on to him tightly. Their hunger for each other intensified as he turned her so that her back was against the post. She lifted her leg to wrap around his hip, and he grunted. He broke free of their kiss, panting, then kissed her neck.

"I'm so glad you came to find me. I couldn't take seeing you dance like that. You're so fucking hot," he whispered in her ear, breathless. "But we can't do this here."

"I want you so bad, August," she groaned as she began grinding on his erection.

"Fuuuck," August gasped. "Lyndsey, we need to stop. We can't do this."

Her hands were on his face. Their lips barely touched. "Why?" she asked, pressing her body into his.

"We're out in public, and we're under the influence," he explained.

"Look around," she said, glancing at the crowd. Everywhere, young couples were pairing off—one couple stood in the center of the group, kissing passionately. Another man stood behind a woman, kissing her shoulder and gripping her hips as he pulled her close. Some other man and woman embraced as they danced. Then the woman wrapped her leg around his, arching her back. Lyndsey watched as he laid a trail of sensual kisses from her chest up to her neck, and she dropped her head back in ecstasy. The air was electrified, and no one was immune. She looked to August. "I think that's the point," she said, her mouth open, pulling him in for another deep kiss.

After a moment, he pulled himself from her. "You're driving me crazy, but I don't think you've done anything like this before."

"So?" she said, reaching for his ass and pulling him back. She began grinding on him again. His resistance was weakening, and he was breathing heavily. "You're so damn beautiful," he said, looking into her eyes. He raked his hand through her hair and pressed himself harder against her, kissing her unrelentingly. His body strained against every curve of her body, and he surrendered with a guttural sound from deep within. He removed her hand from his rear and took a step back. A small, disappointed moan escaped her as her leg slid back down. He pulled her with him, and they started toward the yurts.

———

SHE COULDN'T TELL if he was actually giving in, but she wasn't going to stop him from taking her anywhere he wanted to go.

They were almost to her yurt when Magnus came running up to August and stopped them. "Hey, I need to talk to you about something. It's urgent."

August dropped Lyndsey's hand. "What's going on?"

"It's private," Magnus said, then looked at Lyndsey as if he knew he'd interrupted.

"Um. Okay. Yeah," August said, then looked to Lyndsey. "Give me a few minutes. I'll find you."

"Umm, okay," she said, looking between them. She watched as they walked away.

It struck her as odd that Magnus had his hand on August's back, and she could even swear that she could see the glint of a dark crystal in Magnus's hand.

Not sure what else to do, she took a seat on the chair in her yurt and waited. And waited. After twenty minutes, she went looking for August, but he was nowhere to be found. She searched throughout the camp, but after another half hour, it appeared he was going to be a no-show, and with that, she went to bed, disheartened, anxious, and worried.

The next morning, concern drove her to get up, get out, and get answers to what happened with August the night before. To ease any tension or uncertainty over how she felt about him, she tied the most revealing of her scarf blouses around her neck and left the yurt to search for him. After ten minutes, she found him tinkering with an auto part inside a yurt that served as a garage for their ATVs.

"Hey," she greeted with the most sultry morning voice she could muster.

"Hey," August replied as he continued working. He didn't even look up.

A hard twinge hit her stomach. She moved closer to him, encouraging easier access, but he continued his work. His workspace was strewn with tools, so she wondered how long he'd been there and how much longer he'd be.

"So, um, yeah," she said, placing her hand on her hip, trying to get him to notice her. "That was some night last night."

"Yeah. It was fun," he said, grunting. His biceps glistened as he muscled a wrench.

He looks just as hot as he did last night, but something's off. "So what happened last night with Magnus? What did he want from you so badly that he needed to, you know, interrupt us?"

He stopped what he was doing and squinted his eyes like he was confused. "A funny thing about that…"

"Oh yeah? What?" She hoped this was the part where he made it all better.

"When I woke up this morning, he told me what they needed me to work on over the next few months, like he was continuing a conversation I didn't know we had. I asked him what he was talking about. Then Magnus says, 'Don't you remember our conversation last night?' And I said—"

Her expression fell. "No," she finished his sentence.

"Yep! I can't remember much past that third shot, which I had pretty early on. It's weird how that happened. I don't usually have that kind of reaction."

Crushed, she struggled to breathe. The most amazing night she'd ever had was now hers and hers alone. *He still thinks we're mere friends, while I'm standing here, practically in lingerie like a fool. This is a total train wreck.* She crossed her arms over her breasts. Perspiration emerged as the heat of humiliation came to a boiling point.

He looked up at her. "Are you okay? You don't look so good."

"So you're staying?" she asked. She could hear her voice waver. Never had it occurred to her that she could feel more pain than the day she was set on fire, but August forgetting the night before and not going home with her was a very close second.

"It looks that way. It's complicated, but I still want to meet up when I get back, and I can fill you in."

"When were you planning on telling me that you're not coming home with me? I mean, how am I supposed to get home?"

"I'm going to take you to the airport. Shani is going to stay back as well," he explained.

"So that's it?" Despite her best attempt to hold back tears, they slipped out anyway.

He put his hands on his hips and shook his head. "I'm sorry, Lyndsey, but it's not like I didn't warn you. I did say I had work to do."

She looked away from him. "You weren't referring to this. This feels sudden, and not at all how I envisioned today would go," she admitted, closing her eyes. She could hear how desperate she sounded, allowing embarrassment to saturate every cell in her body.

He put his tools down, and in two steps, he stood right in front of her. "I'm confused, Lyndsey. What am I missing here?"

She wiped her tears with the heel of her hand. She wasn't going to further embarrass herself by reminding him that the night before was proof that there was something between them. "Oh … I don't know. Nothing. Whatever. When do we leave?"

He had a look of pity on his face.

"Don't look at me like that," she demanded. Her stomach dropped, and she felt like she was going to be sick.

"You're obviously hurt. Did I do or say anything last night?"

"No! Please, can we leave as soon as possible? Maybe I can

get someone else to take me since you're so busy!" More tears fell. "You know … I just need to get out of here," she asserted. Then quickly left the yurt.

August ran after her. "Lyndsey, wait!"

She stormed into her yurt, grabbed her suitcase, and stormed back out.

August was standing there, hands on his hips, waiting for her. "Can we talk about what's upsetting you?" he asked.

She continued her brisk walk toward the back of the camp where the ATVs were. "No! Listen, thank you for all you and Shani have done for me. Thank Magnus, too, when you see him."

"Lyndsey." He grabbed her shoulder, and she shot him a look that told him to back the hell off. He immediately let go. "I can't figure it out."

"Then stop trying. You said you have work to do, and that's clear. You were my teacher in a sense, and I was your student, and that's okay. I got what I needed from you, so it's time for me to leave, with or without you."

"I don't see you as a student at all. I can't let you go like this. I feel bad," he said, a strained look on his face.

"Well, not bad enough."

He rolled his eyes. "What is it that you want from me? Do you expect me to drop everything? My work? My career? My life? To run off to marry you?"

The sharp pain in her chest from heartbreak was more than she could bear. "No, August, that is not even close to what I want from you. Don't worry about reaching out to me when you get back." She waited a second, then grabbed ahold of her things again. "Goodbye, August," she said and walked away.

A few feet away, she ran into Magnus and asked if he could take her to the airport. He told her he couldn't but quickly found someone who could. She made her tears appear as though she was sad to leave the camp. She said her goodbyes to

Magnus and Shani, and the rest of the people in the group. She got onto an ATV with her driver and left the Incorporealists and their camp forever.

MAGNUS CAME into the yurt as August was crouching back down, continuing his work.

"How's it going? Everything okay? You seem upset." Magnus asked.

August stopped what he was doing. "Why?" he snapped.

Magnus leaned back against a workbench. "I want to know what happened between the two of you. You both seem angry at each other. What happened after we talked last night? Didn't you go back to her to tell her you were staying?"

"What do you mean by 'go back to her'?

Magnus raised his eyebrows. "Never mind. Just … seeing if you remember anything."

"What are you getting at, Magnus?" He grunted as he tightened a nut.

"When I saw the two of you going at it last night, I realized that I needed to intervene."

August stopped what he was doing. "Hold on … What do you mean we were going at it? Like fighting or …?"

"August, I know you're angry now, but what I did was to help both of you. There is more going on that I can't get into at the moment, but I want to explain before the enchantment wears off."

"You enchanted me? What the hell's going on, Magnus?"

"I stopped you two from completely going off and screwing each other to oblivion."

"Son of a bitch!" August yelled, dropping his tools. "Where is she? Is she still here?"

"No, August, she left."

"Shit! I need to find her." He ran out, grabbed the keys to an ATV, and set out to find her.

He didn't make it on time.

When he returned to camp, Magnus was there to console him.

"The worst part of all this is that after you mentioned what you saw, I began to remember bits and pieces of what happened last night," August confessed. "I *did* give in to her last night, or at least started to, even though I know she's had a crush on me from early on, and even though I fully took advantage of that at first. It was when she broke down and let go of her attachment to those damn turtleneck shirts that I saw the real her, and I fell in love. Fuck! And now she'll never know. She left here thinking I don't feel the same." Tears began to well in his eyes.

"August, there's another reason I interrupted you, and it has to do with a prophecy that came to light while all three of you were here. It's one of the reasons I asked you to stay," Magnus warned.

"What do you mean a prophecy?" August asked, anger in his voice.

"It involves her and her father, but I'm not going to tell you more than that. To save her from the prophecy, you'll need to give her space. She's going to go down a road you need to steer clear of. You will be able to help her, but if you go to her too soon, it'll unfold in catastrophic ways."

LYNDSEY'S PAIN WAS CRIPPLING. She stewed in her humiliation the entire flight home. When she arrived back in California and saw Alastair waiting for her outside by the exit, she could no longer hold back the tears.

"I'm sorry, Grandpa! I'm just so glad to be home," she said, giving him a big hug.

"We missed you, too, Lynds! I hope you found what you were looking for."

"Thanks, Grandpa. I just need a friend right now," she expressed, but then realized that she didn't know anyone who fits that title.

"Let's get going. I'm going to tell you something on the way home that I hope will make you feel better," he said.

He began telling his story as they pulled onto the freeway. "Many years ago, when I was a teenager, I, too, took a trip to Brazil with my family. We were in Manaus on a riverboat tour to see the Meeting of Two Rivers one day. Now I don't know if you know what the Meeting of Two Rivers is, but it's the confluence of the Rio Negro and the Solimões rivers. But the thing that is remarkable about it is that the two rivers do not mix. One is a normal looking bluish water, but the other is the color of coffee. They don't mix due to multiple factors, but one is because they move at different speeds."

She looked at her grandfather. There was longing and pain in his eyes. *Where is this going?*

"Well, it started raining, and my brother and I got into it. He ends up falling into the slower river, and when everyone rushed to his rescue, the boat listed, and I fell into the fast-moving one. Everyone was preoccupied with tending to my brother, so they didn't realize I had fallen in until I was way too far downstream. The run-down charter we were on wasn't fast enough to catch up to me. I ended up on a beach way downstream, and after spending almost two days unprotected in the Amazon, I was rescued by a group of spiritual-type people. They helped me recover, but it was the rainy season, so a family reunion wasn't likely to occur for several days. They welcomed me, healed me, and accepted me as an outsider. They showed me their rituals, and I imbibed on their drink. It was there that I met a girl named Anica. Anica and I fell madly in love, but as you can imagine, when they found out that we were in love … Well, our parents would not allow it, and they tore us apart.

"That doesn't make me feel better," Lyndsey said, frowning and rubbing her forehead.

He raised his hand. "Wait until the end. Years later, when I was in college, we had a chance meeting. She brought me a sacred gift from her group. Unfortunately, she died sometime after, but well before I met your grandmother."

She closed her eyes, thinking back to the arguments her grandparents had had over the hourglass. How he'd hinted it was about another woman. Lyndsey bent over and covered her face. *What have I done?*

"Lyndsey, I know it sounds bad, but—"

"Tell me, Grandpa. Just tell me. What was the gift?" she asked, shaking her head. The last twenty-four hours had been hell for her, and she wasn't sure how much more pain she could endure.

"She brought me an hourglass."

"Oh no, Grandpa," she cried. "I didn't know. I'm so sorry!"

"No, Lyndsey, listen to me. This is the good part of the story. As much as I wanted to hold on to that gift she gave me, I knew she stole it. I knew it was sacred to that group, but I didn't know how to get it back to them. You have no idea how much peace I feel over this. Because ultimately, the time we *did* have together was magical, *despite* the hourglass. I realized that when I saw the hourglass was missing."

"I don't know what to say," she responded. "I went behind your back, and I didn't think about how it would affect you." She slapped her leg in frustration. "I hate myself."

"Lynds, I'm sorry you're still struggling after all this time. Don't feel bad about the hourglass. It's back where it belongs. But, for the future, please ask first. Okay?"

She nodded. "I promise." *I feel bad for hurting you, Grandpa, and I won't do anything to hurt you again, but at the same time, I did what I had to do. Consider yourself lucky, because there will be those in my life who will not be getting such promises.*

As she settled back into home life, she found herself needing to reach out. Brazil, overall, had been an unbelievable experience, minus the devastating heartbreak. However, the most important lesson she'd learned was that people would accept her, and not everyone found her repulsive. She thought about a couple of the friends she'd had and how they'd tried to maintain friendships after the fire, but now she realized that her hatred toward herself was what had caused those friendships to fade away. She logged online and began combing through profiles on Myspace, trying to find them, but it was on Classmates.com that she found her infamous friend, Claudine. Despite her apprehension, Lyndsey sent her a message.

Claudine quickly responded. She was very excited that Lyndsey had reached out, and the two of them made plans to get together and catch up.

They met over lunch at the Beach Chalet. Lyndsey was glad that Claudine came armed with embellished melodramas and salacious rumors. She didn't even mind adding her own lovelorn story to Claudine's catalog of spectacles. She was desperate for a distraction, and she would sacrifice her own pride if that's what it took to rescue herself from her inner turmoil.

By the end of the lunch, Lyndsey had mixed feelings about the meet-up. When she learned that one of Claudine's older cousins, Mason, and everyone in his circle of friends had all gotten married and had babies in 2002, it didn't raise the alarm for Lyndsey. She just focused on how people around her lived everyday lives while she continued to endure one hardship after another.

One thing was for sure—she'd developed new skills that were going to change the course of her life. She was at a crossroads. Only she could decide if she would forever be the victim, subjecting herself to constant treachery with no one to be accountable for it, or be the victor by taking accountability into her own hands to make examples out of those who had oppressed her.

She chose the latter.

5

STARS AND BRANCHES

2019 - 15 YEARS LATER

It was the day before the school year was to start. Lyndsey, now a teacher at West Bayview High School, was in her classroom. She placed a beaded Balinese necklace onto her South Pacific showcase table. The necklace featured three talismans carved out of sandalwood. It was something she'd gotten for herself while she was in Bali a few years back.

She let out a deep breath as she moved to create her final arrangement—the South American display. This year had proven to be no different from last year—or the eleven years before that—so when she placed the yellow scarf onto the table, bittersweet thoughts of Brazil, as well as longing and appreciation, surfaced.

She was grateful that the experience had been so enlightening that it had sparked her interest in anthropology. Not only had she earned a degree in the field, but she'd also earned her teaching credentials so she could teach it at a high school level. Since then, she'd been the Mythology and Folklore teacher at West Bayview High School in Sausalito, California.

She'd never left her hometown. Even with all the tumultuous

memories, she'd stayed. She was alone most of the time, with no one to steer her away from her spiraling thoughts. She knew that over time, her obsession with finding her mother had corrupted her, which in turn, had created another item to add to the long list of the consequences she'd had to pay for her mother's choices. She still held out hope that her reincarnated mother would show up. After all, the town's population was under 7,300, and unless parents schlepped their kids to a private school in San Francisco, most of the kids went to the same schools from elementary to high school. Her mother was bound to show up in the school system sometime.

She still remembered August telling her why her mother would reincarnate near her. Even after fifteen years, she still hung on to those words like they were a promise from a higher power. Her daily life still revolved around that belief. By day, she was a teacher, and by night, a witch. Some would say she was a dark witch, but she would say she was a good witch with rogue-like tendencies. To that day, she still lay in wait for the girl with the star birthmark—the girl who would end up on the receiving end of Lyndsey's fury.

She stepped back to assess her decorating ability. Something was off. She looked through her tote, and there was her missing piece. It was a cup, very similar to the cups used in Brazil to serve the evening drink. She held it close as she thought of August.

She'd had relationships after August, but none of them had lasted more than one or two months because none of them had compared to August.

She put the cup down, hopeful that the new school year would keep her distracted enough that she wouldn't pick up the phone and call him after all these years. *He was the one who made it clear he didn't feel the same way. He has his own life now, and who knows if he even remembers me.*

Rikki Waters rustled through her dresser drawer, searching for her glasses. She hadn't needed to wear them since she'd gotten contacts a couple of months back, but being that she was a poster child for Murphy's Law, and it being the first day of school, one of her contacts had gone missing. She slammed the drawer shut in frustration over her failed search and looked at the clock again. *Shit! I should be out the door any minute. How will I cover up my birthmark when I can't see where to apply my makeup?* She thought as she rubbed the eight-pointed star that laid just under her left collarbone. She threw her long, brown hair over her shoulder as she looked under her bed. If only her hair would stay perfectly in place and cover her mark, but that never seemed to work.

A knock on her bedroom door startled her. Her hair fell forward, getting in the way of seeing clearly, then she bumped her head on the bed frame as she scrambled to her feet. Rubbing her head, she opened her door to find her best friend of ten years, Elle Windsor.

"Nice hair." Elle smirked as she lifted her hand and jiggled her keys. Rikki pulled Elle into the room and closed the door behind her.

"First, love the new piercing," Rikki said. "I don't know. I just love eyebrow piercings. And I love how the loop is similar to your nose ring." She waved her hands to get back on track. "Anyway, I lost one of my contacts, and I can't find my glasses. Can you do your thing and find them?" Rikki asked, spiraling her finger.

"Of course." Elle beamed as if she was a badass superhero. She stood in the center of Rikki's room with her eyes closed, trying to sense where the glasses were.

"I hope you can find them. I need them so I can see where to cover my mark," she said anxiously.

"I don't know why you try so hard. No one cares," Elle said as she drifted about the room.

Rikki crossed her arms. "I'm done being reduced to fake smiling or laughing over everyone calling me 'Morning Star' when I get to school, or 'Rising Star' when I go up the stairs or worse, 'Fallen Star' when I go down the stairs. Then, of course, there's 'Shooting Star' in PE. Oh, and how about 'Lone Star State' if I'm by myself. Or, or … my favorite—'Pop Star' for those lovely times I have a pimple."

Elle giggled. "Those are pretty funny."

"Elle."

"Sorry," she said, turning to hide her smile.

Within two minutes, she'd found Rikki's glasses in her closet next to a pile of neatly folded clothes.

"You're awesome!" Rikki said as she quickly leaned into the mirror over her vanity then dabbed foundation on her mark.

"I thought you liked your mark," Elle asserted.

"I love it, but I don't love having to pretend those old overused, lame remarks are funny," she explained, patting foundation across her collarbone.

"Yeah, well check this out." Elle took a step closer to her, pushing her short, bleach-white hair behind her ear. She pulled her sleeve down, exposing her shoulder, and pointed to the brand new tattoo that covered her own interesting birthmark.

Rikki put down her blending sponge and turned around. "You did it?" she asked, inspecting it. "It looks amazing!" She traced the cascading tattoo of a gnarly tree as it draped over her shoulder and down her tricep. It was multi-layered, with twisted branches and leaves that resembled the brilliant greens, blues, and yellows of a peacock feather.

"Wow! You made that branching birthmark into that? It's so beautiful! The blue leaves perfectly match your eyes. Amazing," she admired.

"Thanks. So when are you going to transform yours?" Elle asked, lifting her sleeve back into place.

"I don't know. But looking at yours, I'm inspired. Maybe after high school."

"In two years?"

"Don't remind me," Rikki said as she finished up. She grabbed her backpack, said goodbye to her parents, and hopped into Elle's Kia to go to school.

***

ON THE VERGE of pressing the trigger and blasting yet another zombie out of the Arizona desert, Caden Brooks's timer went off, alerting him to exit the VR world and enter the real world. Otherwise, he would never make it to school on time. He went into the bathroom and combed his tapered light brown hair, transforming the imprint the VR mask had left behind back to his natural style. When he was done, he grabbed his backpack and waited at the front door for Mia and Blair to pick him up.

His mom, Raylene, came at him with both a camera and little sister, India, in tow so she could post the annual first-day-of-school photo on Facebook. He adjusted his backpack so he could give a proper pose. He put his arm over his little sister's shoulder and just stood there.

His mom had *a look* on her face.

"What?" he asked.

"Fix your shirt so it hides your birthmark," she directed.

"Geez, Mom! I don't see the big deal."

"Because people always ask about how you got that, and when I explain that you got it from an ultrasound when you were in utero, they accuse me of being a conspiracy theorist. I don't have patience for people who are so rigid in their thinking," she defended.

Caden rolled his eyes and raked his hand through his hair.

"Right, right. The ultrasound machine gave me this branching mark on my shoulder. I hear a lot of your' theories,'" he said using air quotes, "but that's a stretch, even for you." He pulled his shirt further up his shoulder.

"It's not a stretch. Come on! That birthmark looks like you were struck by lightning. I wasn't struck by lightning. The only other thing I can think of is that ultrasound."

"But no one else, I mean like *no one*, has a mark like this," he said, pointing to his shoulder. "Come on, Mom, be real."

"Well, how else would you explain why you're so tall when no one else in the family is as tall as you?"

He shook his head in disbelief. "And yet, here I stand," he said, deciding to let it go.

"Yes, you do, my handsome boy! Now smile."

***

ELLE CAUGHT up with Rikki during first break. Rikki was sitting under a tree studying her class schedule as if she was going to be quizzed on it later.

"How's it going?" Elle asked, bouncing on the balls of her feet and grinning.

Rikki lowered her arm. "I only got one' Rising Star'—a record. Yay, me." She grinned a fake grin and rolled her eyes.

Elle sat down. "I mean your classes."

"Oh, yeah. I have to see my counselor about one of my classes at lunch. Why are you so um, happy?" Rikki asked.

"Because this is going to be a good year. I can feel it," she said, closing her eyes and taking a deep, cleansing breath. She shot up. "Will you be at Java and Book later?"

"And miss the annual pilgrimage? You shouldn't even have to ask," Rikki said with a smile.

"You're the best," Elle said.

Ever since Elle could remember, her classmates would

gather at Java and Book after the first day of school for one free drink. The coffee house and bookstore was not only known for being a Sausalito relic, but it had a better view of the bay than any other café along the waterfront. It had been in Elle's family since the 1950s. When Elle's great-aunt, Mozelle, the previous owner, died in a fire, it had been passed down to Elle's mom, Farrah. And being that Elle was an only child, she was next in line after her mom. As far as Elle was concerned, that day could not come fast enough.

AFTER SCHOOL, students flocked to the waterfront and lined up on the stairs just outside the blue Victorian-style building that housed Java and Book.

Rikki walked up the stairs, bypassing everyone, walked in, and sat at the counter. Elle always kept one, sometimes two seats open for her friends when she worked the counter, and rarely did anyone complain.

"Did you get your schedule all cleared up?" Elle asked as Rikki took a seat.

"I did, but now my classes are on the opposite side from where my locker is," Rikki grumbled. "It's a pain to have to go back and forth. But all in all, I got the classes I wanted. What sucks is I already have homework in my AP Chem and AP History classes, so I can't stay long. What about you?"

"I tried to add that Mythology and Folklore class, but apparently that class is only for seniors, so I'm taking horticulture instead, which is fine. I want to learn more about herbs anyway," Elle said as she placed a blueberry muffin in front of Rikki.

Rikki tore off the muffin top and took a bite. She swiveled around to see who else was there. The school gossip, Kendall, sat on one of the cushioned bench seats under one of the large bay windows, speaking with several of her groupies who were positioned all around her. She was annoying as all get out, but she was source number one if you wanted to know what was going down and with who.

CADEN, Mia, and Blair came in and sat at a table under a tall window. Caden sat on the cushioned bench that overlooked the boulevard and the bay. It was their favorite table, and Caden always took the bench seat that faced the counter.

"So glad I got into Japanese. I can use an easy A," Mia said, scooting her chair in. Her shoulder-length, silky black hair swung into her face with each thrust forward. "Although, my parents want me to work on writing Japanese, not just speaking. Anyway, did you get all the classes you wanted?"

"For the most part," he said. "You know, as long as I can still manage the school's e-newspaper, and I'm with my friends— which is pretty much every class—I don't care where they place me." He chuckled. "What about you?"

"I made some changes, but like you, as long as I'm still part of the paper, I'm happy," Mia said.

"On that note, let's talk about the direction of the paper for this year. We should start making the list of teachers to do weekly features on," Caden suggested. "Mia, I need you to update the logo by tomorrow. I plan on having the first issue out by the end of the week. Blair, you could talk to students about their summers, but I also want you to go to Mr. Weiner's class to recruit more writers—" Caden stopped mid-sentence. His eyes followed Ash Carlson as he walked from the entrance of the café toward the counter. Out of the corner of his eye, he saw Blair whip his long, brown hair away from his eyes. Blair was getting irritated.

"Caden," Blair said firmly as he reached over and shoved his shoulder.

"Ow! *Dude*," Caden said, turning back to his two friends. "How do you not know your own strength?" He leaned in. "I don't know what it is about him." He subtly pointed toward Ash, "He bugs the holy shit out of me."

Mia and Blair looked at Caden.

"What?" Caden asked.

"Jealous?" Mia teased.

"Oh hell no," Caden said. Then glanced back at Ash.

"Um, he's hot, especially when he grows that luscious blond hair back after swim team. He's popular and smart." Mia began counting on her fingers. "He comes from the perfect family, with the perfect house, and even a perfect yacht…"

"A little *too* perfect, don't you think?" Caden said, still glaring. "And yet he's trying for Elle? Whose life isn't perfect? She's quirky, and unpredictable." He shook his head. "Whatever. His life."

Blair faked a sneeze. "Sore loser."

Caden leaned in toward Blair. "So, how 'bout you cover cricket, Blair?"

"We don't have a cricket team?"

"Exactly."

<hr>

ELLE WATCHED Rikki stand up as Ash walked toward the counter. "I'm going to get going," Rikki said as she began collecting her things.

"So soon?" Elle asked, her eyes darting between Rikki and the fast-approaching Ash, hoping Rikki would catch on to her *don't leave me alone with him* cue.

"I can't stay. I didn't get enough sleep last night, and I'm determined to have a migraine-free first week of school. I know —it would be a first. Anyway, he's tame," she said, using her head to point in Ash's direction. She stood. "Here, Ash." She patted the stool. "I kept it warm for you."

Elle shot Rikki a look, then smiled as Ash sat down.

"Thanks, Rikki," he said, then turned to Elle. "Hey!"

"Hey, Ash!" Elle replied. She turned toward the sink and pulled a crate of mugs toward her.

Ash stood up and walked around the counter. "Can I help you with that?"

"I got it. Thanks!" she said and hefted the crate onto the counter. She avoided making eye contact with him, but she could feel his eyes follow her every move.

He leaned against the counter and smirked. "I was wondering if you have the notes from Mr. Robertson's class. I left my notebook in AP Calculus."

His blatant attempt to impress was not lost on her. "I do. But it's in the other room. Can I just take a pic of it and text it to you when I get a chance?"

"Sure. No rush. I'll be here for a while," he said, raising an eyebrow as if waiting for her to get the hint.

Looking down, she began wiping down the counter.

"Elle, in all seriousness, I do need those notes, but I would also like it if you would, um, if you would go with me to the football game next week."

<hr>

CADEN FELT his airways constrict as he listened to the uncomfortable exchange between Ash and Elle.

"Just as friends. That's all I'm asking," Ash continued.

Laughable. She's got to see through that.

"Okay. But I can't next week."

Ha ha. She's letting him down nicely.

"But I might be able to the following week."

Caden coughed. He'd never heard her agree to a date with

him before. His lungs constricted as his asthma kicked in. He stood up. "I need to step out," he wheezed.

He eyed Elle as he exited the café, moved into the corridor connecting several shops, and sat on the steps. He pumped his inhaler and held his breath. He closed his eyes as he exhaled.

Mia joined him a short time after. "You get why this is happening, don't you?" Mia asked as if he really should know the answer.

"I care about Elle, but I don't understand why she doesn't see him for the douchebag that he is."

"That's not it," Mia challenged.

"What? You think I *like* her? Well, I don't," Caden said defensively.

"You're not going to convince me otherwise," Mia added.

"I don't think I'd have a problem if Blair asked her out," he said as if he was presenting new evidence.

"That means nothing, Caden. And the sooner you recognize your feelings … Well, I don't know. Perhaps you're better off bottling it up and hoping your inhaler will always be there to give you the relief you're looking for."

"Whatever. I just need space to breathe. I'll head back in in a minute," he assured, staring out at the bay. He leaned his back against the wall and scrolled through his messages until Ash walked out with a sly smile on his face.

"S'up." Ash nodded as he passed by Caden.

"S'up," Caden replied. His eyes followed Ash as he walked down the steps and turned left. After another minute, Caden got up and walked home, breaking his promise to go back inside.

As the semester progressed, things seemed to fall into a rhythm. Rikki maintained her high-achieving trajectory. Caden,

Mia, and Blair continued to turn out The Meridian Voice effortlessly, the school's e-newspaper, twice a week, and Elle breezed through her required classes with the help of her new beau, Ash.

As the holidays approached and finals were on the horizon, the group found it challenging to find time to hang out. Before they knew it, winter vacation was in full swing.

Cheyenne, **Wyoming**
Winter Break

Sitting at the table, Rachel Briggs exhaled a long plume of smoke as she stared at her son, Quinn Axton, who sat across from her. She used her thumb to flick a long ribbon ash as it tumbled into her casino-branded ashtray.

His next bite of his Pop-Tart was interrupted as he let out a small chuckle. She assumed it was over something he was watching on his phone, but the fact that he was listening through earbuds prevented her from knowing for sure. He looked like he was at peace for once, and she didn't know how to break the bad news.

She took a long drag of her cigarette. "Quinn?" she called to him while exhaling.

He looked up.

"I'm not going to be one of those women who just takes it," she stated.

Quinn pulled one earbud out of his ear. "What are you talking about?"

"You get why I kicked Russ out, right? That skank can have him," she spat.

"'Kay." Quinn's response was more of a grunt than an actual word.

"I don't know what else to do," she said, teary-eyed.

He looked back at his phone. "You don't have a choice. Whatever."

"But I know I can't have him here, and the reality is, I don't think I can have *you* here either," she added.

He turned his attention toward her as if to gauge if she was being serious. "Wait. What? You're kicking me out?" Not believing his ears, he leaned back in his chair.

"I just can't care for you the way you need right now. I don't have much of a job n' all. Not to mention, it'll take forever for this to be settled in the courts before I see a penny from that cheap bastard. And look at you. You're depressed, and I can't afford to get you help, Quinn."

He didn't have much of a reaction. He stared at her, arms crossed.

"Go live with your dad," she insisted.

"I don't want to live with Dad. I want to live with you. Wyoming is my home, and it's where all my friends are," he pushed back, shaking his head in disbelief. "This is bullshit!" He leaned forward, placing his elbows on the table over his plate, and dropped his head onto his fists.

"Just finish your junior year with your dad, and I promise you can come back, even if I don't have my shit together. I just need time. I'll be so much better when you come back, I promise."

He shook his head in his hands. "You don't need to be better, Mom."

She studied her son. It broke her heart knowing she was sending him away, but she needed alone time to get into the right headspace. "I really need you to do this," she begged. "You have no idea how hard this is for me."

"Whatever. This is so fucked up!" Quinn pushed his chair back, stood up, and left the room.

"You don't see it now, but you'll look back and be glad you

did this, Quinn." She waited for him to answer. "Quinn?"

A slammed door was the only response she got.

QUINN FLOPPED onto his bed and blared "Last Resort" by Papa Roach in his ears because nothing spoke to him the way music did. Before the song ended, tears rolled down his cheeks. Music was his escape. The beat, the lyrics, and the raging penetrated his body and his mind, compelling his nerves to come alive. It energized him, comforted him, and never, ever judged him.

Live with my dad. Why do I have to go through hell just because she is?

He sat up and texted Sienna, who had been his friend since middle school. *U around?*

wrking, she texted back.

Tomorrow?

Sure.

"I'M MEETING UP WITH SIENNA," he called out later the next day.

"Wait," Rachel said, drying her hands on a dishtowel.

"What now, Mom?" he asked. His hand was still on the doorknob.

She came up to him. "Have you talked to your dad yet?"

His jaw dropped as his grip tightened around the knob. "Holy shit, Mom! You want *me* to talk to him? Are you fucking kidding me?" He faced her and put his hands on his hips. "You want me out?" he asked as he raised his voice, then pointed at her. "*You* call Dad! Until then, I'm not packing shit." He threw open the door and walked out.

This is total bullshit! Anger flared as he thought about how messed up his life was. He had been born in Sausalito, California, to high school sweethearts, Rachel and Mason Axton. Their marriage only lasted seven years. After their divorce, his mom took him with her to Wyoming, where her sister lived. Regardless of her poor choices, he loved his mother, but he resented her for subjecting him to an unpredictable life. Over time, Quinn had developed anxiety over his parents' fighting, which had manifested itself into a fear of flying. Splitting his time between his parents became more than he could take, so he just stopped going back to California. It had been five years since the last time he saw his dad. *Depressed? No duh!*

When music wasn't around to fill the void that festered within, going out with his adventurous friends who did crazy-ass shit was be the next best thing. The thrill of pulling pranks, ditching school, stealing alcohol, or smoking pot was the perfect antidote to his inner tumult.

Sienna Bisset was one of those adventurous friends, even though her background was even worse than his. They understood each other and always had each other's back. They never judged each other, and the shitty situations they got themselves into only strengthened their bond.

The two of them sat on the tailgate of her truck, huddled under warm blankets.

Sienna nudged him with her body. "What's bothering you?" she asked, lighting her joint. Her blonde hair tumbled forward, covering part of her eyes. After a long drag, she exhaled the smoke and handed the joint to him.

"It's my mom," Quinn said, taking a hit.

"Geez. What is it with her now?"

Exhale. "Boyfriend problems. She and Russ broke up. I didn't really care for that one, so that's no big loss, but he had the most stable job and made my mom happy—for a while, anyway." He passed the joint back.

She took a hit.

"I have to leave, Sienna," he said, watching her exhale. "It's just for a short time, but my mom says she needs to get her shit together and is making me go to my dad's in California. She said I can come back in June after my junior year." He took the joint from her and took a hit.

"Oh, man! Really? That sucks," she said, reaching her hand out to rub his back. "When are you leaving?"

"I'm not sure. Soon. Probably before winter break is over."

She shook her head. "Man, I'm going to miss you," she said, turning toward him. "More than you know, especially since we vowed never to go on stupid social media. How else will I see that ugly face of yours?"

He studied her expression. It was as if she wanted to say something else but held back. He didn't want any complications, so he wasn't going to push it. "I'm going to miss you too. The good thing is that Dad has money, so maybe I could get him to pay for you to come out sometime."

They both knew that was an empty promise but went along with it anyway. He threw his arm around her, and she rested her head on his shoulder.

<hr>

When Quinn got home later that night, his mother was in the kitchen on the phone, pleading with Mason.

"Hold on, hold on … Mason, hold on! Quinn just came in," she said and lowered the phone to her chest. "Your dad's on the phone. I told him everything, but he wants to talk to you."

Before Quinn could say "yes" or "no," the phone was shoved into his hand. Quinn set his jaw. "Hello?" Quinn said with the enthusiasm of a DMV worker. Being high certainly wasn't helping this situation.

"Quinn! It's your father."

"I know, Dad," he said, rolling his eyes.

"Your mother is asking that I take you in for a few months.

How do you feel about that?"

"I'm fine with whatever." He could hear the insincerity in his voice. "I don't know. I'd rather stay here, but whatever."

"No, not whatever," Mason said, calling him out. "I would never turn you away. However, my rules are quite different from your mother's," he warned, then paused as if waiting for a response. Quinn wasn't going to give him the satisfaction. "You have to stay in school and maintain a 3.0 GPA. No partying, and you have to go to a therapist," he listed. "Do you have anything to say about that?"

"Do I have a choice?" Quinn asked, shaking his head.

"No."

"Then why ask?"

"Put your mom on the phone," Mason demanded.

Quinn roughly handed the phone to his mom.

"Okay. So I'll bring him this weekend … What?" She shooed Quinn away.

He left the room but stood on the other side of the wall where he could hear her side of the conversation. "I just need a break. Russ was cheating on me, and well, let's face it, you haven't been the greatest support either, so here we are. Are you going to take him or not? … Okay … Fine … Okay. Alright, I said! Geez!"

<hr>

QUINN PUT the last of his notepads in his backpack, then slung it over his shoulder. He sighed, staring at his unmade bed. He hoped it would look just like that when he returned. An uncomfortable twinge in his belly struck him as he feared what would happen if he didn't come back. Shaking the thought away, he swiped his mid-length honey-blond hair away from his eyes, took one last look, and closed the door.

The drive to the airport had Quinn all agitated. Even music

wasn't helping as he rocked back and forth, rubbing his hands along his thighs. "I can't take this. Can we stop by a liquor store or something? I need something to calm my nerves."

"Of course, hun. You can have as much as you like. I don't want you stressed," she said with a devious smile.

"You are *not* a normal mom. Why would you push more than one drink? There's relaxed, and then there's drunk," Quinn said, scoffing as her smirk didn't go away. "Oh, I get it. You want me drunk enough to piss Dad off." Quinn shook his head. "Some things just don't change."

"Oh, Quinn, you know me so well. But I really do want you to be calm, and if that pisses your father off, all the better," she said, lifting her shoulders in delight.

They pulled into Mimi's Liquor. "What would you like?"

"I don't know, Mom," Quinn said, avoiding eye contact. It was one thing for her to know he drank alcohol, but taking a drink order from her underage son was something entirely different, and he was slow to admit he had a preferred drink. "Bud is fine," he said, deferring to the old standby.

"Okay. I'll be right back."

"I'm not going anywhere."

Quinn tapped his knee, waiting for his mom to come out of Mimi's Liquor. He rubbed his legs again as he watched her speak with Mimi herself. He exhaled when she came back to the car with a six-pack of Bud in hand.

"A six-pack, Mom? Really?"

"It was a Mimi's special. I'll finish whatever you don't."

He shook his head. "You can be so WT, you know that?"

"Thank you," she replied, like being called white trash was a badge of honor. "I'm joking. I just want you to be at ease. Anxiety can be a real bitch."

"Uh-huh," he said and cracked open a can.

When they got to the airport, being that Quinn was a minor, Rachel was allowed to walk him to the gate.

"How are you feeling?" Rachel asked.

"Buzzed, but I'm feeling better about getting on the plane."

"Your father will be waiting for you when you get off the plane. Avoid talking to anyone, so they won't know that you've had a few."

"'Kay."

When his row was called to board the plane, he stood up and gave his mom a lingering hug. "I'll miss you, Mom," he said.

"Oh, my boy. I'm going to be just fine. Thank you so much for doing this for me." She patted him on the back, then gave him a loving squeeze.

He nodded and walked to the jetway. He looked back and waved. He couldn't wait for the next few months to pass so he could come back to the only place he considered home—a thought he would eventually forsake.

———

Quinn was glad he'd had those drinks. The turbulence from flying over the Rockies during winter would have pushed him over the edge.

Just as his mother had planned, Mason's flared nostrils were a dead giveaway that he could smell the alcohol on Quinn's breath. "That's just great, Quinn." Mason's jaw was set. "This is so par for the course with her. Are you going to be sick?"

"No," he said, yanking out his earbuds.

"Of course not, because you've been drunk before." Mason took a deep breath. "This is not starting off so well, is it?" He picked up Quinn's suitcase. "Is this all you really have?"

Quinn looked up from his phone. "I wasn't planning on staying that long."

Mason sucked in his upper lip and shook his head in disbelief.

It was a very quiet and awkward ride to his dad's house.

When they got there, Quinn remained standing behind his dad. He didn't know where he was supposed to go. That twinge in his belly reemerged over the miserable feeling of being displaced, and the only person he could depend on to get him through this was this stranger he called Dad. Quinn was frozen as he stared at his dad.

"What? What are you doing? You're creeping me out," Mason said with wide eyes.

Vulnerable, Quinn swallowed. "I don't know where to go," he admitted. His body deflated at the sound of his pathetic words.

Mason raised his eyebrows as if surprised. "Your room is upstairs and to the left. When you're done settling in, I want you to come downstairs so that we can talk about your schedule," he ordered.

Quinn stared at his dad. *This is it. This is now my life. This no longer feels like a favor but more like a punishment.*

Mason took a step back, then gestured for him to get moving. And so he did.

QUINN'S ROOM had white walls and hardwood floors. There was a twin bed with a gray comforter butted up against one of the walls. There was a window next to it and another window that overlooked the driveway. *Welcome home. Is this him giving me space to make this room mine? Or is he being a dick? Probably the latter.*

After a few minutes, he went downstairs and found his dad sitting at the dining room table. A yellow pad and pen were waiting for him at the opposite end of the long table.

His dad shuffled some papers, then took a deep breath. "First, are you aware that winter break is over, and school starts up again tomorrow?"

Quinn nodded his head.

"Tomorrow morning, you will go to school at 6:30 to register for your classes. On Fridays, you will go to Dr. Layla Summers's office after school. She is an exceptional psychologist. I'll also be giving you a phone, so I can keep track of your whereabouts," Mason mandated.

"You'll always find me here because I don't have a car," Quinn interjected.

From across the table, a set of keys came sliding along the dark wood toward him. Catching them, he saw they belonged to a brand new Range Rover.

"Whoa," Quinn said, shocked.

"Call it incentive," Mason encouraged. "Easy come, easy go. Understand? I have to be strict, Quinn, because your mother let you do whatever the hell you wanted. Your grades are dismal, you smoke pot, and apparently, you drink, too, and I won't stand for any of that," his dad said, pointing at his only son.

The chandelier light reflected off the key, twinkling slightly, and Quinn was at a loss for words. "I don't know what I'm supposed to say," he admitted.

"Start with 'thank you,' but I'm looking for action more than I'm looking for words. Okay?"

"' Kay. Um, thanks," Quinn said, still looking at the keys rather than his dad. *I don't know how I feel about this. Is it wrong for me to be okay or even impressed with this? I can just hear Sienna going off on me for accepting such a bougie gift.* He grasped the keys in his hand, closed his eyes, bringing his fist to his mouth. *This is all temporary.* He said to himself to rationalize his contradicting thoughts.

THE NEXT MORNING, Quinn was slow to get out of bed at 5:40, even after hitting the snooze button multiple times. He started moving a little faster when he remembered the dangling carrot sitting in the driveway, waiting to be chased after. When he went to his window to look down upon the beauty that was his Range Rover, he was surprised to see his dad's car still in the driveway. He jumped into the shower, washed his unkempt hair that hadn't been cut in months, then shaved. As he wrapped the towel around his slim waist, he snapped his fingers in frustration. He'd forgotten his clothes in his room and hurried out of the bathroom to get them.

"What the hell is that?" His dad's booming voice startled him in the hallway.

"What's what?" Quinn asked, looking around himself while holding the towel tighter around his waist.

"That tattoo."

"What tattoo? What are you talking about?"

"Right there! That star on your chest."

Quinn placed his hand just above his heart. He wasn't sure if his hand flew there to cover the mark or the pain his father had just inflicted. "Really, Dad? Has it really been that long? That's my birthmark." He pursed his lips, disappointed that his dad had forgotten the times when he used to tell him he must be special because he had such a remarkable birthmark, that because it was in the shape of a star, it meant he could reach to the stars to make his dreams come true.

Mason came closer to inspect it. "Oh, right … sorry. I must have forgotten. It's been a while since I've seen you. And honestly, a tattoo would kind of be par for the course."

"Uh-huh … Please don't assume that you know me, Dad. I'm not the delinquent you think I am."

"You're right. I need to give you a chance to prove yourself," his father said as if he was playing the role of a good parent.

"See, right there." He pointed at his dad. "I don't need to prove myself. I'm fine just as I am." He shook his head. "I'm going to finish up here and get going. I have to register for class." Quinn turned on his heel and left his father's sight.

6

NESSIE

Quinn parked his Rover in what he assumed was the parking lot for West Bay View High but looked more like the backlot of a luxury car dealership. It was a blinding departure from what he was used to. As he ascended into the school, unfamiliar faces moved in and out of his field of vision, none of which made eye contact with him. He could probably light up a blunt right there, and no one would notice. And that would be just fine with him. Each hallway was listed alphabetically and named after famous explorers. The registrar's office was on Cook Strait.

A smiley, middle-aged woman stood up from a desk that had a nameplate with the words *Janice Sheridan—Registrar* etched on it. "Good morning. You must be Mr. Axton. I recognize you from the records your school in Wyoming sent over. Here is your current schedule of classes. If you need to make any changes, you can go to your counselor, Mr. Consuelos, and talk to him about it."

"Okay," Quinn said, checking out the modern architecture of the office. A mural was painted on the wall behind her that read, "Welcome to West Bay View High—Home of the Mariners." The painting depicted a sailor on rough seas, pointing at something with a compass dangling from his hand. Quinn stared at it, intrigued by the compass, which struck him as odd. He thought he could see the Loch Ness Monster painted in the background, but that seemed far-fetched to him.

"Good luck! Enjoy your time here at West Bay View," the woman said like she was very proud to work there.

"Thanks," he replied and walked out. He studied his class schedule, trying to decode it. Some of his classes sounded like they would be taught only at private schools, which piqued his interest. His first class—the school e-newspaper.

Quinn walked through Building B, looking for the class. If it weren't for the open door with a poster of SpongeBob jelly fishing, he would have passed it. Stepping into the checker-floored room, he counted three teacher-sized desks that took up most of the small space. From the looks of it, the room was formerly a joint teachers' office, probably belonging to the classrooms on either side. He stood in a small receiving area by a half-wall with a swinging gate, waiting to be buzzed in.

A guy with short, brown hair and trendy, black-framed reading glasses looked up from his computer. "Hi. Can I help you?" he asked, looking Quinn up and down like he was an alien.

Quinn looked down at his paper, gripping it tighter. "Hi, um, I'm Quinn. I think I'm at the right place," he said, stepping back and rechecking the room number.

A buzz and a click sounded from the waist-high swinging gate, granting Quinn access. He met the guy halfway and handed him his schedule, proving he was in the right place, despite the uncertain look on his face.

The guy studied it, then handed it back to him. Like a switch, his demeanor changed. "Okay, Quinn. I'm Caden, this is Mia, and that over there is Blair. We make up the skeleton crew that is *The Meridian Voice*, but we wouldn't be here without our fellow contributors, so we're appreciative that you're here. Would your focus be on writing or photography?"

"Oh, I didn't know photography was an option. Can I do both?" he asked, looking around the room. The room was pretty cool, with each wall painted a different bold color.

While posters of memes lined most of the walls, one was dedicated solely to the Loch Ness Monster. A massive decal of Nessie was the focal point of the room. Pinned around her were photos, both real and Photoshopped, of students' "encounters" with her. Upon closer inspection, some of the photos were of people dressed up like her. Snorting, it dawned on him that Nessie was the school's mascot. Both vintage and new, toys and other novelties were strewn on most surfaces and even hung from the ceiling.

"You can do both, but in my experience, you're one or the other," Caden warned. "I won't stop you from tryin…" His voice trailed off, looking over Quinn's shoulder in the direction of the door as if waiting for something.

His eyes lit up. "Hey, Elle," Caden said, lifting his chin as if too cool to wave.

A vibration hit Quinn hard in his core. It resonated outward, turning his body into a tuning fork. He slapped his hand onto his chest as it reverberated through his body.

"Hey, Caden!" Elle waved as she, Ash, and Rikki walked by.

As they passed by the room, Rikki suddenly stopped and grabbed her forehead. She felt a charge that started in her head and washed over her body.

"Are you okay?" Elle asked Rikki as she gripped Elle's shoulder.

"ARE YOU OKAY?" Caden asked as he watched Quinn grab the desk for stability.

Quinn nodded his head to prevent undermining his first impression. His eyes darted about as he tried to figure out what was happening to him.

RIKKI FORCED one foot in front of the other.

"Are you sure you're okay, Rikki?"

"Yes. It's nothing." She turned around. "It's probably a stupid migraine aura, and it'll pass." She questioned if that was the truth because auras never felt … good.

AS THE VIBRATIONS DISSIPATED, Quinn was met with concerned looks. He chuckled nervously. "I just felt like an electric wave went through me. No big deal. Right?"

"*Okay*," Caden drew out. "Are you epileptic?"

"No. Really, it's gone. I didn't mean to freak you out. I'm not weird. I promise."

"Oh, no. I'll tell you what's weird—Elle liking that guy she was walking with. I don't get what she sees in him," Caden spat.

Mia laughed. "Who? Mr. 'I'm still hot even after I buzz my hair for swim team'? Well, it looks like their relationship lasted through winter break," Mia chided, never looking away from her computer screen.

"Boundaries, Mia. Ever heard of them?" Caden snapped back, then turned to Quinn. "Okay. Quinn, your first assignment is to photograph the counseling office to show how many people are rushing to fix their schedules. Mia, you're going to cover that as well. And Blair, I want you to cover the club recruitment booths. I'll do a fluff piece on what people did over the break. Let's meet here during lunch for the day's briefing. Any questions?" Caden looked between the three of them. "Great! Happy reporting! Quinn, there's a nice Nikon in the cupboard over there. Let me know if that's too much camera for you. Otherwise, you can use your phone, but I suggest taking Mrs. Wentz's photography class so you can learn how to shoot manually."

"Thanks, man, for the help," Quinn said and grabbed the camera to take it out for a few test shots.

He pointed the camera at one of the hundreds of trees that blanketed the campus. Staring through the viewfinder and down the lens at a tree, a relationship was created between him and this weighted instrument that could only be described as synergetic. The sound and feel of the mirror dropping within as it apprehended a single thread of time solidified its magical power, and he became enamored by its potential. People, nature, even buildings, appeared more meaningful to him, and he was enthralled.

Quinn pointed his lens at the back of a student as they spoke with their counselor. He zoomed in closer and found an expression on the counselor's face that said they cared. Then they tilted their head as if they were listening. The student even sat forward, nodding their head in agreement instead of shame. Back home, if you went to your counselor, it was because you were in trouble. When he peeked into another office, he saw the same thing and was shocked.

During first break, he met up with Blair to check out club recruitment. It was like being at a mini swap meet. There were two rows of booths, but rather than someone pushing you to buy the latest and greatest vacuum cleaner or food processor, students wore the spirit gear of the club they'd pledged their allegiance to as they proudly waved at passersby. Some enticed new recruits with candy and games, while others displayed colorful and creative posters. As Quinn stepped back to get an overall shot, he snorted at how happy the students were and how much pride they had for their school. He looked down, letting his jealousy say what it needed to say, then passed on through the crowd.

"Excuse me?" A female student tapped on his shoulder.

"Yes?"

"Are you with the school paper?" she asked as if impressed.

"Um, yeah." *Weird hearing myself admit that. I've never done anything that got someone else's attention, let alone come to me like I could be of some kind of help.*

"Hi." She giggled. "I'm Zoey, and this is my friend, Kira," she introduced. Zoey seemed like just another student, but Kira looked like she had Down syndrome. "I was wondering if you could take a picture of us. We're from Together We Will." Zoey pointed at the brightly colored club sign behind her and proudly put her arm around Kira's shoulder. Kira's face lit up with a wide, bright smile before Quinn could even bring the camera up.

Click, click.

He grinned as he took down the spelling of their names, and his chest filled up with gratification as he, too, was as proud to be part of something important like the girls in front of him were part of something important.

Quinn hung his backpack on a chair in the kitchen, then grabbed an apple from the refrigerator. He sat down in front of the computer to start his homework. His dad didn't trust him enough to have a computer in his room.

Mason came in a short time later and began fixing himself a salad. "Wow! They got you doing homework right out of the gate. How was your first day, son?"

"It was good," Quinn said as he looked up from his computer. "I'm on the school newspaper, which seems cool."

"That does sound cool," his father said as if mildly interested.

"Yeah. I'm mainly doing photography, so my photos are going to be published, and I'll even get credit."

"Wow!" Mason said, surprised. "It sounds like you had a great first day."

"Yeah," Quinn said, nodding. "I did."

"I'm glad. Don't forget about your appointment with Dr. Summers on Friday."

Quinn scoffed. *The man certainly knows how to take the wind out of my sails.* "I won't forget, Dad," Quinn said, annoyed.

THE NEXT DAY, Quinn was up and ready well before his alarm. *If today is half the day yesterday was, I'll still be impressed.*

When he got to school, he was assigned his locker, located on the second to the last row in Vasco da Gama Canal.

As he approached his locker, he was hit again with a strong vibration. He reached for his chest as the feeling flooded his body. He looked around to see if anyone else felt what he was feeling. All around him, students just went about their days, laughing and talking to their friends, hurrying to classes. No one seemed to be experiencing what he was. *Or maybe they're just used to it.*

He gripped his locker door as his nerves continued to hum. He leaned in to hide behind it and closed his eyes, letting the sensation saturate every fiber of his body. *What the hell is this? Should I be concerned? Is it normal for something that feels this good to indicate something is wrong?*

After a moment, the vibrations faded away. The feeling had come on the same way, and he observed the vibrations hitting him off and on throughout the morning. Sometimes it would happen during passing periods, but the chances of getting hit with the inexplicable sensation were highest when he went to his locker.

He felt compelled to look around to see if there was some electrical or environmental problem. It remained a mystery, perhaps one he wasn't so eager to solve.

RIKKI'S LOCKER was in the last row of Zheng He Channel. When no one was looking, she would lean back, close her eyes, and try to clear her mind as her senses sang in euphoria. *What is happening to me? And why by my locker? Why me? Am I losing my mind? I probably shouldn't be enjoying it. I probably should figure out where it's coming from ...* She took a deep breath. *But not yet.*

Once it passed, she searched around to determine where it was coming from, but she didn't search that hard.

During first break, Rikki explained to Elle what she'd felt. "I can't explain it. It's not a headache. I don't feel any pain or dizziness. In fact, it kinda feels good. What do you think it could be?"

"Are you thinking something metaphysical is going on?" Elle began.

"Metaphysical?" Rikki repeated, tilting her head in surprise at first. "Oh, wait. I forgot who I was asking." She chuckled. "No. I was actually wondering if there was some kind of electrical thing going on, like a short near my locker or something. But then again, I've felt it when I'm not near my locker. I just can't figure it out."

"But it just came on, and only here at school, like this semester? That's weird. Maybe it's hormonal," Elle suggested.

"Maybe," Rikki agreed, considering Elle's notion. "Yeah, I don't know. There's an explanation. I'll figure it out."

"I'm sure you will."

Over the next several days, Quinn settled in. Students began to notice him. With every "Hey, Quinn" or "I liked your photo" he got, the more he owned his status of being a Mariner. The idea of him being an island of sorts faded, and he became more confident in himself. He even began making better friends than he had back home.

"Everything okay?" the guy next to his locker asked.

Caught. "Yeah. Um, just a headache," Quinn lied.

Just as that guy left his sight, Quinn looked around again to find the source of the strange vibrations. He only wanted to identify it—not stop it. Not knowing where else to turn, he decided to elicit the help of those who he trusted with his *condition.*

He entered the newsroom on a vibration high and stood in front of Caden's desk. "I know I might sound like a conspiracy theorist," Quinn started.

"Wait! Have you been talking to my mom?" Caden said with a smirk, never looking away from his computer monitor.

"What? No. Why?" Quinn didn't get the joke.

"Nothing. What's your theory?"

"Do you think there is a story with this vibration thing? Like there's some kind of environmental thing going on?"

"Maybe. Do you know anyone else who experiences it?"

"No."

Caden stopped his typing and leaned back in his chair. "Well, if you find someone else who does, let me know. For now, there's not enough to write a story on. In the meantime, we're going to Java and Book later. Do you want to join us?"

"I can't. My dad still doesn't trust me enough to go out anywhere." He shook his head. "So damn annoying."

"Maybe in your senior year?"

"One can only hope." Quinn hmphed to himself. He couldn't

believe he was suggesting that he might still be there after junior year, but something was starting to change from within. Friends like Caden, Mia, and Blair liked him for who he was and didn't pressure him into being who they needed him to be. They genuinely cared about him as he did them. Looking back, it seemed like his so-called friends back home had only used him to justify their bad behavior. They didn't want to believe they were alone in their delinquencies, but Quinn hadn't understood that until now. Even his therapist had noticed the change in him in such a short amount of time, stating that his depression seemed situational and not chemical, which in turn allowed Mason to start trusting him, and therefore, allotting him more privileges.

<hr>

ON THE FRIDAY before spring break, most of the students, including Rikki, were at Java and Book to decompress after midterms.

"What specialty drinks do you offer for 'hallelujah-my-midterms-are-over'?" Rikki wanted to celebrate with a high-caloric, sugary-sweet mochaccino.

"I'll have the same," Ash said as he stepped up beside her.

"Sit here at the counter. I have just the thing," Elle assured as her eyes lit up.

After a few moments of awkward conversation, Elle presented them with purple, pink, and blue concoctions with Cadbury Mini Eggs lining the saucer plate. "I call it Springtime Sugar Coma."

Rikki's mouth had just closed over the straw when the door chimed and caught their attention.

"Spring break sucks for parking," Caden complained to Mia and Blair while they walked into Java and Book. He saw Ash sitting up at the counter and felt heat rise within him. "It sucks in here too." He made an about-face, bumping into Mia.

"Let's just sit where we normally sit." Mia pushed back against Caden's chest to redirect him from Ash's line of sight.

Caden yanked the chair from under the table and sat. "Elle and Ash are like conjoined twins. Enmeshment is not healthy for a relationship. Just saying," Caden noted. "Maybe we should do an article on the signs of a healthy versus unhealthy relationship."

"Oh, so now you're working to improve their relationship?" Mia chimed in.

"Whatever." Caden hung his head. After a moment, he perked up. "Actually, I have an idea." He took out his phone and texted Quinn. *Can you meet me at J and B? I have an assignment for you. Tell your dad it's school-related.*

K. Give me 15, Quinn texted back.

"Dude, what are you up to?" Blair asked.

"Nothing. Just a small recon job to shed some light on the snake that he is," Caden said, dismissing Blair's accusatory tone.

"Have you lost your mind, Caden?" Mia confronted loud enough for people to turn their heads.

"Stay out of it, Mia!" Caden ordered. He gripped his phone at the sound of Elle and Ash's laughter. Compelled to watch them, hot air blasted through his nose as Ash walked behind the counter and snaked his arms around Elle's waist, slowly nuzzling her neck and slathering his venom. "See? Snake."

Mia tapped Caden's shin with her foot. "You're making me dizzy seeing you spiral like that. I mean, what is it about her that you like so much?" she asked like she genuinely wanted to know.

Caden's harsh stare softened at Mia's question. "She's beautiful and smart, but the kind of smart beyond what you and I have. She's captivating, whimsical, artistic, logical, and compassionate. She has her own thoughts and a way of looking at things that gets you to think. She's a true non-conformist because she considers *everything*. So sometimes she likes something that conforms, and sometimes she doesn't. She's not one of those who call themselves non-conformist when, in reality, they are just being oppositional. And the way—"

"Wow, you've really thought a lot about it," Mia interrupted. "I just thought you were going to say she was hot."

Caden snorted. "So, so much more than that," he said, still staring at her. He exhaled in relief when he saw Elle release herself from Ash's constrictive hold and directed him to sit at the counter.

QUINN STOOD at the bottom of the stairs that led to the entrance of Java and Book, rubbing his chest. Every stair he took, the vibrations strengthened.

Why here? It's been happening at school like clockwork since I started weeks ago, but never outside of school. What the hell is happening to me?

He shook his head to stop his thoughts. He stood there for a moment, waiting for it to pass. If he didn't have to be somewhere, he would bask in the exhilaration. He wanted to close his eyes and let the feeling wash over him, but he was in public, so he soldiered on instead.

RIKKI STOOD up when the buzzing began to overwhelm her. She closed her eyes and immediately sat back down, brushing her fingers along her forehead. She froze, holding her breath as it radiated down her neck and filled her chest.

"Rikki? Are you okay?" Elle asked.

Rikki opened her eyes. She felt like she was in a fog. "I'm fine. I don't know what it is."

"You're feeling that buzzing again, aren't you?"

Her eyes darted between Elle and Ash, hoping to catch any sign they were feeling something—anything, but was only met with mystified expressions. "Yes. And what's weird is that I've never felt it outside of school before," she explained.

Confusion emerged as anxiety mixed with pleasure was more than she could take, provoking her fight or flight response to kick in. She stood up, rubbing the back of her neck. Looking around, she chose flight.

"Yeah, I don't know. It sounds like a migraine aura," Ash interjected.

Rapidly collecting her things, Rikki could feel her emotions reach a boiling point. "It's not that, Ash. You're not a migraine sufferer, so—" Rikki stopped herself from crossing her personal all-out-bitch threshold.

Elle reached for Rikki's arm as if to reel her back in. "It's been going on since the beginning of the semester. I would be freaked out by it, too, especially if it's getting worse. Maybe you should go to the doctor?"

Rikki feigned relaxation under Elle's gentle touch. "I'm not freaking out. It's just never happened outside of school before. I don't think anything's wrong with me. In fact, it's an amazing feeling, but I do need to get going anyway. We'll talk later, okay?"

Rikki leaned over the counter, gave Elle a one-armed hug, and walked out the side exit in the adjoining annex room.

Quinn came in through the main entrance, still rubbing his chest as the vibrations were diminishing.

Elle gave him a quizzical look. "Hey, Quinn! Everything okay?"

"Couldn't be better," he said, spotting a fuming Caden. He headed over to their table. "Dude, what's with the look?" he asked as he took a seat.

"Elle," Mia divulged.

Quinn looked back to see Elle flirting with Ash, then looked at Caden, who was staring at them as if he could send death rays at them through his eyes.

"Wait … you like her?"

"Thanks a lot, Mia!" Caden snapped, rolling his eyes. "I'm never going to open up to you again." He looked back at Quinn. "Yes, I like her. I like her a lot. But to be honest, I'm concerned for her and that guy she's with. Listen, I get that she's not into me, but of all guys, *that* guy?" He glared at them. "There's something about him that I don't trust, and I was wondering if you would do some recon."

"Jeezus, is that what you needed me for?" Quinn asked, trying to gauge if Caden was being serious. Caden's fixed sideways stare was all the confirmation he needed. "Oh, hell no! Caden. There's no story there. I could get in a lot of trouble. I won't do it. Come up with a story. Then we'll talk."

"Okay, okay. I'll find a story," Caden conceded.

Quinn leaned in. "What do you hope to gain from it? Are you going to save her? Do you think she'd even listen? You know, you can either wait for something to happen naturally," he said, looking back at the two of them. They stood there, forehead to forehead, looking deeply into each other's eyes. He turned back to Caden and pointed to them with his thumb. "Or do the obvious thing and move on. Like seriously, dude."

"Well, I still want to know for myself if Ash is the asshole I believe him to be, but I'll find a story. Maybe there's a swim team scandal."

Quinn took a deep breath. "Or maybe there's not. But listen, if you want, I can report on the meets. If any red flags come up, you'll be the first to know."

Caden twisted his mouth. "Yeah, fine, whatever."

Done arguing with Caden, Quinn took a moment to search inside himself, hoping to hold on to whatever vibrations remained, but they had completely dissipated. "Odd," he whispered, disappointed.

"What?" Caden asked.

"Oh, um, nothing. I'm going to head back. I'll look up the meet schedule and let you know tomorrow." Quinn was standing up to leave when his phone began to vibrate. As he walked out of Java and Book, he answered.

"Hey, stranger!"

"Sienna! What's up?" Quinn asked, feigning like he missed her.

"Nothing. I haven't heard from you in a while. Did you fall off the face of the planet?" She sounded pissed.

"I'm sorry, Sienna. I got really busy, and my dad has me on a short leash," he explained. The reality was that he hadn't called because he was having fun, not realizing how much time had passed.

"Uh-huh. Can I come and visit?"

"Um, sure."

"You sound uncertain."

"No, you can come. I'll show you around. There's a lot to do here." Quinn caught himself rolling his eyes at the thought of her visiting. He unlocked his Rover and hopped in, quickly backing out and heading home.

"Okay. I'm going to hold you to that. Are you on any social media now?" she asked with judgment in her voice.

"I'm on Instagram."

"Uh-huh. Of course you are! Thanks for letting me know."

"I'm sorry, Sienna," he apologized again.

"What's with the apologies? I want to come see you. I hope I'll be able to recognize you. Do you still even have long hair?"

"Yes, I still have long hair, but I have it up and out of my face."

"A *man bun*? You've got to be kidding me. You've become a hipster," she mocked. "I bet your username is something like too-cool-for-you-quinn or some shit like that. So tell me, what is it?"

"It's just Quinn-underscore-Axton."

"I just think it's crappy that we said we wouldn't do social media, and yet here you are."

"I'm the photographer for the school e-newspaper, okay? And I've become good at it, so sometimes I share random pics. Whatever. I'm not going to argue with you. I'll call you. I need to go," Quinn said and hung up.

'I hope I'll be able to recognize you?' What the hell was that? he thought, driving home with his elbow sticking out the window. *I can see her being upset over how I've changed over the past three months. She definitely isn't going to get why I like being on the school paper. And then, of course, there's Caden, Mia, and Blair. She would have no patience for them at all.* He took a deep breath to stop the direction his thoughts were going, but it was in vain. *Have I grown away from her? I haven't had a drink or a hit of anything since I've been here, let alone had the desire to. Just hearing her voice is triggering. I should be sad, but I'm pissed instead. Dr. Summers has seen the change in me. Even Dad's coming around. So why is she making me feel like shit? I mean, what if I want to stay and finish my senior year here?* He shook his head. *She can pound sand if she can't be supportive. Ugh! She's in my head.*

Quinn parked his Rover in the driveway and just sat there, his jaw set. "Fuck!" he yelled, and hit the steering wheel. His confusion wasn't going to go away on its own. He squeezed his eyes shut at the thought of how he would confront the crevice that was growing wider and wider between his life then and his life now.

QUINN COVERED the last two of three swim meets remaining for the year. They had both been at visitor schools, but the last one would be hosted at home. Despite Caden's dissection of his stories to find something on Ash, the two meets amounted to a typical swim report and nothing more. Ash was a stand-up guy.

The turnouts for West Bay View home sporting events were some of the highest in the state. The onus was on Nessie, the mascot. Her legendary status was the perfect metaphor for the school's acclaimed aquatic record. And being that this last meet would determine if they would move on to state finals, attendance was expected to be higher than usual.

Elle sat with Ash in the bleachers, hoping to spot Rikki and have her join them for the halftime show. She knew it would be a long shot because that would require Rikki to stop studying—and therefore leave the library—early. Instead, she spotted her horticulture teacher, Mr. Croft, sitting with Ms. Morgan, who she knew from her family's past. Elle never knew how to act toward Ms. Morgan, who always wore either a turtleneck or scarf around her neck even when it was hot outside. Elle always made an effort to be very accommodating the handful of times Miss Morgan had come into Java and Book, but there was—and probably always would be—an awkward vibe between them.

Hey, the halftime show is going to start. Coming? Elle texted Rikki.

Yeah. Just finishing up.

Halftime with Nessie during water polo and football games was such a spectacle that for some, it was the only reason to go to the games. She would slither through the water in long sinuous strides until the beat of the music kicked in, and then she would rock out. The costume was made of nylon, so it was adaptable to land and water. It required three talented people in choreography and water synchronization to maneuver it. One person operated the head, another operated the hump, and the third operated the tail.

Elle saw Quinn arriving late to the meet. He appeared to scramble for a spot poolside, but other photographers had taken all the prime ones. As if thinking outside the box, he found a spot shooting from the three-meter diving board opposite the swimmer's blocks. Judging by the looks given by other photographers, he now had the most coveted spot.

The halftime show was underway. Relief came over Elle when she saw Rikki walking along the bleachers. Elle waved to get her attention. Smiling, Rikki waved back, but then stopped. She reached for her chest—her expression becoming distressed.

Quinn was standing on the diving board, focusing on Nessie, who was underneath him, when the vibration struck him unexpectedly. The impact caused his knees to wobble, which caused the diving board to wave. He reached for his chest, hoping that would stop the sensation, but his camera and lens threw his balance off.

Rikki held her chest while she scanned the audience. Her breath caught when the look of their lively faces turned grim. A collective gasp echoed throughout the room as they witnessed something happening behind her.

QUINN FELL toward Nessie and through the fabric that covered her wiry frame. The material lifted from its frame, enveloping Quinn. He struggled to get out of his entanglement. Gasping for air, the fabric seemed to descend upon his airway, creating a vacuum. Scrambling to remove the fabric and find a way out, the camera twisted around his wrist, repeatedly knocking him in the head. He couldn't withstand the pain any further and used his final seconds of consciousness to save himself.

PANIC HELD Rikki in its grip. Paralyzed, she struggled to breathe as a full anxiety attack came on.

ASH WAS the first one in the pool. The rest of the swimmers jumped in to help free Quinn. He was unconscious when they pulled him from the water. The coaches—both home and visitor —immediately began lifesaving measures. The crowd was silent as people waited with trepidation for some kind of response. Quinn coughed and heaved. Within moments, coaches gave a thumbs up, and sounds of relief reverberated off the walls.

ELLE HURRIED TO RIKKI. "Are you okay? You looked like you were in pain," Elle said as she held on to Rikki's shoulders.

"I can't explain it. I felt those vibrations, but it was solid, and then a wave of panic came over me. I guess because the crowd was reacting to that guy who fell in." Rikki felt so confused.

"You know that was Quinn who fell in," Elle pointed out.

"Who's Quinn?" Rikki asked.

"How do you not know who Quinn is? He's with the school

newspaper and around Caden a lot. He's new this semester? Quinn?"

She shook her head. "I've never met him."

"I could have sworn your reaction was sympathy pain for him. You both reached for your chest. It was kind of crazy."

"Weird," Rikki said, not really believing what she heard. "I hope he's okay." She looked in the direction of coaches that huddled over Quinn as they walked him to the locker room for further evaluation.

LYNDSEY STOOD there in a trance-like daze. A dynamic shift in her world was occurring. Something spiritual. Her eyes slowly scanned the audience. *What is this? Could it be? Is my mother finally here and nearby? I think so, but there's something more.* She began trembling. *Could her lover, Wade, be with her? Are they already together? Damn it!*

"Lyndsey? Are you okay?" Rusty asked.

Her eyes darted to the friend she sat with—the teacher students called Mr. Croft. "Me? Umm, actually, I'm not feeling so well. I think I'm going to go. I'll bring you that herbal tea you were asking about tomorrow, okay?"

"Oh. Okay. Are you sure? Your face is all red." He reached out and touched her arm.

She smiled to not worry him. "I'm fine. I just need to get out of here."

Dread came over her as she weaved her way through the crowd, her hand on her head. She needed to get home, take a breath, and come to terms with the fact that this development had knocked off her trajectory. The rest of the evening would revolve around what she was going to do about it.

"HEY, MAN!" Caden greeted Quinn the next day when he walked into the newsroom. "We're supposed to report the news, not *be* the news," he ribbed.

"That was the scariest thing that's ever happened to me," he confided. "That damn vibration thing came on strong when I wasn't expecting it, and I lost my balance. I know you don't want to hear this, but I'm thankful Ash was there. He got to me first and saved my life."

"I know. The whole school sees him as a hero. Either way, glad to see you're okay." Caden patted Quinn's shoulder.

"I hope they know it was my fault, and they don't get rid of Nessie," Quinn said.

"As of yet, nothing has been said. But expect administrators to be on you for the next day or so."

———

MRS. WENTZ STOPPED by the newsroom to check on Quinn and told him not to worry about the photo equipment, even bringing in a replacement camera and lens. The outpouring of care and concern from friends and strangers proved to be a warm blanket that Quinn had never worn before. It was a pivotal moment for him. He would never have gotten a reception like this back home. Even referring to Wyoming as "back home" no longer felt right. By the last week of school, Quinn told his dad he wanted to stay, and Mason seemed fine with that. His mom was hurt and was reluctant to acknowledge his progress, but she didn't fight his desire to stay. And even though he was looking forward to summer, oddly enough, he found himself looking forward to senior year even more.

7

PEPPER SPRAY

Quinn was relieved to finally take Sienna back to the airport a few days before senior year started. She had been visiting him in Sausalito for ten days, and within the first three days, he began feeling depressed again. She was constantly chipping away at him. It was subtle at first—she mentioned how everyone missed him, how his mom missed him, then she took it up a notch with the guilt, saying things like he was the glue that held their group together, and since he'd left, they'd disbanded. It snowballed from there. She made frequent remarks about how much he'd changed—and not for the better. She even managed to manipulate him into partying and lying again.

"I had a great time! I knew you were still in there," she said as if proud of herself, then took a final hit off her joint and flicked it out the window. "Thanks for having me. Maybe I'll visit during the holidays. That could be a lot of fun, with all your fancy-schmancy holiday parties. We could raise hell."

"Okay," Quinn said, trying to sound alert.

She turned to him. Her soft hair fell to the side as she tilted her head. "Oh, Quinn. Get some rest. You kinda look like shit," she said as if she had nothing to do with it.

Quinn gave a closed-lipped smile. He stopped in front of the terminal, grabbed her bags, and gave her a weak hug.

"Now, Quinn, don't be like that," she said. "Hold on." She bent down to reach into her carry-on bag. She stood up and gave him a handwritten letter. "I know this is old school, but I wrote you something to remind you of us and your real home and how I miss our kind-of friendship," she said sheepishly.

"Thanks, Sienna," he said robotically and took the letter he had no intention of reading before giving her another quick hug.

She stopped him from pulling away from her and gave him a lingering kiss on the cheek, then turned and walked away.

As soon as she left his sight, he got back into the car, stuffed the letter into the center console, and flipped the mirror to look at himself. He had dark circles under his dull, bloodshot eyes. His skin was dry, his hair was slick with oil, and he felt as bad as he looked. He hit his steering wheel in anger. He hated that he'd allowed her to manipulate him, and he was wrong to think he could live in both worlds.

He felt driven to cut his ties with his old life, to cut off the world that even still tried to tear him down. So he drove to the nearest barbershop to do just that. Leaving the top long, he closed his eyes as the buzzing and crudeness of the clippers cut close to the sides of his head. The vibrations jarred his teeth, and when it was over, he stood tall and took pleasure in stepping on the aftermath of his impulsive choice. He exhaled in relief—Wyoming had been severed.

Quinn closed the front door of his home and stood motionless in his entryway. He was depressed and relieved at the same time. Those conflicting emotions overwhelmed and paralyzed him, and he hung his head down. His fresh hair flopped down and covered his eyes. He didn't notice at first that his dad standing at the bottom of the stairs, just feet from him.

"Jesus, Quinn! Are we really back to square one? Nice hairdo," his dad chided.

Quinn set his jaw and balled his fist, not knowing how to handle his emotions. "I … I'm… I'm…" He couldn't get his words out. His hands flew to his eyes and awaited more of his dad's words of contempt.

His dad stood there with his hands on his hips for a minute, watching him, then walked over and pulled him in. Shuttering, Quinn wrapped his arms around his dad and broke down.

<hr>

It was the first day of senior year, and Rikki was in a rush to get going. She tried to open her phone to check the weather, only to find that it had died sometime during the night. "What the…" Following the charging cable, she found it hanging halfway out of the outlet. "Damn it." She shoved the plug further into the socket, threw her sheets off, and plopped down on the chair in front of her computer: rain *and possible thunderstorms.*

"What the hell?" She searched her closet for a proper jacket. "Shit! I'm running late," she swore to herself when she glanced at the time. *Forget the damn jacket.* The day was not off to a good start.

She jumped in the shower and began washing her hair. The shampoo bottle was lighter than expected. Forgetting she was running low, she violently shook the bottle until a single glob shot out. Half of it landed on her foot, while the other half hung precariously from her hand. "Damn it!"

She scrubbed her hair like she was trying to erase it. Thoughts barreled through her mind like a runaway train. *Will I survive senior year? Am I going to get all the classes I need? What about college? Applications? Boys? Will my classes be far from my locker again?* A rumbling noise sounded while she was in mid-thought. The pipes began to rattle and then ceased.

"Shit!" Rikki panicked. "What's with the water?" she yelled, her fingers still entwined in her thirsty hair. It would look like a rat's nest if she didn't get the shampoo out and fast.

There was a knock at the door. "Rikki, sorry! I forgot to tell you they're doing maintenance on the pipes this morning, and the water is off until eight tonight," Olivia, Rikki's mom, said.

"Wow, Mom! I think that's the worst thing I could have possibly heard." Rikki's statement echoed off the shower walls.

"Okay, okay. Hang tight. I think I have bottled water in my car. I'll get that for you."

"A single bottle of water isn't going to do much," she said. Her frantic gesturing flung a single molecule of shampoo directly into her eye. "Shiiit! Aaah!" Blinded, she reached for a towel and rubbed the irritation until her skin became raw. She would not be wearing contacts today.

As expected, the water in the bottle wasn't enough to release her tangles, so a messy bun would have to suffice. Placing bobby pins in her hair, she glanced around, looking for her glasses. It occurred to her, after a cursory look, that she'd left them in her car. *Well, at least that's resolved. Now all I have to do is print my schedule and get the hell out of here, then I'll be back on track, and my world will be right-side-up again.* She tried to convince herself that she could escape Murphy's Law simply by changing locations.

Rikki's cell reception at school was unpredictable, so she always printed out her schedule of classes at the beginning of a new semester. Of course, the printer refused to communicate with her phone and being that it was now only at eleven percent battery power, she was sure that the first-day-of-school gods were out to get her. "You've got to be kidding me?!" she called out as she grabbed a pen and paper to write down her schedule.

She called Elle to apologize for running late and let her know that she would drive herself to school instead. She placed her schedule in her planner and spun around to grab her thin sweater, only to knock over a pitcher filled with cran-blueberry juice. "Damn it! What else, Universe? What the hell else?" she yelled, unintentionally making things worse by trying to wipe the liquid off her white pants, which only made the stain bigger.

"Calm down! You have other clothes. Just go change," her mom said.

Rikki set her jaw. "Well, Mom, all my clothes for school are in the wash, where there is no water!" she bit through gritted teeth.

The mishaps didn't end there. A truck in front of her drove over a pothole, kicking up gravel and cracking her windshield. When she got out of her car at school, cold water rushed into her shoe when she stepped into a puddle. "Shit!" She looked at her phone and saw she was now thirty minutes late.

Under the protection of an overhang at the front of the school, she threw her backpack down to find her schedule. It wasn't in there. "Fuck!" *I bet I left it in the damn car with my glasses, because fuck me, Universe.* She huffed and puffed and marched her cran-blueberry-stained, messy-bunned, legally-blind ass all the way to the office to get a new printout of her schedule because no way in hell was she going back out into the rain.

Shivering, wet, and pissed, she snatched the schedule from poor Ms. Sheridan's hands and stormed out.

She glanced down at the paper. "Period one, AP Physics, building A." She hustled to class and walked in with her head down.

"Ms. Rikki Waters, welcome to AP Physics. Your first lesson: although time is relative, it's constant here on Earth. Try to be on time from now on," Mr. Jamison said in a poor attempt to be funny.

"OMG, Rikki! What happened to you?" Kendall asked because she always had to know everyone's business.

"Not now, Kendall." She slammed her notebook on the desk.

Kendall tilted her head. "Was it the water thing? Did you not get the memo?" she asked condescendingly.

"Seriously, Kendall, shut up!"

"Ms. Waters, is this how it's going to be in my class?" Mr. Jamison called from across the room.

She looked around at all the blurry faces and sank further into her seat. "No. Sorry!"

She spent the rest of the class squinting at the board.

At first break, Rikki surrendered to the Universe, enduring the wind and rain to grab her glasses from her car. She was standing beside her car when she reached inside her backpack for her keys, and like, her schedule, they were not in her backpack.

"Holy fucking shit! How much worse can it get?" Rikki yelled up to the sky. Rain poured even harder. "And what the hell is with the pouring rain? In August?! In California?!" She continued to curse. Throwing her backpack on again, she trudged back through the student parking lot and into the school. By the time she made it to the entrance, first break was over, and people headed to their third period class.

"Oh, Rikki!" Kendall hollered.

Fuck! Rikki took a deep breath and clenched her fist. "What the hell, Kendall?"

Kendall strolled over. "I know something about you that you don't," she teased.

"What about my body language might suggest to you that I'm in the mood for games?"

"Okay, fine. Elle has your keys."

"And I suppose you knew this in Physics, right?"

"You told me to shut up, so I shut up."

"And how do you know they're my keys?"

"Because there's a pink crystal on them, isn't there?"

Rikki pushed past her, subjecting her backpack to another

round of pummeling by throwing it onto the ground to search for her phone. Grabbing hold of it, she looked up at the sky, praying her cell service would cooperate as she called Elle.

Waiting for her to pick up the phone, Rikki reached inside her backpack to look up what class she was inevitably going to be late to next. Relief came over her when Elle picked up.

"Shit, I forgot to turn off my phone. Everything okay?" Elle asked.

"No. What class are you in right now?" Rikki asked just as she flung open her binder and pulled out the schedule that read *3rd period: Modern Mythology and Folklore (L-5) - Ms. Lyndsey Morgan.* "I'm in the Building L in Ms. Morgan's Mythology class."

"Great! I have that too," Elle started. "That'll—"

Rikki hung up the phone. She was beyond caring about being nice and booked it through the deluge all the way across campus to Building L.

ELLE ENDED her call and looked around the classroom in embarrassment over picking up the phone in the first place.

"That was weird," Elle said to Caden's back.

Ash, who was sitting behind her, leaned in. "You shouldn't be answering your phone in class, silly," Ash told her, then chuckled.

"I know, but it was Rikki, and something told me it was urgent."

"How can the ring of your phone tell you it's urgent?" Ash challenged.

Elle shook her head and rolled her eyes.

Caden turned around. "Is she okay?"

"Something's up. I don't know what, but she's pissed, and she totally just hung up on me," Elle said with concern in her voice.

138

She stared across the room at the door, wondering how soon Rikki would show up and in what condition.

"What did she say?" Caden asked.

"She just wanted to know what class I was in." Then it clicked—she had Rikki's keys. "Shit. I have her keys. I bet you she's pissed over that," she said, and reached into her purse to grab them, then put them on her desk.

"Why do you have her keys?"

"She dropped them in the parking lot."

"And she's mad at you for that?"

Quinn, who sat up one seat and to the right of Caden, shook his head. "And this is a friend of yours?"

"It's Rikki. You don't know Rikki?" Caden asked.

"No, but from the sounds of it, I don't think I want to."

Elle leaned over. "Caden, save that seat in front of you."

"What? And have her sit next to me?" Quinn protested. "No, thank you. She sounds like a total nightmare."

"It's either there or the seat in front of you," Elle said.

Quinn looked around as if to find another seat, but none were available.

"Quinn, she's not like that. She's just—"

The teacher cleared her throat, interrupting Elle. She looked up and met the stern eyes of the teacher who was standing behind her desk in front of Elle's row of seats under the windows. She sank further into her chair. "Sorry."

The teacher gave her a slight nod to accept Elle's apology. She walked along the front of the class, stopping in the center between a long table and the whiteboard. "Good morning, class. My name is Ms. Lyndsey Morgan. Welcome to Modern Mythology and Folklore."

As Lyndsey continued her introduction, her head suddenly began to whiz. Something was about to happen. She continued to speak to the class from rote memory as she tried to decipher what was happening to her. What she did know was that it was spiritual, and it was the same feeling she'd felt during the swim meet. Her eyes grew wide as the feeling intensified.

"Miss Morgan? Are you okay?" one student asked.

"Yes. Excuse me while I get a drink of water," she said and walked over to her desk.

Drenched, fuming, and now several minutes late, the vibration Rikki hadn't felt since last school year hit her like a ton of bricks. Her anger leveled up to irate, and she yanked open the classroom door. Looking around the room, she thought she spotted Elle across the room, but some blond guy was blocking her view. She leaned to gain a better visual, and behind Caden, she saw Elle waving at her.

She marched behind the long table at the front of the classroom and raised her hand like a catcher. "Keys!" she demanded, ignoring the fearful expression on Elle's face.

Elle quickly grabbed keys and pitched them to her. As the keys jingled their way through the air, the blond guy raised his hand and caught them, then laughed.

Rikki snapped.

Quinn felt his teasing expression drop the second he saw something in the girl break.

His eyes widened as the batshit crazy girl hurdled the table between them. He scrambled to get out of his seat, but she was already atop his desk, clawing at him. Swerving to dodge her

140

attack, he twisted out of his seat, and suddenly she was on his back, hitting him.

"What the fuck? Give me my fucking keys, asshole!" she yelled as she continued to hit him on his back.

"Okay. Okay." The keys had fallen from his grip. He grabbed hold of the arm she was anchoring herself with and whirled her off his back. She fell on her butt, facing him.

Batshit got back up and charged him. "Fucker! I'm not playing games!"

Quinn grabbed both her arms and crossed them, forcing her to turn her back into his body. "Calm the fuck down!" He closed his arms around her tighter, pulling her into him as she continued to squirm to free herself from his grip.

WHAT THE HELL is going on here? "Hey!" Lyndsey called out. She was losing control. "Kids, I need you all to leave the classroom before you get hurt."

She ran to her desk, opened the drawer, and grabbed her keys with the canister of pepper spray. The last few remaining kids in the class who had wanted to stay and watch what would happen next ran out of the classroom the moment Lyndsey started shaking the canister. She pointed the nozzle at the two entangled students to hopefully scare them into stopping, but they were beyond hearing anything but their own fighting. Still reeling from the whizzing in her head, she didn't know how else to confront the situation.

The guy continued to lean over, holding the girl tight to maintain control.

As Lyndsey held her aim, hoping they would resolve this on their own, her whole world suddenly came to a jarring halt. The moment she had agonized over for the last fifteen years was now right in front of her. As the boy fought against the girl's warfare, their shirts shifted, exposing not just her star birthmark, but his too. Robin and Wade were right there in front of her, and the only thing she could do at that moment—was push the plunger down.

Yells of agony reverberated off the walls. The boy's arms were still clutched around the girl's waist as he fell back, taking her down with him. Their bodies slammed on top of the hard wooden desks, causing the desks and all the items on top to topple over, hitting them on their heads. They were both rendered unconscious.

Lyndsey stood there, confounded and unable to process what lay before her.

Elle and Caden came running back into the classroom.

"Close and lock the door and call 911," Lyndsey directed, never looking away from the boy and girl—or as she now saw them, Mom and Wade.

ELLE JUMPED INTO ACTION. As she made her way to the toppled desks to check on her friends, she glanced over at the opened drawer in Ms. Morgan's desk and saw crystals, oils, a carved wand, and even a tarot deck inside. Her breath caught, disturbed over the number of black candles that were also jammed inside.

LYNDSEY STARTED to tremble when the principal showed up with the school nurse and told the anxious students standing at the doorway to put their phones down, then directed campus security to move them to another room.

"What happened, Ms. Morgan?" Principal Ryan asked as he stepped around the overturned desks. He raked his hand through his black, slicked-back hair, as Nurse Hannah hurried to the kids, who remained unconscious. She immediately administered first aid, checking that their breathing was stable.

"He's starting to bleed on the side of his head here." The nurse pointed above Quinn's ear.

Lyndsey swallowed reflexively at the sound of the principal's long sigh. "They got into a fistfight, Sean. She was enraged, and he was trying to defend himself. I thought he and other students were going to get seriously hurt. I yelled at them to stop, and when I realized they couldn't hear me, I asked all the kids to leave, then I sprayed them with my pepper spray."

"The ambulance will be here soon," he said, looking at the two of them on the floor, just starting to rouse. "I'm going to need you to go home until we get a full understanding of what happened here. You've been here for years, and you're great at your job. You told me you had concerns about the other students' safety, which is great, but I'm still unsure why you chose this action rather than calling security. Hell, even throwing water on them could have been better than this." He sighed. "Ultimately, you're going to have to answer for this, and it's not up to me. Furthermore, Lyndsey, let's pray the parents don't sue, or worse, go to the media."

"Of course," she replied. Lyndsey collected her things and tore out of there.

I don't get Sean. How can he not see that I was protecting the kids? How could he send me home? You know, this might be just what I need, actually. Now I can spend the rest of the day processing what the hell just happened. After all this time. Why am I so shocked? Her mind was in tangles as she made her way to her car. She needed to center herself, consider her options, then move into action.

"Ahhh, man! What the fuck?" Quinn said as he tried to open his eyes. He started to get up, but his head hurt, and that girl was still on top of him, pinning him to the floor. He groaned in pain as he held his head. He felt a warm liquid slide over his ear, and he brushed it away. Blood. *Shit.* He tried to extricate himself out from under her, but the harder he pushed away, the more uncomfortable he felt. Eventually, he gave in, losing consciousness again.

<hr>

The paramedics arrived. As they gently separated and tried to stabilize them, Rikki began thrashing around. Hyperventilation set in.

"I can't open my eyes. I can't see." Her hand reached out, desperate to grab on to something to get her bearings.

The paramedics explained that what they were experiencing was normal and that their vision would return to normal within a couple hours, but Rikki's anxiety boiled over. She was no longer available for a rational explanation of any kind, and before she knew it, she felt a sharp pain in her hip.

"Ow! What was that?"

"We need you to calm down, miss. We gave you a slight sedative so we can provide the care you need. Do you understand?"

They received no answer. She was out before she could formulate a response.

<hr>

When they arrived at the hospital, they were brought to emergency bays beside each other. Only a thin curtain protected their privacy.

Quinn's vision was coming back as they prepped him for a

CT scan since his head had taken the brunt of the assault. They needed to rule out a concussion.

***

Rikki, on the other hand, wasn't entirely coherent. She would fall asleep, wake up, then fall back to sleep. She could hear the machines beeping, papers rustling, feet shuffling, and people talking. It seemed so familiar to her, but when she opened her eyes, she still couldn't see. Oddly, when she closed her eyes, she could see things with a lot more clarity. She didn't know what was real and what wasn't. She looked to her left because someone was there to help her. It was a handsome man with olive-green eyes and an expression of deep concern on his face.

"Wade! Wade!" Rikki cried out.

"Rikki?" the nurse called but got no response. "Rikki!" she yelled louder. "Can you tell me who Wade is?"

"Wade is … he's my—" She could hear the panic in her voice but quickly forgot what had unnerved her. "What? I don't know what I was saying." Rikki drifted back to sleep.

***

Quinn had drifted off to sleep as well. He dreamt of a woman wearing a long, white gown. She had long, brown hair and stood at the edge of a cliff that overlooked the water. He feared she was going to jump. As he took a step closer, he accidentally kicked what he thought was a rock, but when he looked down, he saw it was a crystal. The sound startled her. She quickly looked back at him. The wind blew, causing her hair to whip around her face, and she mouthed something to him. She raised her hand, exposing her palm. An eight-pointed star, just like his birthmark, was imprinted on it. He looked down at his own birthmark. When he looked up, she had turned away from him and was on fire. He was jolted awake by the vibrations he had grown accustomed to.

***

Rikki lurched out of her slumber with a gasp, her nerves humming like the revving of an engine.

"Where am I? I still can't open my eyes! My skin hurts. Where are my contacts? How long will it be like this? And why is that fucking dizzying vibrating or whatever the fuck it is back?" When she got no response, she shifted in her bed. "Hello?"

***

Quinn heard her cries for help, and, in his vibrational haze, he got up and went to her.

***

Rikki heard the curtain be pushed aside. The charge grew even more robust, and she reeled.

***

Quinn stood at the side of the girl's bed as she tousled about. Her hair. It was like the woman in his dream. His heart raced, and he felt compelled to calm her down. Every step he took, the magnetic pull that buzzed through his body amplified. He grabbed hold of her hand and leaned into her, bringing his other hand to the side of her face. Something within them blazed, jolting the girl, who opened her eyes, locking in on his. Tears began to well up in her eyes.

"Shhhh. You're going to be fine," Quinn whispered, and she

instantly quieted. Her breathing slowed, and she nodded, never breaking eye contact.

They sat there for a moment, just looking into each other's eyes. There was something so familiar about her that Quinn's breath quickened, and the tear in the girl's eye that had been teetering on the brink of escape was finally liberated.

"WHO ARE YOU? Do I know you?" she whispered, holding his hand to her face. His eyes, she wondered. Where had she seen those eyes before? Their intensity held an honesty that told her she could trust him wholly and utterly, and she was captivated.

"I'm Quinn." He squinted his eyes like he was waiting for her to connect the dots. "From school?" Then added out the side of his mouth, "And from class this morning?"

Her eyes darted about the room and back to him. It all came flooding back to her. The water debacle, the class schedule debacle, the Kendall debacle, all leading up to the granddaddy of them all: the "I'm-going-to-kick-your-ass-because-you-caught-my-keys–and-then-got-us-pepper-sprayed-in-the-eyes"
debacle.

"Ahh, there it is." The side of his mouth turned upward.

She quickly let go of his hand and scooted back as she sat straight up. "Jesus! What have I done?" she said, bringing the heels of her palms to her eyes. She shook her head. "I'm so sorry! I completely lost my shit!" She let a long breath. "It's just been one train wreck after another," she tried explaining, still shaking her head in disbelief.

"Well, I *did* choose to play 'keep-away' from a batshit crazy girl," he said, the sideways grin of his re-emerging. Her heart skipped a beat.

"Damn, I feel so foolish," she chuckled.

He sat there for a moment. "Can I ask you something? Just

now, when you were calling out, you said that you felt vibrating. What did you mean by that?"

"It's hard to explain. No one I mention it to seems to understand what I'm trying to say, but since the last semester of junior year, I get a dizzying, humming, vibrating sensation that comes and goes. It's intermittent, and I don't think it's something related to my health. If anything, it kinda feels—"

"Like a rush," he interrupted.

"Yes!" she said with wide eyes, recalling the feeling. "Do you feel it too?"

"I do. It's like a vibration that surges from within, then flows right out of me." He used his hand to emulate the feeling coming from his chest and closed his eyes.

"Yes! Yes!" Heat rose within her when he touched his chest. "What do you think causes it?" she asked, dismissing the heat that continued to grow from within.

"I don't know. Sometimes it's stronger than other times. It's what made me fall off the diving board during the swim meet last semester," he said with a pained look on his face.

"I was there, and I felt it then too. I felt the rush, but then it turned to panic." She started to wonder. "Maybe we're ultra-sensitive to something environmental."

"Maybe," he said, looking around the room. "There is something so very familiar here. Like I've been here before."

"Well, weren't you here recently? When you, like, well, you know when...?"

"Yeah, I don't know. I guess," he said but still seemed skeptical. "I'm going to let you rest. I'm sure our parents will be showing up soon," he said, getting up. He took another look around and shook his head as if he couldn't shake the feeling.

She stared at him as he stood. Her emotional high was threatened, and she didn't want him to go. "Hey," she called, and he turned toward her, lifting his eyebrows. She could see that he was on the taller side of average, and even through his hospital gown, she could tell he was fit. If his smooth and toned fore-arms are any indication, then she must be in the presence of a young guy sculpted by the gods. All of him—his eyes, his hair that dangled in front of them, his full lips, chiseled chin, his body, strength, and even the kindness in his voice—all of it added up to someone who was totally out of her league, and an unrequited crush was sparked. "I'm Rikki."

8

BLINDED BY THE LIGHT

Lyndsey paced between her bedroom and her temple room. "She re-enters my life, and not even five minutes go by before she starts fucking everything up," she said out loud while slapping the back of one hand against the palm of the other. *Get it together. What's my plan?*

Step one—a whole lotta ass-kissing. The thought sickened her. *How is it that I have to apologize to the people who have victimized me?*

She quickly called the principal to see if she still had a job. "Hey, Sean," Lyndsey said sheepishly.

"Ms. Morgan," he replied. There was bitterness behind his greeting.

"I don't want to lose my job. How do I make this right?"

"You're a fine teacher, and I hope it works out in your favor. A lot depends on the superintendent and what the parents will do. And although the media hasn't made any indication that they even know, I'm just waiting for the other shoe to drop."

"I understand. Do you know when I might be able to come back?"

"Let's give it a couple days to see what direction this is going to go. But Lyndsey, I want you to think about what happened here. I want you to acknowledge your responsibility and produce a statement of apology," he insisted.

"You can count on me. I really am sorry," she lied. "I'll have that statement for you by tomorrow."

She hung up and retreated to her temple room. She sat on her knees before her altar that was in front of a floor-to-ceiling window with an expansive view of the lush greenery surrounding her house. She lit several black candles and burned some incense that she'd retrieved from the apothecary she had built inside the closet opposite the large window. Reading from her personal Book of Shadows, she cast a Blinded by the Light spell over the principal, superintendent, the school board, and the people in Rikki and Quinn's orbits. The spell would cause those people to feel sorry for her and prevent further consequences.

"Oh, Mighty Spirits of Persuasion:
 Beguile them to see
 That only fairness comes from me.
 Convert their suspicions of my wrongdoing
 Into guilt over their misconstruing,
 Lure them away from the righteous direction
 So I won't be censured to any correction."

SHE WROTE their names on a piece of paper, burned it with one of the black candles, and then burned a cinnamon stick and licorice root. Finally, she soaked the ashes in clove oil. Once the ashes steeped for several minutes, she extracted the remaining liquid in a vial and left to move forward in her plan.

ELLE AND ASH met up with Caden at the hospital in hopes of seeing how their friends were doing. They joined Rikki's parents and Quinn's dad in the waiting room.

"Hi, Elle," Rikki's mom said and gave Elle what felt like a robotic hug. "I'm so glad you're here." She took a step back. "The two of them are just fine and can go home in a couple of hours."

"I can't get over what happened!" Elle said.

"Yeah, we got the play-by-play from the principal. I tell you, that daughter of mine, she can be a real pistol sometimes," Olivia admitted, but there was a dullness in her otherwise bright, happy, brown eyes.

Elle turned to Ash and Caden, wide-eyed, to see if they'd heard what she had. Caden's face also held a look of disbelief. Ash, on the other hand, didn't seem to understand the implications.

"Wow! That's not what I was expecting to hear. I would have thought you'd be on the phone with an attorney to, like, I don't know, sue the school?" Elle said, trying to conceal her shock but failing miserably.

"Oh, yeah, no. I can't tell you how many times Rikki's anxiety has gone overboard and hurt those around her. I've told her that one day, it was going to get her into trouble. Maybe this time she's learned her lesson. I mean, I can sort of hear what you're—" For a moment, there was a glimmer of rational thought in her eyes, but then it switched back. "No, no, yeah … Natural consequences. That's what this is," she said, waving her hand as if to wipe away her betraying thought.

"Do Quinn's parents feel the same way?" Elle asked, scratching the back of her head and trying to see their perspective, but couldn't.

"Oh yes, his dad agrees. We all feel that way."

"That Rikki is to blame?"

"Quinn's no saint," Quinn's father interjected. "He shouldn't have provoked her."

"Oh, um, okay. Have any of you been in to see them?" Elle asked, looking again at Caden and Ash. Caden mouthed "OMG," while Ash's eyebrows were knitted like he was confused.

"Not yet. But they assured us they're fine. They said we could probably see them in a little while," Rikki's mom said.

<hr>

RIKKI OVERHEARD the doctor speak with Quinn about his CT results. She covered her eyes with her arm, and tears traveled down the same trail as her previous tears. *How can I make this up to everyone, especially Quinn?*

The curtain between Rikki and Quinn clung to the backside of a heavy-set nurse. She took a step to the side, taking the curtain with her, and Rikki wasted no time in taking advantage of the window of opportunity to take a peek. Relief came over her when she noticed his bed was further away from the wall than hers was, allowing her the optimal viewing position to study him without getting caught. She shamelessly basked in the fact that he couldn't see her without turning entirely around.

His hair was surfer-like, although the stark tan line around his neck suggested he wasn't much of a sun-worshipper. His artery that bulged from his neck entranced her, provoking her to trace along her nape with her fingertips. Her eyes drifted down his neck to his shoulders, then his chest that moved slowly to the rhythm of his breathing while he listened to the doctor. He exuded strength and protection, and it stirred something from within her.

She closed her eyes to replay the moment she had awoken to his enchanting eyes, how she had felt calm in his presence. The sound of his reassuring voice and the low tone he'd used caused her breath to quicken at the memory. *Who is this guy?*

THE DOCTOR TOLD Quinn that the CT results had come back negative. As he listened to the doctor, a swathing warmth washed over him. He looked around, then turned his head back toward Rikki's bed. His eyes locked with hers. She never looked away, and neither did he. The magnetism was fierce as far as he was concerned, and based on the fact that she was holding his gaze, she seemed to be in the same place he was.

"Excuse me." The doctor looked at the nurse. "Carla, could you close the curtain all the way?"

The nurse moved over and abruptly closed the curtain, causing Quinn to lose sight of Rikki. But like switching from television to radio, the connection remained, even though he could no longer see her. His breathing slowed down as he closed his eyes in contentment.

Even when his father and Rikki's parents came into the room, the line that connected him to Rikki held firm. *What is this feeling? I didn't think there could be a greater high than the vibrations. She's got to be experiencing this the way I am.*

Rustling feet and words of consternation came from Rikki's side of the curtain, especially as they expressed frustration over the inappropriate fixed smile on her face.

"Are you listening?" the parents asked their respective kids.

"Yes, Dad," Quinn replied, then closed his eyes in elation. *She feels it too.*

<hr>

LATER THAT EVENING, Lyndsey looked up Rikki's and Quinn's addresses, then purchased a couple bouquets of flowers. She wanted maximum success with her spell, so she laced the bouquets with the clove oil mixture and began her deliveries.

Her phone rang. It was the principal.

"Good news. The superintendent, the board, and even the

students' parents felt you acted on behalf of student safety. You can come back tomorrow if you would like," Sean conceded.

"Thank you, Sean! I really was," she said, wiping her hand across her forehead in relief over the effectiveness of her enchantment. "I'll definitely be there tomorrow." She hung up just as she pulled up to Quinn's house.

His house was a modest two-story home that overlooked the bay. The driveway was long enough to park behind a Range Rover without blocking the sidewalk. She grabbed the flowers and nervously knocked on the front door. She took a deep breath, tapping her fingers on the cellophane of the flowers in anticipation. She wasn't familiar with making apologies, especially insincere ones.

A man around her age answered the door. She thought she recognized him as being a friend of a friend, way back in high school when she did have friends. "Can I help you?" the man asked.

"Hi, Mr. Axton! I'm your son's Mythology and Folklore teacher. I came here to offer my sincerest apologies for what happened in my class today," she said with as much honey-sweetness as she could muster.

"Oh okay, Mrs...?" Mason asked with no hint of hard feelings.

"I'm Lyndsey Morgan. I hope you can find it in your heart to forgive me," she begged.

"Oh no, there's no need to apologize. They behaved badly, and you did what you needed to do to stop the situation from getting worse. Let me get Quinn."

He left the door ajar as he went to get his son. She snorted again over how well her enchantment was working. *But how well will my plan work? I guess I'll find out once I get something personal from Quinn.*

Quinn came to the door. His hair was wet as if he'd just

gotten out of the shower. His eyes glanced at hers, and then he looked away as if not knowing what to say. "Um, hi."

"Hi, Quinn! These are for you," she said, holding the flowers out for him to take. "I just wanted to make sure you're okay and to tell you that I'm truly sorry for what happened today."

"Um, yeah. It's fine. Thanks for these," he said, lifting the flowers in acknowledgment.

"I hope you'll remain in my class. I know that we got off to a rough start, but time and again, when students vote on their favorite class, my class is always at the top." She was giving him the hard sell. "Even colleges have commended West Bay View for—"

"Do you know if Rikki will stay in the class?" he interrupted.

Her fist balled. She hadn't been expecting him to ask about *her*. "Well, I don't know. Are you asking because of what she did to you, or did all the drama she caused make you like, buddy-buddy?" She tried to maintain her sweetness, but the questioning look in his eyes told her she'd failed.

"That's fine. I'll stay," he said, ignoring her questions.

"Oh, that's great! I'll see you tomorrow then, right?"

"Um, yeah, I guess so. Thanks again for stopping by," he said, then closed the door.

When Lyndsey heard Quinn lock the door, she made her way to his car to look for something personal. She tried the door, and for all that was good and holy in the world, not only did the door open, but she found a handwritten letter signed by a girl named Sienna in his glove box. *Whoa, what is this?* She read the first sentence. A twig snapped. She immediately tucked the note into her back pocket as she looked around to confirm it had been an animal or something other than Quinn or his dad. After a second, she continued a quick search for something more personal to him. *Perfect!* she thought when she uncovered a hair tie that still included a few strands of his blond hair.

She ran back to her car, so proud of herself for the awesome find, but when she reminded herself of her next move, her jaw set as pride spiraled into anger.

On her drive to Rikki's home, she finally realized what she needed to do with Rikki. Quinn's questioning over whether Rikki would stay in her class, she suspected, was driven by attraction. Their love would become a runaway train if she didn't come up with a plan to derail it immediately. On the other hand, the pain of heartbreak is unparalleled, and therefore, *that* should be her ultimate endgame for Rikki. If they never fell in love, they would never know what they were missing and, thus, no heartbreak. *What if I were to get Rikki to remember who she was? She would figure out who Quinn was. If she tried to explain to him that they're soulmates who were sealed in a past life, he'd think she was crazy. But what if he's willing to look past that? He needs to be distracted by someone else. Hopefully, the letter from that girl will be what I'm hoping it'll be. So when Rikki remembers that she's supposed to be with Quinn, he'll already be in love with someone else, which will be the heartbreak and revenge I'm looking for.* She smiled at the clarity of her direction and started singing along with the upbeat music, but as she neared Rikki's door, her attitude darkened.

Rikki's house exuded an energy that reminded Lyndsey of her old home—her loving home before everything went off the rails. She rolled her eyes and shook her head at the idea that—like her mom's past life—she was, yet again, blessed with privilege.

The exchange with Rikki and her parents went just as smoothly as with Quinn's dad. She dreaded asking Rikki the same question she had asked Quinn but knew it was necessary to move forward with the plan.

"Will I see you tomorrow in my class?" Lyndsey asked dryly.

"Is Quinn going to be there?" she asked. Her eyes lit up like she was hoping for confirmation.

"Um, I'm not so sure." She could hear her own condescension. But witnessing the light in Rikki's eyes fade into disappointment was worth the lie. "He didn't say one way or another. Honestly, he might choose to switch classes," she said, crinkling her nose.

And just like that, the light in Rikki's eyes was extinguished, and Lyndsey held an internal celebration.

Rikki shrugged. "Okay. At least Elle and Caden will be there."

"Well, I *hope* so," Lyndsey said, emphasizing the word *hope*.

"Well, thanks anyway for bringing the flowers," Rikki said, clearly saddened by what she had heard. "Good night."

After she left, Lyndsey decided to drive by her old home, otherwise known as the Morgan House Ruins. Her grandparents had placed a gate along the front of the property, but the rest of the perimeter was fenced off with barbed wire, leaving the gutted home as ruins. They had fought with the city but won because the main floor—although nothing more than a façade—still looked intact. It was so symbolic of her life—okay on the outside with a bit of damage, but complete ruins on the inside.

<hr>

LATER THAT NIGHT, Elle went with Ash to Java and Book. Her mom had been covering for her while she was visiting at the hospital.

"Hey, Mom!" Elle greeted and filled her mom in on all the details.

"That's crazy!" Farrah was shocked.

"But Mom, I didn't tell you the craziest part," she started. "When I went back to the classroom to see if Rikki and Quinn were okay, I saw some *things* in the teacher's desk." Elle paused, fearing her mother's reaction to her next statement. "Mom, I think she's a witch."

"What? No. It's probably props for her class. It's a mythology and folklore class," Farrah theorized.

"No, it's more than that. I'm getting a vibe from her. I've always had a weird vibe from her the few times she's come in here. This just confirms it. And this vibe isn't a good one, Mom. I think she's a dark witch," Elle expressed, raising her eyebrows.

"Elle," Farrah said with warning in her voice. "You're going down into that basement, aren't you? Just because you have your great-aunt, Mozelle's name, doesn't mean you have her life. I don't want you going down that path," she demanded. "Not *that* path."

"Wait, what basement?" Elle questioned.

"Forget it, Elle!" Farrah's face turned red and filled with anguish. "I meant it metaphorically like you're heading toward an all-time low," she said weakly.

Elle knew that was bullshit. Her eyes darted back and forth as it finally clicked what that heavily tinted window next to the stairs in front of the building was. She'd always thought it was a storage room for another business because there never seemed to be an entrance to it anywhere in the café. She started to wonder where the door could be hidden.

"Elle?" Farrah raised her voice.

"Right, yes, Mom. You don't have to worry."

"Don't patronize me, Mozelle!" Her mom always used her given name whenever she meant business.

"I'm not! I won't go down '*that*' path," she said, rolling her eyes as she used air quotes.

"Keep an eye on this one," Farrah said, looking at Ash.

"Always," Ash promised, his eyes fixated on Elle.

"Uh-huh." Farrah collected her things in a huff. "Please call me when you're on your way home."

Ash's eyes never strayed from Elle's. As soon as the door closed behind Farrah, he slinked around the counter. Elle playfully walked backward, feigning fear. He lunged toward her, grabbing her by the waist and pushing her against the counter. He began to nuzzle her neck.

"Ash, not here. After closing," she promised.

Ash's expression turned to disappointment as he recoiled. He walked back to the front of the counter and slumped onto the chair.

"Oh, stop! It's like in an hour."

And as soon as she bolted the door and changed the sign to closed, he was all over her. She took his hand and led him to the room just off the side of the counter. The back wall was covered with a tapestry of a woman sitting next to a stream and a bright star above her.

"What is this room?" Ash asked, intrigued.

"This is where my great-aunt used to do tarot card and psychic readings in. I rarely come here, but I'm wondering if the entrance to the basement I've been *forbidden* to go into is in here. Anyway," she said as she began to flip light switches, "we don't offer those services anymore because no one can do readings the way she did."

"And you're her namesake? I never knew."

"I am. I think Mozelle sounds really old-fashioned, so I shortened it to Elle." She walked about the room. A vibrant tapestry of a star over a body of water covered the length of the back wall. She smiled at the pleasant memories of the few times she and her mom had come to this room.

"Were your mom and your aunt close?"

"Kind of. I think they differed when using their psychic abilities, though. My mom has psychic abilities but doesn't believe in them or doesn't want anything to do with them, and her aunt did the opposite, embracing it to the bitter end."

Ash took a seat at the table where the readings were performed. "You never talk about what happened to her."

"Yeah, well, it's pretty much what everyone else has heard." She really didn't want to go into detail with Ash. She walked behind him and slid her arms around his shoulders, resting her hands on his chest.

He immediately responded. Standing up, he turned toward her, his chest heaving with desire as he took a step closer. He took hold of her face with one hand and the small of her back with the other. He pulled her in close to him. She could feel his excitement. He began walking her back until they hit the wall. Their lips met with heated urgency. They moved against the tapestry until the tapestry couldn't take it anymore. It tore off the nails that secured it and rippled down, enveloping the two of them. They broke out in laughter as they made their way out from under its restraints.

"Well, I guess I found what I was looking for." Elle pointed to a Victorian-style door with a vintage knob that required an iron key to unlock it. Luckily, the key had been hidden behind the tapestry as well. "Shall we?"

"I want to fuck you right here on top of this weird, hippy, voodoo sheet thing," he growled.

She laughed. "That's cute, but I'm going down into that basement, like, right now."

"Stay," he begged as he stood behind her, pulling her in close again. He slid his lips along her neck again.

She didn't stop him. His seductive groan in her ear tempted her, but the drive to see the basement was fiercer. The more she reached for the doorknob, the tighter he held her.

"I'm not letting go," Ash said into her shoulder.

She finally got a grip on the doorknob.

"Elle?" Ash said, anger lacing his undertone.

She turned the knob, and Ash's arms sprung open in surrender. "I give up."

"I'm sorry! But I need to see what's down there," she told him as she stared at the door. "Are you coming?"

"Um, yeah, that's a no," he refused. "What do you expect to find down there? More of this hippy, voodoo crap? And then what? Are you going to fight Ms. Morgan because she might be into this voodoo, hippy crap too? I mean, who do you think you are?"

His words stung, but she didn't engage.

Instead, she opened the door, revealing a dark, damp, mildewy space. She pulled her phone from her pocket to light her path. The stairs invited her to enter the unknown, and for some strange reason, she didn't feel scared. She crept along the unfinished hallway toward the room at the very end. A sense of familiarity consumed her. The closer she got, the more she could sense what the room looked like before actually seeing it. Like a magnet, she felt the room calling out to her, and she couldn't resist its bewitching pull. Without hesitation, she opened the door and stepped into it like she would her own house. She even knew that the light switch was awkwardly placed behind the door.

The moment the lights came on, her soul awakened. Awestruck, her eyes drifted from one enchanting detail to the next. Tears stung her eyes, and her skin tingled as positive energy radiated from everything in the room. Each item expressed its own signature vibe, yet it didn't overwhelm her— it charged her. She saw bookcases full of books on witchcraft, tarot, reiki, and self-awareness. There were framed pictures of her family's legacy. Light glinted off crystals that encircled an altar strewn with oils, herbs, incense, and even candles that had maintained their shape after all these years. The floor was an alluring medley of rugs that promised tranquility if sat atop them. Her body shook. Covering her mouth, she felt like she'd finally come home.

"Elle!" Ash called from upstairs. "Elle. Are you okay?"

She was too entranced to respond.

"Damn it! Elle!" Ash didn't wait again for her to respond. He took a breath and headed down. "What the hell is this place?" he asked himself as he neared the entrance.

He stood at the threshold, dumbfounded when he saw Elle, a wand in one hand and a spellbook in the other. "What the hell are you doing?"

She lowered her arms and turned to him. "Oh, hey! I didn't even hear you come down."

"Really? Because I've been calling your damn name over and over."

"Sorry, but look at this place. Can you blame me? It's magical! Literally!" she said as she spun around and laughed a giddy laugh.

"Wait, you're not into this crap, are you?" Fissures began developing on Ash's heart. "Please tell me you're not into this," he demanded.

"Ash? Don't you know me and where I come from? What my skills are?"

Ash stood there, breathing heavily through his nose. "So you're telling me you're a witch? Like a witch with chants and cauldrons and candles and potions and shit?" He looked around and saw a broom in the corner. "Look! There's even a fucking broom!" He pointed and laughed because he didn't know what else to do with his emotions.

"You forgot the pointy hat," she chided.

He raked his hands through his hair, then put his hand on his hips and lowered his head. Heartbreak was setting in. "I … I don't know if I can do this, Elle." He couldn't look back up at her. "This is some freaky shit, and it's not something I can stand behind."

Elle put the wand down and crossed her arms. "So what? Are you going to make me choose?"

The two of them stood there in silence.

Ash was crushed as those fissures on his heart burst. "I don't know. I've got some thinking to do."

"Don't do this, Ash." Elle wasn't sure if she was begging him or warning him.

"I'm going to call an Uber. I just can't think straight right now." He turned away from her and left.

She was torn between staying and relishing in her discovery or chasing after him.

She chose to stay.

9

TEA LEAVES

Quinn shot out of bed early the next morning, still reeling from the events of the previous day. *Those vibrations—I can't believe she feels them too. I really hope she shows up to class.*

A smile emerged on his face but fell when flashes of the dream he'd had in the hospital surfaced. The woman who stood at the edge of the cliff haunted him. She'd raised her palm to reveal the same mark that hovered over his heart.

He shook his head to toss out the dreadful thoughts, then reached for his hair pomade. He cracked it open, and with both hands, smoothed the product through his hair. After slipping on three leather bracelets, he popped open cologne and took a whiff to remind himself what it smelled like, then spritzed it over his chest. Sneezing, he buttoned up his shirt, grabbed his things, and walked to his car with a spring in his step.

RIKKI COULDN'T GO two minutes without losing herself in recalling what had transpired at the hospital. Cleaning her face reminded her of when Quinn had gently touched her cheek. When she brushed her hair, she closed her eyes and recalled the sound of his alluring voice. When she put her mascara on, her thoughts went directly to the moment she had been jolted awake and met the compassionate eyes of a person she had never met, yet made her feel safe. She grabbed her long white cardigan and backpack and left with a warm smile on her face, praying she would see him at school.

Periods one and two painfully dragged along. At first break, Rikki went to look for Quinn but was stopped by Elle, who was disheveled and out of sorts.

Rikki didn't want to stop her search for Quinn, but she knew she needed to be there for Elle. "Hey! Um, Kendall, the annoying yet *informative* gossip that she is told me what happened with you and Ash. I'm so sorry! Are you okay? Why didn't you call me?" Rikki reached out and rubbed her shoulder.

Elle nodded, beginning to cry. Rikki pulled her into a hug. "I'm sorry you had to hear it from Kendall, but I knew you were still recovering from your own drama. It's so stupid. He's so stupid," Elle cried.

"Do you want to tell me what happened?"

Elle pulled away from Rikki and sat down on a planter. She squinted her eyes because she was facing the sun, so Rikki stood in front of her to block the harsh rays. It proved to be the perfect spot because she could listen to Elle while still on the lookout for Quinn.

"Long story short, I found out there's a basement to Java and Book, and I went to check it out. When I got there, it was like I'd stepped into a whole new and enchanting world. It was full of magical things like an altar, and crystals, and books, candles. There was even a wand, Rikki," she expressed with passion. "*A wand.* I was totally into it. Anyway, I guess Ash came looking for me, and he frickin' sees me with the wand in my hand and freaks the hell out." She looked up at Rikki, and even though she was blocking the sun for her, she still brought her hand up to shield her eyes. "I come from a line of spiritual women," she continued. "But you already know that, and as you'd expect, the fruit doesn't fall from the tree, yada yada yada. But he wanted me to like, disavow it, and I wouldn't do that, so he left." She shook her head and looked out across the campus. Tears filled her eyes again. "You know, I'm not sure what I'm upset over more ... him leaving or him rejecting who I really am."

"I'm so sorry, Elle. He didn't know that about you? Everyone knows that you're like a woodland creature," Rikki said.

"Damn straight I am!" She gave an awkward chuckle, and more tears began to fall.

Rikki sat next to Elle and put her arms around her. "This is about someone not liking who you are to your core. It's not as if he didn't like it when you colored your hair or your choice in movies. This is about your essence. You can't be someone you're not, and you can't make him be supportive of something he doesn't believe in."

The bell rang, and Rikki stood up and reached her arm out. "Let's go to class, and you can tell me about this amazing room you found." Rikki was happy that she could be there for Elle, but she couldn't wait to see if Quinn was going to be in Ms. Morgan's class.

QUINN WAS RUSHING to leave the newsroom and look for Rikki, but Caden had other plans. Due to the events that had unfolded the day before, Caden needed details that only Quinn could provide. Even after the bell rang to go to third period, they stayed and continued going over the details.

"Okay! Caden, we really need to go," Quinn demanded, starting toward the door.

"What's the hurry?" Caden teased.

"Nothing. I just want to get to class," Quinn said as he continued three steps ahead of Caden.

"Oh, I think this is about Rikki. 'She sounds like a total nightmare,'" Caden mimicked with a chuckle.

Quinn stopped short and spun around, causing Caden to bump into him. "What's your point?"

"Just pointing out the irony because…" Caden paused as if catching that Quinn wasn't having it. "That's what I do," Caden said out the side of his mouth.

"Well, quit it!" Quinn warned, then turned to continue his brisk walk to class.

"Fine," Caden conceded, then snickered again. "'What? And have her sit next to me?'" he asked quietly.

Quinn shook his head. "Caden, fucking stop," he cautioned half-heartedly, suppressing his laughter, but failing.

RIKKI CLOSED her eyes when the bell rang and dropped her head as her heart sank. Quinn seemed to have bailed on taking the class after all. Who could blame him? She had been momentarily batshit crazy, and the teacher certainly hadn't made the situation any better. She shook her head as she tried to understand. *Didn't we both experience something powerful? Did that freak him out? Maybe I freaked him out. Maybe he caught on that I started crushing on him, and I must have gone from enraged lunatic to freaky star-struck fangirl.* Not only was she heartbroken, but she was mortified over how she'd acted since the moment he caught those keys.

She squeezed her eyes shut. Her belly dropped, and she leaned forward, holding herself. She prayed she wouldn't hurl right then and there and embarrass herself yet again.

Lyndsey was surprised not to see Quinn, too, but when she looked over at Rikki and saw how crushed she looked, a little thrill zipped up her spine.

Nervous, Quinn slowed down as he approached the classroom door and gestured for Caden to enter before him. Caden's tall stature blocked Quinn's field of vision, but as he moved aside, he finally got to lay eyes on Rikki again, and his legs weakened. He knew that she was very attractive, but before that, he'd only seen her explosive anger, then puffy, swollen eyes and smeared makeup in the hospital. What he was seeing now was so much more than he'd expected. Her long, brown hair perfectly framed her flawless, fair-skinned face. Her shimmering blue eyes held an innocence that triggered a drive to protect her from the world's injustices.

When they made eye contact, her eyes grew big with surprise. He focused on ensuring each step was squarely planted or his legs would buckle. She sat in front of Caden, which meant he would be sitting next to her, and he couldn't help but smile.

"Mr. Axton and Mr. Brooks, you had us worried there," Lyndsey poked. "Some more than others," she said quietly, glancing in Rikki's direction.

Rikki's body released tension she hadn't realized she'd been holding. Her hand remained covering her mouth because she didn't want him to see how overcome she was with emotion. To go from feeling like she was free-falling to a jarring halt was enough to bring tears to her eyes. Her body shook in nervous laughter. She felt like a fifth-grader. She drew in a big sigh, thankful that she could compose herself before he took his seat.

"Hey," Quinn said in a low voice as he sat, looking forward.

"Hey," she whispered back.

"I had to stay late in the newsroom," he explained. "I'm glad you stayed in this class."

"I'm glad you did too," she said. She looked directly at him, and when he noticed, she gave him a warm smile.

Lyndsey stood up and addressed the class. "Rikki and Quinn, I know there was a lot of drama yesterday, and I want to apologize. It means a lot to me that your parents have been so gracious and understanding," she said. In reality, she thought they were suckers who had been so easily manipulated. "I also want to apologize to the rest of the class as well. My actions, although reckless, were an attempt to prevent any further injury." She walked behind the table at the front of the class— the very one that Rikki had leapt over the day before like an Olympian. "That said, let's get on with it."

"How are you feeling?" Quinn asked out the side of his mouth as Ms. Morgan spoke about South America.

"Better. You?"

"Better. What other classes do you have after this one?"

"I have to look at my—" She stopped when Ms. Morgan quickly turned toward them.

"Quinn and Rikki, I need you to stop talking," Ms. Morgan ordered.

They looked at each other and stopped, disappointed. All they wanted to do was talk to one another, but the remainder of the class proved to be an exercise in patience. It was hard to be that close and not be able to say anything to each other.

<hr>

THE BELL RANG, and students began collecting their things. Lyndsey needed something personal from Rikki to add to her collection. Her best opportunity would be right after class. She walked over to her desk and glanced around to ensure no one was looking as she picked out a couple saturated tea leaves from the bottom of her teacup.

"Rikki, I need you to stay," she insisted.

Rikki's unmistakable look of malcontent and frustration made Lyndsey drunk with power.

"Ms. Morgan, I have to get to my next class. I didn't even get to check in yesterday. I don't want them to think I dropped the class," Rikki pleaded.

Lyndsey looked outside the classroom, then closed and locked the door. "Come here, sweetie. You have a spider in your hair."

"What? Really?" Rikki began reaching for her head.

"Don't touch! I'll get it. It's in the back of your hair. If you don't know where to grab for it, it'll get lost in your amazing, thick, brown locks," she said as she blocked Rikki's access to her hair. "Turn around." She began to pick at her hair. "He's a quick little sucker," she said to justify her picking and pulling at Rikki's hair. "Sorry, you might lose a few hairs," she said as she yanked at her hair again.

"Ow!" Rikki laughed nervously.

"There I got it. It's smooshed, but I got it." She showed Rikki by pretending the tea leaves were the aftermath of Lyndsey's slaughter.

Rikki glanced at the spider guts as she scratched her head where her strands of hair used to be. "Ew! Thanks!"

Rikki quickly left the class, hoping that Quinn would be waiting for her, but he had already left.

"Damn it!" she said under her breath.

———

Lunch came, and Quinn was searching for Rikki. Just as he began walking toward the quad, he was stopped by Mia, who was under deadline and needed his images from earlier in the day.

"I'm kinda in the middle of something, Mia," Quinn said, looking over her shoulder.

"Quinn, I have a deadline, and I really, really need those images now," Mia demanded.

"Fine," he said, glaring at her.

They both turned and walked back in the direction of the newsroom.

———

Rikki headed to the newsroom to see if Quinn was there, but Elle stopped her again. Rikki felt guilty about how she'd treated Elle during first break, so she gave her the undivided attention she deserved.

The following two periods crawled to the finish line. When the bell finally rang, Rikki grabbed her backpack and bolted out the door and out of the building. Zigzagging through the after-school stampeded, she ran past the office, across the quad, around the gym, all the way to her locker, where she always felt the vibrations. Out of breath, she rounded the final corner and immediately halted. At the other end of the corridor stood Quinn. Her breath caught at the sight. He, too, was breathing heavily as he looked at her with wanting. Her backpack fell to her feet. Exhaustion was not going to ruin this moment for her, and she raced toward him. He began walking, closing the distance, then finally, opening his arms as she leapt into them. The momentum caused them to spin as they embraced like they had been separated for what seemed like an eternity.

"I don't understand what this is, Quinn. I don't understand it," Rikki said with desperation in her voice.

"I don't get it either, but I feel it too." He snuggled deeper into her neck.

"I don't want to let go," she begged.

"I don't want you to," he whispered into her hair.

With closed eyes, the two of them stayed in each other's arms as they swayed. After another moment, Quinn set her down. She kept her arms around his neck, lingering in his embrace. They looked into each other's eyes and nervously laughed. Lowering her arms along his solid biceps caused a charge to surge through her.

"Hi," Rikki said shyly and blushed.

The side of Quinn's mouth turned upward, spurring a quiver in her belly. "Hi," Quinn replied, then smiled widely.

"How is it that we've never seen each other, even after all these vibrations started?" Rikki questioned.

"I don't know, but for whatever reason, logical or not, I think we feel each other. I think the charged vibrations are unique to *us*. It's what I used to find you just now because I feel it here all the time."

"Yes! My locker's over there." She pointed behind her.

He leaned in close to her ear. "And mine is the next row up."

A shiver went down her spine, and her legs started shaking. Quinn noticed. "Are you okay?" he asked, with a bit of a chuckle.

She blushed again and nodded. "Uh, do you want to come with me to Java and Book? Elle is nursing a broken heart, and she has something to show me," Rikki asked without the slightest amount of fear that he would turn her down.

"What do you mean a broken heart?"

"Ash broke up with her last night."

"Really? Wow! I wonder if Caden knows. He didn't say anything. I would've thought he'd be acting like the happiest human being on the planet," Quinn said.

Rikki took a step back, her eyebrows raised in surprise. "Wait, Caden's into Elle? I didn't know."

"Really? I think even Elle knows." Quinn sounded confused.

"I get absorbed in my schoolwork, as you can see—to a fault," she said, fearing he would judge her.

"Got it. I'll have to meet you there. I just have to close up the newsroom, and then I'll head over."

He pulled her in by the nape of her neck and kissed her on her forehead, then turned around and left. Rikki stood there for a moment. The feel of his full lips lingered on her forehead and made every nerve come alive. She grabbed the nearest post to support herself and recover before moving on.

IN HER NEWFOUND PARADISE, Elle stood in front of the vintage bookcase that rested against the green textured wall. Each wall in the basement was a different color—green, which she assumed was for Earth, blue for water, red for fire, and white for air. The bookcase had a beautiful beaded runner on top and was home to several framed photos. They were images of past family members and other people she didn't recognize.

The books on the bookshelf were very personal too. There were old books, family heirlooms, and a few photo albums. What struck her most was a collection of casting books. There were four leather-bound vintage journals—a black and gray one contained spells and potions. A red one was an encyclopedia of crystals, herbs, oils, and candles. A blue one was the casters' code of conduct, ethics, practices, and dispensation. Lastly, the green one that listed her family's genealogy also detailed historical practices and traditions. She noticed a space between the third and fourth journals. She looked around the room for a missing journal, and it bothered her that she couldn't find it.

When she went back to the bookcase, she peeked through the gap the missing journal had left and noticed a stack of composition books tucked behind the journals. She pulled them out and shuffled through them. Each book was titled with a person's name and contained handwritten notes, logs, clippings, photos, and drawings.

The top book, which, based on the date, was Mozelle's last, was for a couple. *Robin and Wade* was written on the cover. Elle traced her fingers over their names, and even though she didn't know them personally, a debilitating feeling of sadness came over her. She took the book into her arms and embraced it as tears fell. When she got a handle on her emotions, she gently put the book back without opening it. All she could think was that she wasn't ready.

Elle looked down at her watch and saw she was late to start work. She grabbed the green journal and ran up the stairs.

THE LETTER

Lyndsey left school immediately after the final bell. She grasped her hair at the top of her head as she drove, thinking of her next step. *I so don't want to go to Java and Book, but I don't have a choice. Nowhere else will I find a book on the intensive spell casting required to get Rikki to remember her past life as part of her current life. It can't be like some disjointed image people often experience in past life regression. No, it must carry the bitterness of all the guilt, anger, and sadness, as if Rikki destroyed my life only yesterday.*

She entered Java and Book to find a sparsely patronized café and no one working the counter. She walked past the bistro tables and chairs to get to the book shop part of the café. Walking up and down a few rows, she found a section revolving around the subject matter of self-awareness, past lives, and even amnesia recovery.

She covered her mouth to hide the heartbroken frown that emerged when she came across another book by August called *The Odyssey of the Spirit: An Examination of the Spiritual Lifecycle.* Her fingertips brushed along the spine. *I wonder how many books he's written. He must be doing really well and is probably very happy.* She hated that she still thought about him. She gripped her turtleneck and looked down in shame. *I would call him in a heartbeat if I knew he wouldn't reject me. I've endured that pain once before—I'll never do that again. He's probably married with kids now anyway.* She closed her eyes tight. *Damn it! I wasn't expecting to be confronted with this today.*

When she forced herself to move past August's book, she came upon a book titled *Vibrations of Whispers: The Book of Impossible Spells*, by Dax Robicheaux. Impressed, she took the book with her to the counter where Elle now stood.

"Hi, Ms. Morgan! What can I get for you?" Elle asked, wide-eyed.

Lyndsey took a seat. "I'll have a Black Eye. I think this is going to be a long night," she said, looking out the window. The sun was still high in the sky, and she was just getting started.

"Black Eye it is," Elle said as she began to move around to make the coffee concoction.

"How's the family?" Lyndsey had never asked her that but thought it couldn't hurt to become friendly with Rikki's best friend.

"We're doing well. How 'bout yourself?"

That 'we both know what happened between our families' elephant could take up every inch of that room, but Lyndsey was fine acting as if it wasn't there and figured Elle felt the same way. "Doing better than yesterday," Lyndsey said with a smirk.

Elle placed the drink down in front of her. "This is on the house." She moved down the counter a bit and opened a vintage-looking green book.

Lyndsey's heart raced. Her eyes widened as she stared at the book. It looked so much like Mozelle's violet journal, other than the color, title, and embossed symbol. She could see that the cover material was the same, and so were the textured pages. It even had the same two buckles that secured the contents within.

"Wow! Where did you get that book?" Lyndsey asked as if she didn't know it was a personal journal.

"It was my great-aunt's."

"Oh, really? I never knew. Could you tell me about it?" She took slow breaths to simmer her escalating emotions. *There's more than one? Is it a copy? Or is this part of a volume of journals?*

"It's just a bunch of rambling notes that I believe my crazy great-great-grandmother collected before passing it on to my great-aunt. I'm reading it because it's fascinating to me, all the things she believed and even practiced," Elle lied as she glanced at Ms. Morgan's choice of books.

"And your great-aunt was really into the esoteric arts, too, wasn't she?" Ms. Morgan's asked with a lifted brow.

"I suppose. I'm not sure. As you know, she died before I was even born." Elle stepped back and leaned against the back counter. She could feel her hands begin to sweat at Ms. Morgan's direct questions.

"I'm sorry, I'm just fascinated by it. You know, mythology and folklore … I teach a little class on it, perhaps you've heard of it." Ms. Morgan chuckled nervously. "But really, maybe the class would get a kick out of you bringing it in."

"Um, well, I think this book is sacred, and I should keep it with the other—" She stopped talking as she realized what she had been about to reveal inadvertently. She began to perspire from panic. "You know, the other stuff from when she passed."

"Elle, are there other books like this one?"

Her attempt to lure Elle was transparent, and she wondered how long she would have to endure it. "I'm not sure. Ms. Morgan, why all the questions?"

"Like I said, I've always been drawn to amazing finds like

that one. It's like being an archeologist and finding a sacred, I don't know, hourglass, or whatever."

"That's oddly specific, but I understand. I see that you're looking at a book about impossible spells," Elle said, changing the subject.

"Yes. It's just research. It's always about research," Ms. Morgan said.

"Is there any topic you're looking for? I might be able to make some suggestions."

"Actually, I'm looking into how to help retrieve repressed memories."

"Repressed memories? Like amnesia? Or trauma?" Elle asked.

"Well, more like past life regression."

"And you think you would find the answer in *Impossible Spells*? Ms. Morgan, do you practice, like, witchcraft?" Elle asked, hoping she sounded merely curious rather than freaked out.

"Oh, heavens no! Like I mentioned before, this is about research," Ms. Morgan said and cleared her throat.

Elle suspected she was lying. "Okay. Well, I probably won't be able to help you." *Nor do I want to.*

"No worries."

The bell at the entrance sounded, and Rikki walked in.

Ms. Morgan's expression turned dark as her eyes locked on Rikki. "I'm going to go ahead and purchase this," Ms. Morgan said, holding up the *Impossible Spells* book.

"Sure." Elle didn't understand her sudden change in behavior. "That'll be fifteen dollars."

Ms. Morgan took out her wallet and swiped her card. She turned toward Rikki. "Hello, Rikki! No more spiders in your hair, right?" She laughed as if she was making fun of her.

"Probably not, since I no longer have enough hair for them to nest in," she quipped, rubbing her scalp.

LYNDSEY FLASHED a fake smile and left the café as quickly as possible. Rolling her eyes, she closed the door behind herself. She struggled to be nice to Rikki and just couldn't help being a bit nasty, even when it could sabotage her own plans. She rushed to her car to process the exchange she had just had with Elle. Her hands locked in her hair as she formulated what to do next. She had to get those other journals. They would have the remaining answers to her questions.

"WHAT WAS THAT ABOUT?" Elle asked, bewildered.

"Well, when I was about to leave class today, she told me that I had a spider in my hair," Rikki explained. Elle's expression went from confused to shocked. "So then she starts picking at my hair to get the damn thing, and after the loss of *several* strands of hair, I was saved," she said, disbelief in her voice.

"Really? That's really weird." Had Ms. Morgan needed Rikki's hair for a spell?

"I guess, but then again, she got a spider out of my hair." Rikki sat down at the counter. "Anyway, Quinn's going to meet me here." Her face lit up.

"Okay, okay. Tell me all about it."

"I don't want to go into detail. I mean, you just had a breakup," Rikki pointed out.

"It's okay. I'm over it. I was more hurt over his bailing because of who I am than hurt over the end of the relationship. I'm proud of who I am. Anyway, I want to know what's up with you two."

"I can't explain it," Rikki gushed. "That vibrating, charged feeling I have? Well, he has it too. It's like a magnetic pull we can't avoid. Shit! That sounds so corny." Rikki paused like she was relishing the thought.

"Wow! That's amazing," Elle said sincerely.

"Anyway, you said that you wanted to show me something."

"I want to show you the basement, but we have to be quick because no one else is here to watch the front."

RIKKI FOLLOWED ELLE DOWNSTAIRS. She stepped inside the room and spun around, looking at all it had to offer. "Wow!" Rikki said, her mouth agape. "I can't get over this. It's so welcoming. Amazing!"

"This was my great-aunt's secret room. She was a full-on witch. It's home to all things Mozelle. Her casting books, candles, crystals, journals. Look here, she has family photos, and over there, she has an awesome altar. You know, since I found this place, I've been coming down and lighting candles before work. I've been working on manifesting a strong and healed heart," she explained, holding her hands to her heart.

"Do you think it was the burning of the candles that got you to get over Ash quickly, or maybe the break up matured you in a way that gave you proper insight? Don't get me wrong. I'm not judging you. I was just asking because I never really questioned my beliefs about these kinds of things. It wasn't that I didn't believe, but I've never really questioned it until now. This whole thing with Quinn seems … I don't know … spiritual? I know you don't think that's weird, but now I'm starting to wonder."

"I truly believe the candles got me to the point of clarity faster than if I hadn't used them. I suppose could I have faith in myself that I would have figured it out eventually, but why put myself through all that wasted time and misery?"

"That makes sense. But what I'm also struggling with is if this is 'otherworldly,' why me?" Rikki was fascinated.

"One thing I've learned is not to question it. Enjoy it, Rikki. Live it and learn from it. Focusing on the whys will drive you nuts," Elle cautioned.

"You're right. And this room, Elle. Can you feel it?"

"What? The love? Yes, I do," Elle agreed.

"And Ash had a problem with it? Why?"

"Because he's a closed-minded piece of shit. I'm glad I figured that out before I really started having feelings for him."

Rikki's eyes darted back and forth. "Quinn's here." They looked at each other as they could suddenly hear people moving about overhead, then turned and ran up the stairs.

As soon as Rikki entered the main room, she stopped and scanned the room. Her heart leapt when she spotted Quinn to the left on the first set of cushioned benches, leaning back against the side of a free-standing bookcase. His head was tilted back against it, with one leg up on the cushion and one arm resting on top of it as he gazed out at the bay. The glow of the afternoon sunlight hit his face and chest such that it created a silhouette, accentuating his masculinity. His facial bone structure was a flawless blend of angular and smooth. Sensuality flowed from his perfect full lips. Awestruck, she covered her mouth, remembering how they felt on her forehead. The crescent shadow in the hollow of his neck made her reach for her own as she glided her fingers along her collarbone. He appeared unaware of how the rays of light filtered through the fabric of his loosened shirt, revealing the contours of his unyielding chest.

She looked around the airy room, noticing other girls sitting at nearby tables, giggling while stealing glances at him—girls who could very well measure up to him more so than she could. Her arm fell to her side, and she blinked a couple times to prevent herself from passing out over the emotional rollercoaster she had voluntarily embarked upon.

Her stomach dropped when he turned his head as if looking

for her. Surveying the crowd, his eyes landed on hers. *Even though those girls might be worthy of him, he's looking for me.* Everything in her periphery suddenly faded away. It was just him and her. Breathless, she waved and walked through what felt like a dream.

QUINN GOT up and watched Rikki sinuously walk across the room toward him. He swallowed hard at the sight and sat for other reasons besides feeling weak-kneed.

"Hey!" she greeted as she took a seat across from him. "I'm glad you're here."

"Hey, yourself."

"Finally, we get a chance to talk."

"Yes, finally."

"Why did it take so long for us to finally meet?" Rikki asked.

Before he could answer, Elle came up and placed two small plates of carrot cake and coffee on their table. "Enjoy! It's on the house," she said with a huge smile.

"She's amazing," Rikki said as Elle walked away.

"I like her too. Anyway, for starters, I just moved here the second semester of junior year. My parents are divorced, and I was living with my mom in Wyoming. She was having problems with her latest boyfriend and ended up kicking him to the curb," he explained, leaning in. "Then she tells me she needs to get her life straight and sends me to live with my dad. I was supposed to go back after junior year ended, but to be honest, life here in Sausalito is better than back in Wyoming. It was kinda rough there," he continued with sad eyes. He looked down and began using his fork to slice into his cake. "What about you?"

She paused like she was uncomfortable digging further into his business, and he respected that. *Wyoming is too much too soon.*

"Well," she started, stirring the cream in her coffee, "my life is nothing but one predictable event after another. Not that I want an eventful life, but there's just not a whole lot to share. I'm just boring."

"Coming from nothing, I wouldn't see it that way. Don't you appreciate what you have?" he asked, hoping he wasn't coming off as judgmental.

"I KNOW I come from privilege, but I just live a very safe life. I don't like to take risks because my anxiety would eat me alive," she said and looked at him as if to gauge if he was okay with her admission. "Does that bother you?" She didn't want to scare him away, but she hoped it might earn her some points toward forgiveness over how she'd acted the day before.

"No. I don't have a problem with anxiety. I have a fear of flying. It's why I never came out here to visit my dad, so I get how fears can stop you from enjoying life." There was a pause, and then a huge smile came across his face.

"What?"

"I guess that explains the overreaction yesterday. The anxiety?"

"Yes. That's what I was getting at. I was having the worst day. I was the embodiment of Murphy's Law." She leaned in like she was preparing for an involved story and animatedly detailed all the bad things that had led up to the moment when she snapped: her phone dying during the night, the water shutting off, the printer refusing to connect, the pitcher shattering, the windshield cracking, the back and forth through the deluge, and having choice words with both the Universe and Kendall. She finally finished with, "And then I completely and utterly lost my fucking shit."

Quinn started laughing.

Rikki didn't know what to do with that because even if he

was laughing *at* her, the sound of his laughter exhilarated her. She shook her head and smiled. "I'm glad you find me so entertaining."

Quinn calmed down. "I'm sorry," he said, fighting to keep from breaking up again. "Truly, if it had to happen, I'm glad it was because of you." There was a long pause before Quinn spoke up again. "I didn't mean to laugh at you," he said, then more laughter burst out of him. "Sorry." He gasped for air. "Yes, I did."

She lowered her head and fought the urge to laugh with him, but lost.

"You have a great laugh," he said when he could speak again.

"So do you," she reciprocated with a smile.

The familiar voices of Caden and Blair rang out as they came through the entrance and headed straight for Elle, who was making coffee up at the counter. Rikki and Quinn looked at each other wide-eyed. Rikki shrugged. She didn't need to ask Quinn out loud if Caden knew about Elle. A shrug was all it took to confirm they were thinking the same thing. The two of them watched from what felt like front-row seats at a dramatic high school play.

⁂

CADEN WALKED TOWARD THE COUNTER, a huge smile on his face and a swagger in his step, Blair trailing behind him.

Blair sped up and edged around him, stopping Caden in his tracks. Blair sucked in his upper lip. "Dude, it hasn't even been a day. You might want to put a lid on the mating dance for now," Blair implored.

"Sure, sure, you're right," Caden accepted. "It's just that I don't want to miss the opportunity."

Blair took a step closer to him. "Listen, right now, that door is closed. When the doors of opportunity burst open, you'll know. But forcing the matter will only leave you locked out," Blair said in a low voice while using gestures to demonstrate his cliché.

When they heard hollers from the other room, he stopped talking, and they looked at each other quizzically.

"Yes! Free at last!" Elle yelled as she slammed open the back door.

Blair's eyes shot over to Caden's. Then he stepped aside as if to offer passage. "After you."

Caden walked over to the counter, again with the swagger. "Hey!" he said to Elle.

"Hey!"

"What's all the excitement about? This wouldn't happen to be about Ash, would it?" Caden asked. Caden and courtship had never been the best of friends because his attempts were rarely reciprocated. He turned to look at Blair for direction, only to catch Blair's facepalm.

"No! Why would you say that? I was excited that I just made the last payment to my mom for a credit card bill," she said as she slammed the bill down onto the counter.

"Oh. Well, I'm sorry to hear about you and Ash," he said, hoping to make her feel better.

"Really, Caden? Are you *really* sorry?" she asked, setting her jaw, then crossing her arms and leaning against the back counter.

"No," he admitted.

"Okay, then is there anything I can get for you? Humble pie?"

"No." His shoulders slumped. He was mortified.

"Then I'll see you tomorrow in class. Okay?" she said with a hint of contriteness.

Caden's walk of shame led him out the door and onto the steps.

Blair gave Elle a harsh look and went after Caden. He found him sitting on the steps, staring out into the bay in a daze of self-hatred.

"You don't have to say anything, Blair. I'll get over it. I always do," Caden said, feeling sorry for himself.

"That was harsh what she said, regardless of your intentions," Blair replied.

"Thanks, but you were right. Brief happiness in the wake of heartache? Well, I really should have known better." Caden drew in a deep breath. "I'm going to give up." Caden stood up and turned to Blair. "I'm going to head home. I'll catch you tomorrow." Caden's head hung low as he walked down the stairs, away from the café.

Blair turned back and threw open the door. "What the hell, Elle?"

His attack grabbed Rikki and Quinn's attention.

"I know, I know. I shouldn't have done that, but really? Did he think I would go running into his arms when it's barely been a day? Does he think I'm *that* desperate to be with a guy? I'll talk to him tomorrow," she assured Blair.

"He doesn't think of you that way, and you should talk to him *now*." Blair refused to calm down.

"I get why you're upset, but I know Caden enough to know when he'll listen and when he won't. Okay?"

"Yeah, whatever." Blair left in a huff, slamming the door behind him.

Rikki and Quinn moved toward the front counter as Elle started to cry.

"Are you okay?" Rikki asked.

"It's just been an emotional twenty-four hours, and I just wish I could be left alone, but I can't."

"Why don't you go rest in the backroom?" Rikki said, lifting an eyebrow. Elle would know she meant Mozelle's secret room. "Quinn and I will stay up here and do the best we can for an hour or two. If we need help, we'll let you know."

"Yes, what Rikki said. Go take care of yourself," Quinn added. "I know you well enough to know that what just happened with Caden wasn't you."

Elle gave a tearful smile. "Are you sure?"

"Yes," Quinn and Rikki said simultaneously.

Elle gave them a quick tutorial on running the counter, then hugged both of them and disappeared.

Quinn took a seat at the front of the counter so they could face each other.

"What do you like to do?" Rikki inquired, leaning forward against the counter.

"Well, I like to listen to music, people watch, go to the movies, hang out with friends. It's weird. The longer I stay here, the more I learn things about myself I didn't know. Like, I would have never discovered photography back home. Or that I can enjoy school. Those are not words I would have ever said because, unlike you—" he looked down, "—I'm not a great student. Um, so yeah," he said. There was a pause as if he was censoring himself. "But since I've come to California, I've become a much better student. I think the school newspaper and good friends made a huge difference."

He's feeling shame. Poor guy. Rikki tilted her head. "Quinn, I'm not judging you. I get that people have different experiences. It sounds like you had it rough in Wyoming. So if you *are* that student, you can trust that I'm not judging."

He nodded with a closed-lip smile.

"Anyway, so what about the school newspaper do you like?"

His eyes lit up. "Caden explains it like being part of a team that keeps students, teachers, and even administrators informed, and I like being a part of that. I like that I can give people visual context to a story or even allow the image itself to tell the story. I kinda like that I'm known for that," he said, his mouth turning up on one side. "And I've made really good friends on top of all that. I don't know, maybe I'm not headed toward a big-league school, but I feel like I could be somebody despite that."

"Is that something you want to pursue?"

"I'm not sure yet," he said. His eyes moved about as he considered her question, then landed back on hers. "Your turn."

"I like everything science and technology. I watch a lot of YouTube or TED Talks related to those subjects," she said proudly, before remembering she was not in the company of nerds. "Um, but I like to go to the movies, too, hang out with friends, read, and I love everything about water—swimming, rafting, sailing, or just looking at it. Perhaps I was a fish in my past life." She chuckled. "But it's hard to find time to do those things because I'm a high achiever to a fault, so you're right, I'm good at school. I'm serious about my studies, and I want to do something where I can help people, like a doctor, nurse, something like that," she said. "I'm not all that creative." She bowed her head in disappointment, allowing her thick, brown hair to fall forward. "We're completely different, aren't we?"

He took his hand and lifted her chin, her hair falling forward on one side of her face. "Well, Ms. Science, what is it they say about opposites? We're not as different as you think, nor do I judge, but I am a firm believer that opposites attract," he said, holding her gaze.

"I couldn't agree more," she said, not breaking eye contact, his hand still on her chin.

"You're so damn beautiful!" he said as if compelled. He looked at her lips that were parted under his thumb. His eyes widened, and he quickly withdrew his hand like he'd been caught thinking something he shouldn't have.

She turned away to hide her flush. Relief came in the form of a couple walking in. Rikki stood up tall and walked toward the couple. "What can I get you?" she asked, wiping the perspiration from her forehead.

"A skinny vanilla latte, no foam, and an espresso, please."

Rikki stood there for a minute, calculating what they'd ordered. She turned and looked at the machines and halted.

"Rikki, do you want me to get Elle?" Quinn prompted.

Her head whirled in excitement, hearing him use her name. All she could do was nod her head.

"Rikki?" Quinn repeated.

She turned to the customers. "I'll be right back. I'm going to get someone to make your drinks." She went to the backroom and called out to Elle.

Elle came and took care of the customers, then gestured to Rikki and Quinn that she had it from there. They grabbed their things and walked out.

"I didn't realize how late it got," Quinn observed while they walked down the stairs.

Rikki drew in a deep breath. "This is my favorite time of year. I love the smell of the sea breeze on a summer night," Rikki said, breathing in deeply through her nose. "Come on." She took off across the street toward the bay, never checking to see if Quinn was actually following her. She wrapped her arms around herself as the chill of the bay breeze whizzed by. She crouched down, reached inside her backpack, and took out her long, white cardigan. She smiled when she looked down and saw the perfect throwing stone at her feet and picked it up. As she looked over her shoulder to include Quinn in on her fun, the wind blew her hair across her face. She began to laugh while moving the wild strands blocking her vision.

Quinn was immobilized. It was too much like his dream. "Rikki?" His heart began pounding as she tried to control her hair. He lost his breath as he rushed to her, fearing she would burst into flames. *Why would that happen? I don't believe in that crap, but then again, vibrations when I'm by someone I've never met? What the hell is happening to me? I need just to hold her to calm myself down and prove that there's nothing mystical about any of this.*

She turned back around to get her bearings, winding up to throw the rock.

Shit! This is when it would happen. When she turns away from me. I need to make sure she's okay.

Quinn caught up to her, grabbed her, and spun her around. "Rikki? Rikki! Are you okay?" He had one arm wrapped around the small of her back, and the other stroked her hair away from her face. His fingers found their way deep within her windblown hair.

"Yes, Quinn. What's wrong?" she asked like she was trying to figure out why there was so much fear in his eyes.

He pulled her into him as he held her with desperation. "Thank goodness you're okay!" He was panting.

She hugged him back. "Quinn, I'm okay! What's wrong? You're freaking me out."

He pulled back. He placed his hand along her jawline and looked into her eyes to assess if she was really okay. He saw concern but not hurt. Still breathless, he said, "I just … I just—" He yanked her closer. There was a brief pause. The gravitational pull was stronger than he was, and he couldn't hold back any longer. "Rikki," he whispered as if begging her to relieve him of his yearning. Their lips fused. It was desperate. Unyielding. They encircled each other, deepening the kiss. It was dizzying, hungry, and fierce. It felt hot. It felt powerful. It felt *right*.

The sound of a foghorn from a nearby ship brought them back to earth. They stood there, forehead to forehead. Quinn's hand continued to hold on to the nape of Rikki's neck while his other arm remained encircled around her waist. Rikki caressed Quinn's face. They both giggled.

"My legs are weak," Rikki admitted.

"I've got you," Quinn replied, then shook his head because his statement felt oddly familiar. "I think." He laughed.

They stood there, cradled in each other's arms for a moment. They kissed again. This time, it was a gentle, lingering kiss.

The foghorn blew again, and they both laughed. Rikki intertwined her fingers with his, and they walked over to a bench and sat down. The cool breeze helped calm down their fevers.

"So what happened back there? Why the panic?" Rikki asked.

"I wish I knew," he said, shaking his head. "In the hospital, I had a dream of a woman standing at the edge of a cliff overlooking the ocean. She had long, brown hair like yours and was wearing this white, long, flowy thing. I don't know what you call it. She turned toward me, and at first, she seemed okay, but then her expression changed like she needed my help. When I tried to help her, she burst into flames."

"So when you saw me in my white sweater looking at the bay, it reminded you of that dream."

"It did. Sorry. I didn't mean to scare you."

"It's okay. The water's like a magnet to me, and I took off without even thinking." Rikki leaned her head on Quinn's shoulder. Her heart filled with bliss, being close to him. It was a new exploration into who she was. She had never experienced these emotions toward any guy before, but that had changed when Quinn came along. It was as if something inside her knew her heart belonged to him, and him only. She laughed at her sappy thought.

"What's so funny?"

"I just thought about how I've never been comfortable with

guys before, but with you, I feel safe, and yet, we only really met like, literally, yesterday."

"Yep. It doesn't seem real."

"Did you have a girlfriend back home?" Rikki wasn't sure if she wanted to know the answer.

"Not really. I had a friend, Sienna, who I spent a lot of time with, and I suppose it could have been more, but then I left…"

Rikki sat up and leaned away from him. "Sienna? I'm guessing she's as beautiful as her name?! I so regret asking." She should know better than to ask a question she didn't want to know the answer to. "So the only reason you're not with her now is because of distance?"

"No … No," Quinn said softly, shaking his head. "What I was saying is that when I left, I realized she wasn't good for me. She came and visited once, and I was miserable." He took a deep breath. "I hear you when you say that we've only known each other for a day, but I feel like I've known you longer, and what I feel toward you, Rikki, is like you said—something I've never experienced before."

"Okay," she said as she laid her head back down on his shoulder. "I no longer regret asking."

AFTER A SHORT WHILE, Quinn heard Rikki's breathing slow down. She'd fallen asleep on him. He, too, closed his eyes and leaned into her. He snorted, pondering if she knew that her love for water carried over to how she smelled. Her hair was an infusion of flowers and the crisp and salty smell of the bay breeze. He inhaled through his nose to fill his lungs with her scent. He held his breath like he had taken a hit. Exhaling slowly, he realized no high could ever match the one he was getting just being around her. It was as if he was experiencing something magical.

LYNDSEY SAT in her living room skimming through *Vibrations of Whispers: The Book of Impossible Spells* to find the perfect spell to cast on Rikki and Quinn.

Time and again, the book mentioned the importance of using personal items to cast curses effectively. She quickly went to her temple room and pulled out the letter that she'd found in Quinn's car.

To my best friend Quinn,

I wanted to get your attention, so I went old school and actually wrote you a letter. Pretty lame, huh? Anyway, the last 10 days were awesome. I know that your dad has strict rules and eppects you to be a "good" kid and get good grades and all and he gave you a awesome car, but when we shared that joint like we used to do in wyoming I saw how happy you were and I was glad to see the old you. I really want you to come back, Quinn. your like my rock and I miss you so much. we all miss you. your mom misses you so much. I wish you could tell us the real reason why you want to stay in ca. you are not you there and I think that's sad. If you come back we can continue where we left off. Apton and Bisset, remember? That's how it all started. we sat nept to each other because of the alphabet order of our last names. Don't you want that again? I know you feel the same way I do, but I think you feel shity if you leave your dad. But just remember, your mom feels like shit to. I don't think your ment to be there. I think your ment to be with me. Please come back. I promise you'll be glad you did. I love you! Please come back to wyoming.

Forever, Bisset

Lyndsey quickly went to her apothecary and grabbed the ingredients to make an elixir. She lit black candles and grabbed a goose feather, dipping the end of it into liquid charcoal, and wrote *Sienna and her family* on the back of a contractor's business card that had been left on her—and everyone else's—doorstep. She rolled the feather into the business card and tied the scroll with both Quinn and Rikki's hair strands. She placed the scroll in a pewter bowl, then poured clove oil on top, and finally lit the scroll on fire with the black candle. As it burned, she chanted:

Oh, Mighty Spirits of Opportunity:
Please provide an enticing proposal
To a family with no income disposal.
The family name is Bisset
And in two weeks will arrive by jet.
Quinn and Sienna will reunite
And Rikki will lose that fight.
Grant passage to the golden state
And turn Quinn's love for Rikki to hate.

Lyndsey's confidence in her ability to cast spells had skyrocketed since the success of her enchantment that had prevented any disciplinary action from the pepper spray incident. Her plan to subject Rikki to the same level of darkness and loneliness that Lyndsey had endured had begun. And with that, she blew out the candle, went to bed, and fell asleep with a smile on her face.

11

CHRYMSONVINE

Rikki awoke to drool on her phone. She'd fallen asleep while talking to Quinn the night before. She put the phone to her ear and heard the unmistakable sound of deep slumber on the other side. Quinn's slow breathing threatened to lure her back to sleep, but when she looked at the time, she shot up. School was to start in an hour.

"Hello-ooo!" Rikki said, with sing-song in her voice.

She could hear Quinn stir. She laughed quietly and closed her eyes, completely taken by his cuteness.

"Quinn-nnn!" she continued her song.

"Rikki? What the heck?" He sighed. "You're still on the phone. You're so damn cute," Quinn exhaled.

"Quinn-nnn, it's time to get uuup." That was her encore.

She heard him fall back to sleep.

"Quinn!" Song over.

"What? Shit! Sorry!" Quinn said, clearly startled.

"Pick me up in twenty minutes, okay?"

"Make it twenty-five," he requested.

"Fine."

WHEN LYNDSEY ARRIVED AT SCHOOL, she went to see her friend and fellow teacher, Rusty Croft. They were good friends and often got into conversations about the healing powers of herbs. He would often procure the organic ingredients, and she, in turn, would create medicinal mixtures, salves, and tinctures for him.

The *Book of Impossible Spells* listed an enchantment called Confluence of Selves. It stated that there was a plant that, under the right circumstances, could effectively bring someone to an altered state of consciousness in which one went beyond just recalling their past life, rather merging their past and present lives. Chrymsonvine was that plant. The problem? It was highly toxic. She would have to put on the charm to get Rusty even to agree to procure it for her.

She strolled into what was considered one of the most efficient and lush greenhouses at a high school in California, if not the whole country.

"Hey, Lyndsey! My favorite patron," Rusty said while gathering material for that day's lesson.

"Hey, Rusty!" she greeted with a smile on her face. She laid the charm on thick as she laughed at his dad jokes and showered him with compliments.

"You are too kind," he replied after she told him that he'd created the most peaceful space she'd ever been in.

It *was* very peaceful, but truth be told, the cave with August was the true owner of that title.

He continued to place the items he was collecting into a plastic bin before speaking up again. "Anyway, Lyndsey, what concoction can I help you with?"

"Do you have the ability to bring in a couple of leaves of Chrymsonvine?"

He stopped what he was doing and gripped the lip of the bin.

"Wow, Lyndsey. You're already in hot water over the pepper spray incident. This is not a smart move, my friend. How do you plan on using it? You know, even touching the leaves can be dangerous."

"I know this is more extreme than my usual ask, but I was going to show it to the class," she said, purposely being vague.

"Show the class what?"

Shit. He's going to push it. "Show the class how Brazilians use the leaves in minimal quantities to open their minds and encourage an open line to their gods," she said, looking at him to gauge if he believed her bullshit. Still uncertain, she continued. "When contained and mixed with indigenous herbs, it illuminates this brilliant purple color. And I don't have to explain how kids learn through experience, do I?"

He crossed his arms. "What indigenous herbs?"

"I have to look up the names. They're ones that you've given me in the past. I can't remember the names offhand, but I have them saved at home." Jesus, this was harder than she'd thought. "Rusty," she said, gently grabbing his forearm. She took a deep breath and willed him to trust her. "It's safe. I have always been protective of the kids' safety. I will place the leaves in a glass container and even wear gloves as I demonstrate. Then I was going to add hot water, which, to my understanding, will kill all the toxins, right?"

"Yes. But know that it's hard to get, and it might take a day or two. And I'm only going to get two leaves, so even if a student ingested both leaves, it wouldn't kill them, okay?" he insisted, looking at her for understanding.

"I respect that. Thank you for even considering it." *Damn, I should have enchanted him to be more amenable, rather than just relying on my charm.*

"This is going to be handled differently than normal. I won't just drop it off in your classroom. I would rather avoid handling it if possible. I'll let you know when it gets delivered. Then you can come and get the leaves from the greenhouse. I'm not sure if you're aware, but the greenhouse has a self-locking timer to keep students from coming in and smoking every damn plant I have in here." He handed her the timer schedule.

"I understand, and I really appreciate it." She took the schedule with a smile. "I will forever remember this," she said as she walked away. "And so will Rikki," she whispered for her ears only.

RIKKI AND QUINN walked into school together holding hands, but the time came when they had to go their separate ways.

"I'll see you at first break," Quinn said as their arms were outstretched, their fingertips hanging on to the last joints. Rikki smiled, turned, and severed contact. Before her arm dropped, Quinn took hold of her wrist and spun her around, grabbing behind her head and crushing his mouth onto hers. Students around them gasped. It was the hottest, most romantic thing they'd ever witnessed.

They missed each other at first break again. Rikki even went down to her locker to see if he was there waiting, but he wasn't. When the bell finally rang, she moved quickly to Ms. Morgan's class. Her heart pounded in her chest as she neared the class-room. When she got there, Quinn was already seated. She smiled and walked quickly to her seat. She could tell the whole class was looking at the two of them.

"Hi," Rikki said, sitting down. A flush came over her.

"Hi." Quinn smiled and shook his head. "You're blushing, and you're still so damn hot."

Rikki glanced over at Ms. Morgan, who was looking at her. There was a weird look in her eye. *Bold* was the word that came to mind. Rikki cleared her throat and settled further into her seat. She wasn't sure what that was about. It was as if Ms.

Morgan was trying to communicate something, but Rikki couldn't decipher it.

The bell rang, and Lyndsey began her lecture series on folklore and the occult throughout South America.

As Ms. Morgan discussed the continent's topography, Caden stood at the entrance with a sheepish look on his face. Shame over being an ass to Elle the day before subdued him. When he walked in with his head hanging low, Ms. Morgan paused. He sat at his desk, then twisted around to face Elle. He opened his hand and presented her with a watermelon Jolly Rancher and mouthed the words, "I'm so sorry." He looked in her eyes, holding his breath, hoping his peace offering would be enough for her not to hate him.

Elle smiled as she took the candy and mouthed, "Me too."

Caden sank back in his seat and turned his attention to Ms. Morgan, who had stopped the class on his behalf. "Sorry."

Rikki was oblivious to what was going on with Caden even though he sat right behind her. She was lost in her recollection of that kiss the night before, how soft Quinn's lips were, and the strength of his arms as he'd pulled her in close, cradling her. Goosebumps formed as she allowed her mind to wonder if there would be a time they would take it further. *Will he be the one?* Being so close to Quinn, she yearned to be in his arms again.

"I wish I could touch you," Rikki whispered.

Quinn's eyes shot directly to hers. He searched her eyes as if gauging how serious she was. He swallowed involuntarily and stirred in his seat. He blinked several times like he was trying to redirect his thoughts, but failed. "Jesus, Rikki. What are you trying to do to me?" he whispered back.

"Rikki?" Ms. Morgan called out, pulling the two of them from their collective musings. "Can you stay after class today? I need to speak with you." It didn't sound like she was in trouble, but regardless, Rikki didn't say another word to Quinn for the rest of the class.

The bell rang.

"Rikki, I'll be in the newsroom at lunch. I'll meet you at your locker after school, okay?" Quinn asked.

Rikki nodded and watched him leave the classroom along with everyone else.

"Crazy how things ended up with the two of you. Who would have thought that your assault on him would bring the two of you together? Weird how fate works." Ms. Morgan chuckled.

Rikki scoffed softly.

"I'm just playing. You make the cutest couple. But that's not why I asked you to stay. I know I come across as odd, but I actually like you, Rikki, and I'm sorry if I've offended you. Anyway, I'll be doing a demonstration in a couple days, and I was wondering if you could do me a favor and pick up some leaves I ordered through Mr. Croft. They will be delivered to the greenhouse probably on Monday. They are fragile leaves from a rare plant called Chrymsonvine. I would pick them up, but I have to leave early every day next week, and access to the greenhouse is limited. Would you be able to do that for me?"

"Sure." Rikki didn't understand why Ms. Morgan had nominated her for the task but felt compelled to comply. "Will Mr. Croft know I'm coming to pick up the leaves?"

"Yes," she said to Rikki. "So on Monday at 3:30, head over to the greenhouse. There's only one table in the greenhouse, toward the back. You'll see three items on the table. A jar with the leaves, an empty jar, and a baggie with a vitamin mixture in it."

"Can I write this down?" Rikki asked, twisting her backpack around to take out her notebook and a pen.

"Yes. Of course."

Rikki clicked her pen. "I'm ready."

"Take the empty jar and fill it with water, and then add the vitamin packet. Stir it and pour the solution into the jar with the leaves. It might react, but just wait until it's done reacting, and then close the lid. You'll have to find Kevin the Custodian, to let you back into my classroom, then just put the jar of leaves on my desk," Ms. Morgan explained. "Did you get all that?

Rikki nodded.

"And for that, I'll give you some extra credit points. Deal?"

"Yes. That's great, Ms. Morgan. Monday after school, I'll pick up the leaves as you've explained." Rikki felt good that her teacher trusted her, and the extra credit wasn't so shabby of a reward either.

When the bell rang, just like the day before, Rikki found herself hustling to her locker, hoping to see Quinn. And, like before, Quinn was standing at the end of the corridor. She ran to him, threw her arms around him, allowing her lips to find his, making their reconnection just as powerful as the day before. She melted into his arms as her lips parted, and he held her even tighter as he delved further into the kiss.

He remembered what she'd whispered to him in class, and heat released down his body. He trembled, his fragile control on the verge of snapping. He needed to disentangle. He gave a slight push, like removing his regulator during a deep-sea dive.

Rikki looked confused.

"You have no idea how badly I want you," he said, breathing hard.

The confusion faded from her face. "I might have some idea," she admitted. "Okay. Don't you have to go to the newsroom? Or anywhere? Like now?"

"Um, yeah. Let's go to the newsroom. I'll show you around."

"Let me grab my backpack, and I'll meet you there."

"That'll work."

The two of them turned away from each other and grabbed their chests as they sought to regain normal breathing.

ELLE WAS at Java and Book in her sanctuary. Every time she went in there, she found something new. This time around, she found Mozelle's tarot card deck. Awe-stricken by its beauty and detail, each card was silhouetted with a vibrant background. She then took the deck with her upstairs to learn more.

CADEN CAME IN, this time with a whole bag of Jolly Ranchers, and placed them on the counter. Elle smiled sheepishly as she walked over and slid the bag toward herself. Caden could have sworn she gave the bag a hug as she placed it under the counter.

"You didn't have to do that. The one you gave me in class was thoughtful enough," she said.

"I know, but I just wanted to make sure you were okay."

"I'm okay. To be honest, I'm more hurt that he broke up with me because I was just being me. I didn't betray him. I didn't lie to him. I wasn't a bitch to him. I liked my great-aunt's spirituality and wanted to learn about it. That, apparently, was the deal-breaker."

"So basically, he didn't know you, like, at all," Caden said, hoping to be the pillar of strength in her time of need.

"Yes! Right?"

"And he's narrow-minded," he added.

"I guess I didn't know him either." She stared off across the room like she was pondering her own statement. "Anyway, I think I'll get over it, probably sooner than later."

"Do you want to tell me about your great-aunt's spirituality?" Caden wasn't a firm believer in those kinds of things, but he also knew this was not the time to challenge it. He wanted to demonstrate what an open mind looked like, but he also just wanted to engage with her. He had given up on pursuing her, so at the very least, he could prove to be a good friend.

"Well, she was a person who could regulate conditions by influencing elemental ingredients," Elle said in all seriousness.

"Yeah. I see. Kinda like saying you're a transparency enhancement facilitator when you really mean window-washer? Your great-aunt was a witch. Got it!" He chuckled, then gestured for her to continue.

She gave a sideways smile that quivered ever so slightly. "Yes. She was a witch." She paused as if needing reassurance. "Are you freaked out?"

"If I was freaked out, my face would look like this." He pointed to his face. It was a mixture of surprise and the aftermath of whiffing something putrid. His eyebrows were raised, eyes wide, nostrils flared, and he didn't blink. After a moment, he couldn't hold it in any longer, and he started laughing over how foolish he must have looked. A flutter in his stomach emerged when Elle joined him. "Seriously, everything you're telling me comes as no surprise. Your style, this café, and your interests clearly point toward an affinity for the metaphysical, and I respect it, and even like hearing what you've learned from it."

"Really? Are you a believer?" she asked as if it really meant something to her if he was.

"Um, I don't know what I believe. I can say that I've never witnessed anything otherworldly before, but I'm curious to hear about what experiences you've had. But listen, Elle, regardless of where my beliefs lie, I will never judge you, and I hope you'll never judge me either."

"Fair enough. That's certainly a better response than my, umm, ex-boyfriend's," she considered, then looked to the side as if trying Ash's new title on for size and then realized it fit. "My great-aunt was a witch, but she was definitely the 'great power, great responsibility' kind of practitioner. I found a room downstairs that was like her sanctuary, and that's where I've been spending some of my free time. There's so much in there. I'll take you to see it some time."

"Nice," he said with a slight smile, tilting his head. "You sound like you really admire her."

Elle leaned back against the counter. "I do. She opened this café to allow believers and skeptics alike to gather and have conversations. She was enchanting. They would come to her for all kinds of advice, spiritual and otherwise, and people always left feeling better than when they'd come in." She smiled a sad smile.

"I'm sorry. I never knew."

"What are you sorry about?"

"That you never had a chance to meet her. She died in that huge fire, right?"

"YEAH. Everyone pretty much knows that's how she died. She befriended a woman who ended up with terminal cancer.

Mozelle became her caretaker, and the fire inspector's report said it was a candle in my great-aunt's bedroom that started the fire. But it remains a big mystery why the woman who was dying, her husband, and another caretaker were all in her bedroom when it caught fire. It kinda makes you wonder what they were doing." She crossed her arms. "And did you know that Ms. Morgan is the daughter of that woman and her husband?"

He placed his hand on his temples. "No. Wait, really? Wow! My mind is blown!" Caden said, ejecting his hands from his head.

She moved closer to him, excitement building within her. Caden was such a good listener. "Yep. That's why she wears shirts with high necks to hide a huge scar." Elle pointed to her neck.

"I wonder if she knows what really went down."

"If she does, she hasn't made it public."

"Is it weird with her?"

"It's a little odd at school. But on the rare occasion that she comes in here, it's always with the proverbial elephant in tow. Which, personally, I don't care how big that elephant is. I just don't know if we'll ever get past it."

"That's a lot to take in. Just know, Elle, your friendship means a lot to me," Caden admitted, lowering his head a bit.

"Well, you're easy to talk to."

Caden hung out for a while longer until the café began to swell with patrons. "I should get going. I'll see you tomorrow, Elle."

"Bye, Caden."

Before he left the shop, he watched her for a minute as she attended to customers. He liked her even more after their talk, and it pained him that she didn't feel the same way, but he was willing to take her any way she would have him. A warm feeling came over him, such that he didn't even need his jacket as he walked home.

<hr>

LYNDSEY STARTED COMPOUNDING her material for the elixir that had Rikki's name on it. She ground up lilac, lavender, and orange blossoms, and placed the powder in a ceramic mortar. She lit two black and two violet candles, then took the newspaper clipping of the infamous fire—a photo of her parents, Mozelle, and Wade—and burned them. She then took the ashes and ground them in with the powder while chanting:

Oh, Great Spirits of Soul Preservation:
Anoint this powder and subject of the ashes
To recall their past life after seeing flashes.
This mixture would be a vessel of transcendence
And remove the veil to the one in attendance.
Provide absorption of one life prior,
Galvanizing the events leading to the fire.
Imprint the intensity of that endless love grown
And become the memory of the one alone.
Only one would remember that greatest love,
The other a memory they're relieved to be devoid of.
The one with the memory of the one life prior,
If attempts to explain would be considered a liar.
The one would forever hold a candle unrequited
To the other whose hatred is now ignited.
Mixture will combine with Chrymsonvine and assist
Allowing enchantment to be delivered by mist.

.   .   .

Lyndsey poured the powder into a sachet and placed it into her school tote.

Two candles burned at Lyndsey's kitchen table, illuminating a single dinner plate. She swiped through her music channel to find songs that fit her current mood, but her mixed emotions made the choice difficult. The last twenty years had been about seeking revenge. What had once been her mission, over time, had coalesced with her identity. She stared at the wavering candles, then reached for her scar, the physical manifestation and constant reminder of her embittered crusade.

As much as she wanted to, she didn't have the courage to reach out to August at times like this when she was thrown. He would have given her excellent advice, which would have erased her pain. Of course, any guidance he would give her would be based on all the lies she'd told him. And if he were ever to find out the truth, he would not just reject her—he would hate her. Lovelorn, she placed her elbows on the table, looked down, and grasped her hair. She took a few deep breaths, then looked back up, compartmentalizing her thoughts and passing the rest of her night with a full-bodied glass of Syrah and haunting chamber music.

1 2

THE MOON BEYOND THE FIRE

Quinn and Rikki piled into Quinn's Range Rover and headed to Java and Book.

"So, what did Ms. Morgan want?" Quinn asked, holding the back of his neck while resting his elbow on the windowsill.

"Believe it or not, she needs me to do her a favor Monday after school. She's leaving early and asked me to pick up a plant from Mr. Croft's greenhouse. She's doing a demo or something next week. I guess she trusts me." She shrugged. "Oh, and get this, she'll also give me extra credit."

When he didn't respond, she looked over to see Quinn glancing at his phone. Rikki leaned to the side just enough that she could see his phone. Sienna. Her heart dropped. "Sienna's texting you?" Rikki asked. She could hear accusation in her voice. "How often does she text you?"

"She texts, but I blow her off," he explained with no sense of defensiveness in his voice.

"Uh-huh." Rikki didn't know what to do with that. *Am I going to be* that *girl? What is wrong with me? We just met, but yet it feels like we've known each other for, I don't know, forever? In reality, we've only known each other a few days, so get a hold of yourself.*

Quinn still didn't look at the text when they got to Java and Book. Her relief, however, was short-lived. Her belly churned at the sound of his phone chiming again. Quinn put his phone on silent without looking at who sent the text. She pursed her lips. *No matter how intense we say our feelings toward each other are, going off on him like a batshit crazy, jealous girlfriend will ruin whatever this amazing thing is over something he has every right to have.*

WHEN QUINN and Rikki walked in, Elle was standing behind the counter and off to the side. She held a finger up to hold them off so she could get one last glimpse of the tarot cards she'd spread out before her. She took a deep breath and stepped away.

"Hey, guys. Can I get you anything?"

"I'll have a blueberry muffin and a chai tea," Rikki requested, then stepped aside for Quinn to order.

"I'll have the sa—" Quinn stopped in mid-sentence as his phone started to vibrate. He looked at Rikki as if he needed permission.

"It sounds urgent. You should answer it," Rikki said as if granting unsaid permission.

"Sorry." He grabbed his phone and walked out of Java and Book.

Elle frowned, looking at the hurt on Rikki's face. "What was that about?"

"Quinn has an old friend he left behind in Wyoming, who happens to also be a girl." She raised her eyebrow. "He says that it could have become something more, but when he came here, everything changed, and he knew they weren't meant to be."

"Do you believe him?"

"I don't have a choice. This is all new, and I don't want to be *that* girl," Rikki said, still looking at the door Quinn had just walked out of. "Whatever. It's not in my control."

"Does she always text and call?"

"This is the first time I've seen it, so I don't know." She drew in a big sigh. "What are you doing with those tarot cards?"

"Aren't they beautiful?" Elle lit up and brought a couple cards over. "These were my great-aunt's, so I'm learning how to read them."

"Looks interesting. I'll be your guinea pig when you're ready for your first reading."

"You always impress me, Rikki. For someone who is so scientific, you are so willing to humor me."

"I think it was Einstein who said something along the lines of, the more he studied science, the more he believed in a higher power. I can see where he was coming from. Something greater than us is responsible for all this wonder," Rikki said, waving her hand.

"Make sense," Elle said as she put together their order. She could practically see the anxiety growing within her friend the longer Quinn remained outside. She laid the muffin and tea in front of Rikki, who hadn't stopped looking at the door. "Are you sure you're okay?"

Rikki turned her attention back to Elle. "No. He said that she texts him, but he always blows her off. But now he's exceeded the 'blowing someone off' stage and has entered the 'we have so much to catch up on' stage," she said, fear in her eyes as she looked at the door again. "I hate feeling like this. He has every right to talk to her. Hell, he even has a right to be with her."

"Rikki, you have nothing to worry about."

"You're right," Rikki sighed.

She sat and ate her muffin and drank her tea while Elle explained what she learned about tarot. "Here. The Moon," Elle presented, then paused. "The Moon isn't that great of a card. Let me pick another," she said and started to put it back into the deck.

"No, it's fine. This isn't an actual reading. Tell me what it means," Rikki requested.

"Okay. Right. This is not an official reading, so no big deal. I can lay out all the cards and explain," Elle said and scrambled the cards.

Rikki grabbed her hand. "Elle, what does the card mean?"

"It's a major arcana card. There are twenty-two major arcana cards. If dealt face up," she hesitated. "It could mean that someone is deceiving you."

Rikki pursed her lips again, then took a deep breath. "Okay. It doesn't necessarily mean me. You just drew a card for educational purposes."

"That's right. If it was an official reading, the cards would have been handled differently, rather than just pulling a random card," Elle said, trying to convince herself. "Really, Rikki, I'm just learning about all this. I could be totally off. This is an art, not a science."

Rikki nodded like she wanted to believe her. "What if it's not upright?"

"If the card was reversed—" she said, turning the card upside down, "—it could mean that you have been dealing with deception and that you are learning from it and moving on."

"Okay. Well, I'm definitely looking forward to a real reading." She looked at her watch. "Jesus! Did he forget about me? He is, after all, my ride."

As if on cue, Quinn walked back into Java and Book. He put his phone in his pocket and sat next to Rikki.

She studied his face, trying to get a reading on how the conversation had gone, but got nothing.

"Sorry," he said, dragging his cold cup of tea toward himself. He didn't elaborate.

"No. It's fine. Is everything okay? Do you have to go to Wyoming or something?"

"No. It wasn't like that. She just really needed a friend, and if I didn't talk to her, she would just continue bugging me." He took a sip, then winced. He avoided making eye contact.

"Okay." Rikki looked to Elle as if seeking approval over not freaking out. "I need to get home soon, Quinn. Sorry to rush you." Her disappointment couldn't be masked.

"Oh, sure. I'll just take this to go," he said, lifting the muffin.

The drive back to her place was uncomfortable. She didn't know what to do with her foreign feelings. She wrung her fingers and looked out the window between the sporadic moments of conversation. She closed her eyes with every ring, vibration, and notification on his phone. And every time Quinn tried not to react, it grated even more on her nerves. *This is so embarrassing and anxiety-provoking. I've never crushed on anyone with such intensity, and now what? I've gone headlong into this without any plan to protect my heart.*

He pulled into her driveway. "Am I picking you up tomorrow?"

"Well, if your phone dies in the middle of the night from all the texts and calls, how would you wake up on time? Or, or, perhaps you can have a phone sleepover with her, and she can get you up." Rikki pulled at the handle to perform a dramatic escape, but the door was still locked. "Can you please let me out?" She yanked on the handle again and pushed on the door as if that would make a difference.

"Rikki, look at me." Quinn waited for her to move her head in his direction, then gently put his hand on her cheek. He could see she wasn't going to look at him.

Her chin started to quiver, and tears fell onto his hand.

"Please. I need you to look at me."

She finally turned her head and looked at him.

"I'm sorry, Rikki. I don't want to hurt you," Quinn pleaded. "And it kills me knowing that I'm the reason for your hurt."

"Quinn, you've done nothing wrong. Really. You have nothing to be sorry about," she said as tears continued to stream. "I don't know what I was thinking. We don't really know each other. I got completely taken by this whirlwind thing, or whatever this is, and I—"

QUINN PULLED HER IN CLOSER. "Listen to me! I'm in the exact same place you're in. I'm taken by all this. No, make that—I'm taken by *you*." He intensely searched her eyes for any sign that she believed him. He held his breath, waiting for her to say something. Anything.

She nodded, and as the remainder of her tears fell, he leaned in and brushed his lips against hers. His heart rate quickened when she reciprocated.

Her eyes were still closed when he looked at her. She even smiled—briefly—until she lowered her head. "Quinn, you had another life, and it's wrong of me to assume you didn't. If you have unresolved feelings for her, I won't stand in your way. But I don't want to hang around while you're working those feelings out."

Air shot through his nose. "Rikki, I don't have feelings for her at all. She's not good for me, but there *is* more to the story. Can we meet up tomorrow, and I'll tell you more?"

"I don't know. Tomorrow's Saturday, so I think I have plans with my family. Maybe on Sunday? Or you can just call me?" Rikki said, then added under her breath, "If you have time between calls."

"Damn it, Rikki! I wish you could see how horrible of a

person she is," Quinn urged, resting his elbow on the windowsill.

"Then why do you even talk to her?"

His eyes darted to hers. "Because!" Quinn raised his voice. "I was just as broken as she was!" Quinn hadn't wanted to admit that to Rikki. He shook his head in shame. "I had no idea what existed outside Cheyenne," he continued, looking out the front window. "I hated myself when I was around her." He closed his eyes as he gripped the steering wheel, thinking of all the things he'd done that he was ashamed of and how Rikki would judge him if she knew what those things were.

Rikki reached out to him, and he grabbed her hand, ceasing its approach. "Good night, Rikki," he said, not looking at her. He unlocked the door, and she got out.

He drove off, hating himself just as he used to.

SATURDAY, Rikki and her parents went boating on the yacht they shared with other family members. Rikki had acquired her love of water from her dad, who worked as a marine biologist. She rarely gave up a chance to get out on the water and always looked forward to helping him navigate. Once out on the water, the family would always eat a meal and play cards. But what she looked forward to most was the few minutes she would spend standing along the railing on the top deck. The calming breeze off the water, the sound of seagulls calling, and the radiant sun as it shined on her face, warming her entire body, was an escape she craved to rid herself of all her anxieties. She imagined that she must have been a bird in a past life—oddly, a songbird. She would stare out into the ocean, pretending to soar toward the sun. If it were winter or spring, the bird she imagined herself to be would instead skim the surface for hours, waiting for a glimpse of a humpback whale or even the occasional pod.

She shook her head in frustration. Her bird felt like it had been grounded. Her escape should have spared her thoughts from going places she didn't want them to go, but she had spiraled anyway. She was angry with herself for recklessly opening her heart with no thought or safety measures put in place for the consequences would that inevitably follow.

"What's with the long face?" her dad asked as he joined her at the railing. "Is this about Quinn?"

"Yes," she admitted.

"What's going on?"

"It seems that it might end just as quickly as it started. I don't know what happened. I've never liked a boy the way I like Quinn. There is an unexplainable connection that seems bigger than us, and he says he feels it too."

"So then, what's the problem?"

"There's a girl back in Wyoming. He says it could have been a *thing*, but then he came here and realized they aren't meant to be. But she calls constantly, and he does nothing to limit the calls. Yesterday, he left me to take her call."

"Hmm, that's not good. I'm sorry you're hurting. But it's not fair to dismiss the life he had back home. And if he says he's not interested in her, then you owe it to him to trust him until he does something to betray that trust."

"I hear your words, and I believe what you're telling me, but I'm struggling with … Well, I'm struggling." Her voice was strained as she clenched her fist. "These are feelings I've never felt, and I don't know what to do with them."

"You have to stew. Sorry," he said, tilting his head and frowning. "It sucks, but you'll lose him if you go off on him every time you have an irrational reaction," he warned.

"Thanks. Not exactly what I wanted to hear, but then again, I don't know what I want to hear."

He kissed her on the top of her head. "I'm going to lower the anchor. Wanna help?"

"Actually, I'm going to pass this time and read my book instead," she said, moving toward a lounge chair.

"We're here when you need us," he assured her.

She nodded and opened her book. Within fifteen minutes, the words started waving on the page.

"Damn it," she said to herself. A migraine was on its way.

<hr>

QUINN SAT at the edge of his bed, looking for some kind of distraction to not call Rikki. Her lack of trust in him was frustrating, and he didn't want to be the one to make the first call, but he just couldn't take it anymore. He gripped his phone tighter, and he gnashed his teeth when his call went to voicemail. "Ugh."

He'd never had to deal with such fierce emotions. Back in Wyoming, when things got difficult, he would meet up with Sienna and smoke pot or drink. Things were different under his dad's roof, and he didn't know what to do with himself. He didn't want to feel his feelings. Not sure what else to do, he grabbed his camera to go on a drive. His phone went off while he was putting his equipment in his car. Looking down at his phone, it was Sienna. *What now?*

"Hey!" Sienna sounded very cheery.

"What's up?" Quinn asked, not matching her level of excitement.

"Oh, Quinn, you don't sound so good. I figure you'd be on cloud nine."

"It's nothing."

"I know you, Axton. You sound like you use some bud," she teased.

"You have no idea." Quinn shook his head, regretting his statement.

"It'll happen, sooner than later, Axton."

"I have to go." He disconnected the call and stood there with his hands on his hips. "Shit," he said under his breath as regret was taken over by guilt.

He shoved his phone into the center console and took off.

WHEN RIKKI GOT BACK into port, she saw that Quinn had tried calling her. She returned his call, only to have it go straight to voicemail.

I see you tried calling. Call me, Rikki texted.

As soon as they got home, she went directly to her room and closed her curtains. Her mom came in with Hershey's chocolates and Excedrin Migraine. Her phone rang just as she was falling asleep.

"Hello?" Rikki answered, without looking who called. She assumed it was Quinn and tried sounding alert so he wouldn't feel bad for waking her. Her chest fell, disappointed it was Elle on the other line.

"Rikki! Guess what?" Elle asked in her usual excited tone.

"Umm," Rikki said, unable to hide her disappointment.

"What's wrong?"

"I have a migraine."

"Want me to let you go? I just wanted to tell you I think I'm ready to read your cards."

"Okay. Yeah. Can we talk later?"

"Sure. Feel better!"

She hung up and tossed her phone somewhere on the bed, then fell back to sleep.

Her phone rang again. She opened her eyes to a darkened room. She squeezed her eyes shut, hoping the pain would cease. She felt around for her phone, then fiddled around with it until she no longer had a choice but to open one eye to find where to answer it.

"Hello?" she said weakly after a dead pause.

"Rikki? I've been trying to get ahold of you," Quinn said as if expecting an explanation.

"Quinn?"

"Yes, Rikki, it's me. Did I wake you or something?"

"My head, Quinn. I'm in a lot of pain." Her voice was strained. "I think I'm going to be sick."

"Shit! Okay. I'm coming over."

Rikki had no response. She put the phone down without hanging up.

"Rikki?" Quinn waited for a response. "Rikki!" Quinn waited again. "Damn it!"

Within ten minutes, Quinn's frantic knocking at the front door got her parents' attention.

The door swung open. Mrs. Waters had a look of concern, and he wasn't sure if it was over Rikki's condition or his beating on the door. "Hi, Mrs. Waters. I'm sorry to worry you. Rikki says she's not feeling well. Do you mind if I see her?" Quinn didn't know what to do with his fidgeting, so he shoved his hands into his pockets.

"Sure," Mrs. Waters said. She began walking him to Rikki's room. "She gets migraines from time to time. It usually resolves in a day or two."

"Oh. I didn't know she got them regularly," he said as he looked around the impressive and warm home.

Rikki's room was up the stairs and toward the back.

"Rikki, hun?" Mrs. Waters knocked gently on the door.

Slow-moving, shuffling sounds came through the door. After a moment, the doorknob clicked, inviting them to enter at their own risk. The door opened on its own as if Rikki was too weak to have adequately closed it.

Mrs. Waters opened the door, and Quinn walked in. His heart sank when he saw her lying there with her back toward the door.

"I'm in the next room if you need anything. Okay?" Mrs. Waters said.

Quinn wasn't sure if that was an offer or a warning. "Of course. Thank you, Mrs. Waters."

She nodded and left the door as weakly closed as they'd found it.

He sat down on her bed and put his hand on her shoulder. "Rikki?" Quinn whispered.

Rikki turned her head. Her forehead was scrunched up as she tried to figure out what was going on. "Quinn?" Her voice wavered with weakness. She twisted her body toward him, then sat straight up and wrapped her arms around him. "Oh, Quinn, I'm so glad you're here. I'm so sorry!"

He held her tight. "Shhh, Rikki, it's okay. I'm really worried about you."

"My head really hurts, Quinn."

A sense of familiarity overwhelmed him at her words. "What can I do for you?"

"Pass me my water, please?"

He obliged. "I'm really concerned, Rikki. Your mom said you get a lot of migraines?"

"I do, and it sucks, but I'm okay. Some are worse than others, and this one's horrible," she explained. She laid back down and took a deep breath. "I'm exhausted, and I don't really feel like talking." She rolled onto her side and brought her knees to her chest.

Quinn's breath caught over the sting of her last statement. "Oh, got it. I just wanted to see that you were okay. I'll get going, but I do want to talk to you." Dejected, he stood up.

"No." She paused. "What I mean is, can you just hold me?"

He exhaled in relief. The side of his mouth turned upward.

"You have no idea how amazing that sounds, but Rikki, sick or not, I can't lay down with you. I don't have that kind of self-control." The thought of lying next to her was more than he could take. He imagined how her body would feel against his, how her curves would conform along the sinews of his body. "I probably should get going."

"Just five minutes. I need a break from the pain," she begged.

What's five minutes? He took a deep breath and slipped into bed with her. His mind and nerves began to whirl, but he wanted to alleviate her suffering. As he pulled her close, the smooth contour of her rear and back complemented his firm build like molten steel poured into a cast. She fit better than he'd imagined. When she moved her hair, the smell of the ocean consumed him. Her exposed neck intoxicated him, and the movement of her breathing impassioned him. "You feel and smell so good," he whispered, trying to sound unaffected as if merely making an observation.

<hr>

SHE COULD FEEL his body stiffen as he made the statement. She reacted as well but focused on keeping her breathing steady. She reached out, rubbing his fingers that rested on her hip, inciting a charge that surged between them.

Quinn's arousal could no longer be concealed. He leaned in and brushed his lips along the nape of her neck, sending another shockwave between and through their bodies. "Rikki," he strained. "I can't take this." His voice was full of lust. "I need to get out of here before I reach the point of no return."

<hr>

SHE TOOK A DEEP, ragged breath and turned toward him. "Thank you," she whispered into his neck and gave him a chaste kiss.

He forced himself to extricate from the physical and mental hold she had on him. He was out of breath. "I don't think I lasted two minutes, Rikki. And yet you don't trust my feelings for you?"

"I'm sorry I doubted you." She sat up on her elbows. Her eyes landed on the vacant space that had been their personal heaven. "My head does feel better, though."

Quinn looked around the dim room and spotted a chair on the other side, beyond the foot of her bed. He pulled it up next to Rikki and sat down, leaning his elbows on his knees and clasping his hands. "Even though we've only known each other for a few days, our bodies and minds respond otherwise. I'm tired of trying to figure it out, and I'm just going to enjoy it for what it is." Quinn reached over and gently pushed her hair behind her ear. "But something *is* going to change, and I'm afraid of losing you because of it."

She sat up. "What is it?" Rikki placed her hand on his as if to reassure him that he was safe to continue, no matter how painful his admission was.

"Sienna is moving to California." He bowed his head to avoid witnessing her disappointment.

She dropped her tender hold on his hand and circled her arms around her knees. The audible exhale that escaped her made Quinn's heart pound. Her hand combed through her hair, and her tightened lips and lack of response tore him apart. "Rikki?"

"Give me a minute to collect my thoughts." She drew in a deep breath. "You know, Quinn, I hear what you say about our mutual feelings toward each other, and I do trust that your feelings run deep, just as mine do. But we haven't established ourselves as exclusive, and I'm not sure I want to be with you while you have unresolved feelings."

"I don't *have* unresolved feelings. I thought I knew what it felt like to—" Quinn knew this was a whirlwind kind of romance, but no way was he going to say the *l-word*, even though it fearlessly circulated his brain. "I thought I knew what it felt like to really, like, be into someone, but I couldn't have been more wrong. And even if we haven't established ourselves as exclusive, well, I don't know about you, but I have zero desire to even look at someone else. It seemed to me that our actions speak for themselves," Quinn challenged.

"So what are you going to do about it? Sienna, I mean."

"I can't *not* interact with her," Quinn warned.

"Why not? Because you relate? Because she reminds you of the good old days? Because maybe, just maybe, she'll change the way you did, and then she'll be perfect? Or are you just scared to hurt her feelings?"

"Stop! It's none of that. But I just can't sever ties with her either. I don't know why."

"Why is she moving here?"

"Her dad got a job. They're going to rent one of those houseboats until they get settled in."

"Wow, so it sounds like it's happening quickly. When?

There was a pause. "The week after next," Quinn admitted.

"Does she even know about me?"

Another long pause.

Rikki gasped like razor-sharp knives had hit her in her chest. "Wow, she doesn't even *know* about me."

"Our conversations have been one-sided, and to be honest, as much as she thinks there's potential between us, she's having a hard time with the sudden upheaval." Quinn knew that wasn't a very good excuse. "She's alone. I'm the only one she'll know."

"You couldn't cheer her up by saying 'Me and this girl I'm *really into*—'" Rikki said, using air quotes to mimic his earlier confession, "'—will do what we can to make you feel at home'?"

He shook his head. "You have no idea how hard this is for me."

"You sound like a broken record," Rikki said. "Listen, deal with it the way you need to deal with it. What I need from you is honesty. I'm struggling with feelings of jealousy, and not just because you two might have become a thing, but because you guys share something, a past, that I don't relate to. So what? You probably ditched class and didn't study. Do you think that just because I don't do those things that that behavior is a foreign concept to me?"

"It's more than that."

"Were you fuck buddies?"

"No!" Quinn bit. He breathed heavily through his nose, frustrated that he wasn't getting his point across.

Rikki's shoulders relaxed. "Then what?"

"We smoked weed, and drank, and lied a lot. We stole things and vandalized the school, peoples' homes. We disrespected people and thought it was funny. And I mean, we did that *a lot.*"

"Well, good for you. Good for both of you. Sorry, but you win. I can't even imagine making friends with someone like that," she admitted.

"So, what does that mean?"

"What I'm saying is that I can't tell you who you can or can't be friends with, but I need you to be patient with me. I'm going to be annoying and all up in your business so I can build trust. Do you get that?"

"Whatever it takes." Quinn stood up and walked around the bed again.

"What are you doing?"

"Giving it one more try," he said.

And even in the moonlit room, she could see his captivating smile, the one that made her melt every time.

"I won't go under the sheets this time," he explained. He moved onto the bed and laid on his back so she could drape her body along his. "What does a broken record even sound like?" he pondered.

"You know, I don't know." They both started giggling, and when they stopped, they looked into each other's eyes and exchanged a few quick kisses. The last kiss lingered, and she moved her leg up the length of his thigh.

Quinn grunted in defeat. "Jesus! How much time was that?" he asked, lifting himself off the bed.

"Thirty seconds," she laughed.

"Okay," he said, adjusting himself. "I'm going to need to go. That point of no return is much closer than I thought."

"You're so hot!" she asserted, still laying on her side. Her hair had fallen over her face.

"That's not helping." He leaned over and kissed her on the forehead. "I'll call you later."

LATER THAT NIGHT, her lingering migraine set off a dream in which she was caught in a rainstorm, lost in a forest. It was nighttime, and she could hear cars passing by but couldn't figure out what direction the sounds were coming from. She started to panic and began running. Her white dress clung to her body as she aimlessly searched. A flicker of light shone in the distance, and relief came over her. The trees began to thin out, and before too long, she was running through the brush. Headlights of a single car came into view, and she ran toward it. She felt saved. She tried to raise her arms to get the person's attention, but she was too wet and too cold.

The lights turned away from her, and she wailed as it began to drive away. She didn't stop; she was determined. Finally seeing a way out, she saw that the car had come to a halt and a man came out. He was backlit, and she couldn't make out if she knew him. He stretched out his arms as if to draw her into his body, but then he turned his palms outward. His wrists were bound with a braided rope, and a star was branded on one of his palms. When she looked back at his face, she was shocked to see it was Quinn. His mouth was agape as if to warn her. Suddenly, the braided rope caught on fire and engulfed Quinn in flames.

She gasped as she sprung up in bed, her heart pounding. She placed her hand over her birthmark and calmed down. It was just a dream. She recalled Quinn's dream while they were in the hospital and thought it strange that they were so similar but dismissed it as the power of suggestion.

13

THE MERGER

Monday arrived, and Lyndsey had barely slept. The thing that had been the bane of her existence over the last fifteen years was finally coming to fruition, and she didn't know what to do with herself.

When she arrived at school, she headed straight to the greenhouse, which was located toward the back of the school. It shared a corridor with a single classroom dedicated to horticulture classes. The eighty-foot-deep by thirty-five-foot-wide greenhouse had only one entrance and exit and was lined with plexiglass windows that, when lifted, meant that the greenhouse was open for visitors.

The greenhouse was filled with a mix of plants indigenous to the region, as well exotic plants. A central path made of decomposed granite extended the length of the structure. Several yards down, two narrower paths branched off and lined the sides of the greenhouse to allow easier access to the plants that grew along the perimeter. Further down the aisle, a region had been cut out to create an oasis. One side had a long park bench between two large planters containing conifers and that season's annuals, and the other side was its mirror image. A wide table stood slightly further back so that students could listen while sitting on either of the two park benches or the four planters during demonstrations.

Lyndsey found Mr. Croft sitting at his desk in the adjoining classroom. "Hey, Rusty," she greeted. "Did the leaves come in yet?"

"Hey Lyndsey," he said, getting up from his chair. He circled around and leaned against his desk. "I ran into a minor problem. The leaves are supposed to be here by lunchtime, but I have to leave as soon as it comes in, so I would prefer if you pick them up in the morning."

That completely screws up my plan. "Um, that doesn't work for me. Can I just pick them up even if you're not here?"

"Um, well…" He was hesitant.

She purposely remained quiet to see if he would cave.

"Well, I guess it should be okay. I'll just leave them in the cupboard behind my desk," he surrendered.

"Thank you, Rusty, for being so flexible," she said enthusiastically, laying her appreciation on thick.

"It's fine. I'll leave the keys and include another copy of the lock schedule in your cubby. It'll also include emergency unlock codes," he explained. "I'm still not totally comfortable with this. If the leaves are still here by the time the first bell rings tomorrow, I'll have to destroy them," he warned.

"I have it handled, Rusty, I promise."

As soon as school let out, she rushed back to Rusty's classroom. She positioned the jars and the "vitamin" pack just as she'd explained to Rikki. And when she was done, she took a step back and crossed her arms. She nodded her head as pride brought tears to her eyes and a smile to her face. There was no turning back.

By lunch, Rikki's migraine hadn't subsided. She went to school to turn in some work, but she felt compelled to stay long enough to pick up the leaves instead of going home.

"Rikki, just have Caden do it. He always stays late after school. You really need to go home and get some rest," Quinn directed.

Rikki nodded and took out her phone. "You're right."

"Great. I'll go get the car."

Rikki slid on her sunglasses and watched Quinn leave for the parking lot. She held her hand to her forehead, praying that Caden would pick up.

"Yo," Caden answered cheerfully.

"Oh, hey. I'm so glad you answered," she said, her voice becoming raspy.

"I'm so glad you called," he said, mirroring her. "What's up?"

"I need you to do me a favor. I have a bad migraine, so I'm leaving early. Ms. Morgan wanted me to get something from the greenhouse, but can you pick it up for me instead?"

"Sure."

"You're the best."

"Well." He chuckled.

"Okay, so there's a jar with some leaves in it on the table in there. You have to add the mixture to the leaves, then bring the jar to Ms. Morgan's room. If her room is locked, then get Kevin the Custodian to open it for you." Rikki's voice cracked. She swallowed to get her voice back.

"Okay. Yeah, just text me the instructions."

"Thanks so much, and, umm…" she said, trying to think if there was anything else. "Oh, and, it has to be done by 3:30. The lock is on a timer."

"Got it. 3:30, greenhouse, treat leaves, bring to Ms. Morgan's class. No problemo," Caden said.

"Thanks."

She hung up and texted him the instructions. *1. Pour vitamin pack into the jar with water but no leaves. 2. Add the mixture to the jar with the leaves. 3. Wait for the reaction to subside. 4. Bring to Ms. Morgan's class and leave it on her desk.*

AT DISMISSAL, Elle pulled out her books from her locker and squatted down to stuff them into her backpack.

"How are you doing, Elle?" Ash asked from behind her, causing her to jump.

She rubbed under her neck to calm herself. "Geez, Ash. You scared me. I'm fine," Elle said as she picked up her book-shoving pace, essentially stuffing her whole locker, including her phone, into her pack, bypassing the what-stays-and-what-goes portion of her exit, all to shorten the length and awkwardness of this encounter.

He squatted down to face her. "I miss you."

Elle's eyes widened in surprise, but she remained silent.

"Okay." He cleared his throat and huffed through his nose. "Don't you miss me too?"

"I don't," she bit and stood up. "You really hurt me."

"I know, and I'm sorry. I just thought that maybe you'd come to your senses."

"Come to my senses? What the hell does that mean?"

"You know, figured out that all that voodoo, hippy crap is a farce."

"What gave you the impression that I felt that way?"

"Come on, Elle. I know you're smarter than that. I feel like this is some kind of protest because of how I acted. I get it now. You win. I want you back," he professed, tilting his head and placing his hand on his chest.

Her jaw dropped. His attempt to be charming was way too transparent, leaving her simultaneously insulted and creeped out. "You couldn't be more wrong," she countered.

"So that's it? You know, you're a hypocrite. You're being just as close-minded. That's not very peace lovin' of you, now is it?" he baited.

"We're done." She threw her backpack over her shoulder and began to walk away.

He stood there with his hands on his hips. "You're a damn freak, Elle!" he yelled for everyone to hear. "Why are you running away when you have a broom?"

Angered, she flipped him off and quickly walked away.

"Oh no! Are you running away to put a hex on me? Stick pins in a creepy voodoo doll of me?" he mocked. His booming laughter echoed in her ears as she rounded the corner.

<hr>

CADEN DROPPED his backpack before the greenhouse entrance, then stepped inside. His mouth dropped, awestruck at the sight of light rays piercing through the ceiling and the windows, the plants standing tall in their glory. He breathed in through his nose and withheld deep in his lungs the serenity that enveloped him. He closed his eyes until he couldn't hold his breath any longer. He shook his head. *Focus on the mission.*

He walked to the back and found the table with everything on it. He opened the baggie labeled "vitamin pack" and poured it into the jar of water. The water turned purple as it began to fizz, and Caden couldn't help but laugh like a mad scientist as he stirred. Chuckling at his joke, he poured the mixture into the jar with the leaves.

The reaction was immediate and relentless, much more significant than he'd expected. Plumes of vapor swirled up, building upon itself until it poured over the boundaries of the jar. Paralyzed, the fumes penetrated his space. He grabbed his chest as his airways constricted. Thrown into an immediate asthma attack, each wheezy breath became more demanding than the previous. He was starting to suffocate. Falling onto all fours, sweating, his heart pounded. Gasping, he made one attempt to call out for help. The distance to the inhaler that remained in his backpack outside the greenhouse was insurmountable. A haze filtered in and seized his vision. His hands clawed against the gravelly floor. The exertion halted him, and he fell forward. Turning onto his back, a black fog emerged along his periphery, swallowing everything it encircled until even the bright blue sky succumbed to its darkness.

IN HER ESCAPE from Ash's assault, Elle found herself heading toward the greenhouse. The word *home* came to mind when the greenhouse came into view, but she quickly noticed that the windows didn't have their usual clarity. Curiously, she peeked through the window. Expecting to see something intriguing, she gasped in horror—Caden lying unconscious on the floor. She bolted to the entrance and threw open the door. Overcome by the dense and fragrant mist, she coughed a couple times but quickly regained stability and soldiered on.

"Oh, no!" She threw off her backpack and knelt beside him. Panic-stricken, she began shaking him. "Caden! Can you hear me?" Elle yelled.

"Inhaler ..." Caden wheezed.

She looked around. "Where? Where's your inhaler?"

Caden gave no response.

"Caden!" she screamed.

His eyes cracked open, and he pointed to the door.

She raced to the entrance. The few coughs that escaped her were not going to slow her down.

A warning in the form of loud beeps, initiating the closing of the windows, was accompanied by the grinding sound of the entry lock sliding into position.

"No, no, no!" she yelled, reaching for the door. She slammed against the release bar of the door with all her weight. Nothing. It was too late. The windows closed with a thud, and the latching of the locks reverberated throughout the greenhouse. "No! Please!" She was hyperventilating and crying as she banged on the window. "*Help!*" she yelled, then started pushing with all her might to force the door open. Behind her, Caden began coughing and gasping.

She stopped and ran back to him. "Caden, you're going to be okay," she promised and dug inside her overstuffed backpack as frantically as she'd packed it in search of her phone. Feeling around for it, she felt it at the bottom of the pack, but it didn't have a sleek feel she was used to. Pulling it out, she squeezed her eyes shut in frustration. Her books must have broken her phone when she'd slammed her backpack down. The screen was cracked and non-functional. "Shit!"

She lifted and cradled Caden's head on her lap.

He searched her eyes for an explanation.

Tears streamed down her face. "We're locked in, Caden," she sobbed.

He reached for her face to wipe away her tears as his own eyes began to water. He nodded. "You can help me …."

"How?"

He began to tear at his shirt.

"Okay. I'll help you with that." She helped him sit up against a planter. Straining to move caused more coughs to escape his constricting lungs. She began unbuttoning his gray shirt and pulled him into her chest as she pulled each sleeve down. When he was free from his restrictive shirt, she gently laid him back against the planter. Her eyes widened, and her hand flew to her mouth, shocked over what was revealed to her.

CADEN MOANED and winced at her horrified expression, and with all the strength he could muster, raised his hand to cover his birthmark. He raised his other arm as if to protect her from being subjected to any more of his grotesqueness. His mother was right. His head slumped to the side in shame, and tears slipped down his cheeks.

TAKING advantage of his weakened state, she moved past his raised hand. His face was pained as she peeled off the hand that covered the mark. It didn't just resemble hers—it mirrored hers, branch by branch. She kept his hand away as she studied it, but then his cough and gasp for air redirected her.

She turned his head to face her and looked into his defeated eyes. "Caden, stop. Use your energy to focus on slow breaths. I can see your color starting to come back."

Caden nodded and tried to turn his head back, but she held his chin, forcing him to look into her eyes.

"I know what you think, and you're wrong. Look!" She began to loosen her blouse. She saw Caden's eyebrows lift. She yanked her sleeve down, revealing her own branched birthmark that was tattooed over.

His eyes grew wide as he stared at her mark in disbelief, prompting his breath to quicken again.

"Shhhh, Caden. It's okay." She searched his tear-filled eyes for understanding. "You see? It's the same thing." His eyes eased, and they smiled at each other.

"I'm going to get us out of here." She stood up, and her vision became wonky. She took a step back to steady herself.

"No use," Caden said, weak, but able to get a few more words out. "Lock is timed." He coughed.

"Caden, tell me what happened," she requested before she splayed her arms to maintain balance. "Woah."

COMPELLED TO HELP HER, he hoisted himself up. "Elle?" His vision started to waver. He lifted his hand to his head as his mind became foggy.

"WHAT'S HAPPENING, CADEN?" Elle's rollercoaster ride was not over, and panic was advancing to a new precipice. She turned to him and saw a face she didn't recognize. It was a man's face, and it began talking to her.

"Mozelle, what's happening?" he asked.

"Who are you? How do you know my full name?" She looked around and saw the greenhouse windows dissipate, the plants morphing into a garden that spread out to become a vista over the bay. A windy walking path invited her to leave, but she didn't take another step. "Caden?"

The greenhouse slowly dissolved back into view, and so did Caden. He was standing with a wild look in his eyes. He was breathing deep breaths in rapid succession as if he'd never had an asthma attack.

Elle reached out to him. "Caden, why are you looking at me like that? How did your asthma go away?"

"Mozelle," he said again, his eyes burning into hers. "What happened? Why did you do that to me?" He stepped closer to her, gripping her shoulders so quickly that she didn't know what was happening. He began to shake her. "What gives you the right to interfere? I trusted you, and you helped Robin betray me?"

"Caden! Stop!" Elle screamed as she pulled at his arms.

His jaw relaxed as confusion filled his eyes. His hand shot up to his mouth. "Holy shit! What am I doing? Elle! I'm so sorry! I'm so sorry! Damn it! Did I hurt you?" he asked, gently placing his hands on her arms again. Elle knew he could see the fear in her eyes. He dropped his arms and turned away from her. Then sat on the bench, pulling his head down between his legs in shame.

Elle took a seat on the bench, putting her arms around him. She lowered her head so she could speak softly to him. "I'm okay, but Caden, I think we're hallucinating."

His body relaxed at the sound of her voice, but he turned his head away. "You're right, and we're stuck in here all night with it," Caden said, shaking his head.

"With what?" she asked, and when he turned back to her to answer, she saw Caden's face and that other man's face at the same time. She shifted away from him, shaking her head to make the other face go away.

He pointed to the jar with the leaves. "I think that's making us see things."

Elle got up to look at the jar. Vapor was still leaking out the top. Her head tilted as she studied the leaves. Something struck her as familiar. Her eyes darted back and forth as she recalled learning about the leaves back when she took Mr. Croft's horticulture class in junior year. The leaves were from a family of toxic, hallucinogenic plants.

"The leaves are poisonous," she warned and took a step back. "Caden, why were you messing with these leaves?"

"Ms. Morgan," he said.

"Wait. Why Ms. Morgan?" She put her hands up to stop Caden from answering. "Forget that. You can explain later. In the meantime, we can't touch them, so let's move the table and get it away from us." Elle stared at the table as it began to transform into an altar she didn't recognize. "Woah! You didn't tell me it was an altar. Do you see that? It's a twinned crystal."

"It's hot in here," Caden said, ignoring her request to look at the altar.

Alarmed by the rasp in Caden's voice, Elle looked over at

him. He stood up from the bench, still shirtless, and put his hands on his hips as he tried to catch his breath. His skin glistened with sweat as his chest heaved. She felt compelled to look away, but couldn't. She had never seen him that way, and she felt her heart pounding at the sight of his tall and muscular build. She forced herself to look at something else as she fanned herself with her hand to cool the heat emerging from within. She cleared her throat, hoping to reel herself back in. "Okay," she said, gripping the end of the table. "Come help me move it." She watched him closely as he walked up and handled the table. Breathless, she was forced to open her mouth at the sight of his impressive form. His birthmark cascaded over his shoulder, and with every movement he made, it moved fluidly with him. And like a light switch, something within her awakened.

SHE STOPPED UNEXPECTEDLY, and he looked up at her. He was awestruck. So consumed with his own crisis, he hadn't realized Elle had stripped down to a camisole. She leaned over to get his attention, exposing the lacy straps and outline of her bra. He lost his grip, causing his side to slip. The jar fell off and broke, filling the space with more fumes. He stood there, his mouth agape.

"Caden!" Elle grabbed his hand and ran back toward the bench.

His wheezing returned as she sat him down. "We'll get through this. Just hang in there," she urged as she sat beside him, slipping her arm under his head and resting her hand on his shoulder. His skin was as warm and smooth as river rock on a hot day. She closed her eyes to allow the feel of skin on skin to calm her nerves, but it only aroused her more. She needed to pull her head out of that space to tend to him. "Shhhh," Elle soothed. She could hear a tremble in her voice and prayed he wouldn't catch on to her uneasiness.

Caden rubbed his chest. "I'm not having a complete attack," he wheezed and took a couple more breaths before speaking again. "But I'll be wheezing for the rest of the night."

"You don't have to talk. Just relax," she whispered. She turned her head to assess the damage of the broken glass, but what she saw was scattered crystals glimmering in the late afternoon sunlight. *Those must have fallen off that beautiful altar,* she thought, then turned her attention back to Caden.

For a few minutes, they remained quiet until Caden stirred, rubbing his eyes. "Shit! I'm seeing the inside of some house."

Elle shot up. "I need to go back to that altar."

"What altar?"

As she headed back to where the broken jar was, Caden immediately stood to his feet, grabbed her by the arm, and turned her around. "There's no altar there. It's a hallucination." They suddenly became aware that they were standing face to face. Caden had an excuse for his rapid breathing, but he didn't know hers. She stood close to him, provoking a reflexive swallow. They looked at each other for a moment, his hand still holding on to Elle's arm. He turned her arm enough for him to study her birthmark. The artwork was exquisite. He swore the leaves of her tattoo began to sway in a breeze that wasn't there.

While he studied her birthmark, Elle did the same of his. The exact same branching. It was remarkable.

As if compelled to do so, they simultaneously touched each other's birthmarks, not knowing their lives were about to change forever.

An electrical charge shot through them, and suddenly Caden was looking through the eyes of a man as he entered his own house. *This is not just some man. This is me. Is this my future? Am I married with a child?* A sense of urgency to get through the house came over him. He stopped and looked at the pictures on the wall. There were photos from his wedding, the birth of his daughter, and even his parents. At that moment, that it struck him. This was not his future—this was his *past*. His past from another lifetime. This wasn't an impression of who he might have been in his past life. Rather, this was a memory.

He saw his daughter standing near the kitchen. "Daddy, I'm scared," his daughter cried.

He stood there, paralyzed, as flashes of his past life merged with his current as if on fast forward. Robin as a radiant bride, the proud look on his parents' faces, the birth of their daughter, Lyndsey.

I had a good life, he thought, feeling good about his past, until the flashes took on a darker tone. The long hours he put in at the office as if he didn't want to go home. *Why would I want to go home? Robin and my parents all wanted what they wanted and never once considered my feelings or what I had to say. I had no control over my life outside of the office.* Images of him pouring himself a drink after drink, smoking, escaping. *Who could blame me? She escaped, too, with all that time spent with Mozelle at the house or at Java and Book.* Memories of yelling insults and criticisms at each other, being at the bar rather than at home when she wanted him there, continued to flood his mind. *If I needed to escape because of how poorly I was being treated, why do these memories carry so much guilt?*

It was the memory of rushing to the hospital after Robin and Lyndsey got into an accident that sent feelings of resentment, fear, and even rage rattling through him. *Seeing* Wade *sitting next to her after the accident was just the beginning. What was my father thinking in hiring* him *as her caretaker? He was there at every turn, from the moment she was diagnosed. And even after I expressed that I didn't want* him *there, she came up with every excuse to keep* him *around. As much as she denied it, I know she was falling for him.*

Recalling holding Robin as she vomited outside their house

and then collapsed in his arms stopped his internal spiral. *I wasn't the best husband. I was the one who belittled her and pushed her away. I can see that. But running into the arms of another man, only to then have our so-called friend, Mozelle, perform some kind of lover's ritual? That was going too far.*

<hr>

ELLE WAS LOOKING through the eyes of a woman sitting at a table, reading a journal in her sanctuary. *I'm looking through the eyes of my great-aunt while she was in her temple room. Why?* As if on cue, her great-aunt got up and looked at herself in the mirror. *Because she is me. I'm the reincarnation of my great-aunt, Mozelle. I can't believe it.*

Elle was inundated with flashes from her past life. She remembered living a life of purpose and sharing her gift of intuition with the community. Tears sprung from her eyes when memories of Robin entered her mind. *She was my best friend, and I miss her. I would've done anything for her, and when she was diagnosed with cancer, I did everything I could to help her. I even set it up so that she and her soulmate, Wade, could find each other in their next life. But it was not without its casualties.* Images of Chris came to mind. He'd tried to help but had failed.

"What the fuck?" Those words coming from a male voice was the last thing she heard in her previous life, and she was momentarily transported back into the room the night she performed the ritual. Caden stood right next to her, and together, they watched everything as if they were in a virtual reality game.

"You ... you betrayed me," Caden accused.

"I'm so sorry. I didn't want to hurt you. I was completely torn, but really, take a look at them, Chris. What do you see?" Elle said.

CADEN FOUND himself standing at the threshold to a candlelit bedroom, looking at *Wade* sitting next to his wife as she lay on Mozelle's bed. "That's what I walked in on, isn't it?"

"Yes. It is," she admitted and slipped her hand into his. "Caden, you're safe with me. Let go of your anger and jealousy."

Hearing Elle's soft voice was a calming light in the dark space he found himself in. Caden closed his eyes. His breathing returned to normal, and when he opened his eyes, the vision vividly came to life. He saw how Wade had cradled Robin with such tenderness and longing. Robin looked at Wade in a way she'd never looked at him. Caden found he could let go of his anger and jealousy. He was able to look at them objectively as if he was watching the Hollywood ending of a sappy love story. He wasn't quite ready to call in a marching band over it, but when he looked inward, a state of peace washed over him.

"I see it now," Caden said. "And what? They're spiritually bonded for eternity or something?"

"Something like that. It was Robin's dying wish to be able to find Wade in her next life," she explained. "I feel awful, but know that she remained committed to your marriage."

"She loved someone else, whether she acted on it or not. It doesn't matter if it was an emotional affair or a physical affair. Her heart belonged to someone else. I mean, she married the guy, and legal or not, for damn sake, that doesn't ring commitment to me."

"Yes, you're right, but she did make an effort to fix it, and then she got sick. If she hadn't gotten sick, and if nothing had improved, she would have ended the marriage. She *did* want to make it work, even after knowing that Wade was her soulmate. That's why she was willing to wait until their next life."

Caden shook his head. "I'm such an asshole. Looking at them, I realize my resentment and anger toward Robin and my parents was misdirected. But it was all me. I'm the only one to blame here. I worked too much, and I drank to avoid facing the truth that I was weak and a failure of a man." He stood there for a moment, then dragged his hands down his face.

"Well, I'm not going to minimize your behavior, and this opens up a whole conversation on personal journeys, but it's not all on you, Chris. This was bigger than you or me. That ritual solidified their reunion as a mated pair in their next life, but they would probably have ended up together anyway. Their connection is *that* fierce. I didn't mean for this to happen, and we all judged you, then eventually just ignored you. But we're here now. We've been given this amazing opportunity to look back at our mistakes and evolve."

"Mozelle, you've always been my lifesaver, and hearing you say those things? Validating my existence? I don't know how to put it into words, but thank you again for being my lifesaver."

They looked into each other's eyes, and both sighed, then laughed as the weight of guilt, shame, and resentment dissolved, giving way to a newfound friendship.

"So what did the ritual entail?"

"It was a spiritual wedding of sorts. I made it easier for them to find each other by doing a handfasting ceremony and ... something else with the wand," she began. Her eyebrows were knitted as if she was trying to remember what else she was doing. "It's weird, but there are holes to my memory I can't quite remember. I was pointing the wand at them..."

Caden's eyes darted to Elle's. "Mozelle?"

"But the ritual wasn't completed ... You came rushing through the door..."

In an instant, Caden and Elle let go of their birthmarks and leapt away from each other. The room shifted back to a green-house, and Chris and Mozelle took their rightful place within Caden and Elle's consciousness. Caden's wheezing started up again, and he began pacing while Elle sat on the bench and pulled her knees to her chest.

"I know what that was," Caden spoke first. "Our birthmarks are the result of me coming in and getting struck in the shoulder by that wand thingy of yours," Caden said, then stopped and looked at her. "Which I'm not angry about," he clarified with his hands up. He swept his hand through his hair. "Jesus! Elle, what *was* that? Was that actually *us*? In a past life? How the hell? How long were we hallucinating? I mean, look! The moon is up and clear across the sky. I can't wrap my head around this."

"Caden, um, yeah. That's exactly what that was. That plant made us remember our past lives." She paused as she thought for a moment, then stood up. "No, it's more than that," Elle said, matching the panic in Caden's voice. "It's like our past and present lives have been fused." As the words came out of her mouth, it connected. "I just figured something out," she began. "Ms. Morgan is behind this."

"She's the one who obtained the leaves, but do you think she knew this would happen?"

"That's exactly what I'm saying. She came into Java and Book and asked me specifically if there was a book that would, in her words, fuse someone's past life with their current life."

"Elle, I don't know where to start with all this," Caden said, putting his hands on his hips and shaking his head. "There's so much to process. I need to break this down. I'm still freaking out. I remember a lot, like my feelings and mindset then, but I don't remember intricate details. I know that I was an attorney, but could I pass the bar? Probably not. Maybe that's why I'm not devastated. I remember *myself*, but it's like I'm watching an old family video. There's a disconnect, kind of like when you meet your parents' old acquaintances from years ago, and they remember some mischievous thing you did as a kid. Maybe you remember, maybe you don't, and it's believable because it's within your character, but, like, you don't have deep feelings about it." Caden's hands were moving as fast as he spoke. His wheezing matched his excitement. "I don't feel like suddenly I'm Chris waking up in some kid's body. I feel like Caden, only now enlightened by the fact that reincarnation exists. Which is a total mind fuck right there." Caden could have continued to dissect his revelation, but when he looked over at Elle, she didn't seem to be in the same place as he was. "Do you not see it that way?"

"For me, it's a little different. I feel very connected to my great-aunt now. Like you, I don't feel like I'm waking up in someone else's body, but we've melded together. And I, too, have missing pieces in my memory. Like when I think about the ritual I performed, I remember I was using the journal that has gone missing," she said. She paused and placed her fingers over her lips. "Come to think of it, that journal was protected. It would have survived the fire." She shook her head. "I don't know what to do about that. None of this was part of the plan," Elle admitted. "I just thought that after Robin moved on, we would remain in each other's other lives. I remember being concerned about how you would handle Robin's death and that I wished you would eventually find your soulmate."

"So you didn't hate me," Caden said with a sideways smile.

"I never hated you," Elle said sincerely, looking into his eyes.

Caden's breath became increasingly shallow.

"Are you okay?"

Caden nodded and held his finger up as he focused on slowing his breaths. "I'm okay," he wheezed.

"Shit, Caden." Elle rubbed his back.

He closed his eyes at her touch. "Seriously, I'm okay. If we reincarnated, then where are Robin and Wade?"

Her eyes darted from side to side as if she was doing a complicated math problem. "I don't know who they are now, but it just occurred to me that there is a composition book that my great-aunt wrote, and it has their names on it. It's in her basement at Java and Book. It's weird how I remember some details so vividly. Probably explains why I was so emotional when I first saw the comp book. Or do I mean, *I* wrote it, and it's in *my* basement? I'm so confused," she said and leaned forward, resting her elbows on her thighs, shaking her head.

"Then, of course, there's the issue of why Ms. Morgan would do such a thing." He placed his hand on his chest, then snorted. "And now for the greatest mind fuck," he warned, "I guess that makes Ms. Morgan my daughter." He leaned back and covered his eyes with the heels of his hands. "Fuck me!"

Elle paced anxiously. She stopped and put her hand on her forehead. "I'm overwhelmed, Caden. We'll have to deal with a crapload of implications once we look at that comp book. I think that will help us put things into perspective, or at least give us a clue as to why Ms. Morgan would do such a thing."

"Alrighty then. That sounds like a plan," he said.

Without warning, pipes with tiny nozzles lowered from the ceiling and began a light rain.

"Ah, shit!" Caden said, crossing his arms and rubbing his biceps.

ELLE WATCHED his muscles flex while he warmed himself. She studied his body as she swiped beads of water off her face, uncertain if it was mist or perspiration. When her eyes finally looked back up at his, he was staring at her like he had been watching her fixating on him. Embarrassed, she felt a blush spread across her face. He'd caught her.

"Um," Caden said and took a step back. "I guess I should put my shirt back on."

She blinked a couple times to redirect her thoughts. "Okay, but you're still wheezing, so won't the constriction of your shirt make it worse?" she asked with no hint of an ulterior motive. "Let me look around to see if there's a blanket instead. Just wait there on the bench, and I'll go see what I can find." She turned away and went further toward the back of the greenhouse. It was getting cold, and she was tired but eager to just be out of his space for a moment.

CADEN TRIED to focus on slowing his breathing. *I've been through worse. Her attention to me makes this so much easier to get through. It's like she's giving me strength.* The misters began to scale back, but it didn't help. He began to shiver, his breathing more labored.

"HEY! I FOUND ONE!" Elle yelled from the back of the greenhouse. When she came back, Caden was on the bench, shivering, wheezing, and his lips had started turning blue. "Shit! Caden?" She rushed to him and threw the blanket over him. She took her socks off and placed them on his feet, but it didn't seem to help. "Caden? Can you hear me?"

Caden nodded.

"I need to get you warm. There's not enough room for me to hold you, and I think that might make your asthma worse..."

Caden's eyes were closed, but he seemed to be aware enough to lift open the blanket and invite her in.

Elle's body came alive, but she fought against it. "I'm only doing this because I think it'll save you. Don't think this to be anything more. Understand?" Elle said it out loud to convince herself as well, then took a deep breath.

Caden waved the blanket to get her to move quicker. He scooted as far against the back of the bench as he could.

Elle gently eased herself onto the bench, leaving a couple of inches of space between them.

Caden pulled her in with one quick movement.

She stiffened at the feel of his hard body, but when she felt his cold skin, she settled further into him. His breathing was strained as he trembled. "I'm sorry, Caden," she said ruefully.

He pulled her in tighter to console her. "My lifesaver," he whispered into her ear.

Goosebumps surfaced over every inch of her skin. "Oh, Caden…" She squeezed his arm, and her eyes pricked with tears. No matter how crappy things had been between Robin and Chris, he'd always called Mozelle that, and she smiled at how special he made her feel.

***

"WHAT THE *FUCK*?!"

Caden and Elle jolted awake and fell off the bench—she landing on her back, and he landing on top of her.

"Ms. Morgan!" they both said. Face to face, Caden leapt off of Elle. He gave her a hand and brought her to her feet.

They both blushed at the nuance.

"What happened here? This place is a disaster!" Lyndsey's body rattled in anger—and in fear.

Caden and Elle sat back on the bench and faced her. She stood there, backlit from the morning sun, waiting for an answer.

"Well, Ms. Morgan, Rikki called me at the end of school yesterday and told me that she had to go home because she had a migraine. She asked if I could come and get the leaves for her. I told her I would, and she texted me the instructions."

The blood drained from Lyndsey's face, and she began to feel nauseous. "Oh no! No!"

"Yeah! So when I came and treated the plants, it threw me

into a righteous asthma attack, Ms. Morgan." Caden's voice was no longer meek.

"I don't know what to say." Lyndsey's hand covered her mouth as she shook her head in disbelief over her epic fail.

Caden's voice got even stronger. "And I don't know how it happened, but thankfully Elle came by because I would have died."

"I'm so, so sorry! Are you okay?" *What have I done?*

"I'm fine, but I really thought I was going to die. My inhaler was in my backpack outside the door, but when they locked, she couldn't get to it. And again, by some higher power, she was able to calm me down and saved me," he said, looking at Elle.

"Elle! I'm so sorry!" Lyndsey was in tears. "I'm so glad you were here."

Elle just nodded. She seemed to be at a loss for words.

"Ms. Morgan, did you know those leaves were poisonous? That they cause hallucinations?" Those words laid heavy on his chest as they triggered a replay of all that went down just hours before. That the woman standing before him had been his daughter. He leaned forward with one hand on his thigh, the other raking through his tousled brown hair. The wheezing started coming back.

"Did something happen?" Ms. Morgan sounded suspicious.

Caden looked at Elle. She pursed her lips ever so subtly, which was enough to stop Caden from saying anything further.

"I need to know what happened!" Ms. Morgan raised her voice.

"What do you think happened? We tripped, we survived…" Caden said.

"Do you remember what you saw?"

"No," they said in unison, looking at each other.

Caden focused his attention back on Ms. Morgan. "Why did you send Rikki in to get those leaves?" he asked.

"I SWEAR I didn't know that would happen!" Lyndsey lied.

"But you knew they needed to be handled carefully," he interrogated.

"Yes, but it's only a problem if you *eat* the leaves." She knew it was a lie but felt a sense of relief knowing that all she needed to do was enchant them into forgiving her. It had worked before—it would work again.

"Well, we can tell you that that's bullshit," Caden challenged, his jaw set.

"What?" Lyndsey didn't appreciate his candor.

"Whatever they told you about the leaves is wrong, and something needs to be said," Caden said.

She exhaled in relief. "You're right! What they told me was completely false. They took advantage of my ignorance, and I'm going to call them now." Feigning indignation, she was thankful they'd paved a way out for her. "I might have to get the authorities. I mean, imagine if something worse happened to you. I just can't believe this," she expressed strongly. "But you're fine, right?"

"Yes!"

"I'm so relieved! Please do me a favor, though. I'm already in hot water over the pepper spray thing. Can we please keep this on the down-low? I truly am sorry, and I'll find a way to make it up to you."

Caden looked at Elle, and she shrugged her shoulders. "Fine."

Lyndsey bowed her head. "Thank you," she said with as much sincerity as she could muster. "I'll take care of this mess. You should really leave now."

Caden grabbed his shirt off the ground, as did Elle.

Lyndsey crossed her arms and covered her mouth as she noticed the matching birthmarks on both his and her shoulders.

The wheels in her head began spinning. *I need to reread the death investigation because I could be in the presence of Mozelle and—holy shit—my father. I never even considered if or when they would reincarnate—and yet... It can't be. If it were them, wouldn't they say something to me?*

"Those marks on your shoulders..." She pointed at them. "What... what are they?"

CADEN LOOKED at Elle again and raised his eyebrow.

"Yeah, um, I saw his birthmark, so I drew one myself to make it look like his, but cooler," Elle explained, studying Lyndsey as if waiting to see if she would take the bait. "We were tripping on the leaves, remember?" Elle and Caden looked at each other, then exhaled when Lyndsey took the bait.

"That's fine artwork," she said, a speculative look on her face. "Now get out of here."

The moment they got out of the greenhouse, Caden dug through his backpack and frantically sucked in several pumps of his inhaler. Elle stood with him. He finally caught his breath and slid down the wall onto the ground. His knees were up, his elbows resting on them. His chin quivered as he covered his eyes. All that happened was more than he could take, and he began to weep.

Elle squatted in front of him and tenderly touched the side of his thighs.

He melted at her touch. He removed his hands from his eyes and opened himself up, inviting her in. She did not hesitate as she leaned in and wrapped her arms around him. She seemed to need to be consoled over the enlightening and unsettling discoveries of the night before just as badly as he did, and she, too, began to break down.

LYNDSEY STOOD IN THE GREENHOUSE, stunned and hyperventilating to the point of seeing stars. This whole time, she'd been so focused on her mother and Wade, she'd never considered that her dad and Mozelle would be hovering around as well. All four of them were in her orbit now. She didn't drink much, but if there was ever a time for her to drink to get over something earth-shattering, this was one of those times.

LIFESAVER

Caden walked into class after taking a couple days to recover. Standing next to Elle's desk, he held his fists out, enticing her to choose a hand. She touched his left hand, and he revealed a red Lifesaver.

Elle blushed and took the candy. Caden stood there with the other hand, still waiting to be chosen. She touched the other hand, and he revealed two red Lifesavers. She laughed, causing him to blush.

"You seem to be doing better," Elle said. She'd also taken a day to collect herself and buy a new phone.

"As do you," Caden said. "So Saturday at eleven, right? At Java and Book."

"Yep."

"It'll be interesting, to say the least."

"Yeah, because it's been such a bore so far."

His mouth lifted on one side, then took his seat.

Rikki and Quinn came in together. Rikki ran to Caden's side. "I had no idea. I'm so, so sorry!"

"It's fine, Rikki. Really," Caden said and smiled as if remembering something good.

"I still feel like shit."

"It was a blessing in disguise."

"Oh. Okay. Great!" she said, looking between him and Elle. She looked at Elle, clearly questioning his comment. She got a smile and nothing more.

Rikki returned to her seat and turned to Quinn. "That reminds me. I had a bizarre dream the other night."

"*Really?*" Quinn flashed a teasing smile and waggled his eyebrows.

"If I had a dream like that, do you think I would call it *bizarre?*" Rikki chuckled. "It was a dream that—" Rikki stopped as Ms. Morgan abruptly called for the class's attention. She looked at Quinn, and the color drained from his face.

"Why don't you take the open seat in front of Quinn there. And what's your name?" Ms. Morgan asked with what looked like a mischievous smile.

"Sienna," the new girl in the room said with a raspy voice. She swept her hand through the top of her unruly blonde hair with light brown streaks only to have it return to its initial position. As she looked up, her alluring blue eyes earned her approving murmurs from many of the guys in the class, and she smiled a knowing smile.

<hr>

Quinn looked at Rikki. She was seething.

"Hey, stranger!" Sienna's smoky voice was as mesmerizing as her eyes.

"Hi, Sienna." Quinn swallowed hard and began to sweat.

"Surprised to see me so soon?" she teased.

"Not really, since you told me that you were coming sometime this week." That wasn't the truth. He'd expected a call from her. He'd expected some kind of warning that she was going to show up. When none came, he'd lowered his guard. He regretted giving her the benefit of the doubt since playing games seemed to be her default mode.

"Fine. Lunch? I need help navigating the school, plus I have so much to tell you."

He looked from Sienna to Rikki.

"What? Don't look at me," Rikki deflected.

Quinn cleared his throat. "Sienna, this is Rikki …" he said without taking his eyes off Rikki. "Rikki … Sienna."

"Hi," Rikki said with the dullness of an old tortoise's shell.

"Hi," Sienna said condescendingly.

Whispers could be heard throughout the class, and Quinn slid down in his chair.

"Well, Axton? Are you going to help me or not?" Sienna waited less than a second before turning to Rikki. "Can I borrow him for lunch?" she asked with an insulting head tilt.

"Sienna," Quinn said with grit in his voice. His unspoken command stopped her from taking it any further. "I'll meet you for lunch."

"I win," she laughed.

Quinn edged up to her and whispered, "Don't be a bitch."

"But isn't that the way you like it? Resist until I break you?" she quipped in a whisper loud enough for the whole class to hear.

<hr>

CADEN TWISTED his head toward Elle when she tapped him on the shoulder with her pencil.

"Look at how Ms. Morgan is eyeing Rikki and Quinn."

Caden studied Ms. Morgan. She just stood there, watching them. The only thing she seemed to be missing was popcorn and a Coke. He was still in disbelief that she was his daughter. The look she was giving Rikki made it seem like she enjoyed seeing the pain on Rikki's face. It triggered a memory of when she was little, and she would do cruel things to her classmates. Had she not changed? And why was she so focused on Rikki? He remembered Ms. Morgan being jealous of other girls, and he wondered if Rikki triggered something in her. Was she so jealous that she would expose her to a poisonous plant?

"ON SECOND THOUGHT, I'LL PASS." Quinn wasn't going to have it.

"You lose," Rikki said under her breath.

"Okay. Sorry! If you call me a bitch, you have to admit there will be pain. Isn't that right, Rikki?" Sienna said in a sickly sweet voice.

"I wouldn't know. No one's ever called me that before."

"My, you're a tame one, aren't you?" she said with wide eyes and raised eyebrows as if surprised Quinn would ever consider someone like Rikki. "Okay then, how about after school?" she asked, looking at Quinn.

"Yeah, no. After school is my time with Rikki."

Rikki sat up straighter and looked at Quinn out of the side of her eye. "It sounds like she could use your help. Go ahead and meet her for lunch."

Quinn felt like he was getting whiplash from the back and forth. "Fine. Where's your next class?"

Ms. Morgan cleared her throat. "Do you have your plans settled now? Can we move on?" she said as if she'd been waiting for them to finish, but oddly, he thought he heard the disappointment in her voice.

IT WAS a beautiful Saturday afternoon in the Bay Area. Quinn had picked up Rikki to spend the day together.

"You'll love Golden Gate Park. I can't believe you've been here for almost a year, and you've never gone," Rikki said.

"Well, my dad n' all. He trusts me more now, especially if I'm with you," Quinn said, and reached over, grabbed her hand, and brought it to his lips. "Thank you for being patient with me. I've made it very clear to Sienna what you mean to me, and she won't be a problem."

"Thanks," Rikki said, staring out at the bay as they drove across the Bay Bridge. It captivated her. She wondered if there were more glimmers of light on the water than stars in the Milky Way.

"Everything okay?" Quinn asked.

Rikki exhaled. "This moment is perfect. I'm with this extraordinarily hot, funny, creative, and fascinating guy who motivates me to be the best I can be. It's a clear sunny day. The sunlight as it hits the water is so serene..." she listed. "I'm completely at peace, Quinn," she said, then closed her eyes and tilted her face toward the sun.

Her beauty leveled him. He craved wrapping his arms around her, holding her close. He pulled into the first vista point after he got off the bridge.

"What's up?" Rikki asked as she looked around.

"Nothing. I just want to share this moment with you." He walked around the car, opened the door, and held his hand out. She slipped her tiny hand into his, and the two of them walked to the wall that overlooked the entire San Francisco Bay. The Golden Gate Bridge was off in the distance, yet from any angle or distance, its commanding stature was nothing short of majestic.

She walked a few steps ahead of him toward the short wall that provided an unobstructed view. The wind blew, and Rikki's hair moved like a sky dancer. She laughed, which made Quinn laugh. He stared at her while she tried to control it. Her beauty and spirit overwhelmed him, and he held his breath as if it could stop time. "Rikki," Quinn called out, releasing his breath.

She turned to him while tying her hair in a knot, then tilted her head when he didn't say anything. She chuckled. "What?" Smiling, she shook her head like he was being silly, then turned to look at the view.

He closed the distance in three steps, spun her toward him, and captured her in a single-armed embrace, his other hand entwined in her hair that unraveled and whipped around. He pulled her in close, their mouths inches apart. "It feels like we've known each other longer than we really have," he breathed. "I'm in love with you, Rikki." His mouth fused with hers and the world around them evaporated. His confession echoed through the kiss, making it as powerful as it was pure. In return, she wrapped her arms around his neck and tilted her head to further possess him. Their mouths moved with fluidity, and together, they were entranced. He opened his mouth to let out a groan, and her legs began to shake.

They broke free, having to catch their breaths. "I love you too," Rikki declared and brought her lips back to his. Off in the distance, they heard snickering and disengaged. She laughed. "I think they'd like us to get a room."

"I'd like us to get a room," he suggested.

She laughed louder.

"I can't put it into words what you've done to me, Rikki," Quinn admitted.

"I'm trembling like a leaf, Quinn. That's what you do to me. I'm so glad that you snatched my keys that day." She snorted. "I guess I shouldn't have kicked your ass…"

"You think *you* kicked *my* ass?" Quinn jested, playfully grabbing her by the waist and pulling her in.

"Actually, Ms. Morgan kicked both our asses."

He chuckled. "Hell yeah, she did."

Rikki grabbed his hand and led him to the wall. "But you know, when all that was going down and you were restraining me and holding me close to you, I knew on some level that you single-handedly had the power to turn my world upside down. At first, I was fighting you because I was pissed, but when you grabbed hold of me, I was wholeheartedly taken by you, and that freaked me out. So with all my might, I resisted. Little did I know that turning my world upside down would be the best thing that's ever happened to me."

"When I was holding you like that, I thought 'damn, she has a nice body.'"

"No, you didn't," she said, swatting his arm.

Quinn turned his shoulder defensively. "I did. I thought, 'She fits. Too bad the body belongs to a girl who's batshit crazy.'" He moved behind her and wrapped his arms around her waist. "Now I have you, and this time, I won't let go," he whispered in her ear. A small gasp escaped her as she wavered like she was dizzy. He chuckled and pulled her in closer. "I've got you."

"Yes, you do."

<hr>

At Java and Book, Elle paced, thinking about the last time she'd had a boy down in her sanctuary—when Ash had freaked out and broken up with her.

"Wow! I've always wanted to know what was behind the curtain. I always thought it was storage. What *is* this place?" Caden looked all around. Not looking where he was going, he bumped into the table where Mozelle used to do readings. "Oops," Caden said and let out a little laugh.

Elle snorted. "Mozelle used to do readings there. Or is it '*I* used to do readings there'?" She shook her head. "You know, I'm my own person," she said, her hand splayed on her chest.

"I'm not possessed by her, so from here on out, I'm me," Elle pushed her hand away from herself, "and she is she." She led him down the corridor and swung open the door. "This is my temple. Welcome to my second home," she announced and stepped aside to allow Caden to enter first.

When he crossed the threshold, his eyes became wide with awe. He took a deep breath. "This place …" he started but was unable to finish his thought.

"It's interesting. I haven't been down here since I realized that I was Mozelle. This is going to take some time to get used to." After a few moments of silence, Elle looked back at Caden. She wasn't sure if he'd heard her.

"It's weird for me too," he said, remaining in the same place, taking it all in. He was like a child who needed to touch everything to gain meaning in a new environment.

"Okay. Let me show you something." She placed a gentle hand on his back to redirect him toward the bookcase that fostered the journals and the comp books. "There are four here, but there are supposed to be five. It really bothered me, but when we got most of our memories back, I remembered that I had the fifth journal with me during the ritual, and it had to have survived the fire because it was protected. And just a theory, but I think Ms. Morgan has it."

"What does that matter? What's the significance of the journal? I guess what I'm asking is, what exactly are we doing?"

"What you and I went through in the greenhouse, I mean, *really* can't be put into words. We were attacked. Maybe we weren't the intended target, but even still, our closest friend is. Do we just sit here and do nothing about it?"

"I'm not suggesting that. I just want to make sure our mission here is clear because I have some theories, and no matter what kind of spin I put on it, what we're up against, Elle, isn't good."

"Fair enough. We need to figure out what Ms. Morgan is up

to, and determine how much danger we're in, and go from there," she explained. "I've never known you to be so analytical."

"It's the journalist in me. Whether doing a fluff piece or an investigative one, it's about asking the right questions—who, what, where, when, why, and how."

"Make sense. I'll keep that in mind," she said and turned her attention back to the bookcase. "So back to your question on why it matters where the journal is. Well, let me be the first to point out that it belongs to *me*, and I want it back. As far as our mission goes, it'll give us a greater understanding of what happened that night."

"I'm still not getting the connection."

"Okay, let me take it back a few steps and bring you up to speed," she said. "Ms. Morgan came to me a little while back, asking me if we had books on merging a person's past life with their current life. She kind of freaked me out, but ultimately she bought a book called *Vibrations of Whispers: The Book of Impossible Spells*.

"I'm listening," Caden said, his arms crossed in consideration.

"It's fair for me to assume that Ms. Morgan ordered those leaves to complete a spell in that book."

"Make sense."

"So, my journalist friend, that checks off most of your questions, except..."

"Why."

"Right," she said, then crouched in front of the bookcase. "So I think the first step in getting the 'why' is to look at what Mozelle wrote. I don't think it's a coincidence that both Ms. Morgan and Mozelle cast spells or performed rituals that involved reincarnation. But why Rikki?" She grabbed the four journals and placed them on the small table toward the side of the room.

CADEN FLIPPED through each of the journals while Elle went back to the bookcase. The journals challenged his belief system. He couldn't see being devoted to spirituality, crystals, or spells, but after seeing what he'd seen, he wasn't going to disregard them either. His eyes followed her as she moved about in her element. *She's so passionate*, he thought. He shook his head to prevent taking that line of thought from going any further.

SHE SLAMMED the pile of comp books down on a table in the corner of the room. "Like I mentioned before, I don't remember writing these, so looking at this will be weird for me."

"We're doing this together, right?" Caden assured.

"Right, right." The front page had Robin and Wade's names handwritten on it like the title page of a fairy tale. Elle chuckled.

"What's so funny?"

"Her penmanship was beautiful. That did *not* transfer over." She giggled, then turned to the next page and read:

I've chosen Robin and Wade because I know them to be true soulmates. I believe this. but I know people will get hurt. so the decision to move forward is a very difficult one.

THE FOLLOWING page was background information about Robin and Wade. What struck them both was that Mozelle had included photos.

"Whoa," they said simultaneously.

"It's weird because I remember Robin," Caden said, "but not with such clarity. So when I see these photos, I can't put words to my emotions. They're all over the place. And I don't remember looking that closely at Wade. He looks almost like a stranger to me. He's more symbolic of my failures than an actual person."

They thumbed ahead and were surprised to see that not only were there several photos throughout but there were samples of plants and hand-drawn diagrams. They looked at each other with wide eyes. What they held wasn't just beautiful—it was sacred.

The next page was about Chris. Elle wanted to skip past it, but Caden stopped her.

Chris hasn't been any help. He just makes things worse. His drinking, smoking, and abusive behaviors have actually become worse, especially since Wade came into the picture. He's out of control, and it's problematic. I don't blame Robin for falling for someone else in her time of need. Chris has been selfish and controlling. He's disengaged and works all the time. He is a good father, so I'll give him that. And he's not absent of any redeeming qualities—he has always been kind to me. I think he likes that I'm always there to cover for him or pick up the slack. I've lost count of how many times he's referred to me as his lifesaver. As much as I like to hear that, it's nothing more than a manipulation. I just think that on some level, he, too, knows he is the one who failed Robin, not the other way around.

Caden's eyes were wide in horror as he reread what Mozelle had written. He hung his head low. "Jesus. I was a horrible person. I mean, it's one thing to be aware that I drank and worked a lot, but it's another to hear what others thought of me. I was seen as a user and abuser and, apparently, an addict. How am I supposed to get past this? I mean, I even called you 'life-saver' like I do now? I was a manipulator," Caden said, pointing at the comp book. He looked at Elle. Her eyes were pained. "What? I'm an asshole, too, aren't I? You think I'm manipulating you, too, don't you?"

Elle shook her head. "No, Caden! I don't think that at all. It's like you said, you remember it like you're watching a home video, but there's a disconnect, right? You learn from past lives, so you're never the same person from one lifetime to the next."

He closed his eyes and shook his head. "No. That's not good enough. I need to take a break."

She grabbed his hand as if desperation struck her. "I'll go with you …" There was fear in her eyes like she feared being abandoned.

Caden raised his hands to stop her. "No. I need to be by myself. I'll be back. I just need some air," he said, looking into her eyes. His brows knitted when he saw an expression of hurt on her face. He placed his hands on her arms as he took a step closer and towered over her. "I promise, Elle. I'll be right back." And with that, he walked out.

***

QUINN AND RIKKI WERE LAUGHING, showing off, and splashing each other while riding pedal boats on Stow Lake. They ate blackberries that grew along the bank and kissed as they pedaled through tunnels. They pedaled up to a multi-tiered waterfall and sat on a bench off to the side.

Quinn stood up and walked over to some stepping stones that led up to the meandering waterfall. A devious smile emerged on his face.

"What are you up to?" Rikki asked, a resistant tone in her voice.

He took her hand and guided her from stone to stone. He let

go of her hand, leaving her on the last stone that lay before a pond that the waterfall cascaded into. He leapt off and landed in water that was far shallower than they'd expected. He chuckled and walked to where the waterfall and pond converged.

"Quinn, are you crazy?" Rikki said, her hand on her hips.

He turned his back to her, then placed his hands against the wall where the water gently flowed down. He lowered his head as he let the fall pour over his body.

Rikki's breath quickened, and heat rose within her. She could see every curve and ripple of his muscles. He exuded sensuality, strength, power, and masculinity. Her heart raced, and she blew out a breath to contain her inner impulses.

He turned toward her and ran his hands through his hair. She covered her mouth to hide her reaction. *Holy crap. This is what it must look like when he takes a shower, minus the clothes.* Her breath accelerated. She turned her head to look away from him, but as if against her will, her eyes refused to follow.

<hr>

QUINN WATCHED Rikki look at him. The look of wanting in her eyes provoked a seductive smirk out of him. He took a measured step closer to her, hoping he still had her attention, but on the inside, he was weakened by her gaze.

She ran her fingers through her hair, encouraging her heavy locks to fall forward, never taking her eyes off him. Taking a slow but deliberate step off the rock, she slinked through the calf-high water. With every step she took, his breath became more and more labored.

They looked into each other's eyes as they stood chest to chest, not touching, just breathing. Water rained down on them. It was incredibly refreshing. Quinn rested his wet hands on both sides of her neck and lifted her chin. She placed her hands on his waist, and he leaned down, parted his lips, and brushed his mouth along hers. He teased her, knowing it was driving her as close to the edge as he was. With the same seductive gentleness, he licked her top lip, and his next breath carried with it a sensuous moan.

Rikki's legs trembled. She lost her footing. Quinn pulled her closer, tighter, and secured her body against his. She buried her head against his chest in embarrassment. He swayed with her and sighed. She made him feel like a man with how she completely trusted him. He nuzzled deep into her neck, just loving how she loved him.

Rikki straightened herself and looked into his eyes, then grabbed his head behind his ears and covered his mouth with hers. It was breathless and sexy, but it was also very slippery, far wetter than it looked in the movies. She pulled her head back and covered her mouth with the back of her hand. "That was really wet," she said and nervously laughed.

Quinn just held her closer and cradled her head. His body shook in laughter as well.

"We're soaked with no dry clothing to change into," she laughed.

"That *is* a problem." He grinned. "I have an idea."

He took her hand and walked back over the stepping stones to the pedal boat. Shivering as they pedaled back to where they had initially embarked, Rikki held on to his arm for warmth. They finally pulled up to the dock at the Stow Lake Boathouse. They climbed out of the boat and dashed inside to find that it had not only a restaurant, but also an elaborate gift shop that sold apparel.

Rikki chose a floral dress that served more as a cover-up than anything else. The alternative choices made it evident that her bra was also a casualty of their frolicking.

Quinn purchased a T-shirt that said, "Stow Your Own Way," with a hand-drawn image from the perspective of looking through the reeds, with a person in a rowboat passing by some herons. When they saw each other, they had a good laugh as they mockingly presented themselves like models during Fashion Week.

"Wait. We're going to need sunglasses," Rikki said and pulled Quinn to the sunglasses display.

Quinn tried on a pair of aviators and tapped on Rikki's shoulder while trying on her own pair. For a fleeting moment, Rikki felt a twinge of panic. She saw a flash of the man from her dream wearing aviators. He hadn't been wearing them in her dream, but the image seemed more like a memory than anything else.

"Rikki? Are you okay?" Quinn asked as if confused by her expression. "Is there something on my face?" He felt around his face.

"No, you're fine. It was just déjà vu. Sorry." She smiled and then took a deep breath.

"Okay. Shall we?" He offered her to take the lead as they entered the café to have a late lunch, and they enjoyed the rest of the afternoon together.

ELLE QUICKLY STOOD up when Caden came back a short time later. He hesitated at the entrance like he needed to be invited back in. Unable to read his expression, she flashed a close-lipped smile to hide the uneasiness inside. "You don't need permission to come back in."

He stepped inside and swept his hair back. "I'm sorry, Elle. Just when I think I've processed everything, something happens, and it sets me back."

She nodded. She couldn't wipe the awkward grin off her face, and she was embarrassed about how transparent she must look. "You don't have to explain, really."

He came up to her and put his hands on her shoulders. "Elle, I'm not Ash. I won't do that to you. You can trust me."

Her body relaxed under his touch. "I will from now on," she said sincerely. "Are you ready to move on, or do you want to continue a different day?"

"No, we can continue."

She led him back to the table. "I looked through the rest of that book. It looks like it's all stuff we already know. It just goes into the events that led up to her deciding to perform the ritual. This page here is like a recipe. It shows all the items that she needed, and then over here, it summarizes the ritual from the missing journal."

"It's so elaborate. A twin crystal, nylon cords, oil, strawberry leaves, candles, a wand. Man, this is some Harry Potter kind of shit," he said excitedly.

Elle gave him a serious look. "Not quite."

"Oh, come on—*a wand*! I want to know what the wand was for."

She turned the page while glaring at him. "The wand was used to harness a lightning strike."

Caden put his hand out to stop her from saying more. "I remember seeing a dark storm swirling over the house when I was driving up. Is that what was happening?" Caden was back to his interested self.

"Yes."

"So what happened next?"

"I think Mozelle used it to brand Robin and Wade, but the details are really fuzzy in my mind." She scanned the page. "What the hell?"

"What?" Caden asked.

She slapped the comp book on the table. "Wow! I'm… I'm shocked!"

"What?!"

"I know who Robin and Wade are."

"You're killing me here. Who?"

"Rikki and Quinn."

"Wait. What? How do you know?"

"It says here that the wand was used to brand stars on their chests, so when they reincarnate, the stars will show up as birthmarks, and when they're near each other, vibrations will radiate from them as a beacon that the other is nearby."

"Damn! So when you turned toward me with the wand, it did more than just scar us. That charge was enchanted when it hit us. Our birthmarks are more than just birthmarks, aren't they?" he asked, looking directly into her eyes as if waiting for her to see it his way.

It can't be what he thinks. I know he wants it to be true, but I won't go there. It wasn't meant for us, and anything more than that is mean-ingless. She shook her head in denial. "The branding part of the ceremony was dedicated to just Robin and Wade. What happened to us was just collateral damage."

"I think that's bullshit. What happened in the greenhouse when we touched each other's birthmark wasn't 'collateral damage,' as you put it."

"Where are you going with this, Caden? Because whatever is between us has nothing to do with what happened before."

"You don't see that maybe we're supposed to be together? I mean, Elle, do you really feel nothing for me? Things went down in that greenhouse and…"

"We were hallucinating," she said, looking away.

"Maybe, but there were some moments that night when I know you liked what you saw, hallucinations aside." He took a step toward her.

She took a step backward, her breathing ragged. "I'm not admitting anything," she said, still finding it hard to look at him for any length of time.

"You're not denying anything either."

She swallowed reflexively. "Can we please, please just get

back to this?"

CADEN PURSED HIS LIPS. He was more encouraged to win her over than ever before. He saw her in a different light now and decided right then and there that he was not going to give up. *This explains everything—including why I've been drawn to her ever since I laid eyes on her. So why is she so resistant?*

"I'm not going there now, so stop with the staring."

"Fine!" Exasperation exited through his nostrils. "Okay, so Rikki and Quinn. How did you figure that out?"

"Rikki has a star birthmark on her chest, right here." She pointed just under her collar bone. "Plus, it says here that the birthmarks, once they're enchanted, create a buzzing, vibrating feeling that serves as a beacon."

"Wow! You're so right. I didn't know that about Rikki, but it all makes perfect sense now." Caden was trying to process all of the new developments. "Alrighty then. So what do you suggest we do next?"

"Well, nothing, I guess, because they're together. I think telling them about all this would freak them out."

Caden shook his head and began pacing. "Man, the implications are enormous. I mean, Rikki and I are Ms. Morgan's parents? That's hard to wrap my head around." His pacing came to a sudden halt. "Wait. I just had a thought. You just said that you think the journal survived the fire because it's protected and that it could be in Ms. Morgan's hands. Assuming that's true and she read the journal, she would know everything that went down. Maybe this is about revenge."

"Revenge? Why?"

"Because in her mind, everything that went down—the fire, our death, her scar—" he counted on his fingers, "—happened because of Robin and Wade wanting to be together. What happened in the greenhouse was intended for *Rikki*. She wanted *Rikki* to remember who she was, but because we went in her place, it happened to us instead."

Elle's eyes grew wide as his statements sunk in. "You're right, Caden. This is serious. But why would she want to do that to only Rikki? Why not have Quinn remember too?"

"Have them *both* remember each other? That doesn't sound like revenge to me."

"Right …"

"But just knowing why she's doing what she's doing isn't enough. Elle, there are a couple things we need to consider. First, what's her end game, and second, we have to believe that she knows we know.

Elle shook her head. "This is a dark witch we're talking about. She has *years* of experience. Confronting her, I think, would be a mistake." She rubbed her forehead. "The best I can do in the meantime is create a protection spell for us, but it'll be weak. That journal of *mine* probably has a good protection spell in it. We need to get that journal back."

"And how do we do that?"

She shrugged her shoulder. "No idea. It's probably at her house."

Caden rubbed his hands down his face. "You warned me. My mind is totally blown."

"Agreed," Elle said with wide eyes.

"Great, well, um, good work today," Caden said. He stood there, unsure what to do with his arms, so he scratched his head. "I guess we'll have to come up with a plan, but maybe not today, so I'm going to get going," he said and turned to leave.

"I'm really glad you came back, Caden," Elle said.

Caden turned around, pulling her into his arms. "Never fear otherwise."

Reciprocating, she wrapped her arms around him, and at that moment, he didn't know if anyone was as happy as he was.

15

LIP GLOSS

Lyndsey grabbed a dry erase marker from her desk, then slammed her drawer closed when Rikki and Quinn walked in, hand in hand, for yet another day. *How are they still together?* Her eyes followed them as they walked across the room, smiling and looking deeply into each other's eyes.

"Pop quiz today," she decided.

A collective moan from the students alleviated some of Lyndsey's frustration over the fact that her plan had become stale. She needed to step up the enchantment. As soon as Sienna walked in late, it clicked in Lyndsey's mind that she needed something personal from Sienna. So when school ended later that day, Lyndsey obtained Sienna's locker information and raided it. Sienna had a mirror on the locker door, a few textbooks, some pens, and highlighters. Lyndsey shoved those things aside and caught sight of a flicker of light glinting off of something in between a couple books. It was as if the heavens had parted and sent a ray of light that shone on the most perfect possession—a tube of Cherry Splendor roll-on lip gloss. Lyndsey held the item to her chest and took a deep breath.

As soon as she got home, she burst into her temple room and immediately grabbed items from her repertoire of herbs, crystals, candles, and oils that she had built into the closet. She hummed as she collected the ingredients for her curse.

She carved Rikki's name on two black candles and lit them, then carved Sienna's name on a red candle and Quinn's name on a gold candle. She tied the red and gold candles together with the remaining strands of hair from Quinn's comb and lit them. In a mortar, she poured pasak bumi oil over aventurine. She added cinnamon, vanilla, lavender, cloves, maguey root, hibiscus, and passionflower. She held the tied candles over the mortar as they bled over the ingredients. She opened the tube of lip gloss and stirred the concoction with the applicator, chanting:

"OH VENUS, praise the sacred goddess of all things passionate, loving, and lustful:
    Anoint this blend that is placed upon each lip
    With lust, passion, sex, and a loving relationship.
    Once Sienna and Quinn's lips caress,
    A re-awakening of his rebellious ways will make him confess.
    He'll admit abandoning Sienna was a mistake
    And believe his love for Rikki was really a fake.
    Rikki's sanity and emotions will plummet
    Because their love knows no summit.
    Quinn's love for Rikki he would permanently sever
    As he realizes he wants Sienna forever.

ANOTHER CLASSROOM DEMONSTRATION would set her plan into action. She went into her garage and grabbed her collection of customary Carnival masks, putting one aside. That one would be reserved for Quinn. She strained the oil and chanted:

. . .

O*H, mighty spirits of illusion:*
When Quinn places this mask on his face,
This oil will induce an illusion to take place.
Sienna is Rikki and Rikki is Sienna, he will believe,
Stirring him with lust only Rikki can relieve.
A single kiss is all he would need,
For my plan, with Venus's help, to succeed.

LYNDSEY ARRIVED at school early the next day to prepare for her lesson—and Rikki's downfall.

"Okay, class. Let's settle down. I want to get today's fun lesson going," As she waited for the students to get settled, she went to her desk and took out the lip gloss and brought it to Sienna.

"I think you dropped this yesterday."

"Thanks! I was wondering where this went." Sienna immediately applied the enchanted gloss, then turned to Quinn. "You like?" she asked and smiled when she saw Quinn staring at her lips as she rubbed them together.

Lyndsey moved back up to the front of the room. "Today is going to be so much fun because we're going to do an awesome demonstration. As we continue our study of mythology and folklore in South America, we are going to celebrate the Brazilian way." She turned on samba music and closed the blinds, then presented the class with the masks they would be wearing. "Welcome to Carnival. This is normally a pre-lent festival originally created by the impoverished, who found a different way to compete with the upper class's more organized fairs. I didn't have a chance to bring in traditional South American food for this kind of celebration. This was a bit spur of the moment, so some things just aren't available this time of year, like a king cake, so instead, I brought in spicy chicken, corn, rice, and beans from KFC. When it gets closer to Lent, we'll have a more accurate celebration." The class energy changed considerably after her announcement. "Now, this celebration just isn't complete without a mask, so I'm going to pass these out. Put them on and let the festivities begin!"

She moved and danced about as she strategically gave out the masks, then she turned down the lights and invited the students up for food.

***

QUINN CLOSED his eyes and absorbed the smell of cloves and cinnamon as he placed his mask on his face. The beat of the music electrified his body and entranced him. He felt buzzed, like when he smoked pot, and he was aroused by it.

After an unknown amount of time passed—maybe two minutes, maybe forty-five minutes—he opened his eyes. He was the last one still wearing a mask. He took it off and scanned the room for Rikki. *That's weird*, he thought. Sienna was in her chair. And even stranger was that she was talking to Elle and Caden like they were friends. He quickly dismissed it when he found Rikki standing at the back of the room. Her eyes were on him, and his lust grew beyond his breaking point.

"Quinn?" Sienna called out to Quinn's back.

"Not now!" he growled as he dismissively waved his hand.

He snaked toward Rikki. He saw the want in her eyes. "I don't know what it is about this setup—the music, the smell—but holy hell, I want you!" He pressed his body against hers.

Rikki didn't hold back. "I knew you couldn't resist."

Quinn grabbed Rikki's hand, and they snuck into the adjoining office that Lyndsey and the teacher next door shared. The office was dark, and Quinn was fine with that. He closed the door, then grabbed Rikki at the base of her head and pulled her in for a mouths-wide-open, tongue-tangoing kiss. If they could climb into each other's mouths to go deeper, they would. Moans and gasps for air escaped as he lifted her onto the desk. His hands reached under her skirt to grab her ass. He was ravenous, and his control was about to snap.

"Yes," Rikki called out, wrapping her legs around his waist.

He shoved her further back on the desk until she was pressed back against the wall, allowing papers and office supplies to crash onto the floor.

"What the fuck?!" Rikki yelled.

Ms. Morgan turned on the lights while the whole class came running in to see what was happening.

Quinn leapt away from Sienna as confusion struck him. "Holy shit! I … I thought she was you! What the hell?" he cried out, wiping Sienna's lip gloss off his mouth. Confusion turned to horror as he watched Rikki's heart shatter like tempered glass. Tears burst out, and she bolted.

Quinn started toward her, but a hand grabbed him on his shoulder.

LYNDSEY PREVENTED him from going any further. "Let her go." She took pleasure in feeling his body weaken in defeat. He leaned back against the desk, resting one of his legs on top. "Going after her when you look like you need a damn cigarette will only hurt her more. Clean up this place, and the two of you will need to stay after class," she said, acting like she was appalled. In reality, this was one of the greatest moments of her adult life. She would never question her ability to get what she wanted again.

She turned around to look at Rikki's little friend Elle, who looked equally shocked. "Elle, go after her. Make sure she doesn't do something she'll regret. And you can all turn around and forget about all this. The party's in there, not out here." She turned back to Quinn and Sienna. "This door will remain open with the lights on while you clean up your mess."

QUINN JUST SAT THERE on the desk, where it had all gone down.

"That was unexpected and fucking amazing," Sienna gushed, moving into him and sliding her hand up his thigh.

He looked at her hand, then removed it with disgust. "I don't know what happened. I thought you were Rikki."

She recoiled at the sharpness of his statement. "I thought that kiss was for me. I thought you'd suddenly realized that you wanted me and that … I don't know, something in you clicked." Sienna rubbed her forehead. "I'm totally embarrassed." She turned her head to blink away her tears.

Quinn lowered his head in shame. "Please don't cry." He'd never seen her vulnerable before. And to add insult to injury, he'd shown her how badly he wanted Rikki. He jumped off the desk and stood tall before her. He lifted her chin. "Please don't feel bad. Really, Sienna, that was a kiss like no other," he said as he looked deeply into her hurt eyes. "I'm so sorry." He closed his eyes, and the feel of the kiss raced through his mind again, but this time it was different. This time, he replayed it, knowing it was Sienna he was kissing, and found himself liking how it felt with her. He opened his eyes, and the wave of guilt and nausea overwhelmed him. Gagging, he covered his mouth. "I need to get out of here," he said through his hand.

"Please don't leave while I feel this bad, Quinn," she pleaded.

"I can't deal with this right now. I think I'm going to be sick." Quinn took off to the nearest bathroom. He turned on the faucet and splashed cold water onto his face. He gripped the edge of the sink. *What just happened?* He looked in the mirror and saw his disheveled appearance. His lips were swollen, and felt compelled to run his fingers along the edges. He replayed the kiss again. His tongue slowly glided along his parted mouth. His heart raced in the pleasure of the memory.

ELLE FOUND Rikki sitting on a large planter. Her eyes were swollen, and she looked dumbfounded.

Elle paced in front of Rikki, her hand on her forehead. "I don't know what to say. There has to be an explanation."

"That image of them together like that is *seared* right here." Rikki pointed to her heart. "I don't get what the hell just happened. 'I thought she was you'? That's total bullshit. I feel sick." She clenched her stomach and bent over as tears streamed down her face. "Just a couple days ago, we had the greatest day in my entire life. We told each other, 'I love you.' And now what? He's confused?" She shook her head. "I really don't feel good." She kept her head low and took in slow breaths.

Elle crouched down to look Rikki in the eye. "I promise we will get to the bottom of this. Listen to me when I tell you that this is *not* supposed to happen. You two are soulmates. Trust me on this one, okay?"

Rikki nodded, then sprang up and ran to a nearby trash can to vomit until she was gasping for air. Elle followed close behind. She held Rikki's hair and rubbed her back.

"I'm not going to survive this," Rikki cried.

"Give me a day or two. I'll get this back on track. I swear to you I will."

ELLE CAME into the newsroom in a huff.

"You saw what happened in Ms. Morgan's class, right?"

"Of course I did," Caden said. "But honestly, it's surprising."

"We need to fix this," she said, crossing her arms.

"How?"

"I don't know. Is this a one-time thing with Quinn or something more? If it's the start of something more, we would need to reverse it."

"Okay. How?" Caden asked, still looking at the computer as he worked on final edits.

"I don't know. I have to look shit up."

Caden finished typing and looked up at Elle. "Let's say you *do* reverse this supposed, I don't know, curse. The problem remains that we don't know what Ms. Morgan ultimately wants. We figure she's out for revenge, but we don't know what exactly she's trying to do. If it's not *this* curse, it'll be another. So until we figure out what she wants, this might be a never-ending cycle," Caden pointed out.

Elle froze in her tracks. "Damn it, you're right. She needs to be confronted. What if you tell her who you are and that you've moved on, then maybe she'll stop?"

He leaned back in his chair, running his hand along his jaw and contemplating Elle's words. "I don't know. It's so complicated, and knowing what she's capable of, all I can say is we need to really consider the consequences of crossing a person like her. Because it won't take much for her to destroy us."

"For sure." She leaned against his desk. "I'm going to look this up. Do you want to help me?"

Caden stopped typing and looked up at her. "You never need to ask, Elle."

RIKKI'S DAZE began to wear off by the time she got home. She looked at her phone again. Quinn hadn't made a single attempt to reach her. She clenched her jaw and chucked her phone onto her bed, resisting the urge to call him. He needed to be the one to call her. *Maybe he's afraid to call because he's humiliated, or maybe he feels like everything's fine and he's waiting for me to call, or maybe he thinks it's over. Maybe I should be the one to call him.*

She texted him and got no response. *Maybe it's on silent, so I should call him.* It rang a couple times, then went to voicemail.

"Fucking shit! What the hell?" She was incensed. "He's sent me to voicemail?" She blew all her air out of her lungs for fear she would go nuclear. "I'm so pissed!" she yelled, choking the hell out of her phone.

"Rikki? Is everything okay?" her mom asked through the door.

"Yes. No. I don't know!" she cried. "I'm not ready to talk about it." She continued to pace. *Maybe he's busy and can take my call now. I'll just wait another hour and then try again,* she thought and set the timer on her phone.

She paced her room. Flashes of Quinn in a lovers' embrace with that horrible, wicked girl ran on repeat in her head. She pursed her lips and picked up the phone—51:07 remaining. *There's no way I'll survive this. I'm going out of my mind. I need a distraction. Homework. I'll do my homework.*

For forty-five painstaking minutes, she did her homework. For the remaining six minutes, she watched the time count down. *It'll take me fifteen seconds to call him and for him to pick up. That'll be one hour.*

She clicked his name. Her breath was ragged as she waited for the phone to connect. It clicked and went straight to voicemail. *"Fuck!"* Tears sprung to her eyes, and she called Elle.

"Hey, Rikki! How are you doing?"

She was so enraged that she could barely breathe. "He hasn't even tried to call me, and when I call *him*, he sends me to fucking voicemail. I don't know what's happening," she yelled and started pacing, hoping that would burn off her hysteria. She was wrong.

"Okay. Breathe. You probably won't get anywhere with him tonight. I know it hurts. The waiting is the worst, but this will get sorted out tomorrow. He's probably just freaked out about what happened and thinks you'll break up with him."

"Right, right. You're probably right. I'll just fucking endure each and every painful fucking minute until then because I won't be sleeping tonight! Fuck!" she shouted.

Rikki heard Elle's deep sigh. "I'm going to help you through this, okay?"

"Uh-huh."

<hr>

IN AN EMPTY PARKING LOT, Sienna and Quinn sat on the tailgate of her truck, drinking beers just like old times. Her lips twisted when she witnessed Quinn look at his phone, then put it back in his pocket. "Was that her again?" Sienna asked as she passed Quinn a beer.

"She's probably freaking out. She can be annoying that way." He took a swig of his beer.

Sienna began tearing the label off her beer. Her ankles were linked as they swung back and forth. "This feels right, Quinn. I'm glad you're here and no longer confused n' all. Right?" She took another swig of beer.

Quinn leaned over and kissed Sienna gently on her lips. He was so drawn to them. They were full and luscious, especially when she put gloss on them. The way they shone, even in the moonlight, made them irresistible. He wanted to lick them. He lifted her chin. "I'm no longer confused." He smiled. "I guess I was looking for you in her, but there's no comparison."

"I don't know what you were thinking, hangin' out with all

the rich kids and their fancy cars and college trust funds n' shit. They aren't our people, Quinn."

He looked down. "I believed I was. I believed it all to be so real. But after our kiss, and after I realized it was *you* I was kissing ..." He took a swig. "I feel like Sleeping Beauty—well, a male version anyway. I was asleep, and now I'm awake."

Sienna slammed her empty bottle down and jumped off the tailgate. "I say we scandalize this town. What do you say?"

"Not tonight. I'm going to head back home."

"Suit yourself, Axton."

Quinn got up and kissed her good night.

His dad was up when Quinn got home and suspected the worst. "She's not here a week, and look at what she's turned you into. I won't put up with this, Quinn. I mean, look at yourself. Your eyes are glazed over like you're looking through me. Rikki is worried sick and has been calling as well."

Quinn set his jaw and put his hands on his hips. Mason could almost see his son's anger pulsing through his veins. With fierceness in his eyes, Quinn turned toward him. "Do me a favor —the next time she calls, tell her I want nothing to do with her, and then stop taking her fucking calls. And after that, you can leave me the fuck alone!" Quinn spat and left the room.

Mason went after his son. "Don't you walk away from me! We're not done talking!" The force with which Quinn slammed his door reverberated in Mason's ears. "You can't stay in there forever. And believe me, we are not through here!"

Rikki was up and out of bed before her alarm went off. No shower, no breakfast, no brushing her teeth, her hair, or even putting on makeup. She even wore the same clothes she'd cried herself to sleep in, which were the same clothes she'd worn to school the day before. She was going to get answers, and fixing herself would only slow down her quest.

She threw her backpack onto the passenger seat, the seat she occupied in Quinn's car when he took her to school. She was hoping that she would find him quickly. She fantasized that he would be waiting for her with open arms and a huge apology. Her whole body hunched forward as dread overcame her when she saw he wasn't in his usual spots. *I can't handle this.* She clenched her fist as her body rattled with anger.

"Rikki?"

Rikki turned around. Elle had a horrified look on her face.

"I know. I know. I look like shit! And before you ask, I haven't seen Quinn, nor have I talked to him, hence, looking like shit," Rikki justified while pointing at her face.

"I'm so sorry. You have to trust me. I'm going to help you, but sadly, it won't be painless."

"I can't take this. I can't take any more of this pain! And it hasn't even been twenty-four hours. This is going to be the death of me," Rikki said as her chin quivered.

"Let's just hope it's all a huge misunderstanding."

"Yeah! Let's hear it for hope!" Rikki said sarcastically as she swung her fist.

Rikki went to her locker during first break. Excitement coursed through her when the vibrations started, but then sank as she rounded the corner and saw he wasn't there. Worse, the vibrations quickly faded as if he was running away. "Asshole!" she yelled. Determined, she lay in wait in front of Ms. Morgan's class.

The charged vibrations began growing, and she drew in a big breath. She saw Quinn down the hall, hand in hand with Sienna. Rikki looked away as her heart raced. She was going to confront him. Her legs began to shake as she stepped into view.

"*You? Really?*" There was venom in his voice. "What do you want?" Quinn held Sienna's hand protectively, pulling her behind him. She clung to him like he was shielding her from a murderer.

Rikki scoffed as she looked at Sienna, then at Quinn. "Can I talk to you alone?" Rikki asked firmly.

Sienna stepped out of Quinn's protective stance. "Oh my, look at you." She giggled, standing up tall. "It sounds like she really needs your help. You can talk to her," Sienna said, throwing Rikki's words back at her. She let go of his hand and kissed him on his cheek. She turned his face toward her and looked him deeply in his eyes. "Tell her what you told me, okay?" she directed. She looked Rikki up and down, chuckled, then walked into class.

Rikki's jaw moved forward, and her breath shot through her nose in response to the rage that coursed through her veins. She closed her eyes to center herself because she feared she would wail on him like she had the first time they saw each other. When she opened her eyes and looked into Quinn's, there was nothing in them. There was no life, no spark, not even anger. He was … vacant. "Jesus! What is wrong with you?" Her question wasn't accusatory. It came from a place of concern.

"Nothing's wrong with me," he replied, sounding just as dull as his eyes.

"Ookaay … Wow! I don't even know what to do with that," she said and scratched her head in confusion. "Um. Well, Quinn … What the hell happened? You kissed *Sienna*," she said, then saw a glimmer of life appear in his eyes. "And then you ignore me? I think you owe me an explanation." She waved her hands. "No, no, let me rephrase that. I *demand* you give me an explanation."

"I realized that she's the one I want to be with," Quinn said.

"Bullshit! You're a damn liar." There was a long pause. Her teeth gnashed as she averted her gaze. She crossed her arms and waited for a response, but she was met with crickets. "Well?" she pressed, shrugging her shoulders.

"Well, what?"

"Fucking tell me the damn truth! Apparently, Sienna knows, and she told you to tell me, so tell me!" Rikki raised her voice. She knew the class could hear her, but she no longer cared.

He just stood there, looking at the ground.

Rikki reached out and touched his shoulder.

His head shot up. Hostility filled his eyes as he batted her arm away. "Don't touch me!" he bit as he pointed a finger in her face.

"He lives!" She was glad to get some kind—any kind—of reaction from him.

He pursed his lips and stood close to intimidate her. "I used you, Rikki. At first, I didn't know I was doing that, but after what happened yesterday, I realized that the kiss wasn't a mistake at all. It was divine intervention. A wake-up call. I was looking for Sienna in *you*, and I could not have been more wrong." He sneered. "You and your money and your goody-goody-ness. Your freaky scientific, anxiety-filled mind of yours is annoying. I don't know what I was thinking. You and your types, you sit on a wall, looking down at all the peasants below with judgment and disdain. The world hates people like you, including me! You bewitched me, and I can't stand being around the person who made a fool of me. There. Does that *satisfy* your need for an *explanation?*"

Tears streamed down Rikki's face.

He bent down to her level and looked into her tear-filled eyes. "It looks like it does. Of course, I can go on if you'd like."

She looked away, ashamed that she couldn't hide how much pain he was subjecting her to. She wiped the tears from her face, but she couldn't keep up with the flow. She took a deep breath to compose herself and process as much as she could within the fleeting seconds she had before he would walk away. She cleared her throat and jutted her jaw. "You sound like you've lost your damn mind," she charged. "I'm a bit dizzy from the labyrinth of bullshit clichés you just spouted out. But really, I think there's something else going on here. I think that you don't believe a damn thing you just said to me. I know that you love me, and I love you. I—"

"Stop! I'm going to stop you right there. I no longer care what you think you know. No, no." He waved his hand to imitate Rikki. "Let *me* rephrase that—I no longer care, period!" He glared and took yet another step closer. "Now get out of my sight!" he threatened.

She took a step closer to him to challenge his posturing. "Or what?"

Quinn laughed at her. "You're a funny little girl. Go run along now."

"The Jekyll and Hyde thing? I'll figure it out. I'm not giving up that easily."

"Oh, brother," he said as he rolled his eyes. "Now who's being cliché? You're wasting your time," Quinn warned. "Go inside, Rikki, before you get a bad grade."

She walked past him and past the entrance to the classroom.

"Where are you going?" Quinn yelled, confusion evident in his voice. "You know, ditching class is a goody-goody felony!"

"Fuck you, Quinn," she called back with a gesture to match the sentiment. She went into the bathroom and hid in the handicap stall furthest away from the door. She dropped her backpack, then slid down the tiled wall onto the floor and cried.

QUINN STROLLED BACK into class with a proud smirk on his face. Everyone's eyes were on him as he made his way across the front of the class. "'Sup," he said, jutting his chin, challenging anyone who might dare question what just happened outside the classroom. He slumped down in his seat.

Sienna spun around in her chair. Her blonde hair flung over part of her face as she cocked her head back. "You're so fucking hot when you defend me like that."

Quinn leaned in. "Axton and Bisset. Just like old times."

"Ah, but this time will be mind-blowing," she promised, using her pen to tug on her lower lip.

A slight chuckle came out of Ms. Morgan. "Alright, class, let's reel it back in." She seemed almost giddy.

"Douche bag," Elle mumbled to Quinn. She stood up, grabbed the hall pass, and walked out the back of the classroom.

AFTER A COUPLE MINUTES, Elle walked into the bathroom. She closed her eyes at the sound of Rikki's weeping. "Hey! Are you okay?"

"No."

"Which stall are you in?"

Elle heard the stall door at the very end unlock and open. Rikki was huddled in the corner.

Elle closed the lid of the toilet and took a seat. "I wish my magic wand could fix this."

Rikki's mouth went up on one side. "So did the whole class hear?"

Elle nodded.

"Great. Whatever. Well, I certainly don't think I'm alone in seeing that he's the one that screwed this up. I mean, really, I'm the victim in all this." Rikki wiped her face. "I never knew he could be such an asshole."

"Trust me, I'm shocked too," Elle said as she remembered the only time Mozelle had seen Wade as Quinn had been—the day he'd confronted Chris in the kitchen.

"But you know what, Elle? The vibrations started again. I think that means there's hope."

"There's more than hope, Rikki. Just be patient. Do you want me to wait with you before going back to class? If you're going back to class?"

"Well, I guess I don't have a choice, being that I'm committing a goody-goody felony." She laughed and cried simultaneously before standing up and taking a deep breath, ready to face the class.

<hr>

RIKKI STOOD with Elle at the entrance of the classroom. Rikki was embarrassed, but she couldn't avoid class altogether. *I might as well wrap this whole crappy moment into one long, crappy day, and hopefully, people would get over it sooner rather than later.*

She could hear the whispers and feel the stares. The heat of embarrassment grew from the inside out as she flushed. She began to perspire and feared that she would finally reach the pinnacle of mortification by passing out in front of the whole class.

"Oh, honey, you don't look so good," Sienna said to her in a baby voice.

"Go fuck yourself, Sienna," Rikki demanded.

"Oh, I don't have to anymore." She chuckled. "Isn't that right, Quinn?"

Rikki tried not to react, but her body did not agree with her mind, and she began to feel sick. She looked at Quinn to gauge his response. He looked at Rikki, but he was looking through her again. A strange smile emerged on his face that didn't reach his eyes. She shivered at the look of it.

"What's wrong with you?" Rikki asked again. "Smile all you

want. You won't convince me that in the last twenty-four hours, you two slept together."

"Made love," Sienna corrected and grabbed Quinn's forearm.

"Shut the fuck up, Sienna. I'm not playing anymore." Her body temperature continued to climb.

LYNDSEY ADMIRED HER WORK. She was proud of her ability to cast spells and make the world hers. Now all she had to do was sit back and watch as her reincarnated mother suffered as much as she had.

"Rikki, is this going to be another one of *those* moments?" Lyndsey asked as she moved to stand beside her desk.

"Rikki? Are you okay?" Caden asked, reaching for her from his seat.

Rikki began to lose color and started to sway. "Something's wrong," she said.

CADEN SPRUNG up and caught Rikki before she hit the floor. He sat down and gently laid her in his lap.

Quinn stood up, his eyes wide, darting side to side as if trying to remember something.

"Déjà vu much?" Caden asked Elle, looking at her for understanding. "Rikki?" he called while tapping her cheek.

The class stood around them to see what was happening.

A minute later, Rikki opened her eyes. She gasped as if startled, sitting straight up. "Where's Wade?" She was panicked. She looked around as if searching for him, but then her body deflated in disappointment. She blinked once, twice, then her eyes were clear again. "Right. I'm in class having the worst day in my entire life," she admitted to Caden.

He gave another look to Elle. "You're right. This needs to be fixed."

"Is she alright?" Ms. Morgan asked, leaning over the desk. Caden could see right through her act, and his body tensed, irritated.

"I'm fine. I'm fine," Rikki claimed as she got up.

"Why don't you take her to the nurse's office?" Ms. Morgan advised.

"I'm fine, really! I just got a little lightheaded. I don't need to go to the nurse's office." Rikki plopped down in her seat.

"Who's Wade?" Quinn asked Rikki.

"What?" Rikki sounded confused by his question. She took her folder and began to fan herself.

"Nothing. Forget it. I don't care," Quinn said, his expression turning indifferent.

"Maybe you should move your seat, so this won't be a problem," Ms. Morgan said, looking at Rikki.

"Why should I move? They're the ones causing the problem."

"I'm *not* going to move," Quinn said defensively.

"Well, consider this a warning."

Quinn and Rikki both rolled their eyes at each other and quieted down. Rikki ignored Quinn for the remainder of the class. As soon as the bell rang, she was up and out.

FOR THE REST of the day, Rikki was miserable. She still couldn't believe how things had turned out in such a short amount of time.

He's got to be on something. The dullness of his eyes and his asshole-ness makes that a viable theory. He said they used to do things like that when they were in Wyoming, and since it's been so long, he must be having a bad trip.

She ran to her locker, convinced of that, and wondered if

now, maybe her fantasy would come true. When she didn't feel the vibration as she closed in on her locker, there was a tightening in her chest. She rounded the corner and saw that she was all alone. Her backpack fell off her shoulder and crashed to the ground. She dropped to her haunches and covered her eyes. She began to wail. She didn't care if anyone came by and saw her. The pain was unbearable.

16

VANDALS

That night, Quinn snuck out of his dad's house and hopped into Sienna's truck.

With a cigarette hanging out the side of her mouth, she reached behind the seat and gently shook a bottle of vodka back and forth to show off the goods she'd stolen from her parents. "I can't read the name," she mumbled, holding onto her cigarette with her lips. She squinted. "I think it's written in Russian or some shit."

Driving along Bridgeway, they passed Java and Book and pulled into the public parking lot. Quinn hopped out, pulled his hood up, and made his way to the convenience store. His skin crawled as the store clerk watched his every move. He was tempted to steal the mixers and Visine, but the store clerk was just waiting to pounce. He paid the clerk, then jumped back into Sienna's truck.

"Park over here," Quinn directed, and she pulled in front of Java and Book. Swig after swig, chase after chase, the clarity of their world became blurred.

Sienna climbed over and straddled Quinn. "I think we should fuck with Rikki," Sienna suggested.

"What do you have in mind?" Quinn asked as he placed his hands on her hips, but it didn't do much for him that she was on him like that. Perhaps he was too drunk.

"I don't know. I want to kick the bitch's ass, to be quite honest. I mean, who the hell does she think she is? That fainting act in class? Give me a fucking break. She wants you, and we need to show the little bitch that she can't have you." She leaned in and nuzzled his neck.

"She annoys the shit out of me, but I don't want her to get her ass kicked."

She sat up. "Okay, maybe that's a bit strong. I say we just have a talk with her. Set the record straight. Tell her she needs to get the fuck out of that class and out of our lives."

Quinn considered it. "Umm, I don't want to go to her house, but I bet you I could get her to come to me."

"Okay. Call her," she demanded with a bit of a bounce.

Quinn called Rikki and put her on speaker.

"Hello? Quinn? What time is it?" Rikki asked. Her voice was raspy.

"Were you sleeping?"

"I guess I fell asleep studying."

Sienna snickered at Rikki, and Quinn waved his hand to get her to stop.

"Are you okay?" Rikki asked. "You don't sound so good."

"I'm totally fine," he slurred.

There was a long pause.

"Why are you calling?"

"I want to see you."

"Okay, why?" Rikki sat up, threw the sheets off her, and ran to her closet. *Maybe he's going to tell me that Sienna slipped him some drug, and that's why he acted like such a dick.*

"Meet me in front of Java and Book," Quinn directed.

"It's late. Can't you just come here?"

"No," he said abruptly. "I want to see you where we first kissed."

Rikki took a moment. "Oh, um, okay. I'll be there in twenty." She changed out of her sweats and put on green, wide-legged pants and a white blouse that hung off her shoulders. After thinking about it for a moment, she grabbed her white sweater as well.

Sienna rolled her eyes as he hung up the phone.

"What?" Quinn asked.

"'The place where we first kissed,'" she mimicked. "I never knew you could be so cringy."

"Hey, I got her to agree to meet up with me, didn't I?" he said, then yawned.

"Am I boring you that much?"

"No. The drinks are just getting to me."

Rikki pulled into a small parking lot a few doors down from Java and Book. She checked the stairs in front of the café, but she didn't see Quinn. She closed her eyes to try to feel the vibration. It was faint but could tell he was nearby. She walked across the street to where they had shared that incredible moment.

She looked around and saw nothing, Then dropped down onto the bench they'd sat on that night. She straightened her blouse and patted down her flyaways. Suddenly, she felt a strong pull of her hair, and she cried out in pain.

Sienna had a firm hold on her hair, and she wasn't about to let go. "Hey, Rikki!"

"What the hell? Where's Quinn?" she asked as she tried to reclaim her hair.

"He's in my truck. He's exhausted from drinking and screwing all night."

"Liar! Fucking let go of my hair!"

Sienna yanked her hair, and she cried out again.

Quinn was jolted awake as his birthmark started to sting. The vibration was more extreme than he'd ever felt. "Son of a bitch!" He grabbed his chest. Rikki was not okay. He rushed out of the car to find her, but as the evening air hit him, he remembered he was with Sienna. Like waking from a dream, his feelings for Rikki faded with every step he took.

"What is it that you want?" Rikki asked. Her head was canted as Sienna's grip became more aggressive.

"Quinn and I have decided that you need to get out of our lives."

"And you don't think you've already made that clear?" Rikki asked as she continued to try to get Sienna to let go.

"Look at you. All dressed up. Hair and makeup all because he called you. You clearly aren't getting the message. You better find a way to get out of our class, out of our school, out of our town. You know … disappear."

"Okay," Rikki surrendered, holding on to Sienna's hands in hopes of loosening her grip.

Sienna yanked her hair again. "You can't get rid of me that fast. We're just starting to have fun."

Rikki closed her eyes as tears tumbled down her cheeks. She

dug her nails into Sierra's hand to gain control over her hair, but Sienna only yanked harder, and this time, she pulled Rikki up and walked her toward the water.

"Please let go of my hair," Rikki begged. "I won't resist." Sienna yanked her hair again, and Rikki yelled out. The vibrations started to grow stronger. "Quinn!" she yelled. "*Quinn!*"

"Shut up, you little bitch! He's passed out asleep," Sienna said, still pulling her along.

"Where are you taking me?" Rikki asked.

Sienna held her hand down, so Rikki was bent over as they walked. "I'm going to tie your hair to that dock."

Rikki saw her chance for an escape when she kicked up a rock. She grabbed it and purposely fell forward. Yanking and twisting Sienna's arm, she was forced to turn around. With all her might, Rikki smashed the rock onto Sienna's toes.

Sienna yelped in pain as she let go to grab her foot.

Rikki got up and made a run for it.

Sienna tried to run after her but fell. She reached for her toes as they bled over her fingers. "You bitch!"

Rikki ran all the way back to her car. Out of breath and shaking, she struggled to get her keys out of her purse. She was whimpering and panicking, then felt a hand on her shoulder. She dropped everything, turned around, and shoved whoever was there. Then she began swinging her arms, crying out as she lashed out.

"Rikki! Rikki! Stop!" Quinn shouted. He grabbed both of her arms. "What's going on?" he urged. He almost sounded like he was concerned. His alcohol-laced breath was like a toxic cloud that burned everything in its wake.

"Get her away from me!"

Sienna limped her way over and looked at Quinn. "What?!"

"What the fuck, Sienna? You were supposed to wake me up! You hurt her?"

"No!" Sienna acted offended by his accusation.

"Yes, you did!" Rikki yelled.

"Well, that's because you hurt me first. Look at my toes!"

Quinn looked down at Sienna's bloodied toes, then turned to Rikki with that same disdained look he had when he'd gone off on her in school.

"I hate you so much!" Rikki sobbed, looking at Quinn. "How could you do this to me?" Her voice was hoarse from screaming. "Please," she implored. "Please, just let me go. This is torture."

Quinn let go, and Rikki fell to her haunches, wailing into her hands. "I hate you, Quinn! I hate you so much!"

<hr>

Quinn walked over to Sienna. "This is not at all what we talked about. We were just going to tell her to leave us alone. But this? This is far from okay. You took advantage of me being passed out." His voice was raised. "Get a grip, Sienna! I might love you, but your cruelty will be our undoing."

"She's a drama queen, Quinn. It's what she does to get your attention and what brought us to this place to begin with," Sienna said, pointing at Rikki.

"I need you to leave!" Quinn ordered.

"I'm your ride, remember? I'm the one riding you all the way home," Sienna yelled, looking at Rikki.

"I'll Uber."

"I'm not leaving you here alone with her."

Rikki stood up. "You have nothing to worry about. You can have him," Rikki spat. "But I won't let you bully me into leaving that class. I need it to graduate."

"You think you're tough right now because Quinn's here? Don't fool yourself. He's not rescuing you, Rikki. He's rescuing *me* from losing my shit on—"

"Shut the fuck up, Sienna!" Quinn yelled.

"Please take your lover's quarrel somewhere else." Rikki's sobs turned into hiccups.

"Sienna! Fucking go!"

"There are going to be consequences for this," she said, looking at Rikki before she turned and limped back to her car.

"I wish you would go with her. You've hurt me beyond anything I could imagine," Rikki begged. She shook her head. "I mean, really, Quinn? *Her*? Like, just a few days ago, we told each other how much we loved each other. And now we're like this."

Quinn had nothing to say. His eyes grew dull again.

"Do you really not remember how you felt?"

"I just want to make sure you're not going to say anything. Alright?"

"Ah. Okay." She nodded her head and sucked in her upper lip. "I have no words." She got into her car and drove off.

***

ELLE CLOSED Mozelle's journal titled *Spells and Potions* and called Caden.

Caden picked up on the first ring. "What's up?" he greeted, slightly out of breath.

"Hi! I know how to get Ms. Morgan to talk. There are two spells we can use. One would lure her to Java and Book. The second is an enchanted tea that would compel her to tell the truth. What do you think?" Elle bit her lower lip as she waited for Caden's response. She wasn't sure what Caden would think of her plan.

"Yeah, no, that sounds good. When do you plan on doing this?"

"As soon as possible."

"Do you need me to help with anything?"

"Can you be there too?"

"Of course. Whatever support you need."

She smiled at his reassurance and hung up.

Standing in her sanctuary, she was nervous. She felt clumsy and lost. She lit incense and meditated while holding a red jasper stone to stabilize her energy. When she finished, she felt very connected to Mozelle and was confident her plan would work.

Elle collected a white candle, Ms. Morgan's yearbook photo, citronella oil, lemongrass, and a quartz crystal. She carved "Lyndsey come to Java and Book" onto the white candle, then rubbed the candle with citronella oil. She folded the yearbook photo, placed it in a ceramic bowl, added lemongrass and a couple drops of the oil, then lit it on fire. Holding her quartz crystal close to her third eye, she chanted:

"I APPEAL to thy guides of influence:
  Compel Lyndsey Morgan to come to Java and Book
  Over a curiosity that will drive her to take a look.
  She will come about an opportunity
  And upon arrival, drink my enchanted tea.
  Organic conversation will flow
  And she'll tell us the things she doesn't want us to know."

FOR THE TEA, she collected ground cloves, mint, lemongrass, ginger, cinnamon, rosemary, and lavender. She mixed all the ingredients and placed them in a coffee filter that she tied with twine, then chanted:

"I HONOR thy beholders of faithfulness:
  This tea is to compel to speak truth from a teller of lies.
  Lyndsey has fooled Rikki and Quinn with her disguise.
  The two of them are hand-fasted and eternal soul mates,

SHE LOOKED at a photo of Mozelle. *Now I have to just wait for her to take the bait. Why am I questioning if this is the right thing to do?* She felt conflicted because she was uncertain what made her different than Ms. Morgan. "Motivation," she said out loud to herself. She and Ms. Morgan were on opposite sides of the good versus evil spectrum. Pride came over her as she recognized that what she was doing was for the common good.

THE DAY after Rikki's run-in with Sienna, Rikki hung her head low as she entered Ms. Morgan's class with a transfer request in hand. She'd decided to surrender her pride and ask to be moved to another course.

"Oh, Rikki. I'm so sorry that you're having a difficult time. There's nothing *I* can do for you. It's not really up to me. It's up to admin. And I'm positive they will deny you." She leaned and held out her hand to list the reasons why. "We're several weeks in, you need a social science to graduate, last I looked, the other classes that would fit the bill are full, and I know you—having to play catch up this late in the game would be really stressful." She scrunched her face, but there was condescension behind her expression. It was as if she took delight in Rikki's disappointment over being stuck in her class.

Rikki slammed her backpack onto her desk. "I tried," Rikki conceded to Quinn and Sienna. With her jaw set, she slumped into her chair and dug through her backpack for her notebook.

"You really should be the ones to leave if I'm that much of a threat to you," she said without looking at them.

"You think that's the reason we asked you to leave this class?" Sienna laughed.

"It's just that you're just a reminder of my blindness," Quinn admitted.

Rikki turned to Quinn. "It's just that," Rikki mimicked, "you remind me that that's not my problem," Rikki snapped back.

Ms. Morgan cleared her throat, looking pointedly at Rikki. When she finally had everyone's attention, she explained that the South America unit would be coming to an end in the next week.

Elle raised her hand. "Ms. Morgan, what got you interested in mythology and folklore?"

<hr>

LYNDSEY NEVER GOT questions like that. Most people came and went in her life with no interest in who she was or what made her tick, so she indulged herself in the moment. "It's an interesting story because it wasn't something I had a strong interest in when I was younger. I, um, I lost my parents in a fire, as most of you might know," she said. "So I went to live with my grandparents, who have been all over the world. I was fascinated by all the rare artifacts they collected and displayed. One piece struck me in particular. It was this beautiful hourglass that intrigued me. So I went to Stanford's anthropology department to see if anyone knew about this amazing timepiece. Anyway, I met August Cariso." She paused and thought about him—about how much she'd loved him—then realized she'd just been silent while everyone looked at her. "Sorry." She shook her head to move on.

"Oh, Ms. Morgan, you were in love with him?" a student pried.

She hesitated. "We had some good times. But basically, he told me about the significance of the hourglass, and before I knew it, I was on my way to the Amazon to deliver the piece to a tribe who had been missing it for forty years or so. Anyway, the experience was so amazing that I decided to devote my life to learning about cultures, myth, folklore, rituals, and even magic," she said, wiggling her fingers to the class. The whole class was captivated by her story. They wanted to know more, but some of those memories were too painful, so she stopped there.

Elle and Caden looked at each other, wide-eyed as if they'd had the same thought.

"August?" Elle mouthed to Caden. He shrugged.

After class, Ms. Morgan stopped Elle. "Hey. Do you have *Trees Through the Forest* by August Cariso at the café? I think there's more to the title, something about the Amazon. I can't really remember, but he talks about witchcraft. I figured you might have it."

"Maybe. Let me text my mom, and she can check," Elle said.

"Okay. I can even swing by sometime today," Ms. Morgan said. A slight smile emerged that lit up her face. "Man, I haven't thought about him in some time. I would love to read that book again."

"Um, sure. I'll be there at 4:30 today," she said and looked down at her phone. "My mom has one in stock called *Trees Through the Forest: An Examination of Myths and Folklore of the Amazon*, by August Cariso."

"That's the one," she said as if surprised and impressed. "I guess this means I'll be stopping by later."

"Sounds good." When Ms. Morgan walked away, Elle turned

and mouthed, "OMG!" to Caden, who mouthed, "I know!" right back.

"What are the odds? I swear that wasn't planned," she said, raising her eyebrow in surprise. "So, can you come to the café at 4:30 tonight?"

"You never need to ask."

After school, Rikki sat in her car, mindlessly watching students leave the parking lot as it dwindled to just a few cars. She finally blinked and closed her mouth, not knowing how long she had been frozen in place.

Flashes of Quinn holding her tight after he professed his love to her that day at the lake popped in her head. As if against her will, she texted, *Hi*, to him.

Two minutes went by. It went unread.

Her head slumped down in defeat. "Why can't I let go?!" she shouted at herself while gripping the steering wheel as if she could choke it. She pressed her head to it, hoping the physical pain would replace her emotional pain.

It didn't.

When she got home, she dragged herself through the front door.

Her mom came to her and held her. "I know it hurts, and nothing I say can make it better, but one day, you will meet the right person, and it will all make sense."

"I can't imagine that. I mean, Mom, our connection was spiritual. It was bigger than us. And he just flips a switch? I'm mean, he professed his love for me! I'm so confused."

"So, do you think something else is going on?"

"No. I guess not. I was fooled because I opened my heart so wide and so blindly. I thought that he was the one, Mom. I know I'm young, and he's my first love, but I felt it down to my core."

"I'm so sorry you're in so much pain. I wish I could just put a Band-Aid on it," her mom said with sadness in her voice.

I don't want a Band-Aid. I want Quinn.

Rikki nodded her head and cried. She wondered if she was going to dry up for all the crying she'd done.

***

ELLE GOT to the café at four to prepare for Ms. Morgan's arrival. She located August's book and laid it on the counter. Then she hurried down to her temple room to grab the infused teabag. She stopped when she saw a quartz crystal on top of her altar. She picked it up and held both the crystal and the tea bag to her chest, then closed her eyes, sending positive vibes to enhance its strength—something she recalled practicing another lifetime ago, and it brought a smile to her face.

Caden arrived at 4:15 and hung out at the counter. "Don't be nervous. You'll be fine."

Elle paced and fidgeted in anticipation. Her breath caught every time someone walked in.

"You've got this," Caden encouraged.

Ms. Morgan arrived just after 4:30 to find the book already waiting for her on the counter. She picked it up with a deep look of fondness. "Thanks for having this ready for me," she said, her fingers moving over the title.

"Of course!" Elle paused. "Let me get you some tea. It's on the house."

"Okay. Sure." Lyndsey sat at the counter and studied the front and back covers. She paused longest on August's photo and let out a sad sigh.

"Here you go." Elle laid the tea in front of her, then looked at

Caden. Eye contact was all she needed for reassurance. He nodded, then looked at Ms. Morgan.

She held the cup with both hands and blew across the top. She lowered her head as if taking in the aroma, closed her eyes, and took a sip.

A tingling sensation radiated from Elle's hands to her head – there was no turning back. So what do you think of the tea?" Elle asked.

"It's a bit heavy on the cinnamon. Do you have raw sugar?"

"Sure," Elle said, turning her back to her, smirking at Ms. Morgan's honesty as she pulled down the canister of raw sugar. She poured some in another teacup, so Ms. Morgan could add to her liking, and placed it in front of her teacher. "So that's the man you went to Brazil with?"

"Yes, it is. 'Course, he's about twenty years younger in this photo. He's probably fat and gray now, but back then, *oof*. He was hot."

"You were in love with him?"

"I was. But it was unrequited."

"Damn, I feel ya," Caden said sincerely, then looked up to see them both looking at him. His face turned bright red. "Did I say that out loud?" He raked his hands through his hair.

Elle snorted at his innocent interjection that had warmed her from the inside out, then turned her attention back to Ms. Morgan. "That's too bad. Is he still at Stanford?" Elle asked.

"I don't know. I haven't spoken to him since Brazil. It's not that we had a falling out, but it was clear that he didn't feel the same way I did. I don't know, sometimes I think about reaching out to him. He helped me get through my self-hatred. I used to be ashamed of my scars, and he helped me believe that I'm still a good person," she said while looking at her reflection in her tea. She stared at herself as if momentarily lost in thought. "Your great-aunt made me a tea similar to this one, years ago. My mom was taking me to school when she had a seizure and crashed the car. When I came home from the hospital, Mozelle gave me a tea that calmed me down. It was nice, but then things got all screwed up." Ms. Morgan took another sip.

"I just want you to know that there's no hard feelings on my end if you want to talk about them. You can just let me know if I'm being rude for prying."

"Thank you for that. I don't want to hold it against you. The anger I feel is mainly toward my mother for having an affair and Mozelle for encouraging it."

"Oh, I didn't know that," Elle lied. Hearing Ms. Morgan use Mozelle's name with bitterness made Elle shutter. Painful as that was, she was proud of herself that Ms. Morgan was playing into her trap.

"When my mom got sick, your great-aunt, who was my mom's best friend, became a caregiver for her. She worked alongside another nurse, who my grandpa hired. He was the nurse my mother had the affair with. I don't know how physical it was, but at the very least, it was emotional. My dad worked hard to provide, and that was the thanks he got?"

Caden eyed Ms. Morgan as she spoke of Chris. He pursed his lips and tilted his head as if bracing himself to hear, yet again, what a horrible person he was in his previous life.

"Perhaps he wasn't a great husband, but he was an amazing dad and provider. He didn't deserve to die. And I certainly didn't deserve to live in the hell that was created in their wake. Do you know the level of pain a burn victim goes through? It's unimaginable. The baths to scrape off the scabs, the special garments, and nerves that fire off unexpectedly or become numb—and why? Because my selfish mother, who I *did* love, took a lover in her remaining days? And so what? I'm just supposed to move on with my life? Just accept that the hell I've been through is nothing but an unintended mishap? It's infuriating, and I hate her for it."

"Wow. This is all very shocking. I'm so sorry," Elle said

sincerely. *Hearing this from her perspective is painful. Mozelle never thought to consider Lyndsey. She'd figured she would grieve the loss of her mother and move on.*

"When the fire happened, I was in the kitchen. The house was built into a hill, so when you entered the house, you were on the second floor, where the kitchen, living room, and main bedrooms were, and below were more rooms. When my mom got really sick, Mozelle moved into one of the bedrooms downstairs. At some point, she found out that my mom and this nurse guy, Wayne—no, Wade—were in love. And it wasn't like she discouraged it. It wasn't that she even ignored it. No, she decided to encourage it! I don't know why. Perhaps a dying woman's final wish. I'll never know. But it went beyond just encouraging the affair—she actually *married* the two of them. And still, that wasn't the worst of it. She performed a ritual in which she branded them as soulmates so they could find each other in their next life."

She's not wrong. Elle was starting to see Ms. Morgan in a different light. "I'm just blown away."

"So I'd been in the dining room with Wade, who was helping me with my homework when Mozelle came out and said my mom needed to talk to him. I remember being so happy that she was awake because it was near the end, and we thought that she would never wake up. I thought I would have a chance to talk to her at least one last time, to tell her I loved her and that I would be strong and brave. Anyway, after a few minutes, I saw Wade carry my mom downstairs. He told me that Mozelle was going to perform Reiki and that I should stay in the kitchen. It seemed strange to me because she had had a Reiki treatment earlier that day. So I called my dad." Lyndsey had a faraway look on her face when she paused for a moment. Then she took another long drink of her tea.

Elle gave her a refill as soon as Ms. Morgan put her cup down—encouraging her to drink more and stay a while longer.

"Then some freaky things started to happen. I was paralyzed and didn't know what to do. I was just thirteen at the time. My dad came rushing in and told me to stay upstairs. It seemed like seconds passed before the whole downstairs was on fire. I started to run downstairs to see what was happening, but I couldn't get to them. That's when the banister fell on me, and I got this *nasty* scar. I ran out of the house while I was still on fire and rolled under some bushes. I didn't know that all four of them had died until I stumbled upon their body bags on the way to find my parents."

Tears filled Elle's eyes. *Jesus—no wonder she's full of anguish.*

"You don't have to be sad. I appreciate your empathy, but it's all in the past." Ms. Morgan took a deep breath. "The interesting thing is that to this day, no one knows about the ritual. I figured it out because I was able to salvage two things." She counted with her fingers. "The journal Mozelle was reading during the ritual and a twinned crystal she used for their 'wedding' or whatever that was. Later, I worked up the courage to read through the journal. Even though some of it was burnt, a lot of it was readable, and that's how I figured out what happened."

"So that's why you were curious about the journal I was reading. Because it was probably from my great-aunt."

Ms. Morgan nodded her head. "I've carried that story with me for so long, and I've never told anyone. I'm sorry to have placed your great-aunt in a bad light, but she did a bad thing, and so did my mom, and many lives were changed as a result of it."

Elle swallowed reflexively. "I don't know what to say. Do you still have those things, the journal and the crystal?"

"Yes. I have them at home in my temple room."

"You have a temple room? Nice!" Her insides tensed from all the new details.

"I do. You should come by some time."

"That would be really cool. Thanks again for trusting us to

open up like that. You definitely cleared up things that have been a mystery in my family for a very long time."

"Of course. Can I take this book home with me? I'll bring it back in a couple days."

"Please, take it. It's yours."

"Great. I'll see you tomorrow," Ms. Morgan said. She slid her empty teacup to the edge of the counter and walked out with her head held high like a weight had been lifted.

THE MOMENT LYNDSEY stepped outside the café, an uneasiness came over her. She replayed what she'd said to Elle and was concerned that she'd overshared. It was as if she hadn't wanted to share that much, but was compelled to.

She eventually dismissed it as being paranoid. Caden and Elle had been genuinely interested and absent of any ulterior motives.

ELLE WATCHED Ms. Morgan drive off, then turned to Caden. "I don't even know where to start with this. My emotions are all over the place."

"How about congratulations on a successful enchantment?" It took everything he had not to run up to her and give her a huge hug.

"Thank you, Caden." She paused, then relaxed as if his kind words anchored her. "You're right. But I didn't expect both the journal *and* the crystal to survive. That crystal can break the curse. I remember it all now."

"How would it break the curse?"

"When the two of them are near it—or better yet, touch it— they will be reminded of their past life and why they love each other. They'll essentially get a download of Wade's and Robin's memories."

"Whoa. That's cool."

"Yes, so we need to get that crystal. Otherwise, it'll all be for nothing."

17

BACK TO SCHOOL NIGHT

The next day, Rikki woke up with a migraine and couldn't get out of bed. She grabbed her phone and saw a text from Quinn.

Lose my number.

Then she saw a text from a number she didn't recognize.

It was a photo of Quinn and Sienna kissing, with *I win* underneath it.

She never knew that there was something more painful than a migraine. "I hate him so fucking much!" She covered her mouth and ran to the bathroom to vomit. She felt like shit, but she wasn't sure if it was the migraine or Quinn. Either way, she was *not* going to go to school.

THE BELL RANG while Quinn and Sienna were still sitting in the school parking lot, taking turns putting eye drops in.

Quinn got a text from Caden. *Staff meeting at first break.*

"Shit," Quinn said.

"What?"

"I have to go to a staff meeting at first break. Sorry. It'll have to wait until later."

"That's okay. I'll go with you," Sienna told him.

"Okay," Quinn gladly agreed.

<hr>

CADEN'S MOUTH dropped open when both Quinn and Sienna walked into the newsroom giggling. *Something's off. He's never that giddy. Could they be high?*

He stood up from behind his desk. "What so funny?" Caden asked to test his theory.

"Shoehorns," they said at the same time.

"Honk honk," Quinn said in a high-pitched voice out the side of his mouth, and they both started laughing again.

Fucking Quinn. Exasperated, Caden raked his hand through his hair. "Okay. Well, um, Quinn, this is a staff meeting, and since Sienna is not on staff …" Caden trailed off, hoping Quinn would fill in the blanks.

Quinn just stared at him blankly.

Caden drew in a big sigh and scratched the back of his head. "It means she can't be here."

Sienna's exaggerated frown didn't help relieve Caden's anger. "I'll be right outside," Sienna said as if she was going to miss Quinn in the brief amount of time they'd be apart.

"Okay. He'll be out in fifteen minutes." Caden waved and flashed a condescending grin as he watched her leave the room. His eyes darted back to Quinn, who was still waving goodbye to her. "Really?" Caden questioned, his eyes wide in surprise, then took another deep breath. "Anyway, I'm hoping I don't regret this, but I have an odd request. Do you know how to pick a lock?"

"Actually, Sienna is better at that than I am."

"Wow, it's pretty sad that you know that." Caden shook his

head. "Um, yeah. I'll have to think about that. But for right now, you're my go-to."

"What's this for?" Quinn asked, then looked back at the window cutout on the door as if checking on Sienna. He blew out a sigh of relief when he saw her head popping up and down, stealing glimpses of what was going on in the newsroom.

"Jesus, Quinn! Focus!"

He turned around after blowing a kiss in her direction. "Sorry. I'm here. Go on."

Caden put his hands on his hips. "You're pissing me off."

"Sorry. Sorry. You have my undivided attention," Quinn said, then stood at attention.

"Uh-huh." Caden took a breath to settle his anger. "I need to get something from a friend's house. They borrowed something from me, but they went on vacation, and I need it now."

"What is it?"

"It's a key of sorts, but—"

"Ooh, a key," Quinn interrupted, then stared out in space like he was caught up in some sort of twisted Indiana Jones fantasy.

Caden grunted, "Focus, Quinn." Caden snapped his fingers and waited for Quinn to return to the conversation.

Quinn shook his head. "Sorry."

"Maybe this is a bad idea."

"No. Please, I want to help," Quinn said, then pulled up a chair to give Caden the attention he deserved.

"Okay, because you can't fuck this up."

"I promise."

"Fine. All you need to do is get me through the door. You don't even have to stay."

"When?"

"Wednesday at 5:30. I'll send you the address."

"Okay, but it might be me *and* Sienna who come."

"You can bring the whole fucking football team if it means I can get through that door quickly. But don't actually bring the whole football team. You get my point." Caden paused. "You *do* get what I'm saying, right?"

"Yeah, right. Just me and maybe Sienna."

"Geez, Quinn, I really need you sober for this."

"You have my word," he promised.

After the meeting, Caden ran into Elle before Ms. Morgan's class. "Did you get my text?"

"I did. Sorry I haven't responded, but I think the Back to School Night thing would work. How are we going to break in?"

"Sienna and Quinn—you know, the school delinquents. Surprise, surprise, they know how to pick locks. Well, she does more than him."

Elle's lips twisted, and she crossed her arms. "Sounds risky."

"They won't know it's Ms. Morgan's house. I lied and told him I need to get something back from a friend who's on vacation."

Elle's arms remained crossed as if still uncertain.

"Seriously, he was high when he came in today. I could have told him I needed a wooden stake to kill a vampire, and he would have bought it," Caden added. "Man, I can't wait until this is over. Wasted Quinn is damn irritating. But I did tell him he needs to be sober and that they can leave after they get the door open."

"Once we get the crystal, how do we get them together?" Elle asked.

"I think the greenhouse would be perfect, like what happened to us. But rather than poisonous leaves, they'll have the crystal."

"Ooh, I like that idea," Elle said. Her eyes shifted from left to right as if she was building on Caden's idea.

"What?"

"Just let me put more thought into it," Elle said and nudged him into class.

Lyndsey's stomach dropped as Caden and Elle entered her classroom. Recalling how she'd overshared that night at Java and Book pained her. *I told them too much. My gut is firing off all kinds of warnings. I can't tell if something bad is happening or if this is because I shared something so personal with my students. I could just kick myself. What came over me?*

By mid-morning, Rikki regretted staying home. Her boredom led her down memory lane, and she missed Quinn terribly and hated herself for it. It was wrong. She tried to hold on to the words her mother had told her. *Pain is part of the grieving process. It will start to get better. But what's preventing you from moving forward is feeling guilty over wanting him back, even after all the crap he pulled. It's normal when you first breakup to focus on the good and justify the bad, but the sooner you realize that you're better than that, the sooner the true healing process can begin.*

Back to School Night was only a couple hours away, and Caden and Elle were parked down the street from Ms. Morgan's house. Caden watched through binoculars as Ms. Morgan pulled out of her driveway. He texted Quinn her address, which he'd gotten after paying on an online people search site.

They waited for traffic to die down before exiting their car and heading to the house. Once there, fearing their presence would look suspicious, they crouched behind the hedges that obscured the front door from the street as they waited for Quinn and Sienna.

"They should be here any minute," Caden whispered to Elle.

"I'm not sure if you noticed the door on the side of the house, but I think that'll be the best door to go through."

"Sounds good," Elle whispered back.

Quinn and Sienna walked up the driveway. Caden exhaled in relief when he saw they were clear-eyed. "Okay, let's move," Caden said, his voice still low. They snuck around to the side of the house and unlatched the iron gate.

QUINN STARTED WORKING the lock as Sienna directed him. Progression into the next phase of their plan sounded with a click. Quinn stood up with a proud smile on his face and opened the door to a mudroom. For the briefest of moments, Quinn saw a flash of a radiant Rikki standing by the bay the night they kissed. He gasped as he tried to catch his breath, then shook his head to regain focus. *What the hell was that?* He looked at Sienna to see if she'd noticed his unexplained reaction.

"Everything okay?" Sienna asked.

"Of course," he said and kissed her for reassurance, uncertain as to who needed it more, him or her.

CADEN AND ELLE moved past the two of them. "Thanks. We'll catch you later," Caden dismissed.

The smell of musky incense was overpowering, and there was no escaping it no matter where you were in the house. It was a wonder that Ms. Morgan didn't smell like incense when she was at school. As soon as they crossed over the threshold, they felt like they'd entered a vortex of darkness, depression, and loneliness. They crept down a hallway with dull, mustard-yellow walls bare of any photos or art. Dirt seemed to have piled on from years of neglect. On the right was a family room with more seating than Ms. Morgan probably had friends. On the left was the first of two bedrooms. It was as bare as a classroom during summer break, completely absent of life. The walls were a flat white that yearned for love and attention. In between the bedrooms was a bathroom that had dirt and black gunk surrounding the sink, toilet, and tub.

"What the hell?" Caden squinted his face in disgust.

It all changed when they entered the second bedroom. It was the liveliest of all the rooms, yet the most disturbing. It was her temple room and clearly belonged to someone with vile intentions. The artifacts that she had collected in her travels exuded malevolence. Creepy masks hung on the dark red walls, and figurines of twisted gargoyles were strategically placed around the room. Pentagrams, black candles, and glass drams of people's personal things were lined up along the windowsill. The closet had a small shrine with a pewter hourglass but was relatively plain compared to what was embossed on Mozelle's journal. It was surrounded by shelves of candles, incense, herbs, a wand, crystals, and oils.

Elle stood in place and held her arm out to stop Caden from moving as well. "This room is protected. Don't touch or move anything unless absolutely necessary. We just need to find the crystal and leave."

"This feels like some kind of modern-day Indiana Jones kinda shit. Are the walls armed with poison darts if we remove the crystal?" Caden asked, only kind of joking as he studied the walls.

"Probably not," Elle replied, distracted.

"*Probably?*" Caden shouted.

"Shhh. No. There are no poison darts. But if she suspects, she could ask the right question to the right source, and it would be revealed to her who was here."

"This is not good, Elle. Not good."

"Look harder, Caden."

They both looked and tried not to touch anything. Elle spotted the journal as if it beckoned her. She removed it from the shelf and began taking photos of the sections they needed.

Caden stood in her closet, glancing at all the items on the shelves. "I'm going to have to move some things. I don't think the crystal is in plain sight," Caden said like he was asking permission.

"If you don't have a choice."

"Don't you have that ability to locate things?"

"Yes, but mainly in places I'm familiar with or for a friend. And even then, it's not a hundred percent."

Caden saw a pewter jewelry box and opened it with care. Purple velvet covered the box's contents. "I think I found it," Caden said and gingerly walked the box over. He waited for her before removing the fabric. She clung onto him, not knowing what to expect, as he slowly peeled the velvet away. There it was —the crystal—untouched and pristine.

Elle closed her eyes, and a flash of Robin and Wade appeared in her mind. The flashes were of memories she'd never witnessed, as if the crystal was giving her a gift for liberating it. She saw Wade holding Robin as he helped her out of the car. She saw Robin's face light up when Wade came to her in the garden. She saw Wade carrying Robin as rain poured down on them, their emotions palpable. Tears of both happiness and sadness swelled, but it was when she saw the two of them during the handfasting ceremony, how he held her and looked deeply into her eyes while their world around them disappeared, that the tears broke free, and she began to sob.

Caden wrapped his arms around her. "I get it," Caden admitted. "I know why Mozelle did what she did. It went beyond wanting to be together. They *need* to be together."

Elle nodded her head against his chest as relief came over her. "Oh, Caden," she said as she nuzzled further into him.

He held her tighter, gently rocking. "Come on. We're taking a risk staying here." He pulled his head back to gauge how she was doing.

Elle looked up at him. It was like being back in the greenhouse. They were having a moment, and they both knew it, and they just stood there, allowing it to happen. Caden swallowed hard as he swept a tear off her cheek, then took a deep breath and released her. They both took a dizzying step back.

Caden turned and took the crystal from the box. He replaced it with a lightweight polished rock that had been hidden away as if exiled from the rest. He placed the velvet back over it and, ever so carefully, put it back. He took Elle's hand, and they snuck out the way they'd come in.

On Lyndsey's drive home from Back to School Night, she couldn't let go of something Elle's mother, Farrah, had said to her about her daughter.

"I have concerns that this class is influencing Elle to follow in my aunt's footsteps," Farrah complained.

Lyndsey didn't know what to do with that. "And what path is that?"

"You know, 'witchcraft,'" Farrah said using air quotes.

"Well, I can assure you I don't teach witchcraft." Not "how to" anyway, *she thought. "I merely tell stories, discuss customs, and encourage tolerance," Lyndsey explained. "Has she said that I teach witchcraft?"*

"No, but since taking this class, she's started to obsess over my aunt's magic and esoterica."

"Okay. What does that look like? Like, has she joined a coven, has

her behavior changed, or is she just looking at things?" Lyndsey asked but could hear interrogation in her voice.

"I just see her going down into Mozelle's old room at the café too often. To honor my aunt, we've left it untouched, but I'm thinking of packing it all up."

"Wow, there's another room at the café?" Lyndsey's eyes lit up, knowing she'd hit the motherload. The remaining journals must be there.

"Yes, well, it's more like a basement."

"Oh, okay. Well, she's doing great in class, but if you'd like, I can stop by, and you can show me the room and, I'll give you my opinion." Lyndsey poured all her energy to get Farrah to say 'yes.'

"You're always welcome at the café," Farrah said, sincerely.

"I appreciate that. But listen, my experience with kids this age is that they're trying on different interests to see what fits. That being said, if it seems like she's talking to 'spirits,' or burning incense, or collecting herbs—things like that—she might be practicing. And it's a personal choice how you want to handle that, but please understand, I don't even talk *about witchcraft in my classes." That wasn't a* complete *lie.*

As she pulled into her driveway, Lyndsey redirected her thoughts to having a glass of wine and reading August's book. She choked as she entered her home. The energy had been defiled. Holding her breath, she glanced around to spot clues as to who the violator was. The disturbing presence was so pronounced that she grabbed a silver candlestick and proceeded to check if the miscreant was still there. The instant she stepped foot into her temple room, the candlestick slipped from her hand. She grabbed her hair at her temples—this room was the most desecrated, and yet everything was exactly how she'd left it. The remaining spectral signatures—two to be exact—still lingered, and her mind went straight to her students. Caden and Elle, more precisely. The timing of her unintended confession to them could not be ignored. She swung open the door to her closet and snatched the pewter jewelry box. She flung open the lid and let out a deep sigh of relief. The velvet cover was still there, covering the crystal. Even though nothing seemed to have been taken, the landscape of the game was changing, and she was going to have to reassess who she was really dealing with.

———

AFTER SCHOOL THE NEXT DAY, Quinn and Sienna were hanging out in her truck in front of Quinn's house. "Where's the bud?" Quinn asked her.

"Look at you," Sienna said as if trying to embarrass him. "I'm always the one to encourage *you*," she continued. She tilted her head at him. "Is there something bothering you?"

Quinn needed to rid himself of the image of Rikki in his head. *I can't shake the vision of her. She hates me just as much as I hate her, so get a grip.*

"I think we should mess with Rikki," Quinn suggested as he lit up the joint.

"I'm kind of over the whole Rikki thing. Aren't you? Why are you still focused on her?" Sienna asked. There was accusation in her tone.

"I'm not focused on her. I just think it's fun, and she's an easy target." Quinn's voice was high-pitched.

"Okay."

"Okay? Like now you're okay with it?" Quinn asked. *The sooner I face this, the better.*

"Sure, why not. What did you have in mind?"

"I don't know, but let's go to her house. I'll figure something out," Quinn said with a sinister smirk.

When they arrived at Rikki's house, the gate on the side of the house was ajar. He slipped through the opening, but as Sienna tried to sneak through, she bumped the gate, triggering it to auto-close, locking them both in the backyard.

They both stopped for a second to see if anyone would catch them. They heard nothing but music coming from Rikki's upstairs bedroom. They quietly moved under her window, and Quinn picked up a small rock and threw it at the glass.

RIKKI THOUGHT she heard something hit her window. She paused Billie Eilish's "Lovely" and looked outside but didn't see anything. She turned away when another rock struck her window. She threw open her curtain—nothing. She remained at her window to see if it would happen again. Her mouth dropped when she saw Quinn and Sienna collecting rocks and throwing them at her window.

She slid the window open. "What the fuck, Quinn? Stop being an asshole and leave, or I swear I'll call the police!"

From out of nowhere, Sienna ran up to Quinn and began kissing him, and he responded aggressively. Still lip-locked, he looked up at Rikki as if to gauge his success at hurting her. A sinister squint emerged like he was proud of the results.

Rikki shook her head as she rolled her eyes and closed her window.

QUINN DISENGAGED FROM SIENNA. *She can't just roll her eyes and walk away from this. I'm not through with you. You invade my thoughts. I'll invade yours!*

He moved Sienna aside, then picked up a large rock and threw it, shattering Rikki's window.

Bitch! Stay out of my head!

BROKEN GLASS FLEW PAST RIKKI, slicing her shoulder. She gasped in pain as she slapped her hand over the wound that immediately began to ooze blood. "Son of a bitch!" she grunted. "This hurts. Are you trying to kill me?"

Enraged, she tore down the stairs and flung open the door. "You're not getting away, you fuck!"

QUINN FELT pain like he had when Sienna was hurting Rikki. It was centered near his birthmark, and the vibrations grew strong. "Shit!" he said, his breathing temporarily strained.

"Let's get out of here," Sienna said, and started to run, then turned and saw Quinn still standing there, grasping his shoulder. "Come on, hurry!" Sienna yelled as she tugged at Quinn.

They twisted the knob of the gate, but it was locked.

"Shit! It must have locked when it closed. Let's just jump it," Quinn suggested. As if on its own, the gate unlatched, and they were freed.

Their laughing over their liberation was cut short when they were met with blazing eyes full of fury. Rikki was in a rage.

Her breathing was heavy as blood streamed down her arm. "Look what you've done," she said through gritted teeth. She pulled down the strap of her shirt and showed the laceration.

Quinn froze when he saw something on her chest just under her collarbone. It looked like his star, but it was covered in blood, and his weed-laden vision prevented confirmation.

Rikki saw his look. "Sooo? What the hell are you going to do about it?"

"Here we go again with the theatrics. What? You want us to pay for it?" Sienna bit.

"Are you *stupid?*" Rikki asked. "Quinn, is she stupid?" Rikki just stood there and stared at them.

Sienna scoffed. "Whatever. Let's go," she said and tugged at him again.

As Quinn passed her, Rikki stopped him with her bloody hand, leaned in, and whispered in his ear, "I wish you would just fuck off and die."

He looked into her eyes and saw that not only was she serious, but they lacked connection anymore. She had let go. That vision of her flashed again in his mind. He tried to stop himself from holding on to it, but failed.

***

Rikki saw a brief look of horror and guilt on his face, and then it went away. "What the fuck are you looking at? Can't you feel her tugging your leash? Are you stupid too?"

Rikki's dad stormed outside. "What's going on?"

Quinn's face drained of color at the sight of her father's anger. He turned his head as if making sure Sienna was still there, but she was halfway down the street. He swallowed hard. "We ... we were messing around, sir, and I accidentally broke Rikki's window," Quinn said, then lowered his head. "I apologize, and I'll pay for replacing it and any other costs." Quinn surprisingly sounded sincere.

Her father protectively pulled Rikki behind him. Standing tall, he invaded Quinn's personal space. "You did more than just break her window," he growled. "Are you okay, sweetheart?" he asked, maintaining his intimidating stance.

"I...I don't know." Her voice was small.

He gave Quinn a death stare, then turned toward Rikki. "Let's take a look at the cut."

She pulled her shirt sleeve down again, and Quinn strained his neck as if he wanted to see how bad the cut was.

"What the hell are you doing? Admiring your handiwork?" Rikki's dad snapped.

"No, sir. I was just looking to see—"

"See what?" Rikki yelled.

"Leave now before I call the police," James said through gritted teeth.

Quinn turned around and left.

"It doesn't look like you'll need stitches, but let's get you cleaned up."

Rikki and her dad moved to the kitchen sink, where he took a cloth and cleaned the wound. He placed a bandage over her arm as Rikki lost herself in thought.

"What are you thinking about?" her dad asked.

"Nothing. It's just this whole Quinn thing is … I don't know. Something's not right. I don't recognize him, especially since *she* came into the picture. Sometimes when he looks at me, it's like he's looking *through* me. His feelings didn't just go from 'I love you' to 'I'm no longer interested.' They went to 'I loathe you,' but I didn't *do* anything to him. Like just now, he was being an asshole—" She saw her father look up at her. "Just calling it like it is. But you know, for a split second, there was this look in his eyes he was *there* again. Like a look of panic and shame, and then it went back to vacant."

"What are you trying to say?" James asked as he continued to wrap the bandage around her arm.

"I think he's having some kind of emotional crisis that he doesn't have control over." She paused. "I don't know. I'm trying to move on, but when I saw that look in his eyes… I just don't know. Whatever battles he's dealing with, I hope he works it out soon."

"All I could say is that until he does, you need to stay away from him."

"I'm trying to, but he keeps showing up."

"Sorry, I must have left the gate open. I didn't notice him coming in," her dad said as he finished applying the bandage.

"It's fine, Dad. Thanks," She stood tall and kissed him on the cheek.

OON THURSDAY BEFORE SCHOOL, Elle and Caden met up in the newsroom.

"Okay, so you're going to text Quinn to meet you at the greenhouse after school, and I'll do the same with Rikki," Elle directed. "Then we get the key from Kevin the Custodian? Right?" Elle confirmed.

"Well, he'll unlock the doors for me, but he won't give me the key."

"Of course. And also, remember to collect their cell phones before going in. Say something like the sprinklers might come on and ruin their phones," Elle instructed.

Caden nodded as he followed along. "The next hurdle is, according to the ritual, they need to have rose oil on their hands to activate the crystal. How would they know to put rose oil?"

"It's not required, but it's more effective if they do, and since there's no room for failure, we'll just have to get them to put the rose oil on before they go in." They laid out the rest of their plan, determined to save their friends. "My goal is to get them to grab the crystal at the same time. Might not be exact, but it'll be close. This probably goes without saying, but we need to standby at first if it looks like they will kill each other. At that point, we'll step in and try something else. I just think that making this as organic as possible will be far more effective, and we'll get a lot less resistance, but I'm open to suggestions."

"Well, I'm impressed. I've got nothing," Caden admitted. "I think it'll be fine."

"Alright, then. Tomorrow it is!" Elle made fists. "Let's do this!"

"Yep. You're the lifesaver," he said and flashed a smile that made Elle blush.

Friday after school, Caden had Quinn meet him in the newsroom.

"So what do you need? A crystal? And it's in the greenhouse?" Quinn asked as he stood before Caden's desk.

"Yes. It's for a story I'm working on. I just need you to photograph it, but the deadline is 4:30. Otherwise, I'll have to fill it with something boring, like library dues or some shit like that. I'll walk you over there now."

"Can Sienna come?"

"No!" Caden shot down. "Which reminds me—you'll have to leave your phone outside because there is an automatic sprinkler system, and I don't know the schedule."

"Can't I just put it in my pocket?" Quinn asked. He was very uncomfortable with leaving his phone behind.

"Do you really want to take that risk? It's just a few minutes. I can wait outside while you do this, sheesh!" Caden shook his head, his eyes wide.

Quinn grabbed his equipment and a camera hood in case the sprinklers went off, then left with Caden to the greenhouse.

Caden texted Elle. *I feel like this should be called Operation something or other. Lol. On our way. Wait five minutes.*

Rikki was at her locker, packing her books for the night when she noticed Elle quickly texting.

"Everything okay?" Rikki asked.

"Umm, yeah. Actually, I need a huge favor from you, and I think it's going to help Quinn," Elle said. "I found out that Mr.

Croft has a rare crystal collection, and I believe one of the crystals can help Quinn. I know that Mr. Croft just used the crystal for a demonstration, but I don't know where in the greenhouse he left it after his lesson. I can't get it because you have to be the last person to touch it for the ritual to work.

"Wow. Really? Okay. I'll take care of that," Rikki said, glad she could do Elle a favor. "I hope for his sake it works."

"Oh, I'm pretty certain it will." She chuckled. "I'll walk you to the greenhouse now. It also requires that I put rose oil on your hands, and here's the box to put the crystal in, so you don't have to worry about anyone touching it."

Rikki took the box. "Sounds good."

Elle texted something that made her smile.

18

THE GREENHOUSE EFFECT

uinn was struck with another vision as he and Caden neared the greenhouse. It was the woman from his dream holding out her palm with the eight-pointed star on it. *What was that mark on Rikki's chest the other day? What if it was a star, like mine?* Shame flooded his body, and he stopped, shaking his head, hoping that would throw it out of his mind. The vision dissolved.

"You okay?" Caden asked.

Quinn nodded. "Yeah," he said, and they continued walking.

As they stood at the door to the greenhouse, Caden put his hand out. Quinn reluctantly put the phone in his hand.

"And why the oil again?" Quinn asked while Caden sprinkled the rose oil on his palms.

"Because it doesn't like human oils."

"Ah. Okay. And where is it?" he asked, rubbing his hands together. He looked at his hands, impressed that they were still pretty dry.

"I'm not totally sure. I think it's toward the back. Just look for it. It shouldn't be too hard to find."

"Okay. I'll see you back at the newsroom." He grabbed his camera bag and faded into the beauty of the foliage.

<hr>

ELLE APPROACHED the greenhouse with Rikki a few minutes later.

"Hey, Caden," Rikki said.

"Hey, Rikki. Thanks for helping Elle out. I would help, but you know, this greenhouse and I have a history," he said with a mocking grin on his face.

"I'll never get over that, Caden," Rikki said, guilt evident in her voice.

Elle took Rikki's phone, citing the same reasons that Caden had. Elle added a drop of rose oil to Rikki's hands, then advised her that time was of the essence.

Once Rikki had passed through the doorway, Elle and Caden looked at each other and smiled. "They have no idea what's in store for them," Caden said.

"I feel like a proud parent," Elle said with a chuckle.

<hr>

RIKKI ENTERED the greenhouse and was struck hard with vibrations. She quickly retreated back to the entrance.

"What's going on?" Elle asked when she cracked open the door, panic in her voice.

"Quinn is here," Rikki whispered.

"So?" Elle mimicked her whisper.

"So I don't want to face him."

"Rikki, I really need you to do this for me so we can help Quinn. It's really, *really* important," Elle said, raising her voice just a bit.

"What if he's in here with *what's her face*, and they're, like, having sex?"

"Hey, Rikki," Caden interjected. "I saw Quinn go inside, and he was alone."

"Why is he in here?"

"I don't know, but please, please do this for me," Elle begged.

"What if *what's her face* shows up?"

"She won't. She's busy at the moment," Caden said, raising his eyebrows with a devious smile.

"Fine!" Rikki said as loud as a whisper could go. She turned back around in a huff and began her quest.

QUINN STOPPED for a moment when he felt the vibration of Rikki coming closer. He ducked and hid behind a tree in a planter. "Shit!" he whispered to himself. He spotted her and saw that she was looking for something. *Is she looking for the same thing?* "Shit, shit!" He scouted out his next move.

RIKKI COULD FEEL that Quinn was close, but she still didn't see him. She wondered if he was avoiding her. *Damn it! Why is he here? It couldn't be for the same reason, could it?* She shook her head to remove the paranoid thought.

A loud tone sounded, and the ceiling windows started to close. Rikki looked around to see if the sprinklers were going to start, but when the windows began to close, she panicked. "Shit!" she called out and ran as fast as she could toward the entrance.

Quinn flew past her, the echoing sounds of finality prompting him to pick up the pace. He reached for the bar to freedom on the door, but his efforts were in vain. The green-house was locked for the night.

"Fuck!" he yelled, yanking on the door and slapping his hand on its window.

Rikki started banging on the window, calling out to Elle. Quinn joined in and yelled for Caden.

CADEN AND ELLE were in Mr. Croft's classroom, watching the drama unfold before them on the CCTV. They even broke out the popcorn and sodas. All they had to do now was sit back and watch their brilliant plan unfold.

QUINN PUT down his camera bag and turned to Rikki. "Tell me, why are you here?" he demanded.

"I was looking for something. Why are *you* here?" Rikki demanded back.

"I was hoping to harvest some tulips."

"Uh-huh, in September? And you need your camera for that —why?"

"Because … tulips in September!" he cited, with a conde-scending smirk on his face.

They glared into each other's eyes. That was all the confir-mation they needed before they tore back down the path. "I need that crystal more than you do, Quinn!"

"I need it to meet a deadline. And stop saying my name!"

"What deadline? It doesn't look like you're getting out of here anytime soon," Rikki said, then realized her own doom.

"Caden will come looking for me and let me out," Quinn said as if to purposely exclude her from the rescue.

"Let just *you* out?"

"Sorry, sister, you're on your own."

They searched over, under, through, and in between planters, pots, trays, and beds, and came up with nothing.

"Stop!" Rikki yelled, winded.

"What?" Quinn asked, out of breath as well.

"When I find it, I'll let you take a couple pics, and then you have to give it back to me. It's really, *really* important. Deal?"

Quinn stopped for a moment and looked her up and down as he considered what she asked. He crossed his arms and rubbed under his chin. "Hmmm," he contemplated. "I want you to take off your top," Quinn said, out of the blue.

"What the fuck?"

"I need to see something," he said, spinning his finger at her chest.

"Hell no!" She could feel her face turn red with anger. "I want you to listen to the words coming out of my mouth," she said, exaggerating her words. "I would never, ever, *ever* give you the satisfaction of *ever* seeing what's under this." She moved her hands down her body in a way that she knew was damn sexy, regardless of what Quinn currently thought of her. "If you ask me again, I'll finish you the way I wanted the first time we met."

"*Oooh!*" Quinn said sarcastically, complete with shaking hands.

She turned away from him. With her hands on her hips, she assessed what she had already covered and decided looking along the floor would be a fresh direction. She got down on all fours and started crawling to continue searching for the crystal. "If only Sienna knew what you just asked me. I think she'd freak out." Rikki imagined Sienna's face when she learned of Quinn's proposition.

"I don't think she'd care," he said as if that was a good thing.

"Really, Quinn? I've said this before, and I'll say it again —*her*? Really?"

"Just shut up, and let's find this thing."

"I'm just saying that if you were to aim higher, you would end up with trash. No, worse. You would end up with the insects that eat the trash." She paused and laughed. "No, no, wait! You would end up with the shit-eating decomposers that feed off the insects that eat the trash."

"Rikki, you bitch! Shut the hell up!"

"Shit-eating decomposers," she said under her breath and started cracking up.

Suddenly, the heavy weight of potting soil fell onto her head. She looked up and saw Quinn standing there with an empty container. Rikki shot to her feet. She was no longer laughing. She looked around to retaliate and found a hose with a trigger nozzle.

"Fuck you, Rikki, if you do that! I have my phone on me!" Quinn held his hands up. "I swear to you, I—". Water hit him square in the mouth. He was knocked back but not knocked down, and the second he got his bearings again, he charged her, tackling her to the ground. They were face to face. Water dripped off his honey-blond hair onto her face. She grunted as she tried to free herself from him. She looked around for something to defend herself with, and just as she was turning back to spit in his face, he took soil and rubbed it all over her face. She kneed him in the crotch. He rolled off her, holding himself in pain. As she sprung up to run away, he grabbed hold of her ankle. She refused to let him take her down again. A trowel was on the table, and she stretched to get a hold of it, but he had a vice grip on her ankle. With every ounce of strength, she pulled her leg, and he let go. Flying forward, she hit the ground on her belly in front of a long table.

On the floor just past the table, a large, empty plexiglass tube used for root and soil demonstrations laid before her, and inside was the crystal in all its splendor. She slowly looked back at him to see if he saw what she saw. A mischievous grin grew from his lips to his eyes. The crystal shined through the tube like a beacon.

They both sprung up and ran around to opposite sides of the tube. Rikki got there first and reached inside but couldn't get to it. Quinn tried to put his arm through, but his wet sleeve prevented him from making any progress. He stood up and threw off his shirt. He only needed a couple more inches to grab and make it his.

Rikki's eyes grew wide at the sight of his bare chest, and she became paralyzed with shock over what was unveiled. The birthmark on his chest was exactly like hers.

"Jesus, what's with the look?" he asked as if offended. "I'm not trying anything. My wet shirt won't allow me to reach down this tube."

"Your, your …" Rikki pointed.

"My *what*, Rikki?"

"The mark on your chest."

———

QUINN ROLLED HIS EYES, laid back down, and reached down the pipe. Rikki extended her arm as far out as it could go. Quinn's fingers touched the crystal, but the residual soil on his wet fingers caused it to slip forward enough for Rikki to grab. They both stood right up and moved to the front of the table. His heart pounded when he witnessed her pupils dilate to the edge of her crystal blue irises.

"Rikki?" His voice was full of unease.

As if in a trance, she stepped over to him.

He stood rigid in fear, panting, as she grabbed his wrist and slapped the twin crystal onto his palm. A blinding bright light illuminated the room and enveloped them. Beams of light shot out of both the crystal and their birthmarks. Their bodies shook as they journeyed somewhere they had never seen before.

RIKKI OPENED her eyes to an emergency room. A man with striking green eyes locked in with hers, but there was a look of deep concern in them.

"I'm Wade Kenton, Mrs. Morgan. Dr. Morgan called on me to make sure you were taken care of. I'm right here if you have any questions. But you're out of surgery and doing great."

QUINN OPENED his eyes to find himself standing on a deck overlooking a garden that stretched out to an amazing view of the bay. A strikingly breathtaking woman stood in the garden, looking out. She closed her eyes, allowing the sun to hit her face. The wind blew through her long, chestnut hair. Her white gown flowed in the rhythm of the breeze. She began swaying, and he thought she was going to faint.

Damn it! I shouldn't have allowed her to go on her own!

He began to run to her but stopped when he saw a beaming smile emerge on her face. Quinn's eyes watered at the sight of the goddess that stood in the garden before him.

RIKKI FOUND herself wrapped in Wade's arms. He was helping her out of a wheelchair. The feel of his arms around her waist caused a charge to travel through her body, and she became dizzy. Guilt struck her. She knew she shouldn't have strong feelings for this man.

Quinn found himself crying as Robin was being rushed into emergency surgery. He hadn't had a chance to say goodbye. Why had his heart chosen her? He tried to ignore his feelings, but the more he resisted, the stronger her hold on his heart.

Rikki found herself walking through the brush. It was raining, and she was cold, confused, and lost. If she surrendered, she would die. In the distance, lights from a car moved past her like a spotlight, and she ran toward them. She raised her arms to flag them down but could only raise them slightly. Despite her poor attempts to get their attention, they still stopped. A man got out of the car and ran to her. She thanked the heavens when she recognized Wade, then collapsed into his arms. His embrace, strength, protection, and warmth was the life force that kept her alive. He had rescued her, and she wanted so badly to tell him she loved him, but she was going to die, and he didn't feel the same way. Rikki cried out.

Quinn was there too. He held Robin in his arms, relieved that he showed up when he did. He had saved her life a few times and wondered if she realized that she'd saved his too. Being raised by people who ignored him, like they might some stray dog, he'd long believed himself to be invisible. That was until Robin came barreling into his life and proved over and over again that he was anything but. She had proven to him that he shone blindingly bright. And as he brought her to his car to warm her up, all he wanted to do was make the pain stop—both his *and* hers. He had resisted falling in love with her, but every time he was near her, she would do or say something that made him realize that he *was* a man of value, and his resistance weakened. Then when he disrobed her to warm her up, and she responded by wrapping her arms around him, pressing her bare breast into him to siphon his warmth, shame came over him. All he wanted to do was to take her and demonstrate how much he loved and yearned for her. She didn't make it easy for him to give up hope when she spoke to him like she needed to tell him something. He never heard what she wanted to say because Chris showed up. He wrestled with the thought that maybe she was going to confess her love for him, and for a split second, he bought into the fantasy that her love *was* as strong as his. However, his fantastical thoughts evaporated as hope descended into sadness and anger when he placed Robin in Chris's arms, rendering him lost forever.

THE TWO OF them were in a bedroom. Rikki could feel Robin's heart growing weak as the end neared. It was finally safe to tell Wade how she really felt—how he was her life raft when she had been drowning in the storm surge that was her life. She strategically waited for the last second to confess her love so that the pain of his rejection would be short-lived. Nervously, she preemptively told him that he needed to continue with his life as planned—get married, have children, and leave this chapter behind.

"I fell in love with you … With every fiber of my being, Wade, I'm in love with you," Robin professed.

Having the scene unfold before her, only now enlightened about his mutual feelings, she understood why, at that moment, he had turned away from her. It had been an attempt to contain his feelings, and when he'd failed, he turned to her and immediately dispelled her belief with his own declaration that he, too, was in love with her. Before she could utter another word, he grabbed her, covering his mouth with hers with fervor and intensity and love.

Rikki felt her heart come alive again. If she were to die at that moment, she would die knowing that she'd experienced the greatest love.

THEY BOTH FOUND themselves in Mozelle's bedroom. Their hands were bound in a handfasting ceremony that Mozelle officiated while they looked longingly into each other's eyes, reciting their vows of eternal love for their current lives and all following. They held the crystal that would become the custodian of all their thoughts and shared memories from the moment they laid eyes on each other to that very moment. Then Mozelle took her wand and summoned a bolt of lightning, branding them on their chests. Paralyzed by the charge, their love was sealed.

But then Chris barged in and was struck by the stream of light coming from Mozelle's wand. They saw the room burst into flames, and Wade instinctively threw his body on top of Robin's to shield her from the fire.

IN AN INSTANT, they were back in the greenhouse. Their eyes locked.

Quinn gasped. His face erupted with horror and shame. Stepping backward, he held his hands up, tripped, and fell back. "No!" he screamed. "No! Jesus! What the hell have I done?" He shook his head, rolled onto all fours, then collapsed onto his haunches, burying his face in his hands. "I've lost you. I know I've lost you. What have I done to you?" he squalled.

A deep frown emerged on Rikki's face as she placed a trembling hand held her chest, pained over his brutal cries of anguish and regret. Crushed, she ran to him and wrapped her arms around his shoulders, but he was inconsolable.

"Shhhh. Quinn, it's okay," Rikki whispered in his ear and stroked his hair. "Quinn, it's okay. I'm right here!"

"I can't believe what I've done to you!" he bawled. "I think I'm going to be sick!"

Rikki continued to whisper in his ear, rocking him to reassure him of her forgiveness. "Shhh," she said with a tremble in her voice. "Oh, Quinn, my Wade." Tears burst from her eyes.

Quinn twisted around and drew her into his arms. They held on to each other and cried for a long while.

"I've missed you, my Robin," he sobbed. "So damn much."

"I've missed you too."

"Oh, Rikki," he wept. "I'm so sorry! I'm so, so sorry! I've hurt you so much. How could I have done this to you? To my soul-mate? I swore that even if you slipped away before the ritual was complete, I'd find you, but look what I've done to you instead."

"Quinn," she said firmly. She grabbed his face. "Please look at me. I forgive you," she reassured, but all he did was look back down and shake his head. "I'll prove it!" She unbuttoned her blouse just below her bra, then took his hand and laid it on top of her birthmark. He lifted his eyes to hers. They stared into each other's tear-filled, puffy eyes and remembered their past and current love.

"Your mark! That's why you freaked out when I took my shirt off. I can't believe we found each other," Quinn said.

"I can't believe it either."

"I thought I saw your mark the other day, but I wasn't sure. You know, when I … Fuck! I hate myself!" He grimaced, and tears continued falling.

"So that's why you asked me to take my shirt off."

"Yes."

She reached toward his birthmark, and he reached for hers. They closed their eyes and lowered their heads toward each other as warmth flowed through their bodies. More memories of both their previous life and present life came flooding back.

They opened their eyes, immediately finding each other.

"I love you so much, Rikki."

"And I, you, so, so much, Quinn," she said. Her eyes drifted down to his lips.

Quinn looked away. "I can't get past what I've done to you. I hurt you. I told you I hated you. I called you a bitch. I ignored you and kissed another girl in front of you. Jesus! I'm so ashamed."

"And now that you won't kiss me, you can add rejection to that list."

He shook his head as if he was giving into his shame, then swung around to look at her. He reached over and caressed her face with his hands. Ragged breaths escaped him as he looked into her eyes. A pained expression surfaced like he was battling within himself whether or not to give in to his desire. He wilted, looking down. "I'm not rejecting you. I'm sparing you. Thinking about what I've done makes me sick to my stomach."

Tears rolled down her face. "Quinn, something happened to you that was beyond your control. It was like you were possessed. I can't explain it any better than that. Most of the time, when we *did* talk, it was like you were looking through me. It was like you weren't there. When all this happened just now, my suspicions were confirmed. Do you believe me?"

Quinn looked into her eyes and wiped her tears. "Why would someone want to do that to me?"

"Maybe Sienna did what Mozelle did, but in an evil way."

"I doubt that. She's not very bright. She can be a bitch, and that's about her only talent."

"Well, she was bright enough to get you into her bed." She put her fingers over his lips, regretting what she'd said. "Please forget that I said that. It hurts me to think about it, and it's so not my business." She stood up and turned away to hide her grieved expression.

Quinn turned her back toward him. "I didn't sleep with her, okay?"

"You don't have to make me feel better. Please forget that I brought it up."

"No, I want you to know. It just didn't seem right, and at the time, I didn't know why. I just figured it was because I was usually high or drunk or both," he said with regret. "But now I know that somewhere deep inside, it would have been a betrayal. It all makes sense." He tilted his head as if something else had occurred to him. "You know, Caden needed me to break into his friend's house to get something while they were out of town. Now that I think of it, I bet you he was getting the crystal because as soon as I opened the door, I had a flash of who we were, just like when I was coming over here. The first time, it freaked me out because I wanted to resist seeing you in that way, but then I became obsessed with it. That's why we went to your house that day—I was trying to convince myself that I was supposed to be with Sienna. When we came in here, that feeling came over me again."

"I could feel you were here, too, but I wasn't getting flashes."

"Maybe because you didn't need to be reminded," he said, rubbing his hands down his face. "I swear to you—I will never forget again."

Rikki exhaled in relief, and Quinn brought her in for a hug. He kissed her on top of her head.

"Why do you think that Caden and Elle worked so hard to set this up? I don't understand how they know about this." Rikki stepped back. "I mean, I suppose Elle could have found out about it because she has access to all of Mozelle's things. Maybe she stumbled upon it."

"When Mozelle found out about us, she mentioned she had a

comp book about us, and she was going to show it to me. But then, well, you know."

"How do you remember so much?"

"Well, you were kind of out of it. You were the greatest thing that had ever happened to me, and I don't plan on ever forgetting it, no matter what lifetime I'm in," he expressed, looking into her eyes. His breath became rapid again, and he turned away from her. "Do you not remember a lot of it?"

"I remember the important parts. I remember how you held me that night and that I had been longing for you to touch me for so long," she said. "I remember how right it felt, even though I was married and had a daughter—" She covered her mouth.

"What?"

"I can't believe this." She shook her head, and tears poured out of her eyes again.

"What, Rikki?"

"Ms. Morgan, Lyndsey— She— I can't say it," she cried. She removed her hand from her mouth. "She's my daughter," she choked out.

Quinn stood there with his hands on his hips, staring at her as if he was processing what she had just said. "The thirteen-year-old girl I helped with homework is now the teacher who pepper-sprayed us? Holy shit! I see it now."

"Ms. Morgan— Oh, this is weird. She's behind this? Like all the bad stuff?" The pieces were starting to fall into place. "Why?"

"Do you think she knows who we are?"

"Well, that would explain a lot. But why not be happy that I'm back in her life? Which brings us back to how Elle and Caden are involved in this."

"Do you think it stems from when *they* were here in the greenhouse?"

"I don't know, but we need to get to the bottom of this,

because whoever did this to you doesn't want us to be together, and won't stop until we're apart."

"But now we have the crystal. Do you remember the crystal during the ritual?" Quinn asked.

"Some parts of it. I know the crystal is sacred to us, and it worked exactly as it was supposed to," Rikki replied, gazing into his eyes. "It got us to remember how we fell in love." Her eyes moved to his full lips again. They were ever so slightly parted, and she sucked in her bottom lip, wishing he would read her suggestive cue to take her already. Defeated, she drew in a deep breath to center herself. "But I still want to get to the bottom of what happened to you and why." She turned on her heel and began walking toward the entrance.

"Where are you going?"

"To see if there's a way out."

Quinn followed behind her.

THE SWAY of her hips exuded sensuality, enrapturing him, and something within ignited.

She turned to see how far behind he was trailing. Her hair fell in front of her face.

Quinn's self-control splintered when her entrancing brown eyes found his. A simple stroke of her soft skin, or merely holding her hand, would be just enough to satiate him. Driven, he reached for. As his fingertips touched hers, his control shattered. He grabbed her wrist, spun her around, and covered her mouth with his.

HIS DESPERATION for forgiveness was behind the fevered kiss. Grabbing onto the sides of his face, she opened her mouth, inviting him in, and he unapologetically responded to her craving with unrelenting passion. She connected with him again, and it awakened her. Her nerves came alive, making her dizzy, and her legs started to shake.

Without disengaging, he picked her up and walked toward the back. He put her down on the bench where the table with the crystal was.

"I'll never get over how you react to me. It weakens my control that much more," he said in her ear. There was an ache in his voice that made her shiver.

He sat next to her, and she climbed on top of him, straddling him, causing him to catch his breath. "What are you doing, Rikki?" he asked, his voice strained.

"Oh," she said and began to shift off him but stopped as if struck by another thought. "I love you and believe everything you're saying, but until we get this figured out, no way am I going to set myself up for the heartbreak I just endured. You might think your love for me is strong enough, but you're wrong." She leaned in and gave him a gentle but lingering kiss.

He pushed her away. "Really, Rikki, get off of me unless you're going to get off *on* me."

"Sorry." She blushed and moved off him. "You lead the way," Rikki said and stepped aside.

When they got to the entrance, a note had been slipped under the door.

Quinn opened it.

We're so happy for you both! By now, you've seen things that require time to process. We have more to tell you. The auto-lock is on until 6:00 a.m. That crystal belongs to both of you. Don't lose it! Welcome back, Robin and Wade! There are blankets in the cabinet at the back of the greenhouse. Also, we'll cover for you so your parents won't worry.

Your friends forever, Chris and Mozelle, aka Caden and Elle

· · ·

RIKKI CLOSED her eyes in shock.

Quinn wiped his hand down his face and covered his mouth. "Well, I guess that explains why they know so much." He paused. "I don't even know where to begin with that."

"Well, it looks like we have all night," she said, looking around. "Shit! I hope there's a bathroom in this place, or else I'll have no choice but to give these plants some very special fertilizer." Rikki laughed at her own joke.

"I have special fertilizer, too, but it's not meant for plants," Quinn joked back, then cleared his throat. "I, uh, guess we're here for a while."

"Let's get the blankets." She grabbed Quinn's hand, and they walked to the back of the greenhouse. They opened the cabinet and found blankets, flameless candles, pillows, an umbrella, jelly donuts, bottled water, and condoms. "Wow, they went all out—and without Mr. Croft knowing. That's impressive."

"I guess we're going to sleep on the benches." Rikki began to get up, a blanket in hand, but Quinn caught her wrist to stop her.

"Let's just sit here for a bit and talk. We can set that up later."

They sat cross-legged, facing each other as they ate their jelly donuts.

"So I guess that Caden and I were married in our past life. So that would make Ms. Morgan our daughter," she said with a patronizing look on her face. "I wonder how they remembered who they are."

"I guess we're going to hear all about it when we see them next, which will be weird."

"The whole thing is weird. I remember myself as Robin, but I'm not her either."

"I feel the same way."

"So what now?"

"Fucking get Sienna out of my life."

"I hate when you say her name. If we have to talk about her, can we just call her 'what's-her-face'?"

"Yes, of course. Anyway, I'll deal with her."

———

HE WATCHED as she bit into the donut, only to then take her fingers and sweep them across her lips. When she put her middle finger in her mouth to suck the remnants of the jelly filling, his body came alive.

———

SHE WATCHED him stare at her lips. Her mouth lifted on one side, and she repeated the movement.

He looked her in the eye as if to gauge her motivations. "What are you doing, Rikki?"

"Me? Nothing," she said with a devilish smile. When she went in for another bite, the jelly squirted down her chin and onto her chest. "Shit!" She laughed, snapping out of her flirtation. Embarrassed, she began to clean herself. Before she could, he moved in, breathing heavily with aching want in his eyes.

She was taken by surprise when she saw the unstated desire in his eyes. Her breath quickened, and she gave him a low, breathy answer. "Yes."

He licked the jelly off her chest. The touch of his tongue on her skin sent shockwaves through her body, and she threw her head back, cradling his head as he moved up to the side of her neck, and a moan she didn't recognize escaped from deep within her.

He pulled her in close, and she wrapped her legs around him. He looked into her eyes and wiped a remaining drop of jelly off her chin. "Like a dream, I can recall the night I rescued you in the rain. I wasn't supposed to notice your body under that white dress of yours, but it was soaking wet and see-through, so I did. If the situation were different, I would have taken you then."

"I've had a mixture of memories and actual dreams about that night. Each time I think about it, well ..." She looked down in embarrassment. "I feel something." Taking a deep breath, Rikki stood up and walked down the aisle to turn off the lights. She adjusted her clothing to be as similar to what she'd worn that night as possible.

Quinn activated the flameless candles.

Rikki walked back and stood a few feet away. She began to unbutton her shirt.

Quinn swallowed hard.

"My shirt isn't quite like my dress that night, but maybe you can help me remember the parts that were fuzzy for me."

Quinn stood up and walked up to her. "Well, you were shivering and weak. I began to walk you over to the car, but you had a hard time walking." He picked her up as he had that night. "So I carried you."

Rikki leaned her head back, allowing her shirt to slip further off her shoulder, nearly exposing her nipple.

"No bra?" Quinn's voice was weak. He cleared his throat. "You remembered?"

"Yes, it's in my back pocket." She laughed. "Just go with it."

"Jesus, Rikki!" His husky voice warmed Rikki's body, and she melted into him. He took a deep breath. "Okay, so I brought you to the car and sat you in the passenger seat," he said as he gently put her down on the bench. "I began to warm you up by putting the heat on, but your clothes were wet, and you were freezing. So I had to take your clothes off." He leaned over her.

She looked up at him. Her breath caught as he looked down at her, slightly opening his mouth to catch his own breath.

Desire burned in his eyes. He smiled, confirming her eyes were saying the same thing.

"Do it," Rikki whispered.

"Are you sure? Rikki, we don't have to do this if you don't want to. I mean, you just said—"

She placed her hand on his chest. She could feel him tremble under her touch. "Never mind what I just said. I want you. It's weird because I know in this life, I've never done it, but when I reflect on my past life ... Let's put it this way: the day I confessed to you, and you kissed me, had I not been on my deathbed, I would have cheated on Chris. Now here we are, free as can be, and I want you as badly now as I wanted you then."

Quinn swallowed hard and kneeled before her. "Okay, um, so I asked you to take off your dress, but you could only get it up to here." Quinn slid his hands up her thighs, stopping midway.

A shiver traveled up her spine, making her head buzz at the touch of his soft hands. She unzipped her jeans and slid them down her legs. Quinn stood up to help pull them off her feet and drop them on the floor. As she went for her panties, Quinn kneeled before her again. Then placed his hands on the sides of her thighs to stop her from continuing.

"You weren't able to take those off, so for historical purposes, I'll take them off for you." His warm hands glided further up the side of her thighs, gently wrapping his fingers around the delicate lace and slowly pulling her panties past her rear, down her legs, and off her feet. He stood up, dropping her undergarment onto their growing pile of clothing.

Leaning against the back of the bench, Rikki threw her head back. Her breath was ragged in anticipation of his next move.

He stood over her and grabbed the bottom of her button-down shirt, then stopped. "I tried to help you out of your dress." He slowly exhaled. "But you drove me right to the edge when your leg fell to the side, and your legs were spread apart like you wanted me."

"Like this?" Rikki allowed her legs to fall to the sides.

"Yes." There was a rasp in his whisper. "Like that." He let go of her shirt, placing both hands on the back of the bench, then leaned in and laid kisses along her neck. "Rikki, I'm not sure how much more of this I can take," he admitted, exhaling with a moan into her ear.

She took her nails and drew them up his neck, enticing a seductive grunt. "What happened next, Quinn?" Rikki's voice was breathy and low.

He pushed back from her. Looking her in the eye, he left one hand on the back of the bench and used the other to trace along her jaw. "I gently moved your leg back." He reached down to close her legs, but she stopped him.

He swallowed hard, then grabbed the sides of her shirt again. "I pulled your dress off." He slowly lifted her shirt over her head. "And just like now, there was no bra." He knelt back down between her opened legs and laid slow kisses along her thighs, then her belly, and then to each nipple.

Rikki's breath caught. She bit her lip as she held his head.

His tongue worked her breasts until Rikki couldn't take it anymore. She pulled his head up and brought him to her mouth. It was a deep, hard, and passionate kiss. They were hungry for each other and groaned into each other's mouths. Rikki began to unbuckle Quinn's pants, pulled them down, and grabbed hold of him.

He gasped. "Fuck, Rikki!"

He stepped out of his pants, scooped her up into his arms, and carried her to the blankets on the floor. He laid her down and caressed her naked body. His mouth was on hers again as he reached between her legs.

"Damn, you're so ready for me," he whispered into her mouth.

"I need you, Quinn."

He reached for the condom and put it on, then hovered over her. "I can't wrap my mind around this. A span of two lifetimes has led up to this. I love you, Rikki."

"I love you, too, Quinn."

Quinn lowered his body onto hers. They looked in each other's eyes as Quinn pressed himself against her entrance.

Rikki let out a grunt.

"Shit, are you okay?"

"Yes, Quinn. Please don't worry."

He closed his eyes as he moved deeper into her, and then deeper. "You feel so good," he moaned.

"Don't stop," she whispered.

She gasped, then they groaned in unison as he slowly delved all the way in.

She grabbed his ass to prevent him from moving. He held himself there and looked in her eyes to gauge if he should continue, waiting for her body to ease. She blew out a long breath and relaxed under his commanding body.

Rikki moved his ass to set the rhythm. She felt mind-blowing pleasure and burning pain simultaneously, but as Quinn continued to gradually glide in and out, the pleasure took over. Her legs intertwined with his, allowing him to plunge further into her.

She reached around the back of his head and pulled him to her mouth. He ravaged her as they moved together.

The feeling of skin against skin ignited their lust. It was then that their birthmarks connected, and they saw flashes of how they viewed each other, both past and present. They saw each other's thoughts and fantasies. It was when she saw what had gone through Wade's mind when he'd found Robin sleeping on the deck that Rikki's pleasure exploded. She called out Quinn's name. He held her tight as her waves of pleasure encouraged him to meet up with her.

His breath was heavy, and sweat beaded on his chest. His muscles flexed with each drive, and the veins in his neck emerged as he strained. He moaned as he lost himself in her.

She melted into his vulnerability, making her forget any discomfort she had left. She knew at that very moment that he truly and deeply loved her.

"I can't hold on much longer." Quinn's voice was barely audible as he buried himself further into her.

"I've got you," Rikki whispered in his ear.

His control snapped.

She held him tight as his body shuttered through his release. His grunts and gasps for air made her head spin.

He kissed all over her face and neck as he continued to throb inside her. "Are you okay?" he asked into her neck as he tried to catch his breath.

She nodded. After her heart settled down, she turned in to him. "Better than okay," she admitted, kissing his neck. "That was not how I remember it being." She laughed.

"Same," he said, raising himself up on his elbows, smiling a knowing smile. "We're going to be trouble."

"Indeed we are," he said and kissed her.

They cuddled close the remainder of the night and fell asleep in each other's arms.

<hr />

AT SIX O'CLOCK THE next morning, a tone sounded, the doors in the greenhouse unlocked, and the sprinklers went off. Rikki and Quinn were tangled together as they woke but did nothing to separate themselves.

"I don't want to leave. I want to be here against your body forever," Rikki groaned, curling further into Quinn.

Quinn kissed her forehead. "I don't want to get up either. Let's just stay here until they kick us out."

"Ugh! I don't want to get in trouble, and if we get caught, they'll know exactly what we did. And then they'll tell our parents, and it'll stain the most amazing night."

"It *was* amazing," he agreed.

Rikki started laughing and buried her face in his chest.

"What's so funny?"

"I told you that you'd never have this." She waved her hand along her body. "You know, after you asked me to take my top off."

"'I want you to listen to the words coming out of my mouth,'" Quinn said in his best attempt of sounding like Rikki and laughed.

Rikki hit him and laughed too. "But really, at the beginning of the night, I would have never guessed in a million years that the night would end up being … so … absolutely perfect."

"Absolutely," he repeated.

"When can we be together again?"

"We need to find Elle and Caden because—well, because *OMG*. Then let's find a place where we can be together."

"Okay." She moaned. "I can't let go. Five more minutes."

"Five more minutes."

Caden's leg was bouncing a mile a minute as he sat at the counter at Java and Book. "Have you heard from them yet?" Caden asked as Elle was finishing up an order.

"They said they would be here in a few minutes. Chill," Elle said.

"How easy is that for you to say? They'll love you. But me? They're going to hate me."

"I'll protect you."

"Right … Lifesaver," he said while nodding his head, then

flashed her a bright smile, which fell when he heard the front door chime.

"Chris!" Quinn yelled. "I think you have some explaining to do!"

Caden's heart pounded, and he turned toward Quinn. "Hey, guys!" Caden's voice wavered.

"I'm just playing." Quinn laughed and gave Caden a hug. "Thank you," he said sincerely.

Caden closed his eyes and exhaled. "No, thank you." Caden's eyes pricked with tears.

Quinn let go and turned to Elle.

Caden's heart started to pound again when Quinn stepped aside and saw Rikki. "Hey?" Caden began to perspire.

Rikki placed both hands over her heart. Tears welled in her eyes as she threw her arms around Caden.

"I'm so sorry!" Caden said, stifling a sob.

"No, Caden, please don't be sorry! I'm to blame. And I wouldn't be with my soulmate if it wasn't for you. Thank you … Chris!" Rikki said, her body shuddering.

Rikki turned to Elle and gave her a big hug. "I don't know how I will ever be able to repay you."

"You never have to worry," Elle said. "I've missed you, old friend."

"I missed you too!" Rikki sniffed.

They all took seats at a table near the window.

"So I guess it worked …" Elle smirked at the double meaning.

Quinn and Rikki looked at each other and smiled. Quinn reached for Rikki's hand under the table.

"There are other things that we need to catch you up on," Elle said, suddenly all business. "Beyond the fact that I'm Mozelle and Caden is Chris, something else happened that night that was unexpected. When Chris, you know, barged in, I was startled, and I accidentally shot him with the charge. What you might not know is that the charge also hit the mirror behind him and bounced back into me. If you remember, that charge was meant to seal your marks."

"We were all there, so I'm sure most of us remember," Quinn said.

"Well, Caden?" Elle invited him to pull down his sleeve as she did hers.

"Whoa!" Quinn remarked as their own birthmarks were revealed.

"Wow, so are you like us? Are you soulmates?" Rikki asked.

"Um, well, it's, uh—" Elle stammered.

"It's complicated," Caden interjected, and he shoved his sleeve back up.

"That charge was dedicated to you, so what we got was …" Elle tried again to explain.

"Sloppy seconds," Quinn blurted.

"Hey!" Caden snapped.

"Sorry, man."

"It just made it so that we're not physical magnets to each other like you guys are. And I mean that literally, not like an insult. But Caden and I, we've been through a lot, and that definitely plays a role in how we feel about each other," Elle explained.

"So we figured out who we were similar to the way *you* figured it out. It happened in the greenhouse when Ms. Morgan—I mean, Lyndsey, our daughter—" Caden stammered, looking at Rikki. "How weird is that?"

"I'm sorry, I'm going to interrupt here because it is *very* weird, Caden. I'm not sure how to process that you and I have a daughter and, at the same time, don't. We did in a past life. I guess this is why we aren't supposed to remember our past lives. It's such a mind fuck. Were we not good parents? I have a daughter who hates me, yet I've never had kids." Rikki shook her head in bewilderment.

"I guess the 'Reincarnated Parents of Children Who Hate You Even Though You've Never Had Kids' support group probably didn't get a high enough turnout to sustain membership, so we're it," Caden joked.

There was a long pause as everyone absorbed the bizarreness of their new reality.

"Well, anyway," Caden continued, "what I was getting at was how Elle and I figured out who we were when I went to pick up the leaves that day. It was intended for you, Rikki."

Rikki gasped. "Shit! I'm so sorry."

"No, don't be. I'm glad it happened. One thing I concluded was that when I was Chris, my anger was misguided. I was jealous, and the truth was, it wasn't because I was in love with you, but because our relationship was yet another thing I'd lost control over. I knew it then, and I can see it now. You two are truly soulmates, and I'm very happy for you both. Honestly!"

Quinn grabbed Caden's shoulder. "That means a lot to us."

"So now we have to catch you up on Ms. Morgan's role in all this. After the fire, she went back and found Mozelle's journals and your crystal," Elle said. "The problem is that she read the journal and figured out everything that happened."

"So this is all about revenge?" Quinn asked.

"That's what we're suspecting," Caden replied.

Rikki leaned forward and placed her elbows on the table. She buried her hands in her hair. "It's all my fault. That's why she concocted the whole greenhouse plan. It was meant for me."

"Yes, to get you to remember your past life," Elle said.

"So she knows who Quinn and I are, and she doesn't want us together. Wow. How did you figure all this out?"

"Mozelle left behind comp books that explain what she was doing. She kept these books for clients who required her more specialized services."

"So I guess you found that she wrote something about me

and Quinn—well, Robin and Wade," Rikki corrected. "That'll take time to get used to."

"Well, the real question at this point is what is her end game?" Quinn asked.

Caden leaned in. "To ruin each and every one of us."

19

DEMANDS

Quinn parked his car in front of Rikki's house. He needed to be a man and apologize to her parents. He took a deep breath and walked up to the front door. His hand was shaking when he reached to knock on the door. He had not gone beyond the point of no return. He counted to three in his head, then gave a firm knock on the door.

The door swung open. Mr. Waters stood there with one hand gripping the side of the door and the other on his hip.

Heat flushed through Quinn's body, provoking a hard swallow. "Hi, sir. I'm here to apologize for my behavior. I hope you can understand that I've been going through some personal issues. I can assure you that I will *never* do anything like that again. I understand if you're not ready to forgive me, but I hope over time you'll see that I only want to make Rikki happy," Quinn explained.

Rikki appeared behind her dad. Rikki appeared behind her dad, hovering just far enough away that she wasn't intruding.

Mr. Waters lowered his arms. "Well, Quinn, thank you for your honesty and for working up the courage to let us know. As you can guess, our trust in you has been broken, but we have faith in Rikki that she will make good choices."

Rikki walked Quinn back to his car after their talk. "Thank you for that. My parents will come around."

Quinn nodded his head. "Now off to What's Her Face's," he said, rolling his eyes.

QUINN PULLED up to Sienna's house and finally replied to the multitude of texts Sienna had sent him over the last several hours. *Come outside. I'm in my Rover.*

Her blonde hair was pulled up in a ponytail, and she looked like she hadn't slept. She hopped in. "Where the hell have you been?" she asked, slamming the car door behind her.

"I've been with Rikki," he admitted with confidence.

"Really?" She pursed her lips. "And why is that?"

"The blinders were removed. That's about as clear as I can make it."

"That's kinda what you said about me. So what? You're breaking up with me?"

"Yes."

She huffed through flared nostrils. "You are such a *dick!*" she yelled. "I think she has something on you. I'm going to figure it out. I'm not giving up that easily."

"She does *something*, that's for sure," Quinn said with a smile.

"Uh-huh."

"She has my heart. I'm sorry I led you on. I wasn't myself."

"So that's it?"

"That's it."

"Fuck you. There will be hell to pay," Sienna threatened.

Quinn's expression turned dark. "I won't stand for your threats. But you know that I have proof of the crap you pulled in Wyoming that will get you put in prison. Don't fuck with us, or your days of freedom are numbered."

"This isn't over," she said as she threw the car door open in a rage and slammed it behind her before stomping her way across her driveway.

BEFORE SCHOOL, Lyndsey went to the greenhouse to drop off a medicinal salve that she had made for Mr. Croft's dog. The dog had a chapped nose, its skin cracking and bleeding. She found Mr. Croft sweeping up potting soil that had been dumped on the floor.

"Everything okay?" Lyndsey asked.

"Kids got in over the weekend," he said, dumping a dustpan of soil into a garbage container. "Nothing was stolen or anything, but they made a mess."

"Oh no. I'm sorry. Do you know who it was?"

"Yeah, it was that kid who almost drowned last year and a girl with brown hair," he said as he continued to sweep.

"Quinn and Rikki? How do you know?"

"I don't know their names, but it was caught on the CCTV. It looked like they were looking for something, and then they started horse playing. And I think they found what they were looking for, but it was weird, because whatever it was, it let out this pulse that screwed up my CCTV."

Lyndsey's stomach churned over the new development. Trying to suppress the need to hurl, she grabbed the hair at the base of her skull. She closed her eyes to center herself. Taking a cleansing breath, she finally spoke up. "They're in my class. I'll see to it that they're reprimanded. Can I see the tape?"

He stopped sweeping and rested his hand on the top of the broomstick. "Well, what I didn't realize is that the pulse messed the with equipment, too, and it ate the tape as it was playing.

Now both the machine *and* the tape are ruined. Which means I have nothing to take to admin. I can't imagine what I have in here that could do such a thing."

"I don't know," she lied. "I'll get to the bottom of this."

"You're a good friend. Thanks."

SHIT! Did they get the crystal? I thought I checked it. I need to get out of here. She claimed she was ill and walked off-campus. She about died when she saw Rikki and Quinn kissing in his Rover. Fueled by rage, she got into her car and sped the hell out of there.

When she got home, she tore into her temple room and threw open her closet. She snatched up the pewter jewelry box and flipped it open with such force, the velvet cover flew off and exposed a rock where the crystal was supposed to be. It fell from her hands and crashed to the floor, twisting the hinges that had held it secure all these years. She stepped back, grasping her hair above her forehead. "Fuck you! You think you can outsmart me?"

She had been blindsided. She scrambled around, trying to think of her next step. She had to break things down in her mind. Elle came to mind first. *She's behind a lot of this because she obviously remembers who she was and the strength of her power, I'm guessing. She needs to be quieted. An apathetic enchantment should shut her up long enough for me to focus on Rikki. Since Rikki and Quinn have the damn crystal, and since Elle has probably protected it by now, bringing Sienna back into the picture won't work. It will have to be something that physically stops them from being together.*

She got online and looked up all kinds of curses that would physically stop people from being together. She came across a condition called allodynia—an illness in which a person feels physical pain from things that are not typically painful. *When Quinn touches her, she will endure physical pain.*

First and foremost, they were going to be given the honor of a private lesson on what happened when you crossed a witch. From there on out, it would be no secret who had turned their lives upside down.

Lyndsey needed another day before stepping back into the classroom. She wasn't ready to face them or her failures. She reached out to Farrah and asked if she could come by and look at the room.

"Of course. I'll be here for another hour, then Elle will be here," Farrah said.

"I'll be right over."

When she got there, Farrah brought her down to Mozelle's room. Stepping through the threshold, Lyndsey set her jaw and balled her fist as she immediately felt Mozelle's presence. She stood in the center, surveying the room. It didn't take her long to spot the other four journals and a mediocre collection of oils, herbs, candles, and crystals. Looking at the altar, she humphed and rolled her eyes unimpressed.

"What do you think? Is she too far gone?" Farrah asked.

"Well, based on the ashes in the mortar, burnt wicks on various colored candles—some of which are black—and fresh herbs, I would say that she *is*, in fact, practicing. If it really bothers you, you might want to consider an intervention or just lock this place up and throw away the key. It's expensive to replace all this, so that should put a stop to her starting up again."

Farrah covered her mouth, visibly shaken.

"Don't be too upset. You're doing the right thing."

ELLE EMERGED from cleaning the bathroom when she heard her mom and Ms. Morgan come through the back room. Anger flared in her, and she began to perspire when she realized they'd been in the reading room.

"Where were you?" Her voice wavered, making it evident that she was nervous, and she hated herself for that.

"She asked to see the basement, so I showed her," her mother said as if she did that all the time, and Elle should know better.

"You *what?!* Why would you show my *teacher* my *room?*" Elle saw stars, her body buzzing in anger. Her private and magical paradise, her safe and happy place, had now been polluted by the worst person possible.

"It's not like it's your bedroom. It's not really your room at all," her mother maintained.

"My apologies," Ms. Morgan said like she was reading a script. "I didn't mean to intrude. Your mom invited me because of the subject matter of my class, and she thought I'd appreciate it. It's quite an amazing room. Full of beautiful *crystals* and *journals*," Ms. Morgan said, flashing a condescending smile.

"It's supposed to be a *private* room, not something that's open for daily tours, regardless of whose room it *really* is, Mom!"

"Whatever. I'm done talking about this," her mother threatened with narrowed eyes, then turned back to Ms. Morgan. "Ms. Morgan, it's been a pleasure. I apologize for Elle's behavior. I need to head out. I'll see you at home." She grabbed her things and left.

Elle saw Ms. Morgan's fake smile drop as soon as the door closed behind her mom and turned toward her. There was fury in her eyes. "That was quite a room, Elle," Ms. Morgan said, taking a seat at the counter. "Oh, and by the way, I need you to send your customers away and get Caden, Rikki, and Quinn to come here right now." There was a threatening tone to her voice.

Elle's mouth dropped as she felt the blood drain from her face. "What for?" Elle needed to hear Ms. Morgan say the words.

Ms. Morgan leaned in and tilted her head. "I'm sorry, let me rephrase that. I need you to get *Chris*, *Robin*, and *Wade* here, right the fuck now," she said with a cold smile. "I'll be in the reading room. You just let me know when they get here."

Shaken, Elle put out a sign saying the café was closed for a private gathering and please come back later. Fearing Ms. Morgan would know how freaked out she was, Elle moved into the annex to call Caden.

"Hey. What's up?" Caden's voice was loud as he spoke over the pumping music blaring in his car.

Elle swallowed. Unbeknownst to him, she was about to turn his optimistic world on its head. "She knows."

The music went silent. "Elle? What's wrong? Your voice is off."

"Ms. Morgan. She knows everything, and she wants to talk to all of us. How soon can you, Quinn, and Rikki get to the café?"

"Elle, are you safe?"

"Yes, but she asked that I clear everyone out."

"Fuck!"

Elle could hear Caden hit his steering wheel.

"I'm heading there right now. I'll call Quinn and Rikki to meet us there. I'll be there in two minutes, even though I'm ten minutes away. Don't talk to her. Just stay where you are," Caden directed.

"I'm okay. I've got it handled. I'll see you in a few," she assured and hung up the phone.

Caden burst through the door within the two minutes he'd promised. "Where is she?" he demanded.

A flush ran through her body. Caden stood there with balled fists, his chest rising and falling in rapid succession. She knew she needed to talk him off the ledge, but her mind was still buzzing at the sight of him, and for the first time, she recognized Chris in Caden. *That is who Chris should have been—protective but not jealous or possessive, dependable but not flaky, and willing to put others' needs first, rather than run off to work or drink when the shit got real.* She shook her head to stop her line of thinking and finally raised her hand to calm him. "She's in the reading room and will come out when we're all here."

Caden put his hands behind his head and paced. After several minutes, the place was cleared out, and Quinn and Rikki had arrived. They stood at the counter while Elle walked toward the reading room to let Ms. Morgan know they were all there. Before she could get there, though, Lyndsey swung open the curtain that separated the two rooms and stepped out in a huff.

"Go sit over there." Ms. Morgan pointed to a table for four near the windows. She walked over to the entrance to ensure the closed sign was up, then made her way over to them.

"Mom, Dad, lover, and witch," Ms. Morgan said, pointing to who was who.

"We're only trying to protect ourselves," Rikki said as a defense.

"Let's talk about this, Lyndsey," Caden called her by her first name as if hoping she'd see him as her dad instead of her student.

"There is *no* talking happening here. No matter what or how you say things, there will be *no* negotiating!" Ms. Morgan said animatedly.

There was silence all around.

"I'm sure by now you understand how each of you fucked up my life. Mom, you and your *lover*, Wade, carry the most blame. Mozelle, you hold a great deal of responsibility as well. Really, the only innocent person here is Dad, but—"

"Lyndsey, you don't understand," Caden interrupted.

"Listen. You're siding with *them*. You're innocent, but

not *that* innocent, so shut the hell up!" Ms. Morgan's eyes were full of rage. "These are the things that need to be done to stop the inevitable pain that each and every one of you will bear. First, you will *not* leave my class, and I will see to it that you don't. It's a lot easier to control you that way. Next, I want my damn crystal back."

Quinn stood up. "Fuck you, that crystal belongs to us!" he yelled.

"No negotiating, *Wade*! You have *no* say in any of this. You are *nothing*. You should have *never* come into our lives. This is a family meeting, and you need to shut the fuck up before I hurt you!" There was no stopping her now. "Anyway, I want *my* crystal back, and I want the rest of those journals. Mom, I want you and your playmate to *never* be together again, and I want *you*, Mozelle, to stay the hell out of it! Stop practicing witchcraft! Once you've done those things, then I'll drop it. But make no mistake, all the bad things that you endure from here on out are because I've made them so. Until you give me what I want, believing you're safe or that Elle will cast your way out of this will only result in greater pain. I *will* win!"

The four of them just looked at her, shock evident on their faces.

"That's all I have to say. See you all in class!" Ms. Morgan turned around, flipped the "closed" sign to "open," and stormed out.

"WELL, THAT WAS UNEXPECTED," Caden said after a long pause.

"She's not going to get a damn thing!" Quinn contended.

"How do you expect to stop her?" Rikki asked.

"Can't you place some kind of protection thing on us?" Quinn asked, grasping for straws.

"I can try. She's very powerful, but let me do some research," Elle said.

"Okay. We'll leave you to it," Quinn said.

They each said goodbye to Elle, then the three of them got into Caden's car and drove off.

Quinn sat in the back with Rikki. "She won't get to you. I'll do everything in my power to protect you."

"We're all vulnerable," Rikki said.

"Yes, but Rikki, her anger is really focused on *you*."

She nodded and spent the remainder of the ride staring out the window.

LYNDSEY WAS ON A RAMPAGE. She sewed four dolls of their likenesses because she was no longer fucking around. She grabbed ingredients to begin her enchantments.

"OH, mighty spirits of health and sickness:
Quinn and Rikki cannot be in each others' heart.
Consequences will be swift until they are apart.
Rikki will acquire allodynia only to Quinn and his touch,
Causing her to suffer pain, excruciatingly much.
There will be no cure to this curse.
Only I can put this hex in reverse."

SHE BURNED needles in her solution and stuck them all over the Rikki doll, then she took two more and put them in the ears of the Elle doll and chanted:

"OH HAIL the rulers of care, love, and hate:

Render Elle powerless and take away her emotion.
Removing herself from this drama is an encouraging notion.
Her friends' attempts to bring her back with charms magnetic
will be fruitless, for she is perpetually apathetic."

CADEN WAS at home finishing homework the next night when Elle called him.

"Caden?" Elle cried. "I'm sorry for calling you like this again."

"Elle? What's wrong?" He demanded an answer. The sound of her voice was immediately clear to him—this was a distress call and one that he would never expect her to make unless it was dire. The urge to kick the ass of whoever did this to her overwhelmed him.

"Something horrible happened."

"Are you hurt? Where are you?"

"I'm fine. I'm at the café."

"I'm coming to get you!"

Caden rounded the corner within minutes and saw Elle standing on the sidewalk. "Get in!"

Her eyes were red, and she could barely get her words out between sobs.

"Elle, you're killing me here! What's wrong?" he asked as he drove aimlessly down Bridgeway.

"I— I—" she sniveled, "I went to research a protection spell, and I couldn't get into the room!" she cried. "I went to my mom, and she said that she'd sealed the place up. Like sealed it metaphysically because she knows what I've been doing, and she wants to put an end to it. I've always known that she had the gift, but she never uses it because she thinks it brings in evil. I tried to explain it to her, but she accused me of being crazy!" she explained. "I can't believe this, Caden!"

He pulled into an empty lot that provided beautiful views of the bay. He got out and quickly went onto her side of the car. He pulled her out and into his protective arms.

She cried as he held her close. "I failed, Caden. Now everyone is going to suffer because of this."

"We'll figure this out, Elle," he said into her ear, pulling her in closer.

Her body calmed in his embrace. "My mom's fear is all based on some abusive crap her dad pulled that she can't get past. Now we all have to pay. I don't know what's going to happen."

"We'll find a way in. Or get someone else's help. Maybe we can give her a fake crystal, or maybe Quinn and Rikki can pretend they're not together. We'll figure this out," he promised.

"Thank you, Caden. I guess I'm not the only one who saves people around here."

"I don't know about that. You'll always be my Lifesaver," he said and loosened his arms so he could look her in the eye to gauge her emotions. He regretted moving that way. The wind blew her white hair over her eyes, the lights from the city and off the bay glistened in her blue eyes, and her red lips were swollen and sensuous. He wanted her but refused to make a move when she was so vulnerable. The second it became apparent what was going through his mind, he completely let go and took a few steps back. He shoved his hands deep into his pockets and turned toward the water to re-center himself.

"Are you okay?" Elle asked.

"Of course. But that's supposed to be my line."

"I'm feeling better. You know, you were the first person I thought of when I was upset because ever since the greenhouse, you have a way of calming me down," she said as she circled around him, then stood toe to toe with him. She looked up at him, then forced her arms through the space between his securely planted arms and his body, encircling them around his waist.

"What are you doing, Elle?" Caden was suddenly very

nervous, no longer the white knight he'd been when he first picked her up. His breath was jagged.

She took one of her hands and swept his brown hair off his face, then traced the side of his head with her fingernails. He closed his eyes in ecstasy.

He opened his eyes to find her looking right at him. "Please, Elle. Don't," he whispered. He could barely contain himself.

She didn't listen and placed her hand behind his neck. "I need you to kiss me," she whispered.

His body was shaking as his control started to crumble. His mouth hovered over hers. "Elle, you're upset. You don't—"

It was when she said, "Please," that the dam broke, and his lips landed on hers, taking her in completely. He thought about this moment all the time but never thought it would actually happen. Heat traveled from his birthmark, throughout his body, overwhelming him. He started to worry about what she was doing to him. She didn't feel the same as he did. This was going to be a devastating fall for him, and he wasn't sure if he would survive it. He pulled away.

Elle looked confused. "I thought you wanted me."

"Can't you feel my body trembling?" he admitted against his will. "But I can't handle knowing you're not in the same place I am. I'm too weak, Elle. I can't just be in the moment like you."

"It's not that I'm not in the same place you are. It's that I'm scared."

"Of what?"

"Caden, I'm a free spirit, you know that. But it's the birthmarks. You feel 'stronger' toward me because you got hit harder than I did. It makes me wonder if I have *any* free will at all. Or is this something that's manufactured? What I fear is that my feelings are a result of other forces. I need to have control so that when I'm feeling compelled to give in, it's because I made that choice."

"And you haven't quite made that choice. So then why are you taking this further?" Caden questioned.

"Because I'm starting to lose that battle," she said, but her eyes didn't show fear—they showed lust. "And continuing to dissect my feelings is draining." With that, she pushed him against the hood of the car, grabbed his head, and plunged her mouth onto his. Her tongue forced its way through, parting his lips and drinking him in as if her survival depended on it.

He reciprocated by picking her up and turning her so that she was now sitting on the hood. She wrapped her legs around his waist and yanked him closer. He grabbed her ass, pulled her in, and pressed her against his arousal, causing both of them to moan at its declaration. He needed a breath and began kissing her neck while she leaned her head back and slid her fingers along his scalp. He wanted to take her right then but knew on some level that it needed to stop there. He let go of her rear and placed his hands on both sides of her, pressing his forehead to hers. "If we weren't in public and if I had protection, I would take you right here and now," he said, out of breath. "So I'm going to drop you off at home or wherever you plan on staying, and I'm going to go let off some steam."

She grabbed his head and kissed him on his forehead. She sighed in resignation. "You're right," she said, then slid off the hood of the car.

Out of breath, Caden put his hands on his hips and dropped his head. "Where to?" he asked as she opened the passenger side door.

"Take me to Rikki's," Elle requested.

He wiped his hands down his face and shook his head, hoping that would help him change tracks. He took a deep breath, opened the driver's door, and slid into his seat.

There was an awkward silence for a few minutes as Caden drove to Rikki's house until he couldn't take it anymore. "So, is it going to be weird at school tomorrow?" Caden asked, clearly insecure.

"I hope not," Elle said.

"Then I'll say this now. I really, really like you, Elle. I've been crushing on you probably since you shot me with that bolt that branded me. This mark has so much more meaning to me now, and I want to display it to the world." He could feel his face fall in sadness. "But for my own sanity, I'm going to step aside."

"Wait …What? So this is some kind of preemptive strike against me? Are you *that* afraid of getting hurt? I could have sworn I felt that you had a pair." Elle's hand was on her chest like she was trying to heal her heartbreak.

"I will be waiting for you when you truly choose me. But I can't be in a situation where the scale is so unbalanced," Caden said as he put the car into park in Rikki's driveway.

Elle threw open the door. "This is not normal, Caden!" She slammed the door shut and walked away.

Rikki was so out of it when Elle showed up that she made Elle set up her own blanket and pillow. Elle even tried to tell Rikki all about what had happened between her and Caden, but she was out cold.

The following day, Rikki could barely get out of bed. She complained that her head felt foggy, and she just wanted to sleep. Elle was still disappointed that she couldn't talk to Rikki about the night before.

"Are you going to go to school?" Elle asked but got no response. "Rikki?" Still no response. She went to shake Rikki awake, and upon touching her, could feel she had a fever. "Rikki?"

"It's freezing in here," Rikki whispered as she pulled the covers up to her chin.

"Rikki, I think you have a fever."

Elle went to Rikki's mom to tell her that Rikki was sick. When they came back to her room, she was sweating profusely. Her mom got a thermometer and a cold compress. Her temp was 105.

"She doesn't get fevers. I'm going to take her to the ER," her mom said, then left the room to get Rikki's dad.

"Rikki? Can you hear me? Your parents are going to take you to the ER," Elle said, hoping to get a response from her.

Rikki began to moan. "Where's Wade?"

"He'll meet you there."

"Am I going to die?"

"No, Rikki, we're not going down that path again. Nod that you hear me."

Rikki nodded. "I don't feel so good, Mozelle."

RIKKI'S MOM rushed her to the ER, where they admitted her and began a battery of tests. When Quinn heard that Rikki wasn't doing well, he raced to the hospital. Her mom told him that they were running some tests and that she had an infection of some sort. She tried to reassure him that Rikki was going to be okay and that she'd be able to go home within the next day or two, but Quinn was still uneasy. Rikki had woken up a couple of times before he'd gotten there, but she had remained asleep since he'd arrived. He stayed by Rikki's side throughout the day. When he returned from lunch, he brought in a collection of magazines like he had in their previous life in hopes of bringing a smile to her face once she woke. He took a seat next to the bed and grabbed her hand as she slept. She began to stir and withdrew her hand. "Wade?"

"I'm right here," Quinn said softly and took a deep breath.

Rikki opened her eyes. "Hey," she said, affection in her voice.

He knew he looked like he hadn't slept. His eyes felt dry, and he assumed they were bloodshot. When he swept his hands through his hair, he cringed at the feel of oils building up. "I've been so worried about you. Are you feeling better?"

"I always feel better when you're around." She tried to smile. "What happened?"

"The doctor said that you have an infection of some sort. He said you'll have to be here for another day because the fever might come back. They have you on heavy-duty antibiotics."

"Did they say what kind of infection it is? How did I get it?"

"He didn't tell me. Your parents might know." The unspoken truth lingered between them—this unknown illness with an unknown origin may have been the work of Ms. Morgan. "I'm going to step outside and call Caden and Elle to let them know how you're doing."

"Don't leave me," Rikki begged.

"I'll be just outside the door." He kissed her on the forehead, but she recoiled.

"Are you okay?"

"Yeah. It felt like you shocked me with your lips," she said.

"Weird. I didn't feel anything," Quinn dismissed. "I'll be right back."

Quinn called Elle and told her that Rikki was awake and seemed to be doing okay, minus a few minor things, like repeatedly referring to him as Wade and not being as touchy-feely as she usually was.

"Are you guys going to come by after school?" Quinn asked.

"Caden probably will. I'll see her a different day." Elle's voice was distant.

"Um, okay. I'll let her know." Quinn hung up and went back to Rikki.

ELLE CAUGHT up to Caden before they got to Ms. Morgan's class.

"Hey," Elle said flatly.

"Hey." Caden didn't like the sound of her voice.

"Rikki's in the hospital with some infection. They don't know what it is. I just got off the phone with Quinn, and I told him that you might swing by after school, but I'll go see her a different day." Her voice was monotone.

"Okay. Is everything okay? Are you still mad at me?" Caden hated that he was so weak with her.

"Actually, I'm over it. You were right. I need to figure things out," she said matter-of-factly.

"You're *over* it? Just that quick? We were on the verge of having sex the other night, and you're *over* it?" Caden was angry. He refused to believe her. "So glad I did what I did."

"Whatever, Caden," Elle said with no real emotion.

"Yeah, whatever."

They walked into class at different times. The moment Caden stepped into Ms. Morgan's room, it occurred to him that maybe this was her doing. *"Make no mistake, all the bad things that you endure from here on out are because I've made them so."* He pursed his lips at the memory and quickly walked over to his seat, avoiding any eye contact with Ms. Morgan.

"Hey," he whispered to Elle.

She paused, then turned her head toward him and just looked at him blankly. She raised her eyebrows impatiently for him to get to the point.

"Do you think this is *her* doing?" Caden said, using his eyes to point to Ms. Morgan.

"What? Us?" Elle said, holding in her laugh. "I don't think so. I think she's planning to subject us to something far worse than this."

Caden grunted from the pain of her words. "You know, it's

one thing to say you're no longer into me, but now you're just being cruel."

ELLE ROLLED HER EYES, and Lyndsey caught sight of it. *The curse is working.* She glanced over at Quinn and Rikki's empty seats. *I hope that means my curse is working on Rikki as well.* Soon enough, she'd have everything she wanted, and she could live peacefully knowing that they had paid as high a price as she had.

After class, Lyndsey stopped Elle and Caden.

"So, how are my demands coming along?" Lyndsey pushed.

"I'm so over this," Elle said. "My mom sealed my room shut, and I'm not seasoned enough, nor do I remember enough, to work outside that room, so you got what you want. I'm not practicing. Can you leave me alone now?"

"What about my journals and my crystal?"

"We don't have your crystal, and the journals are locked up," Caden jumped in.

"Well then, you have your answer. Until I get all that I've asked for, you should sleep with one eye open."

"Whatever," Elle replied.

"Why is that your response to everything all of a sudden?" Caden asked, accusation in his voice.

"Hmmm, I'm sensing some tension here," Lyndsey said with a smirk.

"Can I go now?" Elle asked.

"You two can go and have a *great* weekend," she said with the sincerity of a flight attendant wishing her one-millionth passenger safe travels.

RIKKI STAYED in the hospital for a couple more days. Quinn found himself frustrated because Rikki's skin was still sensitive, and no matter what the doctors said, Quinn believed it was personal.

The day before, Elle had finally come to visit. She'd given Rikki a long hug, and Rikki had tolerated it like normal. Then a social worker had come in and touched her, and she'd had no problems with that either.

But when the social worker left, Quinn had reached for Rikki, and she'd shied away from his touch, yet again.

"I don't know what it is. When you touch me, I feel pain. I can't explain it," Rikki said.

"We need the doctor in here," Quinn demanded.

THE DOCTOR SPOKE with Rikki's parents and explained that she had developed a condition called allodynia. "The pain is very real to the person suffering from this," the doctor said with an odd look on his face. "But what is atypical here is that it seems to be specific to one person—her boyfriend. Do you know if something major happened between the two of them? She may have manifested the trauma."

"He did start dating another girl and treated Rikki horribly. He even threw a rock at her bedroom window, and it shattered, leaving her with a deep cut. But they seemed to have worked things out," Mr. Waters said.

The doctor shook his head, clearly at a loss. "I don't know what to tell you. The good news is that so far, it hasn't spread to other objects."

Rikki's parents explained the condition to both of them.

She shook her head like she was overhearing more bad news. "So you're telling me that because we had a rough patch, my body is reacting this way?" she asked, bewildered.

"Mr. and Mrs. Waters, can I speak with Rikki alone?" Quinn asked.

WHEN THEY LEFT THE ROOM, Quinn struggled with not being able to throw his arms around her while she blinked back her tears.

"Damn it, Ms. Morgan! This is her doing. I know it is." Quinn raised his voice.

"This is bad, Quinn. This is really bad. I can't live like this," she said, her voice wavered. "I thought that Elle was going to protect us. What happened?"

"About that. Elle told Caden that her mom freaked out and sealed the room with all the things she needs." Quinn's expression was pained.

"So she can't help us until she gets back into that room?"

"Right," Quinn said, raking his hands through his hair in frustration.

"What else are you not telling me?"

"I'm not sure if this is Ms. Morgan's doing or not, but Elle seems to have dropped the whole thing. She says she's 'overall this drama.'" Quinn swore under his breath. "I don't know. Maybe if I tell her what's going on—how bad it really is— somehow she can help." He rubbed his forehead. "I'm grasping as straws here, Rikki."

She nodded, then hung her head low, shaking it in defeat. She looked back up with such despair in her eyes. "I need you as close to me as possible, Quinn. Just for a second." There was desperation in her voice as she opened her arms. "I'll just endure it."

Quinn got up and gently pulled her bedsheets up to prevent skin-on-skin contact. He sat on the bed and placed his hands on both sides of her body and awkwardly leaned into her, not knowing where it was safe to put his arms. He felt her stiffen and hold her breath. Her body started to shake. When he looked up, her eyes were squeezed shut, and the grimace on her face was of sheer agony. He immediately leapt off her.

She cried out in pain. "Get off me! Get off me! I can't take it!"

"Rikki, open your eyes. I'm not even on you!"

"Then why is it getting worse?" she yelled, writhing in pain. She was panting. Her eyes shot open, spotting Quinn across the room.

Now *he* was the one in agony.

"What are we going to do?" she asked, pausing between words.

"Rikki, I love you. This has to be part of Ms. Morgan's game. Please, we just need to hold out a little longer." Quinn was desperate.

"I love you too. And I miss you," Rikki whimpered.

Her parents came running in. "What happened?" her mom asked.

"Did you touch her?" her dad accused.

"I—I— Yes," Quinn admitted, lowering his head.

"I asked him to," Rikki defended.

"He should know better," her mom said, then turned to him. "It's time for you to leave," Mrs. Waters ordered.

His head shot up as he stood tall. "Can I at least say good-bye?" Quinn was rapidly entering panic mode.

"Dad, please. It's my fault," Rikki pleaded.

Jutting his jaw, her dad broadened his shoulders and moved into Quinn's space, forcing him to move back.

"Dad! Stop it. He did nothing wrong!"

Quinn looked her in the eye and put his hand over his birthmark. He hoped she understood that was as close to a loving goodbye he could give.

"Leave now!" her father yelled.

Quinn closed his eyes in defeat. He swallowed his anger,

turned, and walked away. He looked back to get one last glimpse of her. Then the door slammed shut. He felt like his air supply had been severed. Walking away, he felt the vibrations startup. He stopped, grasped his birthmark, and squeezed his eyes shut. "Why are you letting go?" he asked quietly through gritted teeth, hoping he could will Rikki to have faith.

Quinn? Is that you?

Quinn's eyes widened hearing Rikki respond to him in his mind.

You can hear me?

I can hear you in my mind.

Woah. It's our birthmarks. Listen to me, Rikki—I can feel you letting go. Please don't let go. Promise me, he demanded in his head.

There was no response. He wasn't sure if that was because she refused to respond, or if their connection was weakening. He feared the latter as the vibrations showed no end in sight. "Damn it!"

2 0

THE RIKKI AND QUINN SHIT SHOW

Rikki stayed home for a week to recover, but she video chatted with Quinn daily.

"Elle's attitude is getting worse," Quinn said during one of their conversations. "Caden and I are thinking about going to another metaphysic to see if they can remove the curse. What do you think about that?"

"Sounds good. Have you found someone?"

"Not yet, but probably by this weekend."

"I miss you, Quinn." Rikki looked down in defeat.

"I miss you too. Just hang in there. I'll be there holding you soon enough, and I'll never let you go."

CADEN AND QUINN started the weekend by visiting a psychic by the name of Miss Brenda. She claimed that she'd have no problem lifting the curse. Her plan was to burn and bury some black candles. Her fee was $200—not including the candles— nor did it guarantee that it would work the first time around. She offered them a deal to purchase in bulk, which was followed by strongly suggesting that if they didn't do it soon, they'd have bad luck for years to come. They thanked her for her time, paid the $120 consultation fee, and left.

"Okay. That was a ripoff. Maybe we shouldn't look at the ones that advertise or that tourists go to," Caden suggested.

"Where are we going to find one then?" Quinn asked.

"I wonder how easy it is to find a coven. It's not like we want to become members or anything. We just need some direction."

"Maybe the Meetup app?" Quinn suggested.

"Okay. I mean, this *is* San Francisco, right? How hard can it be?"

Their adventure continued throughout the weekend. They visited spiritual and new age shops, coffee houses, bookstores, and even a yoga class. They were either told they didn't know of any or that it was a clandestine group and no visitors were allowed. One suggested that they be careful because rubbing a coven the wrong way might bring them the bad luck that Miss Brenda had talked about.

They reconvened at Java and Book to debrief. They stood third in line to place an order.

"Dude, we're so out of our element. I don't know how we're going to find a coven who will help us," Quinn said.

"I don't know what we're missing either. When we sit down, I'll Google it," Caden said, looking around to make sure Elle wasn't there.

Caden felt a tap on his shoulder and turned around.

"I'm sorry to bother you. I couldn't help but overhear what you were talking about," the man said. He was a tall and middle-aged man with straight brown hair and blond tips. "My name is Thomas. I used to work here ages ago," he said, waving his hand. "Anyway, I don't normally do this, but intuitively, I don't think this is just a chance meeting." He looked between the two of them. "I happen to be a leader of a coven. Can you tell me what help you need?"

Caden and Quinn turned to face him. "Wait. Did you work for Mozelle?"

Thomas placed his hands over his heart. "Yes. I did," he said. A deep frown emerged on his face. "May her ever-loving soul rest in peace."

"Yeah, about that," Caden said.

After they got what they ordered, Caden and Quinn sat on a couch while Thomas sat on the adjoining chair in a corner of the adjoining annex room. Quinn and Caden brought Thomas up to date on why they needed help. Before they knew it, Thomas invited them to come to his house after the ceremonial portion of his coven's weekly gathering.

They went to Thomas's coven's gathering the next night, held off 18th and Hartford in the Castro district. The group called themselves the Coven of the Crescent of Spectral Light, which was comprised entirely of married gay men. Their gathering took place on the bottom floor of their tall, Victorian-style home. The dark, polished-wood hallway led them to a wide archway of a large front room with a grand fireplace, white walls, and sprawling exposed wood beams that lined the ceiling.

The smell of burnt sage was briefly hard to escape before it dissipated completely. Burning candles had been strategically placed in spots that looked more elegant than ritualistic, while the fireplace mantle held a goblet with a knife inside.

Quinn looked at Caden, who shrugged.

It was a small group of five couples. The two men sitting on a long couch opposite the fireplace moved to either side of the couch. One patted the brown, overstuffed leather cushion, inviting them to take a seat. They obliged.

An African American man turned to face them. "Thomas has told us a little about what you are going through, and we are so impressed with your bravery. You are like heroes to your friends, and I hope one day they see the lengths you went through to help them. If not, we're here to help with that too." He winked and chuckled. "I'm just joking." He sighed. "Okay, not really." He laughed again.

Caden and Quinn laughed nervously.

"The look on your faces," commented an Asian man who was sitting on the arm of a red velvet chair adjacent to the couch, pointing at them. "You're both so cute. I could just eat you up!" he said, clasping his hands.

"You guys are awesome," Caden said.

They became fast friends and spent most of the night telling them all about their past and current lives. The members shared their own stories of their past and present lives. They also offered great relationship advice and told them their door was always open.

"I'm so glad that Mozelle is back and that it seems like maybe she's finding love in this life?" Thomas hinted.

Caden nodded and smiled bashfully. "One can hope, right?"

"Indeed," Thomas said and giving Caden a knowing look. "Once you get through all this, we would love to have you all come back and hang out with us."

"We would really like that," Caden promised.

Toward the end of the night, Thomas and his husband, Samuel, were able to tap into the source of the curse. They were advised that the curse was extraordinarily strong and well protected. "I'm sorry to be the bearer of bad news," Thomas said. "It's virtually impossible to reverse this unless you can get the caster to change her mind."

"Virtually, but not absolutely?" Quinn clarified.

Thomas nodded and sighed. "Is there anything or anyone she values?" Thomas asked.

"August," Quinn and Caden said simultaneously.

"What's in August?" Thomas asked.

"Not the month—the *man*. The only man Ms. Morgan ever loved," Caden said.

"Then you need to get on it, like, yesterday. He, my friends, is the key."

<hr>

THE FOLLOWING Monday at school was a challenging day. Caden saw Elle talking to some guy he didn't know. He was tall, with brown hair and brown eyes, and if someone were to compare Caden to that guy, they might think they were related.

"What the hell?" Caden said to Quinn during first break.

"I don't know what she's doing with that guy. I haven't seen him around, have you?" Quinn asked.

"No." A sneer emerged on Caden's face as he continued to stare. Elle glanced over at him, then averted her eyes back to the mystery guy.

When the bell rang, the guy placed his hand at the small of her back, whispered something in her ear, and laughed. Then they walked to class together.

Leaving Quinn behind, Caden left to confront Elle. He got as far as the hall of Ms. Morgan's classroom. "Elle!" He called out.

"Hold on. Let me deal with this," Elle told the mystery guy, then headed over to Caden. "What?" she snapped.

He took her arm and pulled her aside. "What the hell are you doing?"

"Oh, him? That's Fin. Yeah, um, we're kinda dating."

"Bullshit! Since when?" Caden stood there with his hands on his hips.

"Since this weekend, and it's not bullshit," she said, looking at Fin suggestively.

"How can you be so blind? I mean, geez, look at him. He's like me, well, before the upgrade. And this attitude of yours? It's all Ms. Morgan's doing. How can you not see it? How can you not see that your closest friends are suffering because of that woman? It's just like she promised. How do you not feel any desire to help us?"

"What do you want me to say?" Elle asked plainly.

"'What do I want you to say?'" Caden repeated, his voice getting louder with every word.

Fin walked over as if to assess the situation. "What's your problem, man?" Fin said, puffing up his chest and invading his space. "If she has nothing to say to you, she fucking has nothing to say to you."

"Fuck you, asshole. If you knew her, you would know she can take care of herself, you fuck!" Caden confronted and shoved Fin away.

Elle quickly got between them and stood between the two men. "Stop!" she yelled. "Fin, I'll see you after school. I've got this!" she said, gesturing for him to move on. When he was a good distance away, she looked at Caden with fury in her eyes. "I know you're in love with me. I know you're jealous of Fin. I know Quinn and Rikki are having issues. What else is new? But Caden, you're the one who said you were stepping aside. That's on you, not Ms. Morgan."

Caden's mouth dropped. He raised his arms in disbelief, then took a step closer to her. "Really? I know you, Elle. I know you better than most. I know that you're the most compassionate person I've ever met. I know it's true now, just as it was true before. It's your soul's true self. Fin and this apathetic attitude is completely against your character, against the essence of your very soul." He took a deep breath. "Please, Elle. Please remember that about yourself because we really can't do this without you." He was begging.

"I think that you're getting 'being compassionate' mixed up with 'being a tool.' I'm not a tool! And now I'm done with this!" She turned and walked away.

Caden swept his fingers through his hair and let out an exasperated breath as Rikki came walking by. Quinn was twenty steps behind.

"Hey, welcome back," Caden said as he gave her a big hug. He let go when he saw how sad Quinn looked at the gesture.

"What's wrong?" Rikki asked.

"Elle. That's what's wrong," he spouted before walking into class.

RIKKI WAITED for Quinn to enter the classroom first. She made her way to her seat, hoping that she could at least sit next to him. For a few minutes into Ms. Morgan's lecture, she seemed to do fine, but she started feeling pain in her head as the minutes passed. She put her hands to her temples to alleviate the pain, but it didn't help. She started feeling nauseous, then began sweating. She did everything she could to get to the end of class. No way was she going to be the center of attention yet again.

"Rikki, are you okay?" Quinn asked, moving his hands as if trying to find a spot where he could touch her, but failed.

She shook her head as her face began to turn red.

"What do you need me to do?"

She lifted an unsteady hand to stop him from doing anything more while covering her mouth. But her eyes said it all —she was in distress.

"Rikki, damn it. Get some help," he implored in a loud whisper. "I can see the veins in your temples throb." He started to fidget in his seat, shoving his fingers through his hair and clasping them behind his head as it hung low. He hit the desk with his fist.

Rikki leaned away from Quinn. "Stop it, Quinn. You're making this worse." She eyed the door in the back, planning her stealthy escape.

"Quinn?" Ms. Morgan called. "Everything okay?"

"I don't think Rikki is feeling well. She should go to the nurse's office."

Rikki gripped the top of her desk and gave Quinn the stink eye for ignoring her pleas.

"Rikki, are you okay? Do you want to go to the nurse?" Ms. Morgan asked. "Quinn, why don't you walk with her?" she suggested with a raised eyebrow.

Quinn looked at Ms. Morgan with ferocity in his eyes. "She says she doesn't want to go."

"Thanks a lot, Quinn," Rikki bit. She looked at the clock. Five minutes left, and the class wouldn't have had to know. Her breath was ragged as her body trembled and stomach clenched. The agony worsened with each second that went by. She had never endured pain like that before. Even when compared to the pain from cancer in her previous life, this was far worse.

The bell rang, and everyone got up except for Quinn, Caden, and Rikki. Elle left with the rest of the students.

Rikki moved away from Quinn and doubled over. Caden came to her.

"What can I do for you?" Caden asked, his hand on her shoulder.

"It's unbearable!" she yowled. A warm liquid slid out of her nose. She wiped it. She stared at the blood as it trickled down her fingers. "Oh, no."

"Let's get you to the nurse's office. Can you stand up?" Caden asked as he held his arms out to support her.

"Please ask Quinn to go away," she whispered.

QUINN SAW Caden's "you need to leave" look. He took his cue and turned to go. On the way out, he stopped as he was passing Ms. Morgan. "You won't win," he challenged.

Once in the hallway, Quinn took several steps back to give Caden and Rikki space. She looked at Quinn with such pain in her eyes. She covered her mouth and ran to the nearest trash can, where she threw up. Caden was there to hold her hair back with one hand and rub her back with the other. Quinn's chest was heavy, making it hard for him to breathe.

He remembered going through this with Robin—the pain he had endured while watching Chris be there for Robin. Even though Chris's care had been adequate at best, he'd still gotten to be there for her.

When Rikki was done, her body became weak, and her legs gave out. Quinn took several steps toward her to catch her, but Caden was there first. He swooped her up, cradling her, and she wrapped her arms around his neck. He began to walk toward the nurse's office, and Quinn could see Rikki's body relax with every step Caden took.

As soon as they were out of view, Quinn kicked the trash cans, knocking them over, then punched the lockers. "*Fuck!*" he yelled as he gave a locker another hard punch. He turned and slid down to his hunches, covering his eyes with the heels of his palms.

Later, Quinn went to the newsroom to submit his photos for the day and find out what had happened with Rikki. He found Caden in his usual position, fact-checking or editing on the school's computer.

"So what happened?" Quinn asked, handing Caden an SD card.

"Nothing. I just brought her to the nurse. As you'd expect, the farther she got away from you, the better she felt. I think she was one hundred percent by the time we got to the Nurse Hannah's office, but they sent her home anyway."

His jaw was set as he nodded his head. "Well, I'm glad you were there for her," he said, trying to hide his jealousy.

"Sorry, man."

"It's not your fault. Anyway, what's the latest on this August guy?"

"Well, it looks like he still teaches at Stanford. The problem is that I need Elle to come with me."

"Why?"

"Well, I won't know what to do if he tells me how to cast some spell that will free us from all this. It's like speaking another language. She can conceptualize it far better than me. Then if she decides she wants to modify it, she can ask him questions right then and there. Plus, this might be a one-time thing. What if he can only meet with us once? It's just not worth the risk that I won't be able to explain it right to her, no matter how good my notes are."

"So, how are you going to get her to come with you?"

"Don't know yet. That'll be quite a hurdle."

"I'll try talking to Elle too," Quinn volunteered.

"Well, good luck with that. She pretty much said we're using her and that she wants out."

"How does she not see what's really happening?"

"You have to remember, it wasn't that long ago we all had that same thought about you," Caden said, shrugging his shoulders.

"You're right, but even then, you would think she would see the similarities."

"Yeah, I don't know what to tell you," Caden said.

"How are you feeling?" Quinn asked Rikki over video group chat. Caden was on as well.

"Better," Rikki replied.

"So I'm going to call the university tomorrow to see if August is available for an appointment," Caden briefed.

"Uh-huh," Rikki grumbled.

"What's with the discouraging attitude?" Quinn challenged.

"I'm exhausted, and it's just one obstacle after another," Rikki said as she rested her chin on her hand. "I'm going to go now. I guess I'll see you at school tomorrow ... somehow. I'm like a depressing and rare piece of art to you, aren't I? One that you can't touch. Anyway, I don't know what else to say." She logged off without waiting to hear their responses.

Rikki went up to Ms. Morgan at the beginning of class the next day. She wanted to have her seat changed.

"I know you want to see us suffer, but if you make me sit by Quinn, it'll literally kill me. Isn't it enough that we will probably never be able to be together again?" Rikki whispered. "Because I'll tell you something—"

"Fine. You can sit in the front, there in the first row." Ms. Morgan pointed at the seat, then touched Rikki's arm. "This isn't mercy," she said with a calculated smirk on her face.

Rikki took her new assigned seat, then looked over at Quinn. He was staring at her with a mournful look on his face. She jumped when her phone vibrated with a text, only to see that he'd texted, *I miss you!* Rikki gave a slight smile but didn't text back. Part of her welcomed the space. She could listen to the class lecture, even though it was straight out of the mouth of the one person who was going to destroy her life. *Ms. Morgan is going to win.*

After class, Elle walked out without saying anything. Rikki's heart sank.

"Elle!" she called out.

Elle slowly turned toward her.

"You were going to walk out of the class without even asking how I'm doing?"

"How are you doing?" Elle asked like she was bored.

"I'm better. So are you walking away from our friendship too? I thought I meant more to you than that."

"I just need space. I've been stripped of my identity and

threatened. Like I told Caden, I'm over it. I did what I could, but now I'm moving on. I suggest you do the same."

"But why does that mean moving on from me?" Rikki started to tear up.

"Because you're stuck in suspended animation, Rikki. I do care about you, but I'm over getting involved in the "Rikki and Quinn Shit Show". I'm sorry. I know this means that you'll lose Quinn, but my needs come first. I hope one day you'll understand." Elle walked away and joined Fin.

AFTER SCHOOL, the three of them video chatted again.

"I'm feeling diseased and isolated," Rikki said.

Quinn scoffed like he was annoyed. "What's the latest, Caden?" Quinn said to get the debriefing underway.

"Um, well, August Cariso is on sabbatical, and they don't know when he'll be back, but typically it's a year-long break. They won't give me any details—not when he left, not where he went, not how to get in touch with him. I did leave a message saying, 'You don't know me, but you know my teacher, Lyndsey Morgan. It's imperative you call me back.'"

There was a long silence.

"Rikki?" Caden said as if it was her turn to say something.

"I surrender," she said. "I'm completely spent. I can't even cry about it anymore," she added.

"Fuck that. I'm not giving up! Rikki, I'm not giving up!" Quinn yelled. "I'll figure this out."

"Maybe we should just give her the crystal," Rikki said weakly. "It's not the crystal that defines us. It's *us* who define us."

"Giving her the crystal would be devastating. She'd probably destroy it, and we'd probably forget everything that's happened. The crystal is something that's supposed to be with us in every lifetime. You want to give that up over a damn hurdle? A hurdle that can be cleared if we give it time?" He slammed his fist on the desk he was sitting at.

She shook her head.

"Rikki, I will wait a lifetime if I have to!" Quinn yelled, hoping to wake her from her despair. Her expression remained distant. He lowered his head, grasping the top of his hair. "Damn it! It pains me that you don't want to wait, like at all."

"Guys, let's end this here before you say something you can't take back," Caden mediated.

Lyndsey paced along her hallway, occasionally going into her temple room like she was going to do something, then turning around and leaving because she didn't know what she what that *something* would be. She was growing impatient. *I want this settled already so I can go on with my life. I need to light a fire under them.* She snapped her finger. "Fire as in heat. That's it." She had to get Rikki and Quinn near each other for a good amount of time. Enchanting an oil that would make Quinn irresistible to Rikki was a good start. *She will be so intoxicated with lust for him that it'll consume and even fool her into believing she can rise above the pain, only to discover it'll never get better. She can't "mind over matter" herself out of it. And they'll be compelled to give in to my demands.* She reentered her temple room, this time fully knowing what she was going to do.

Quinn walked along the corridor to his locker. He could feel Rikki nearby. He closed his eyes at the thought of her being close. He recalled the feel of her body under his. A frown emerged at the idea of being unable to do anything about that. He stood in front of his locker until he felt her leave. When he went to open his locker, he recoiled like an over-torqued spring. There was an oily substance coating the lock. He winced and rubbed his fingers on his pants. "What the hell?" He ran to the bathroom and washed his hands. "Bitch!" He prayed that whatever Ms. Morgan had planned, he was able to thwart it.

Lyndsey's eyes followed Quinn as he entered her class late. As he moved past Rikki, Lyndsey glanced at her just as she began to fan herself.

Lyndsey stopped mid-sentence, watching Rikki's leg sensuously swing back and forth as she played with her hair while sneaking a peek at Quinn. Lyndsey smirked, proud of her handiwork.

"Ms. Morgan?" a student called out.

"Sorry! I got distracted by my own work." she laughed and then continued with the lecture.

Rikki texted Quinn, *I miss you.*

I miss you too, was his reply.

Rikki's mind began to wander to the night in the greenhouse —how the cords of his muscles had moved with every drive. His moans when he buried himself deeper into her. His vulnerability when he came.

The bell rang, jolting Rikki out of her reverie. She got up and left the class without saying anything. She was flustered and embarrassed. For the rest of the day, and even after she got home, whenever she had a moment's peace, she allowed herself to become entranced by the need to have him inside her again.

Hey! Is everything okay? You left class in a hurry, and I haven't seen or heard from you, Quinn texted.

She called Quinn. "I'm fine. I want to see you. I don't know what's happening, but I feel better than I have since I got sick. I want to see if I've gotten over it. Can we meet up?"

"I don't know if that's such a good idea," Quinn said hesitantly.

"How will I ever know if we don't try? I'll get better. You said it yourself."

"But it's not a disease, Rikki. It's a curse."

"Please," Rikki begged.

She knew she was breaking him down. He sighed. "Where do you want to meet?"

"My parents aren't here."

"Um, yeah, okay."

<hr>

QUINN WAS THERE by eight o'clock. He heard her invite him to come in. When he opened the door, she was standing at the top of the stairs wearing a button-down shirt. Quinn swallowed hard. Her silhouette showed through her shirt, making it clear she wasn't wearing anything underneath it.

"What are you doing, Rikki?" Quinn asked, trying to fight his arousal.

"Come on up. Let's see if we can do this."

He started up the stairs and tripped a bit when he saw her shirt fall off her shoulder. He stopped to gauge her reaction. "I want you to step all the way to the back of the hall toward your room."

Rikki did as she was told.

At the top of the stairs, he took a few steps toward her, then stopped. Her rapid breathing made him stand still.

"I'm okay, Quinn," she encouraged, but there was uncertainty in her voice. If she felt anything, she chose to ignore it as she strode toward him.

"Rikki, what are you doing? You need to slow down!" he said, moving backward, looking behind himself so he wouldn't trip and fall down the stairs.

"I'm so hot for you. Whatever pain I'm feeling is nothing compared to my need to have you inside me again."

"No, Rikki. I'm not going to chance it. I thought you just wanted to see if we could be a little closer." Quinn put his hand up. His breath caught when he bumped into the railing.

Rikki began to unbutton her shirt so that it still covered just enough to tease, but not enough to maintain Quinn's control.

He stopped resisting and just stood still against the metal railing as his breath quickened.

Her lips lifted on one side as she looked at him with victory in her eyes. "Take off your shirt."

"Rikki, please ..."

"I can't do it for you." Her voice was low and full of lust.

Quinn unbuttoned his shirt but didn't take it off completely.

She growled at the sight of his chest heaving with longing. She took a few steps closer, closing the gap. She felt something, but it wasn't enough for her to stop. She lunged and adhered her lips and her body to his. He instantly closed his arms around her.

It was as if she had fallen on a beehive, and the bees had invaded her mouth, stinging her lips, gums, tongue, and throat. She was being stung on every inch of her body that came into contact with his. She shrieked in pain, and he threw her off of him.

"Rikki! Rikki!" he shouted, running to pick her up off the floor.

"Don't touch me! Get away from me!" she yelled as she waved him away. She was in hysterics. Still on the floor, she curled up like she was taking cover and cried out. "I'm in so much pain!" She rocked back and forth, holding herself close and shivering.

Quinn ran down the stairs, trying to get as far away from her as he could. He paced, not knowing what to do next. "I don't get what just happened. Please talk to me, Rikki!"

She moved to the top step and sat down. Her face was swollen and red as she buttoned up her shirt. "I'm utterly mortified," she said, unable to look him in the eye.

"Please, please, don't be. If we weren't under this curse, I would have taken you the moment I saw you at the top of the stairs."

"You were right. This was Ms. Morgan's doing. It started in class. I kept thinking of that night in the greenhouse, and I got myself all worked up, like I was a slave to my hormones."

"Welcome to my world," Quinn quipped.

She covered her eyes as she continued to weep. Quinn lingered fifteen feet away from her. "She did to me what she did to you and *what's her face*. I want you so bad, and she knows it. I want you inside me like you were in the greenhouse, and it's literally impossible. I can't live another life like this. To be around you and not touch you? I just can't!" She sat there, wrapped in her shirt, trying to calm herself down. "She wants me to lust after you—not that I don't already—but I would never do what I did tonight."

"That's a disappointment. You're sexy as hell, and that was really hot." His eyes drifted like he was replaying the image, then shook his head. "No, tonight will be an image to carry me through many, many lonely nights, let me tell you. No man could be this lucky."

"My point is that she wants me to yearn for you but not be able to touch you."

"So, are you going to let her win?"

"I don't see a choice. She made her point. I get it now."

Sadness emerged from her pain. "Please go, Quinn, before you hurt me again. Please." She got up and left his sight.

"I'm not giving up!" he swore and left.

IN CLASS THE NEXT DAY, Quinn confronted Ms. Morgan.

"I know what you did to Rikki yesterday," Quinn said.

"And you're welcome," Ms. Morgan chuckled.

"You're nothing but a one-trick pony. You're desperate and weak, and it won't take Elle long to recognize what you've done with her is the same as what you did with me."

Ms. Morgan's expression turned angry. "Even if she gets it, she's too far gone to care."

"We'll see about that. We're not giving up."

"Oh, no. It's already happened. You just don't know it yet, and I'm growing impatient. Now stop fucking with me and give me what I want. Or next time, there'll be no pleasure, only pain. Now class is about to start, so get in your seat."

Rikki showed up late. She didn't even look at Quinn.

Avoiding me? Quinn texted.

Avoiding pain, so that's a yes, she replied.

Enraged, after school, Quinn went to Java and Book to speak with Elle. When he arrived, he saw she was with Fin. *Painful to see them together.* He couldn't imagine how bad Caden must feel.

"I need to talk to you," he said with no pretense of being happy to see her.

"You too?" Elle rolled her eyes.

"Are you so obtuse that you don't see what Ms. Morgan has done to you is the same as what she did to me?" he asked, hoping his harshness would rile her up. "And you've just allowed her to win. All that work you've done, not just for the four of us, but for all her future victims, was all in vain. Really, Elle, you're such a disappointment." He waited for her to respond, and when she didn't, he continued. "The silent treatment. Uh-huh. Too proud to admit that what I'm saying rings true. Hopefully, it won't be too late by the time you remove your head out of your ass." Quinn set his jaw. His eyes burned with outrage, and he stormed out.

Rikki stood at the bottom of the steps, which stopped Quinn dead in his tracks for several reasons. "You scared me. I didn't feel you coming." His rage was so intense he hadn't noticed the vibration.

"Caden told me I would find you here," she said flatly. "Let's go across the street."

She walked in front of him, wearing that infamous white sweater as she made her way to the park where they'd kissed for the first time. *Well, in this lifetime,* he thought. As she moved away from him, he felt the vibration start up. His body sunk in weakness because feeling the vibrations meant one thing—they were working to bring together what was falling apart. *It's par for the course, so why am I surprised she's going to break up with me?* He stopped for a minute, taking in her beauty and remembering that night there on that bench.

"By your expression, I'm guessing Elle continues to be a dead-end?" Rikki asked, looking out at the water. Dark clouds were moving in over the bay, and she wrapped her sweater tighter around her body.

"She won't help. She doesn't even believe that Ms. Morgan is behind all this," Quinn said. A shaky breath escaped him. "Rikki, I can't let go."

"The way you made me feel yesterday, Quinn, it's like I know it's not your fault, but I found myself becoming angry … at you. You have no idea the pain I'm in, physically and emotionally."

"You don't think I have an idea of your emotional pain? Really? I sometimes think I can't *breathe* without you. You're my world, Rikki, and I can't lose you." He shook his head.

"I'm thinking of going to private school for the remainder of the school year, so there won't be this longing for each other."

Jutting his jaw, he shook his head and put his hands on his hips. His breaths were sharp as they escaped through his nose. "Not seeing you makes the longing worse," Quinn challenged.

She turned and looked at Quinn. "You'll get over it," she snapped.

"Why are you angry with me?"

"Because you want to protect me, but you won't let me go because of *your* pain, not mine," she said with such sharpness—he was surprised he didn't start bleeding.

"You're absolutely right. I *was* being selfish, but I also believe this will be reversed any day now. And to me, it feels like you're giving up so easily. I mean, it's only been a couple weeks."

"For me, it's nonstop torture. If I'm not living it, I'm dreaming it. It's all day, every day for me. I wish just hearing you breathe was enough for me, but I want more. Quinn, you'll always be the love of my life. But maybe we're not supposed to be together in this life. Maybe we have to wait again."

"So that's it? You can walk away, just like that?" He sucked in his upper lip, shaking his head. "Don't do this, Rikki."

"At school, please give me my space. I will also let Ms. Morgan know that she can check another thing off her list of demands. Eventually, we'll need to part with the crystal as well. I just need to take this one step at a time."

"This is so fucked up!" He turned away from her, then picked up a rock and chucked it.

"Goodbye, Quinn." Rikki stood and walked away.

"*Fuck!*" he yelled, and collapsed onto his knees.

Every day, Quinn came to school looking worse and worse. He neglected to shave. He looked pale, gaunt, and depressed. Rikki didn't look much better either. Even Elle took notice.

"Every day, I think it'll be the day you wake up and start taking care of yourself, but every day, I'm shocked to see that you look worse than the day before," Elle said to Quinn one day outside class.

"And every day, I think it'll be the day you wake up and realize that Ms. Morgan is behind all this and that you hold the key, but every day, you seem to care less than the day before." Quinn's comeback was harsh. "You're like a tease when you say things like that because you *can* help, but you don't. I wish you wouldn't even talk to me."

Elle's heart wilted at his words. She wanted out of all the drama, but she didn't want to see her two friends suffer. She reached for Quinn. "Quinn, I …"

Caden came running into class and sat down. He leaned in as he wheezed but had a huge smile on his face. "August called!"

"I want to help," Elle blurted out.

Caden and Quinn heads spun toward Elle and looked at her with speculation. "What?"

"Okay, I don't want to get *too* involved, but Quinn, you look like death, and you're kind of freaking me out. So I'll listen to what you have to say, Caden."

"Um, okay, yeah, great! Let's just meet at the café after school," Caden said.

"Sounds good, but in the meantime, let's not mention it to Rikki. I don't want to get her hopes up about something that might lead us nowhere. But August had good news for us, right?"

"That's the impression I got from the tone of his voice," Caden reassured.

That afternoon, Caden and Quinn sat at the counter at Java and Book and waited for Elle's undivided attention.

"Okay, so I got a call this morning from August. He said that he was out of the country, but he will be returning this weekend. He said that he hadn't spoken to Ms. Morgan in like eighteen years and that things hadn't ended the way he hoped. I told him that we heard of him when she talked about his book to the class. I could swear he was happy to hear about her. I told him that she's in trouble and that we need his help. I asked if we could meet with him in person … and he agreed," Caden explained.

"He agreed?" Quinn asked with excitement in his voice.

"He agreed," Caden confirmed with a huge smile.

"So when does the meeting take place?" Elle asked.

"On Sunday. He seemed concerned and wants to get to the bottom of it as soon as possible." He turned to Elle. "You say you want to help? Here's your chance."

"I'll go, but I'm not making any promises. I just can't stand seeing you like this," she said, looking at Quinn. "I'll hear what August has to say."

"That's all we've been asking," Caden said, then turned to Quinn. "I think you should stay here. We're not sure what to expect, and you're our only point of contact should anything go wrong."

"That's fine."

Caden turned back to Elle. "I'm guessing you need to get Fin's permission." Caden couldn't help but be patronizing.

"*Really*, Caden? I just agreed to go with you, and you *still* go and pull that shit? He probably *won't* be okay with it, but whatever. He's just going to have to trust that I won't betray him."

Those words hit Caden hard. He felt a crushing feeling in his chest. It was an unexpectedly rude awakening to know that this road trip wouldn't do much to mend their fractured friendship, let alone offer any chance for a romantic encounter. He only had himself to blame because he was the one who had chosen to step aside.

"Okay. I'll come by early on Saturday. Be prepared. It might be an all-nighter. I expect some things will be going down." He blushed at how bad that sounded. "That didn't sound the same in my head." He laughed nervously.

Elle snorted. "I was gonna say—"

Zinged again.

THE MIRROR

Caden pulled up to Elle's house and texted that he was outside waiting. Wearing black gradient sunglasses, she walked out in a black halter that complemented her shoulder-length white hair, with torn gray leggings and black combat boots. Each confident stride confirmed she was the star of every young guy's fantasy of hotness and self-assuredness, but she wasn't a fantasy. She was real. Caden blew out a breath and white-knuckled the steering wheel. He wasn't sure if he would be able to contain his feelings.

She slid in. "Where to?"

He swallowed reflexively. "Um." He blinked a couple times to snap himself out of his headspace. "Yes. That would be Lexington Hills," he announced while putting the address into the GPS. "Looks like it'll take about an hour and a half to get there. Last chance to change your mind," he jokingly warned, then locked the doors. "Now youse can't leave," he said, quoting *A Bronx Tale*, then flashed a huge smile.

"Let's get outta here," she said as if she was looking forward to it.

Forty-five minutes into the ride, they got hungry and went through an In-N-Out drive-through.

"Will you be eating in the car, or are you taking it home?" the young teen asked over the intercom.

"In our car," Caden said.

"So that'll be one double-double, one single with cheese, a Dr. Pepper, a chocolate shake, and two fries animal style," the teen confirmed.

"That's right."

Caden parked in a shaded area for them to enjoy their meal.

"So, do you want to address the elephant in the room now or later?" Caden poked as he handed Elle her fries.

"Are you calling Fin an elephant?"

"Um, yes. Yes, I am."

"What's there to talk about? He likes me, you stepped aside, and there you have it."

"Do you like him?"

She could have answered him but took another bite of her hamburger instead.

"Hello?" Caden wasn't going to let it go.

She swallowed. "I don't know. Are you going to make this an uncomfortable trip?"

"I just want to make sure we're on the same page, so there aren't any misunderstandings." Caden could tell that he was slipping into territory even he wasn't comfortable with. "Anyway, did you bring anything with you to take notes or prepare if you need to cast something?"

"No, because I said I was just going to listen. I made no promises," she said defensively. "Did you misunderstand me?" she asked, throwing his words back at him.

"No. You've made it quite clear you just want to listen."

"What do you mean 'quite clear'?" she asked as if she was rearing for a fight.

"You just want to be passive about the whole thing. I'm not

judging; it's just an observation." Caden paused. "Okay, It's a bit of a judgment because passive is an improvement compared to where you were a couple days ago."

Elle took a deep breath but said nothing. She was quiet the rest of the ride there.

They arrived at August's home around noon. It was a beautiful two-bedroom home surrounded by woods.

A tall, salt-and-pepper man came out and warmly greeted them with firm handshakes and a brief hug. His skin was tan and smelled of incense.

Caden and Elle were utterly enamored with the interior when they entered the home. It was lined with books everywhere. Any space books didn't cover—his immense collection of artifacts did.

"Any part of the world you *haven't* been?" Elle asked.

"Buffalo, New York. I've never been to Buffalo," August said. They couldn't tell if he was joking or not.

"You have a beautiful home," Elle complimented.

"Thank you. I've been in this house since I started at Stanford," August said with pride.

"Really? So you even raised your family in this house?"

"No. I, uh, I never married," August admitted. "Sometimes I feel like I'm married to my job and my books. We certainly have that similar love/hate dynamic of an old married couple. I won't even get a Kindle for fear of betraying my tangible, old, bound books."

Elle walked about the room, looking at the pictures displayed on the walls, bookcases, and shelves. "Wow! Is this Ms. Morgan? She looks so young with her hair in a braid and that top she's wearing. You would never see her in something like that," Elle commented after finding a photo of her and August standing by a yurt surrounded by tropical forest. "Aww. And you're not even looking at the camera. You're looking at her. That's so sweet."

"That is us. We were in the Amazon Rainforest. I remember that moment vividly too. The tragic thing about that photo is that she's never seen it. I don't think she was even aware that I was staring at her." He gave a closed-lipped smile and shook his head as if not knowing how they ended up that way. "She had come out of her yurt that day, and she was just illuminated from within."

"You said on the phone that it didn't end the way you were hoping?" Caden asked, taking a chance. He didn't know if jumping right in would help or hinder the purpose of them being there.

Elle seemed to disagree, though. She whipped around and glared daggers in his direction. "Jesus, Caden, let the man be. Don't go hounding him about—"

"No, it's fine. She was a feisty one." August chuckled, then looked away. "I don't know. I was kind of an ass. But being in a remote, secluded area for that length of time, and the journey we shared? Well, we had our moments together," he said with the kind of smile people flash to hide pain. "She left without me, and I always felt awkward about calling her. That was a lifetime ago. How is she doing? I'm guessing she's mentioned me because, well, you're here."

"She did mention you. She teaches Mythology and Folklore at our high school. She brought your book into class once, and when we asked how she knew the author, she lit up. She said nothing but kind words about you. She said that you helped her get over her insecurity about her scar and that the trip to Brazil left such an impression that it was the reason she continued to study anthropology," Elle explained.

August humphed like he was impressed. "Wow, I love hearing that," he said with a smile, then the expression on his face turned to concern. "So what about her brought you here today?" he asked, inviting them to follow him.

HE LED them to a remarkable kitchen, not because it had an impressive collection of appliances and granite countertops, but because it was designed to worship the sunlight. Rays of light poured in from the ceiling. The table was located in the adjoining solarium that showcased the sweeping deep forest that surrounded the house.

"This is enchanting," Elle said. "You have such a respect for nature."

"Took the words right out of my mouth," Caden agreed.

"Thank you. Take a seat while I make us some tea. Any requests?"

They both shook their heads.

August hummed while standing at the stovetop that faced the table, allowing him to observe the two concerned students. He could sense that even though they were admiring the scenery, they avoided looking at each other. It was when the kettle went off, startling them both, that they finally looked at each other. A serious expression emerged in their lingering gazes. *He likes her, she secretly likes him, but they're angry at each other.* He could practically visualize some of their past exchanges.

The instant he placed their cups in front of them, the tension broke. They laughed nervously like they'd been caught, triggering both pleasant and not-so-pleasant memories of Lyndsey.

"Tell me what's going on," August started as he took a seat.

"Okay. Just know that you might not like what you hear. But we wouldn't have come to you if we felt that she was a lost cause. We're hoping you can be the one to bring her back," Caden explained.

August leaned back as dread laid heavy in the pit of his stomach. *What has she gotten herself into?* "Um, okay," he said, then crossed his arms as if to brace himself for bad news.

"She's become a dark witch."

He sat up, planted his elbows on the table, and rested his forehead on his hands, shielding his eyes. "You know, that was the one thing I was hoping you wouldn't say." August raked his hands through his hair. "How do you know?" he asked. He could hear the distress in his own voice.

"Well, it all started with her mom."

"I'm familiar," he said. "She told me that her mom and dad were soulmates and that when her mom was dying of cancer, there was a curse placed on her parents that prevented them from ever finding each other in their next lives. It was the doing of one of her mom's caretakers, a witch. It's why she came to me. She wanted to learn how to find her parents when they reincarnated to reverse the curse."

When he was met with silence, August looked between the two kids. Their mouths were agape. August's heart raced. "What?"

<hr>

"Um, yeah. That couldn't be further from the truth," Caden said firmly, sweeping his hand as if to remove any further misinformation.

"No way," August said with a smirk on his face. He leaned back and crossed his arms, clearly confident that he knew better than they did.

"Really." Caden took a deep breath. "August, I'm Lyndsey's dad. I *am* Chris. This here next to me is Mozelle, the one who performed the ritual." Caden paused, staring at August as he waited for him to absorb what he was saying.

Still skeptical, August looked between the two of them. "Odd. Go on."

"The truth is that my wife, Robin, Lyndsey's mother, *did* find her soulmate, but it wasn't me."

"So you're here to seek revenge?" August inserted.

Caden put his hand up to stop August from taking that thought any further. "No. Since Elle and I have remembered our former selves, it's become obvious to me that my former wife did, in fact, meet her soulmate. And there *was* a ritual performed, but for Robin and her soulmate, Wade. After the fire, Lyndsey found Mozelle's journal and discovered the truth. She's on some twisted quest to prevent Robin and Wade from being together. That's why she sought you out. The hell she's paid as a result of her mother's supposed betrayal has led her down this dark path of revenge."

"I mean, it all makes sense," August said and shook his head, looking out the window. "I'm still shocked. I knew her to be kind and thoughtful. Feisty. She was definitely a feisty one," August said and sighed.

"Yeah, you mentioned that. I wish we could say the same. She has unleashed her wrath since she found out that we figured it out. She has allowed Rikki, who was Robin, and Quinn, who was Wade, to find each other and fall in love, only to rip them apart. She nearly killed me, and she's cursed Elle," he said.

Elle just sat there with her arms crossed.

"She's caused our best friend, Elle, here," Caden said, turning toward her, "who we care about so much ..." He paused. *Please listen to me.* "Sorry, Elle is gifted, and Lyndsey knows that Elle can stop her, so she cursed her to become apathetic and resistant to helping us. It was only after seeing how devastated Rikki and Quinn are that she decided to come for the ride to listen to what you have to say." Caden's chest became heavy over Elle's lack of reaction to what he was saying. He turned to August. "Can you help us? I didn't know who else I could turn to, and I worry the more time gets away from us, the more frustrated Ms. Morgan will become, leading to greater trouble for all of us and her. She is incredibly strong."

August stood and put his hands on his hips, exhaling in defeat. "She had me fooled."

Caden needed to reel August back in. "She was, and still is, lost. But she told us the impact you had on her. That was *real*. She told us that she never contacted you because she believed you didn't feel the same way. We think that you can help her and also help us."

"I'm not sure what I can do," August said, staring at the woods just outside the window.

"You can start by lifting the curse on Elle. Are you able to do that?"

"How long will you both be staying?" August asked.

"We can get a hotel if this is going to take longer than a day," Caden said.

"That won't be necessary. I have an extra room and a sofa bed that you can use. This is a lot to digest, and I need to meditate to get some clarity. In the meantime, please make yourselves at home." He drew in a sigh, then left the room.

After fifteen minutes, August came back. His demeanor had changed from needing clarity to determined. "I want to help."

"That was fast," Elle observed like she was impressed.

"I think I can bring her back," he said, then looked at Elle. "Can you give me something personal of yours? A couple strands of hair would do."

Elle pulled a couple strands from her hair and gave them to August.

"Give me ten minutes. In the meantime, please step outside on my deck and enjoy the sights. Or better yet, check out my herb garden. I have some of the rarest species of basil. I invite you to take a taste."

Caden and Elle walked out onto his deck. There were stairs down to a path through a wooded area that wound around the large property. A patch of sunlight hit the basil crop like a spotlight.

"So, what are your thoughts?" Caden asked as he handed her a basil leaf.

"I think he can help Rikki," she said, smelling the herb and then nibbling on it.

"What about you? Do you think he can help you?"

"I mean, I guess if I needed help, he could," Elle said with a shrug.

"If you think you don't need his help, then why did you give him your hair?"

"I didn't want him to feel bad. I'll end up pretending that it worked too."

Caden scoffed. "Uh-huh."

"Sorry, but it's the truth. I don't think anything is right with me," Elle said, enjoying her basil.

"Wait, what? What do you mean by that?"

"I mean, I don't think anything is *wrong*. Seriously, Caden!" she yelled. "Why do you think that if I'm not fawning for you, it means there's something wrong with me? Why do you think I don't care?" She pointed harshly at him.

"Elle, it's okay," he said with his hand up. "You're not into me. It's all my fault. It has nothing to do with some evil, dark witch that wants nothing but to siphon every drop of happiness we have. It has everything to do with me stepping aside, a mistake I will never repeat."

She crossed her arms. "Answer the question! Why do you think I don't care? I want to know!" She started to pace, hyperventilate, and cry. "Why?" she sobbed.

"Elle! What the hell is wrong with you?"

"What's wrong with me? *What's wrong with me?* What's wrong with *you*?!" She stopped and looked Caden in the eye. She continued to hyperventilate, then suddenly stopped abruptly. Panic struck, and she covered her mouth. "Oh no! No!" She shook her head and ran away. She stopped a short distance away and yelled, "Damn you, Lyndsey!" then fell to the ground.

"Elle!" Caden bolted over to her. She was out cold. He scooped her up in his arms and carried her to the house.

As he made his way through the foliage toward the house, Caden noticed August standing on the deck, Elle draped over his arms.

"Ah. Too much?" August asked.

"I think so," Caden said, relieved that Elle's odd behavior was from August lifting the curse. He guessed the basil leaf was the catalyst.

"She'll be okay. I guess I'm a bit outta practice," August admitted but didn't seem too concerned.

Caden walked into the room, still holding Elle, and looked around for a place to put her down. August pointed to the sofa across the room.

<hr />

SHORTLY AFTER, Elle started to rouse. At first, she didn't realize where she was, nor did she care. She was in the arms of someone who radiated heat, strength, and concern. She wanted to bathe in the feeling. Anxiety about figuring out where she was thwarted her brief visit to heaven, and she opened her eyes. She met the eyes of the Adonis that was holding her. Those striking blue eyes seemed familiar to her. She squinted her eyes in hopes that she could place them. She felt bereft when the man released her from his hold and put her down onto the sofa.

"Elle?" Caden called softly.

Elle's eyes grew wide in shock. "Caden?"

"I'm right here," he continued, his voice calm and captivating.

She gasped. "Holy shit, Caden!" She shot up and threw her legs over the side of the sofa. She grabbed his wrist. "Fucking shit! I fucked up," she admitted. Caden's expression was of deep concern, and her body wilted in shame. She reached out and put her hand on his cheek. "I'm so, so sorry!"

Caden held her hand to his face and closed his eyes. "I'm just glad you're back."

"That's not good enough. Somehow, I will make it up to you and Rikki and Quinn."

"It's not your fault," Caden said, then pulled her into his arms.

Her head started to swim, and she melted in his embrace, encircling her arms around him and holding him close.

She looked up at August, who was across the room, and mouthed, "Thank you."

He held up prayer hands in response.

Caden released his hold and sat back.

"That was— *Wow*. August, you are a master, " Elle gushed.

"I'm glad I could help. Speaking of which," he said, pulling up a chair and leaning in. "I want to help get Lyndsey on the right track. I know what she's capable of, and I know she'll listen to me."

"Great, then an evil witch intervention it is," Caden joked. "What about Rikki and Quinn?"

"Let me put some thought into it. By tomorrow, I'll have a clear plan," he promised. "In the meantime, relax and enjoy the beauty that surrounds you."

CADEN WAS anxious to give Quinn the good news and excused himself to August's guest room. He paced back and forth. "August is going to help us!" Caden blurted before Quinn could say hello. "And Elle is back to herself too."

"That's great news. I've got to tell Rikki."

"We need to hold off on that, just until tomorrow when we

have a clear idea how we're going to handle all this. Elle and I are going to spend the night here, and then hopefully, things will be set right in the next couple days."

"Thanks, Caden. You're a good friend."

"Hey, I know you would do the same for me."

Caden came out of the room and headed back out to the deck. He leaned against the railing that overlooked the forest that was August's backyard. As the sun hit his face, he closed his eyes and breathed in the fresh, pine-laden air. He was relieved to have Elle back and felt confident that she would see that Fin was all wrong for her.

"Hey!" Elle said. She leaned against the railing next to Caden. "I feel like shit."

"Please don't. We're all vulnerable to Ms. Morgan's power. I don't know what changed your mind about coming here, and I probably shouldn't ask. I'm just glad you did," he said.

She gently rubbed his back. He tensed up when she rested her head on his arm. Goosebumps formed when she began tracing his fingers with hers. "Thank you," she whispered.

His breath became uneven. He shook his head in frustration over being weak around her. She was just thankful, and her touch was nothing more than her way of showing that. He tried to resist looking into her eyes, but he did anyway. Her eyes were on his, then moved down to his lips.

"Elle ..." he breathed, then looked away.

"A mistake you won't repeat." She cupped his face to assure him it was safe.

Just like that, he crumbled. She was choosing him, and he wasn't going to fear the pain that might follow. Every nerve in his body hummed as he succumbed to her sensual touch. She pulled him closer. He stared at her lips as his mouth hovered over hers. He needed her to succumb too.

"No, I won't repeat—" he said, parting his lips. His heart pounded as her mouth gently swept against his—his breath catching the implications. He wrapped his arm around her waist and slid his hand into her hair to truly kiss her.

"Lunch!" August called out from the kitchen.

Elle and Caden immediately pulled back. Their chests heaved as their hearts continued to race.

"Come on in," August waved at them.

Catching their breaths, they obliged.

He served them a fresh-from-the-garden salad. "I'm glad you're feeling better," August said with a smirk. "Anyway, I think I know what we can do to help your friends. Rikki and Quinn will need to be together when performing the reversal ritual. I'll write down all the ingredients you'll need and the order of operations step by step. But to start, you'll need two reversal candles, which are candles you can burn from the other side, some of my special basil, a mirror, and Rikki's favorite flower, if you happen to know it, otherwise you can use passionflower, which is in my garden too.

Meanwhile, I'll talk to Lyndsey. That's where the mirror comes in. It's a special mirror. When she looks into it, she will see peoples' perspectives of her, as well as her true beauty," he said, then paused as if thinking about her. He shook himself out of it and dug into his salad. "A mirror on your end will deflect any further assault on you and, with a few other additions, should reverse the curse."

"Okay. Simple enough. Elle and I will get on that after lunch."

THEY COMBED THROUGH THE GARDEN, looking for the required herbs. When Elle came in contact with a passionflower, she stopped. The environment around her shifted to her temple room. A younger woman with tan skin wearing a yellow tube top and skirt was standing in the middle of the room. She pointed to Brazil on a world map, then pointed to the journals in Elle's bookcase. She reached for her journals and comp books, but they disappeared before she could get to them. Crystal dust came showering down over her. She heard Caden call out to her.

A hand grabbed her and pulled her back.

"Why are you standing in the sprinklers? Are you okay?" Caden asked.

She looked around. Her mouth was opened, but no words came out as Caden and the garden came back into view. Whatever that was, it was different than what she had experienced in the greenhouse when she was hallucinating. This was like being in virtual reality. It had felt so real to her.

"Elle? Are you okay?" Caden asked again, shaking her a bit.

Caden came into focus. "I think I just had a vision. I've never had that happen to me."

"Jesus, Elle. You scared the hell out of me. I thought you were having a seizure or something," he said, then stepped back, bent over to grab his thighs, and took a deep breath. "Okay. I'm okay now. A vision? What did you see?"

"A young woman standing in my temple room. She pointed to Brazil on my world map, then to my journals and comp books, but then they disappeared. I think I need to move the comp books and journals. I just want to finish up what we're doing here and then leave early in the morning. August is going to need to get me into my room."

That night, August lit the fire pit, and they relaxed in each other's presence. August told stories of his adventures. Caden shared what happened in the greenhouse, and Elle inquired about her emerging magic skills.

When it was time for bed, Elle went to the guest room, leaving Caden as he was putting blankets down on the sofa. So much had happened during the day that she couldn't turn her mind off. She wondered if Caden was going through the same thing. *I think I know Caden enough that if he wanted to talk more about things, even after we kissed, he would be knocking on my door.* She stared at the door for a long time, hoping he would somehow reach out to her. *What am I thinking? He's also the logical one. He's probably thinking it's just not a good time, especially at the home of someone they had just met.* By 2:30 in the morning, she finally let go of her thoughts and went to sleep.

THE NEXT MORNING, Caden came out of the bathroom and jumped, startled that Elle was standing there.

"Sorry! I didn't mean to scare you," Elle said, stifling a laugh.

"I hope you weren't standing there long." He scratched the top of his head like he was embarrassed. "Um, but now that we're here," he said, looking around, "with no interruptions. I just wanted to say that I really wanted to talk about all the things that went down yesterday, but I don't think this is the time or place."

She chuckled a bit. "I figured as much."

"What's so funny?"

"I just know you, Caden. I know what makes you tick, and it's so different from me. That's not a bad thing. But you're right. We'll have time later."

The two of them walked into the kitchen.

"I hope you found the accommodations to your liking," August said, never looking up as he circled his table, moving small crystals around.

"What are you doing?"

"I'm preparing, planning, and strategizing. I'll explain in a bit," he said and stopped. "Follow me. Right now, I need you to soak in a protective and anointed bath made of rosemary, rose, and peppermint oils."

He went over to a buffet next to a floor-to-ceiling glass

window in the sunroom. He crouched down and pulled open the doors. The doors' inside were lined with a collection of oils, tinctures, rocks, and bound sage. The shelves held candles, incense, crystals, tarot decks, and goblets. He guided his fingers along the oils, pulling out the ingredients and creating a mixture in a cruet. Then he took out a candle, a bowl, some incense, a quartz crystal the size of his hand, and a bundle of sage and placed them on the surface of the buffet before closing it. He filled the bowl with water, lit the candle and incense, and then stood back.

"You two will take the mixture I created and dip them or hold them over the four elements I collected. Water is water, the candle is fire, the smoke from the incense is wind, and the crystal is Earth.

Elle and Caden stood before the buffet. Elle picked up the bottle, and Caden placed his hand over hers. They looked at each other and smiled, then glided the bottle over the stand-in elements.

"You could have done it one at a time, but I like the team-work," August said with a smile.

They turned away from each other as if embarrassed.

August waved a wand with a crystal on the tip and began chanting. He called for helpful spirits from near and far, new and ancient, to chase away all the negativity and bring in light, positivity, protection, and triumph.

"So for the bath, you don't have to do that together," he chuckled.

Elle and Caden blushed.

He explained the soaking process and sent them on their way. When they were both done, they joined him back in the sunroom, where August had prepared some tea for them.

"Regarding getting back into your sanctuary, I want to speak with your mom first because I think she'll be the path of least resistance for releasing the protection," August said.

"Okay, but if she finds out what I've been up to, it might make things worse."

"After all we've been through in such a short amount of time, have you lost faith in me that quickly?" August asked, feigning offense.

"I see your point," Elle said meekly and took a sip of tea.

He brought out the crystals he had been strategizing with and showed them the course of action in detail. When they all felt ready to execute the plan, they collected their things and left to go back home, with August following close behind.

When they got to Java and Book, Farrah was wiping down the counter in preparation for the next customer.

"Oh, hey!" Farrah greeted. She averted her attention from Elle and Caden to the hip and attractive older gentleman in boho garb and artsy necklaces following behind them. "Who is this, Elle?"

"Mom, this is August. August, this is my mom, Farrah."

"It's nice to meet you," the man said graciously. "This place is stunning. No, bewildering," he commented, rotating as he walked. "I think of myself as a book connoisseur—well, snob actually—and if I'm impressed, well, that truly says a lot. Well done."

"Oh, well, thank you," Farrah said as she touched her forehead.

"Mom!" Elle whispered loudly. "Jesus, get a grip."

"How do you know my daughter?"

"Can we sit?" August invited.

"Of course. How can I help?" she asked as they walked to a quieter part of the café.

Elle and Caden remained at the counter and ate while August and her mom spoke.

"What do you think they're saying?" Elle asked.

"She's saying, 'I'm so glad you like the place. You should check out my bedroom,'" Caden said in a high-pitched voice.

Elle slapped him on the shoulder. "Idiot, my parents are still married."

Caden laughed. "Oops. Okay, sorry. Now August is saying, 'You know, I grow the most amazing basil on the planet,'" he said in a deep sultry voice. "'You do?'" Caden said in that high-pitched voice. "'Yes, I do. I also have the most amazing kitchen with the most amazing solarium, and I'm also the most amazing wizard because I have been taught by the most amazing shamans in the entire amazing world,'" he continued, then laughed out loud. He looked at Elle, who didn't seem to appreciate his humor.

"You know, he saved our lives," Elle said.

"Elle, I'm just playing. August is working his magic, and everything will work out. I have trust in the most amazing wizard." He laughed again, looking at Elle. His heart leapt when she nodded in agreeance and smiled back.

"Oh my gosh. He's coming over here. It's too soon. We're doomed," Elle said anxiously as she straightened herself up as he approached.

"It's all done," August said, clasping his hands.

"Really?" Elle asked, bringing prayer hands to her chin, giving a discreet but excited round of applause. "I don't get how you did it."

"Sometimes the magic is in the words you use, not the spells you cast … just saying," August said with a wink.

Elle smiled along, quickly realizing why women were drawn

to him. It was so tragic that Lyndsey was so lost that she would probably never have August. He was way too good for her.

Farrah came over and hugged Elle. "I'm sorry, Elle. I didn't realize," her mom said, sadness in her eyes. "I'm going to go down now and unseal the room."

"Thanks, Mom," she said, perplexed. She looked at August.

He shrugged.

Elle hurried down and stepped into her sanctuary. Her body vibrated as she took a deep breath. She felt like she was home and wanted to share the moment with Caden. She turned to get him, and her breath caught. He was already waiting right outside the threshold. Her hand went to her mouth to gain control over her emotions, then grabbed his hands and brought him in, wrapping her arms around his waist. "Now I really feel like I'm back," she said as she looked up at him.

He cupped her face as he looked at her. He moved a strand of her hair behind her ear and looked deeply into her eyes. She swallowed, waiting for him to make a move. He bent down and gave her a gentle kiss, then another with a little more assertiveness. He looked at her for acceptance. She looked at his lips. His gentleness caved as his mouth came down on hers in a declaration that he was no longer holding back. Her lips parted, and he wrapped his arms around her to pull her in closer.

August cleared his throat.

Caden and Elle let go.

"Jesus, August. It's like *every* time!" Caden said, out of breath, raking his hand through his hair.

"There will be more time for that later," he waved dismissively. "But right now, we have a job to do," August said with his hands on his hips. He looked around. "An amazing room, by the way. The light energy is quite arresting." He nodded like he was impressed.

THEY STOOD at the circular table in the corner of Elle's temple room. Caden grabbed a piece of paper from an unused comp book and began drawing out the plan. He started by explaining the layout of Lyndsey's house, and they agreed that they should enter from both the front and the back. August believed that the element of surprise would work in their favor. Their objective was to get her to reverse what she'd done to Rikki, stop her abuses of black magic, and open up to the possibility of redemption.

During that time, August explained to Elle step by step the process of reversing Rikki's curse.

"I'll need a wand, right?" Elle asked as she went to her altar and picked up Gladys, Mozelle's sacred wand. It was made of birch wood that was braided, with a spherical cavity near the top, allowing a quartz crystal to sit at the tip. She put it in August's hands. "It's okay. You can touch it," Elle encouraged and closed his fingers around Gladys.

"Exquisite. This is an exceptional and powerful instrument. Ho-ly cow!" he expressed, drawing his fingertips up and around the striking form of the wand. He closed his eyes, and after a moment, spoke up. "You need to get reacquainted with Gladys. She misses you very much," August said on behalf of the wand.

He opened his eyes and placed the wand back into Elle's hands, closing her fingers around the wand as she did his. "Close your eyes," he directed and clasped his hands around hers as if he was marrying her energy with the wand's.

A light emerged in her hand, and she felt a buzz through her body— prompting her to question if that was what Rikki and Quinn feel when they are near each other. It was euphoric. More memories of Mozelle flooded her mind as if presenting her life from birth to death. She saw flashes of her grandma, Lucia, that she had been so close to, holding her tight. She saw her family, including her wayward brother, Rex. She remembered when she first started working at Java and Book and her mother showing her the ropes. She experienced again the emotions and physical feelings she felt the first time Lucia brought her down to the sanctuary room in which she was standing. She saw one of her first comp books written for Alastair and Anica, and her last one that was for Wade and Robin.

A tear slid down her face, and when she opened her eyes, she saw the auras standing around her and felt spirits embrace her. Stronger vibrations coursed through her body as the spirits infused theirs with hers.

"Caden, let her be," August said.

She felt hands clutch her shoulders. "Elle, are you okay?" Caden asked.

She removed Caden's hands from her shoulders. She closed her eyes again and blew out a deep breath before opening them again. "I'm here. I'm back. And I'm the oracle I was always meant to be," she declared.

"That's my girl," August said, holding Caden back. "I'll give you a moment to collect yourself. Caden and I will wait for you upstairs."

Caden stood there for a moment. There was concern in his eyes, but it wasn't concern for her—it was concern for *them.*

"August, can you give me a moment with Caden?"

August looked at his watch. "Fine. Please make it quick," he insisted, then turned and left.

She walked up to Caden, whose head was down, and placed her hand on his cheek. "You look how I felt when you left here the other day, and I was afraid you wouldn't come back. Listen to me. Nothing between us has changed. We're just getting started," she emphasized and laid a gentle kiss on his cheek. "I'll see you up there." He closed his eyes and held her hand that caressed his cheek. He nodded and left with his head up.

As she let her newly discovered sense of self wash over her, she remembered the vision she'd had at August's. She wasn't sure what the vision was communicating, but she was compelled to take all the journals and comp books back to her house before meeting back up with August for their final showdown.

———

By 5:30, they pulled up to a house a couple doors down from Lyndsey's.

"Are you ready for this?" Caden asked Elle, his hand on the door handle.

"Ready as I'll ever be."

"Let's do this."

Caden and Elle got out first and headed to the front door. August waited for them to go in before heading toward the house's back entrance. Lyndsey opened the door slightly.

"What do you want?" she asked. She looked pale and exhausted.

"Let's talk about bringing this to an end. We have the things you've asked for, but we want to talk before just giving you everything," Elle said.

Lyndsey crossed her arms and looked down her nose at them. "Prove to me that you have the crystal."

"Let us in, and I'll show it to you," Elle lied.

Lyndsey hesitated, then stepped aside and let them in.

"I think we need to talk about expectations," Caden said as they stepped into the front entranceway.

She scoffed and closed the door, then stood before the two of them. "You really think you're in a place to make any demands? Give me the crystal," she said, swinging her finger between the both of them.

"Okay, okay," Elle started. "We don't have it with us, but I know where it is, and I can get it as soon as we're done here."

Caden stepped forward. "I just want to talk to you, Lyndsey. Will you listen to me, as your father? Will you give me that?"

Lyndsey thought about what he said. "Fine. Say what you need to say." She whirled her hand to encourage him to get on with it.

Caden drew a nervous breath to allow his memories of being Chris to saturate his mind. "When I think of Chris, I know that I *was* him, but it's like remembering a very vivid dream. In the dream, I'm aware of who I am. I feel and remember the feelings that were Chris's, but I still consider myself a separate person from him. It's kind of hard to explain. But the distinction is important—because when I'm talking to you now, I'm talking to you as Chris, not Caden."

Lyndsey stood there with her arms crossed, but he could tell he was reaching her. She was actively trying to fight tears.

"I love you, Lyndsey, very much. I love that you really became something special and that you help engage kids in a subject that's a challenge for most. I love that you have passion, drive, intelligence, and beauty."

"But …?"

"But you're a complete disappointment. You used your strengths and twisted them to help yourself in this crusade you have against your mother. The thing that happened in the greenhouse was damn scary to go through, but I walked out with a new memory and a new identity." Caden swallowed the lump in this throat. "I'm so sorry that you were raised with my alcoholism. I'm so sorry that you had to witness me verbally, mentally, and emotionally abuse your mother. We were wrong for each other, and it's so clear to me now. I had no control over my life, and that was more important to me than owning up to my failures as a husband and a father." He blew out a shaky breath. "I don't blame your mother for falling for another man, and after realizing that they really *are* soulmates, I'm the one who is at fault for the fire, not your mother. I will go a step further and let you know that they have my blessing to be together. But I have also asked for forgiveness for my transgressions and for putting us in this situation. So, my sweetheart Lyndsey, I'm going to ask the same of you. Can you ever forgive me?"

Lyndsey still stood with her arms crossed. "There's nothing to forgive, and you're not going to convince me that any of this is your fault. Thank you for explaining yourself to me, but I think that Caden has corrupted you into thinking that what Mom did was okay. Had you survived the fire, I don't think you'd be saying the things you're saying now. And so my actions are somewhat to protect Caden because I know you're in there, Dad. Please see that my actions are for *you*. I'm seeking the revenge you would have sought had there never been a fire."

Caden felt a heaviness in his chest over how twisted Lyndsey had really become.

<hr>

"REALLY, Lyndsey? Do you really think you're working on your father's behalf?" an accusatory voice came from behind Lyndsey.

She froze. Her chin quivered as shock hit her hard. "August," she whispered, then slowly turned around. She trembled as her hand flew to her mouth. Shaking her head, tears burst out.

August took a step closer. He looked just as attractive as the day she met him but with some gray mixed in his hair and stubble. His warm brown eyes were as bright as ever, and he was actually standing there, scolding her of all things, like nothing had changed. She became that naïve girl again and wanted him to wrap his arms around her and let her know how proud— The second that word popped in her head, she wanted to vomit. *Does he know the truth?*

She put her hand out to stop him. "What are you doing? Why are you here? Why ..." She sobbed into her hands.

He came and pulled her in his arms. "Shhhh, Lyndsey. Shhhh."

She broke down in his arms, and he held her shuddering body close to his. "I'm so sorry, Lyndsey. I was a coward when you needed a hero. I failed you."

"That's not true. That's not true at all," she said, then loosened her hold. *Why is he here, out of the blue, saying these things?* Something in her mind clicked as she figured out what was happening. This was some kind of intervention.

She shoved her way out of his embrace. "What am I doing? You're here to change me. You're here to get me to *be* good and *do* good." Disdain coursed through her blood, making her eyes burn with fury. She turned to Caden and Elle. "You!" She pointed to Caden. "I won't forgive you. I will never forgive you! I protected you, and *this* is how you repay me?" She turned back around and was confronted by her reflection in a mirror August was holding up. It was the size of a single window pane that covered him from head to waist. "What is this? Are you trying to bewitch me?" she asked, struggling to look away.

She could see August motioning to Caden and Elle like he had things under control and that it was okay to leave. "Get to Rikki and Quinn."

Through the reflection in the mirror, Lyndsey saw Caden nod and immediately pull Elle out the door.

As if against her will, her eyes drifted back to her reflection. Excerpts from her past, present, and future played like a movie before her. She clenched her jaw as bitterness consumed her while she was forced to watch and relive all her misdeeds. She saw her anguish, her mistakes, her hate, and her corruption—but she also saw how August saw her. His adoration when she'd stepped out of the yurt the day she shed the bondage of shame that were her turtleneck shirts. The anger he'd used as a shield to deflect his attraction to her. The care and attention he'd put into the wand he'd carved for her. But like knives in the chest,

she felt his disappointment when he'd learned of her transgressions.

This is a trap. Snap out of it!

She lifted her hands to her ears and shook her head to pull
herself out of it. "No!" she yelled. The mirror began vibrating.
The ground started to rumble, and cool air began to circulate.

August gripped harder, but as her anger escalated, so did the
tremors. The shaking roared through the house, forcing doors
to slam shut, glasses to rattle, and light fixtures to swing like
pendulums. Her anger was developing a mind of its own as
Lyndsey remained transfixed by the mirror.

"Lyndsey!" August yelled. "Don't do this!"

She could make out August's cries, trying to save her.

"I love you!" he shouted.

His love was pulling her out of her trance-like state. It felt as
if she was hanging off a cliff by a thread, and against the odds,
he was there pulling her up, determined to yank her into his
arms and save her. His voice, which had sounded faint before,
was now loud and clear. She looked up at him, and for a split
second, she could see in his eyes that he was pleading for her to
choose him.

"That's it, Lyndsey. Come back to me," August called out.

Lyndsey watched in horror as the mirror began to crack and
splinter, sizable spiderwebs forming on the glass and disfiguring her reflection. Lyndsey reached out. "August!" The mirror
shattered under the pressure, causing shards to fly away from
her—and into August. He slumped onto the floor. "Noooo!"
Lyndsey screamed and ran to August. "Oh no, no, no!" She
cradled him as he bled from his chest, his neck, and even one of
his eyes. Blood spewed out of too many places for her to know
how to even begin to save him. Trembling, she grabbed her
phone from her back pocket and dialed 911.

"911. What's your emergency?"

Sobbing and barely able to speak, Lyndsey responded,

"There's been an accident." She gave her address, but she dropped the phone when she heard August gurgle. He was looking at her with an odd combination of fear and sadness.

"Please, August! Stay with me! I'm so sorry. I didn't mean it. I love you, August! I love you!" She wept and held him as the warmth of his blood pooled around her.

He lifted his hand and reached for her face. His pained eyes looked longingly into hers. He gasped as he tried to speak. "I know. I know it was an accident, and I know you love me," he whispered, then coughed. Blood started oozing out of his mouth, and his eyes rolled back.

"Damn you, August! Stay with me! Don't close your eyes. Please!" she begged. "You had me. I believe you," she sobbed. "I don't know why the mirror broke like that. Please!"

"See me. I'm walking in …" With a final shudder, he breathed his last breath.

Her wails of anguish echoed through her derelict house as she rocked him back and forth.

Paramedics, firefighters, and police, too many to count, scrambled throughout her house. They found her cradling August as she sat in his blood. They tried to remove her from him, but she resisted and cried. She was barely coherent, but they needed her official statement, so the police took her in.

What just happened? she thought on the way to the station. Sights and sounds were distorted, just as they had been when she'd woken up under gnarly bushes after running out of her childhood home, still ablaze, the night of the fire.

She grabbed her hair and pulled her head between her legs. *"I love you,"* she could hear him say inside her head. Even after all these years, his voice was so memorable, and for the tiniest of moments, she was that young, naïve girl falling for an amazing man again. His confession felt like the most miraculous thing she'd ever heard from the only person she'd ever loved. *He was reaching out to me, and it was the greatest moment in my life, only to be shattered like that mirror within mere seconds, becoming the worst moment of my life. Even worse than the fire.*

Why? Why do bad things happen to just me? My mother—plain and simple. She's destroyed my life's promise. Because of her, I'm disfigured, and now the only person I have ever loved is dead because of her and her selfish choices. She held herself as she shivered even though she wasn't cold.

Lyndsey's shock and sadness quickly spiraled into a dark rage. *I haven't done enough. As soon as I leave the station, I will take care of Rikki with a more permanent solution.*

Lyndsey was escorted to a room with a table. Tears poured down her cheeks, and she whimpered as August's confession, his attempt to rescue her, and the mirror shattering played on a loop in her head.

"We're sorry for your loss, Ms. Morgan," one of the officers said after taking a seat across from her. "Do you want anything to eat or drink before we get started?"

"No," Lyndsey whispered.

"Very well. Can you tell me what happened?"

She nodded her head. "August was helping me move the mirror. He was holding it up, and he didn't realize that the sun was reflecting in my eyes and blinding me. I held my hand out to stop the sun from blinding me, and I tripped and fell hands first into the mirror," she cried, recalling the shards as they'd impaled August. "And the glass, it shattered all over him."

The officers continued their questioning for an hour, and in the end, they told her that her statement and the 911 tape were consistent, so she was free to go.

"Thank you," she said and walked out of the station.

Elle called Quinn while she rode with Caden to the greenhouse.

"Elle?" Quinn answered with uncertainty in his voice.

"Hey, Quinn," she said enthusiastically. "I'm back. I feel terrible. You were right, and I'm sorry."

"Listen, you don't need to apologize to me. I totally get it. I'm glad you're back to your old self."

"So we have all we need to make this happen. Let's meet at the greenhouse tonight at 7:00."

"I'll be there," he promised. "Wait. How are we going to get in? Isn't it locked?"

"I have Gladys."

"Who's Gladys?"

"My wand," she said like he should have known.

"Oh. Okay. See you in a bit," Quinn said and hung up the phone.

She then called Rikki. "Hey. I'm back!" Elle said with confidence.

"What do you mean you're back?"

"Caden and I met up with August. He's going to help us, Rikki. So much has happened, but for right now, I have almost everything I need to reverse Lyndsey's curse on you. Meet us at the greenhouse at 7:15 tonight. Quinn should be there too," Elle said with enthusiasm, but then there was no response. "Rikki?"

"Um," she started. "I'm glad you're feeling better. You sound like you're back to your old self, but I don't think I can do this. It'll kill me if it doesn't work, Elle."

"August is very powerful. He told me what I need to do. We'll be at the greenhouse, so it's large enough that you can stay back and not feel any pain while we work the reversal. We've got this, Rikki."

"Okay," Rikki said. "Wait, how are you going to get into the greenhouse? Isn't it locked?"

"Seriously, Quinn asked me the same thing. I have Gladys."

"Who's Gladys?"

"Holy shit, she's my wand," she said with a slight laugh to

hide her irritation. She lowered her phone and turned to Caden. "Have I not mentioned her before?"

Caden shook his head.

"Fine. I guess I haven't mentioned her before. She's been with me since I was Mozelle, and she's as beautiful as she is powerful."

"Oh. Okay. Alright. I'll head over."

"I know you're depressed, but please have faith. You and Quinn will be together."

"Thank you, Elle," Rikki said sincerely.

HOPE FILLED Rikki's chest that Elle could reverse the curse and things might work out after all. She quickly dressed in jeans and a bell-sleeved, white blouse that crisscrossed over her breasts and tied on the side, then headed down the stairs.

"Where are you off to?" her mom asked.

"I'm heading to the greenhouse at school. I'm meeting up with Elle, Caden, and Quinn."

"Quinn? Why Quinn?" her mom quizzed.

"I think there's a chance of getting back together," Rikki said with optimism.

"Uh-huh." Her mom sounded skeptical.

"I was the one who broke up with him, and it was for reasons that you don't know about. I don't have time to explain, okay? Please trust me."

She grabbed the crystal and her backpack and left the house.

BY THE TIME she got to school, night had fallen. Crickets chirped, and frogs croaked as she trekked across the freshly watered lawn. Beyond a small group of trees, she could see the greenhouse glowing with candlelight. The same feelings she felt the first time she looked into Wade's eyes surged and enveloped her. She recalled laying in a hospital bed, bombarded with beeping machines, people talking, and papers rustling. It had all faded away when a man with the most alluring green eyes she'd ever seen assured her she was in good hands. It was as if he'd cast a halo over her. One that protected her from the chaos that swirled around her like a cyclone. The greenhouse and the people inside—the people she loved—radiated with the same halo, and she rushed toward it.

She could make out Elle and Caden's silhouettes as they moved about, but Quinn's was most prominent as he paced along the windows with his hands on his hips, toward the front. By the time she came through the entrance of the dimly lit greenhouse, Quinn had moved back to where Elle and Caden were. He raked his hands through his hair, closed his eyes, and blew out a long breath like he was thankful she showed up.

Simultaneously, they took a step toward each other, then halted, as if both were fighting the urge to run to each other like they would after school by her locker.

As she walked further into the greenhouse, she was hit with a flash of Wade serenading her in the hospital. She smiled over the crystal doing its thing.

"Country roads, take me home," Quinn sang and smiled over the shared memory. "You brought the crystal, didn't you?"

She nodded and smiled back. "Hi," Rikki said shyly to Quinn. It seemed like it had been a while since they'd spoken to each other.

"Hi," Quinn replied. The side of his mouth turned up.

Her heart leapt at the sight of him. Then she blew out her breath when a hint of pain buzzed through her. She took a step back. "Sorry, this is about as close as I can tolerate," she cautioned, then squatted down, reaching into her backpack to take out the crystal. "I wasn't sure if this was necessary, but I brought it anyway."

"Wow! I need something personal from both of you. This crystal is perfect," Elle said as she took it from Rikki and studied it for a moment.

Elle had created a beautiful altar adorned with crystals, herbs, oils, and two candles. She had laid out a familiar tapestry, which triggered the memory of their handfasting ceremony.

Elle lit the dried sage as she stood behind the altar, sifting through pages of notes she'd taken while August explained each step of the ritual. Quinn stood in front of the altar with Caden by his side as if he was Quinn's best man. They both faced Rikki, who remained down the aisle, a few feet in front of the entrance.

"Aww!" Elle said with a thoughtful smile. "So right now, I'm creating a tincture that will be infused into a bath you will each soak in separately," she explained as she compounded together lemon, crab shell powder, and Himalayan salt. She took a black candle and broke off the bottom. She carved Lyndsey's name into it with the tip of a quartz crystal, held it upside down, and lit the newly exposed wick. As the wax dripped into her mixture, she chanted.

I CALL *upon you spirits of light and fairness:*
    Rikki and Quinn have been cursed with a powerful spell.
    I beg thee, turn this blend into water from your magic well.
    They are fated to have a love that will last
    Based on being sealed by an oracle in their life past,
    They are victims of a powerful witch who is not sane,
    In which Quinn's touch causes Rikki tremendous pain.
    Your ability to anoint my blend
    Will bring this evil curse to an end.

. . .

SHE PLACED the blend into two separate vials of rosemary oil. "Next is the bath. There is a large basin with water. It's not heated. Just saying—this isn't the Four Seasons," she chuckled. "I'll put the anointed blend in the water, and then Rikki will go first."

Elle brought Rikki toward the back, behind a planter with a tree in it. Rikki undressed and stepped in. Shivering, she took a deep breath of the floral scent, then submerged herself. The cold water felt lustrous against her skin and made her feel resilient. Her hair floated down along her shoulders, and if she didn't need to come up for air, she would have remained. Pulling herself up, she took the sponge Elle gave to her and smoothed it all over her body. She leaned her head back one last time, then stood up, and Elle wrapped her in a towel.

"Okay, Quinn. You're up," Elle called out.

QUINN AND CADEN stepped behind the planter.

Topless, Quinn made quick work of his button fly. "I can feel a change already," Quinn said, stepping out of his pants and into the basin.

"I'm happy for you, man," Caden said, stepping aside.

"Shit, this is cold." Quinn crossed his arms across his chest and rubbed his biceps. He squatted down, held his breath, and plunged his body back. Closing his eyes, he let the smooth water wash over him. He felt cleansed of the curse, cleansed of Sienna and his misdeeds, as well as his dad's judgment of him. Despite being submerged in the frigid water, he felt warmed by Rikki's love, and he resurfaced a renewed man.

Lyndsey rushed home to prepare for Rikki's demise. She packed a backpack with a couple long cords, paralyzing powder, a wand, knife, black candles, enchanted water, respirator mask, and her pestle and mortar set, along with all the cash she could find. Once she placed everything in her car, she rushed to her temple room and lit three black, two red, and one gold candle. She summoned the spirit guides who could give her the most precise direction to Rikki.

As the candles burned, she stood in front of the shelves with her crystals and oils. She let out a shaky breath and reached for her wand, the very one that August had carved for her. The one that, over the years, she had corrupted by inviting vile spirits to leave their impressions on when they assisted in granting her twisted requests. *Strength.*

"It's not my fault!" she shouted, hoping that August would hear her. "I wouldn't have to do this if it weren't for *her!*" Tears tumbled down her cheeks. "I'm sorry, August, but I don't see any other way around this."

She sat before her alter, hovering the wand over the candles.

I summon the keeper of the missing:
  Come and show me where Rikki is right now,
  And I will honor thee with my fealty, I vow.

Shortly after she chanted, a spirit of a pale, emaciated, and menacing looking little boy appeared before her. Without saying a word to her, he reached a bony finger out and touched her temple, revealing plants sitting on tables behind windows. She stood up. "They're in the greenhouse," she said and rolled her eyes. *I should have known.*

She went to the kitchen, took out a knife, and sliced her forearm. The blood flowed into her mortar. Then she placed it on the altar as an offering to the vow of loyalty she had just made to the young spirit. She lowered her head as shame came over her. Desperate, she knew this wouldn't be the only depraved spirit she was going to appeal to in such a way. "Thank you for this, young keeper of missing souls." She took her blood and used it to burn out the black candles, then left, not knowing when she would be back.

She pulled up to the side of the school closest to the greenhouse. She dug out the paralyzing powder, wand, gloves, and respirator mask from her backpack. As she moved closer to the greenhouse, light flickered from the back. Peering into the window, she covered her mouth in shock. It was the night of the fire all over again. Elle was standing behind an altar full of items Lyndsey could see were being used to reverse her curse. In front of the altar, Quinn and Rikki stood opposite each other on the edge of a circle with burning candles inside it. They were just a few paces from each other as they smiled and looked longingly into each other's eyes. It was as if she was witnessing their wedding, complete, with Caden as the best man. *You've got to be kidding me.*

RIKKI AND QUINN had not been this close without pain since she'd been cursed. Breathing heavily, the two just stared at each other. Then they walked around the candles as Elle directed. After the third time, they reached out to each other. Their fingertips were millimeters away when wind swiftly blew through the greenhouse, causing the candles to burn out.

A fog smelling of burnt car oil surrounded them, reducing their visibility to mere feet in front of them.

"What the hell? Rikki, are you okay?" Quinn asked, waving the fog away so he could see her.

The sounds of glass and ceramic breaking echoed

throughout the room, followed by muffled screams, then the sound of something being dragged.

"Damn it! I can't see. Where are you, Rikki?" Quinn demanded.

"Lyndsey's here," Elle bit.

"I'm just going to have a chat with Mom here," Lyndsey growled. "If you try to follow me, I will fuck you up with enchantments."

Quinn quickly moved toward Lyndsey's voice. He could make out shadows of Lyndsey dragging Rikki's limp body and continued toward them.

"Quinn, stop!" Elle yelled.

Ignoring her warning, he reached for Lyndsey. "Rikki!"

Lyndsey dropped Rikki, reached inside a sack she had on her hip, and turned toward him. She motioned like she was blowing him a kiss. He was instantly showered with a powder that stopped him dead in his tracks, and he collapsed to the ground.

"What did I just tell you? Thanks for the head start," Lyndsey bragged, sliding Rikki's body through the entrance. "So predictable. By the time he's able to move again, I will be so far gone, you won't find me in time," she touted and slammed the door.

<hr>

STUNNED, Elle looked around. The fog had diminished enough to allow her to make out shadows. She could hear Caden inhaling pumps of his inhaler behind her. She turned toward Caden, who was bent at the waist, trying to catch his breath. She placed her hands on his back to offer whatever help he needed.

He waved his arm up and down as if to say he had it from there. "I'm okay," he wheezed.

"Okay?" She looked him over to assess if he really was fine. "Then I need your help. Do you think you can do that?"

Caden nodded. He drew in a deep breath, stood up tall, and stepped toward her. He peered down into her eyes. "Name it," he said like he was ready for the challenge. He was breathing heavily, but she wasn't sure if it was because he was still recovering or if it was for another reason.

Jesus, he's standing here in front of me, exuding some kind of protective strength. I see it now. The Adonis that held me yesterday wasn't a dream. It's part of who he is. His resilience at that moment caused her to pause, and she had to shake her head to get back on track. "Go get the car. I'll get Quinn moving again," Elle directed. "Oh, and turn on the lights on the way out."

"On it," Caden said. He left, flipping on the lights over the plants along the perimeter, which wasn't all the lights, but it was enough to work with.

Racing to Quinn, she found him laying on his side. His eyes were closed, and he was drooling. "Quinn! Quinn!" she called out as she kneeled next to him. "We need to get out of here. Rikki needs your help." He opened his eyes but remained quiet. "Quinn! Damn it! Find the strength!" she yelled, shaking him. "Hold on." She ran back to the altar, grabbed her wand, and returned to his side. Standing over him, she gripped the wand with both hands and swirled the air. The room darkened as ominous clouds spiraled over the greenhouse.

I SUMMON a strike of a lightning bolt
  Please awaken Quinn with a slight jolt.

LIGHTNING STRUCK the spherical chamber of her wand. "Woah!" Her jaw dropped in disbelief over what she'd just done. Trembling, she pointed the wand at the ceiling. "Quinn! Wake up!"

she yelled. Lightning discharged out of the wand, spreading along the ceiling like spider legs. Thunder boomed and rattled the windows.

Quinn gasped for air and shot up. "Where is she?" He began coughing.

"Quinn, look at me," Elle pleaded. "I need you to focus and remember who you and Rikki are. You hold the answer to where she is," Elle said, pointing to his chest.

He grabbed his birthmark and closed his eyes.

Honking from a car just outside the greenhouse startled Elle and Quinn. They looked out the window—Caden had driven his car onto campus and up to the greenhouse.

Elle grabbed Quinn by the shoulder. "You can continue searching in the car," Elle encouraged. "Let's get our Rikki back."

22

DUEL OF WANDS

Moaning, Rikki started to struggle with the cord tied around her wrists. "Where are you taking me?" Rikki slurred.

"Son of a bitch." Lyndsey banged on the steering wheel. "Shut the fuck up!" At a stoplight, she reached her gloved hand down into her pouch and took a large handful of powder. Rikki tried to raise her hand to defend herself but couldn't stop Lyndsey as she puffed the enchanted powder into her face, paralyzing her again. Her head fell back. Only her watery eyes were able to move.

Lyndsey continued weaving in and out of traffic. She began raging. "August died because of *you,* you bitch! None of this —*none* of this—would have happened if you had just kept your legs closed. I'm done with the games. It comes to an end tonight, *Mom!* This ends *tonight!*" She pointed at her hysterically, then slammed her fist on the steering wheel. "I'm sending you back to a place where hopefully your soul's memory will be wiped, or if you reincarnate, it will be where no one knows who you are. You won't even know who *you* are. That birthmark will be gone, and so will *this*." She reached in her pocket and held up the crystal.

Dread cascaded from Rikki's head, down her spine, and through her body. She began perspiring as tears tumbled down her face. *What have I done? I shouldn't have brought the crystal. Where is she taking me?* she wondered as Lyndsey serpentined through the residential streets of Sausalito. Rikki looked at Lyndsey to gauge how far gone she was.

Lyndsey's eyes darted to hers. "You wretched woman. Is there anything you can't take away from me? The love of my life died a violent death today, and you're to blame," she said through gritted teeth. "I can't take any more of this. Your deception, your choices—they all have consequences that *I* pay, and I'm losing my fucking mind!"

This is game over, Rikki thought and squeezed her eyes shut. *They're never going to find me. I have no idea where I am.* Her stomach clenched like she was falling, and her head felt like it was spinning. She was going to be sick. *Another lifetime where we can't be together, or worse—she succeeds in erasing my soul's history. Was that moment in the greenhouse the last I'll ever have with Quinn? With my Wade?*

<hr>

Driving toward the waterfront, Elle turned to Quinn, who was sitting in the backseat. "How are you doing, Quinn? Any vibrations?" Elle asked.

He shook his head as he continued to clench his birthmark. "Come on, Rikki. Where are you?" he pleaded. "Ugh! Damn it!" he yelled, lurching forward as if that might make the difference. "If she does anything to Rikki ..." he warned, then hit the car door. "Fuck!"

"Stay focused, Quinn," Elle appealed as they made their way to Bridgeway.

"Go through the lights," Quinn demanded.

"Doing what I can, buddy. We want to get her back as badly as you do."

"Really?"

"Focus!" Elle yelled.

Caden looked at Quinn through the rearview mirror. "Listen, you're no help to her all pissed off and shit. Take a deep breath. Close your eyes and focus. She needs you, Quinn."

Quinn swallowed his anger. "Okay." He took a deep breath. "There have been times that I could feel when she gets hurt, but she's never been this far away," he said, squeezing his eyes shut. "Just be quiet for a sec."

He slowed his breathing and relaxed his body, then called out Rikki's name in his mind and waited for a response.

"WE'RE HERE," Lyndsey said as she pulled up to an abandoned house. "We're home, Mom. Don't you want to see what they've done with the place?" she asked condescendingly as she hung a parking permit over the rearview mirror.

Rikki's birthmark started to tingle. It was the first thing she had felt since Lyndsey had paralyzed her. She could hear Quinn calling for her. She tried to lift her hand to touch her birthmark, but that connection wasn't online yet. She tried to move her head. Although slow to move, she was relieved that she could roll her head toward the birthmark and mentally called out to Quinn.

"I've got her!" she heard Quinn shout. *Where are you?*

Quinn! Oh, Quinn! You can hear me? I don't know where I am. She said something like, "We're home. Let's see what they've done with the place." We're in front of an abandoned house. I guess it's permitted parking here because she placed one over her rearview mirror. I'm not sure why she has that. There's a gate in front of the driveway. Looking up the driveway, it's surrounded by trees and shrubs. At the top, I can see a house with wood panels and large windows. There's vines all over the house like it's not maintained very often. And none of the lights are on. It looks really dark inside. Oh, Quinn. I don't know if any of this helps. The worst part of this is that she has the crystal. I'm so sorry!

WE'LL FIND YOU. *Just hang in there.* Quinn then relayed what Rikki told him.

"Our old home," Caden pointed out. "She's probably still allowed to go there, and that's why she has the parking permit."

"I don't remember where that is. Do you?" Elle asked with panic in her voice.

"I don't remember!" Caden slammed his fist against the steering wheel.

Quinn was in the zone. His body remained relaxed as he maintained his connection with Rikki. *I'm so relieved you're still with me. Tell me what's around you.*

"Ow!" he heard Rikki yelp.

Quinn's birthmark shocked him, and he grabbed it to stop it from getting worse. "She's in pain. Shit! I swear I'm going to kill Lyndsey."

"Okay, Quinn. Don't let your anger slow you down," Elle said, scrolling through her phone. "I'm looking on my phone for that old article on the fire. Hopefully, it'll give us some idea where she's at."

"I'm going to turn onto some residential streets. You just keep looking on your phone. Quinn, keep it up!" Caden encouraged.

With her backpack over her shoulder, Lyndsey jerked and pulled Rikki by the long cord that was firmly tied around her forearms and wrists. She dragged her through an overgrown garden, then climbed down a pathway that was so full of gnarly, thorny shrubs, it was almost non-existent. To their right stood a concrete structure—ruins of what had stood there once before.

"Look familiar?" she said and yanked Rikki so hard, she fell forward. She placed her backpack in the corner and went to work.

Rikki closed her eyes and called out to Quinn. She took a deep breath as she figured out where she was. "We're at our old house off Cressida," she said out loud, hoping that Quinn could hear her.

"Ha! So you do remember." Lyndsey pulled her around a couple concrete walls and stopped in front of what used to be Mozelle's room. The room had concrete beams across what used to be the ceiling. Lyndsey took the cord and tossed it over the beams to create what looked like a pulley.

She's going to hang me, Rikki realized. *If I try to run, she'll just paralyze me again.* She gagged and bent over as she hurled. Nothing came out. She whimpered, trying to catch her breath. *Such a violent death, but I'm not ready to give up. I'm going to fight until the end.*

Lyndsey started pulling on the cord, hoisting Rikki up by the ties that bound her wrists. She stopped pulling when she was a foot off the ground. She wrapped the cord around the exposed structure where the two adjacent windows used to be.

Rikki grunted at the pain. "Lyndsey! Listen to me. I didn't mean to fall in love with Wade," she rasped. "Nothing actually happened between us. Your father and I were wrong for each other, but we tried to work things out—for you. We loved you so much. Why can't you see that?" Rikki implored.

"Because you still didn't have to act on your feelings," Lyndsey said as she took the excess cord and shaped it into a pentagram beneath Rikki, then reached into her pocket and took out a knife to cut off what remained of the cord.

She's going to perform a ritual. "I never acted on my feelings. It was a deathbed confession, that's it. Mozelle just made it so that your father and I could be with the right people in the next life. Is your selfishness so great that it's blinded you?"

"*Me?* Selfish?" Lyndsey stopped what she was doing and heaved the cord, taking Rikki up higher by the arms.

"Aah!" Rikki cried.

QUINN RECEIVED ANOTHER JOLT. "Jesus! She's not doing well!" he exclaimed. "Hold on, Rikki. We're coming to get you."

She's losing her mind. Please hurry! Rikki said out loud.

LYNDSEY KNELT on the ground as she was placing the final candle beneath Rikki, then stopped mid-movement when she heard Rikki speak out loud. "Who are you talking to?" Lyndsey quizzed, putting the candle down. She shot up and approached Rikki with the knife, then held it to her throat. "Who are you summoning?"

"No one!" Rikki cried.

Lyndsey took the knife and lightly traced it along her neck before noticing her birthmark. She remembered what the journal had said about the power of enchanted birthmarks. "Interesting choice of words. Kind of what you'll become—no one. You will be nothing but a shell by the time anyone gets here," Lyndsey promised and slashed her birthmark with the knife.

Rikki cried out before Lyndsey shoved a rag into Rikki's mouth.

446

"Fuck!" Quinn called out in pain.

"What?" Caden looked over at Quinn. "Quinn! Your shirt…"

Quinn looked down and saw blood oozing through his shirt. "Shit!" Quinn's eyes darted back and forth. "I got her. I got her! I can feel the vibrations. We're getting closer."

LYNDSEY RUSTLED through her backpack and took out her wand, and anointed water. She turned toward Rikki, raising the wand and water as if presenting it to a higher power, and chanted.

"I SUMMON THEE, custodian of souls:
Rikki has been granted an unnatural ability.
I request you wipe her soul, for she's a liability.
She has used this gift only for evil,
And formulated my life's upheaval.
Choose a punishment you see fit,
And I will honor you with loyalty and submit."

WHEN SHE FINISHED, she threw the anointed water on Rikki's body, crouched down, and lit the cord on fire. She stood back, satisfied with her work, but unsatisfied with the fact that her anger hadn't seemed to dissipate. *What the hell? This is it. The moment that I've spent over half my life waiting for. She's going to suffer for the hell I continue to live. So what am I missing here?*

"Lyndsey!" August appeared as an apparition.

"August?" She looked him up and down. He looked young again and dressed the same night they kissed. It distracted her. *Ignore him. Stay on task.* "I can't deal with you being here."

"And why is that? Let me help you, Lyndsey," he begged.

She had passed the point of no return. "Leave me alone. You can't save someone who doesn't want to be saved."

"That lingering anger you feel is because the source of the problem lies within you, *not her."* He pointed behind him at Rikki.

"Oh, fuck that psychological bullshit!" She shook her head. "It's something else. I know it. I just need a moment to figure it out."

<hr>

ELLE PULLED up in the front of the house, ignoring the permitted parking sign. Quinn bolted out of the car before it came to a complete stop. Even though his birthmark was bleeding, he could feel Rikki was nearby. Elle and Caden weren't far behind. They met up once they got to the top of the driveway, then ran down the side of the property that led to the back.

Muffled screams caused Quinn's heart to ache.

They rounded the wall and saw it all. Rikki was hanging by her arms as flames waved dangerously close to her legs. She had a gag in her mouth and was crying hysterically. Lyndsey was mumbling to herself while she circled around Rikki. She was grasping the top of her head as if something was not going her way.

They stepped back and huddled as they began to come up with a plan, when Lyndsey's mumbling stopped. A condescending laugh bounced off the walls. "Aww, Rikki. Would you look at that? The cavalry has come to save the damsel in distress." Lyndsey snickered, then suddenly stopped. "Sorry, these openings are all protected. Look," she invited. "You should be able to see your reflection like you would a glass pane. Either way, you're in for quite a show."

Quinn leaned over to see if it were true. Not only did he see his reflection, but he saw Lyndsey lift her wand and chant while she worked up an electrical charge. The sound of static crackled through the room, and a controlled stream of lightning emerged out of her wand, striking the cord that held Rikki as she continued to cry out. Lightning crawled up the cord and along the ceiling.

By the time Quinn looked back at Rikki, she was no longer crying, and her head was slumped over.

"Rikki!" Quinn yelled, reaching his body toward the room.

Caden's arm quickly hooked Quinn at the waist and yanked him back. He pointed his finger at his face. "Get your emotions in check. You're not thinking straight, and you're going to screw this all up."

Elle turned her attention away from Lyndsey toward the guys. "Listen. The opening isn't protected from me because I enchanted the room when I lived in it, so it should know me for as long as it remains standing," Elle whispered. "We need to disarm her. I say all three of us enter together. Quinn and Caden, you take care of Rikki. I'll corner Lyndsey."

"She's cut Rikki, which probably means she has a knife," Caden said.

"And I have Gladys," Elle reminded them as she took her wand out from her pocket.

"Sounds good. Let's go," Quinn said impatiently.

Caden shook his head. "I don't know. I think we're being impulsive here."

"I'm open to suggestions, but we don't have all frickin' day," Elle asserted. Neither Caden nor Quinn spoke up. "Alright then. Are you ready to kick ass?" She turned and led the guys to the threshold. Elle merely blew on it, and their reflections vaporized. "Sorry, Lyndsey, but these walls know me, and they protect *me*!" Elle yelled triumphantly, pointing to herself.

Lyndsey growled. Her eyes burned with rage as she moved backward to the opposite corner where the openings of the two adjacent windows used to be. "I wouldn't step any closer,"

Lyndsey warned and pointed to the center of the pentagram. Their crystal sat in the center. A single ray of light stretched from Rikki to the crystal as if tethered together. "Rikki's soul is attached to the crystal. One strike of this wand will pulverize the crystal—and Rikki's soul." Lyndsey grabbed hold of the cord that was keeping Rikki suspended and jerked it hard enough to make the skin on Rikki's arms rip and bleed. Rikki didn't respond. "See? She's not crying out in pain. That's because her soul is weakening and growing more dependent on that crystal!"

⁂

Quinn could still feel her soul fading, but it wasn't completely drained yet. He was reassured when he saw a tear escape from her eye.

Quinn pointed to his birthmark. "Rikki's not as weak as she's saying. I say we call her bluff," Quinn whispered loud enough for Caden, who stood next to him, and Elle, who stood a few steps ahead of them, to hear.

Elle turned her head. "On three," she said quietly out the side of her mouth. "One. Two. Three." Elle hurried to the corner opposite Lyndsey.

"Stop!" Lyndsey yelled. She held out her hand to stop Elle's advance. Then took her wand and pointed it directly at the crystal. Static snapped all around as sparks fired from the corners of the room. Immediately, her wand siphoned the energy and expelled a charge that hit the crystal and lit up the room. They were blinded momentarily. A piercing crack came from the crystal as the light funneled into it. The longer she worked her wand, the more the crystal splintered.

Caden and Quinn charged toward her.

SHE REDIRECTED the charge at Caden and Quinn. Her determination, fury, and the help of the pentagram allowed her greater power. The charge paralyzed them before she lifted them off the ground and threw them out where the French doors used to be.

CADEN ROLLED DOWN THE HILL, hitting his head on a rock on the way down, before everything went black.

QUINN HIT the razor wire on top of the fence that lined the sides and back of the property. His body tangled within it, impaled in the spirals of spikes. The slightest movement, even his breathing, deepened each piercing puncture. He felt warm liquid slide down his face, arms, and legs. "Fuck!" he yelled out in anguish. *This isn't it. This isn't the end.* Grasping at his shirt, he grunted and yelled out in pain as the razor wire sliced further into his skin. He refused to surrender.

HEAVING IN ANGER, Elle, who had moved closer to Lyndsey while she was distracted with the guys, gripped her wand and began swirling it in the air. Elle's emotions gave her greater focus. Her inner Mozelle came to the surface as she harnessed more power than Elle had ever had before.

Elle watched as Lyndsey scrambled to find her next course of action. Lyndsey reached in her pouch and collected a handful of the powder she'd used to immobilize Rikki. In her hand, the powder swirled in unison with her wand, and she fired it in Elle's direction. The force blew out the candles, leaving only a couple candles outside the pentagram still lit, preventing the room from dropping into total darkness.

Elle tried to dodge out of the way, but the cloud enveloped her. She collapsed, rendered helpless.

Lyndsey directed her wand back to the crystal. It vibrated violently. The fissures widened. She took pleasure in the misery that besieged her surroundings … until August appeared again. His face was pain-stricken, looking at her in disgust.

"This is *me!*" she shouted at him. "Nasty is as nasty does."

"You're not lost!"

"And I'm about to prove you wrong!" Lyndsey yelled, then lifted her arm to finish off Rikki. Gripping the wand with both hands, a charge blasted out, striking the crystal. An earsplitting ring sounded as a bright light erupted from within as it cracked and then blasted into pieces. She froze in disbelief. Her trembling hand continued pointing the wand at the remnants of the shattered crystal.

Bloodied arms reached through the window opening, wrapping around Lyndsey's neck and covering her mouth. Her body was yanked backward through the window. Quinn threw her down to the ground. Straddling her, he held her wrists with one hand, and tore the wand from her hand with the other, then pressed the wand against her neck. She squirmed beneath him, but her attempts to free herself were in vain. The anger mixed with adrenaline that pulsated through him was no match for her.

Elle laid on her back on the rough floor, staring at the ceiling. Flames from the two candles flickered in her periphery. The

452

sounds of Quinn and Lyndsey struggling and the fact that she could not move to help out, made her sick to her stomach. The sounds of tearing caught her attention, and she looked to Rikki just as her bloody, hanging body plummeted to the floor. Tears tumbled down her cheeks, and she closed her eyes. *Get up, Elle!* her inner Mozelle yelled. *There's no time for self-pity or surrender!* Elle's eyes flew open. *Stand up, Elle! Stand up!* Her leg twitched, then her arms. She needed to act quickly and used her legs to roll onto her belly. With all her strength, she stood up. With each step she took to help Quinn, her nerves awakened, and soon she reached the outside.

THE CHARGE from Lyndsey's wand was like a live wire. Sparks continued to fire from the tip, and Quinn could feel vibrations hum through the wand.

Lyndsey stared at the wand as if commanding it to fight against his assault as he muscled the wand toward her face.

"Bitch! I'm going to kill you!" Quinn vowed.

Elle staggered to Quinn and threw her arms around him. "Stop! Stop!" she commanded. "You can't kill her. Rikki needs you right now. I've got this!"

"She needs to die!" Quinn was unrelenting and grunted as he strained to keep the wand moving toward Lyndsey's face.

Elle held him closer and whispered in his ear. "Please. You need to save Rikki. I will take care of Lyndsey," she assured and raised her own wand to prove it to him.

He caved. Still holding Lyndsey's wand, he yanked his hand from Lyndsey's grasp and shoved the wand into Elle's hand. He lifted himself off Lyndsey. "Show her no mercy," he said and climbed back through the window to get to Rikki.

His breath was caught in his chest when he saw her slumped over in a heap. The two candles outside the pentagon remained burning, as if unaffected by all the activity happening around them. He ran to her, fearing the worst. Not knowing if she could handle his touch, he reached for her anyway. He pulled her into his arms. She was lifeless.

"Rikki?" His voice was weak. He could see her chest moving up and down, but her eyes were closed. He placed his hand on her cheek. "Rikki!" he willed.

She opened her eyes, but they were dead. No color or life came from them as she looked around aimlessly.

"Oh no, Rikki," Quinn urged her to wake.

She continued to randomly scan her surroundings but focused on nothing.

"Fuck you, Rikki," he said through gritted teeth. "You can't leave me." He raised his voice, desperately trying to get a reaction from her. Any reaction.

Nothing. Quinn rocked her. She was right there, laying in his arms, and yet he didn't know how to reach her. No matter how much he touched her, called to her, shook her, she remained vacant. He opened her blouse. His teeth clenched over the brutality inflicted on her birthmark as it continued to ooze. Compelled, he placed his hand on top of it. At contact, weak vibrations channeled down through his hand but faded before it could surge through his body. He removed his hand and grabbed hers, bringing it to his own birthmark. The vibrations intensified.

"That's it, my love! Come back to me! Come back to me!"

The vibrations remained weak. "Damn it, Rikki. You can do this."

He looked around and saw shards of the crystal all around. Still cradling her with his left arm, he reached out with his right and grabbed two pieces of the crystal. He placed one fragment on her birthmark and the other in her hand. He took her hand, brought it to his mark, and then pulled her in.

Skin-on-skin, crystal on crystal, light emitted from their marks and lit up the room. The energy that burst out of them blew through the place like a shock wave.

"Rikki!" Quinn hollered. He looked up to the heavens, and tears began to spill from his sore eyes. A hand touched his face and wiped his tears. He looked down. Rikki was looking right at him. "Oh, no! Please, I'm not hurting you—"

Rikki shook her head, and Quinn pulled her to him with lightning speed. "Rikki!" he cried.

Rikki tried to wrap her arms around him, but her arms fell back down as if they were too weak to lift.

"I've got you, and I'm never letting go. I'm never letting go!" he sobbed.

"You have me," Rikki whispered.

They cried together in each other's arms for a very long time.

<hr>

PINNING LYNDSEY'S wrists with her knees, Elle, now in possession of both wands, began to strip Lyndsey of her casting abilities. She waved both wands together and chanted:

FAITHFUL CURATORS OF BALANCE:

Lyndsey is a dark witch who abused her power, and people were harmed.

She is a danger to herself, others, and our kind and needs to be disarmed.

· · ·

Elle siphoned the power of Lyndsey's wand into her own, leaving the wand nothing but a twig, which she broke and threw into Lyndsey's face.

Lyndsey struggled to free herself. "You think you've won. Magic or not, I *will* get my revenge," she promised.

Elle rolled her eyes. "Good luck with that."

She called out to Quinn to bring a cord.

After a moment, Quinn came out to her with a cord in hand. "Rikki's okay," he said, handing it to her.

"Great. Help me restrain her, and then I need you to check on Caden. I don't know where he went," Elle instructed.

***

Quinn ran in the direction he and Caden had been thrown. He hurried along what used to be the footpath where he'd realized that Robin was his soulmate, all the way down to where the chain-link fence lined the property. There, he could see Caden lying face down in the dirt. Blood pooled around him.

"Caden!" Quinn called out and ran to him. He saw he was breathing and shook him, but Caden was unresponsive.

"I'm calling 911!" he yelled loud enough for everyone to hear.

In less than ten minutes, police, paramedics, fire department, and ambulances were on the scene.

***

Elle stood over Lyndsey, who remained restrained while sitting outside the house where the fight occurred. Her eyes followed the paramedics, several in number, as they passed her by with Caden on a gurney. Her heart sank at the sight of him. One person was squeezing a bag to force air into his lungs, while another seemed to be ensuring his stability. Every part of his body was either strapped, pinned, or swaddled to render him immobile. She wanted so badly to be with him, but it was going to have to wait.

In addition to the bumps and scrapes she'd incurred, her exposure to the paralyzing toxin concerned her most, and she needed to be examined. Unfortunately, that, too, would have to wait—staying with Lyndsey until the police could take her away removed any chance of getting the immediate medical attention she wanted.

Lyndsey remained uncharacteristically quiet, but she frequently glared at the wand in Elle's hand.

"What?" Elle challenged. "Why are you staring at the wand like that?"

A smirk emerged on Lyndsey's face. "What you've done with the wand …" she said darkly.

Two police officers walked up to them before Lyndsey could finish what she was going to say. They made her stand and placed handcuffs on her before removing the cords and walking her to the police car.

Elle followed close behind. "Finish what you were going to say," Elle demanded of Lyndsey.

As they sat her in the car, Lyndsey looked at Elle. "Nothing. I was just admiring what you've done to that wand. You know what you've done, don't you?" Lyndsey asked, but there was grimness in her voice.

"Sure I do," Elle lied. All she had known in that pivotal moment was that Lyndsey needed to be stripped of her power. Never had she considered any consequences to her actions.

Lyndsey's eyes moved to Elle's. "I think you're lying. Look it up in one of those damn journals of yours."

A cop closed the car door before Elle could respond. He turned to her. "You really need to get checked out," he said and pointed her in the direction of the ambulance.

Holding the wand in her hand, she considered Lyndsey's

warning but dismissed it. Lyndsey was just messing with her mind. Even still, she made a note on her mental to-do list to look it up later.

She didn't want to take the wand with her to the hospital now that she wasn't sure what it was capable of. She quickly went to her car, hid the wand in the glovebox, then locked the doors before casting a protection on the doors. She glanced at the sign that read, 'Zone 1 Resident Permit Only—7 a.m. to 7 p.m.' She looked down at her watch. 9:05. *I'll be back before then,* she thought and walked back to the paramedics.

———

ELLE LAID in the ER for hours. In addition to the nurses and doctors that moved from one bay to another, the police presence could not be ignored. Then came the parents.

Farrah and Shane came in, giving Elle a big hug.

"I'm so glad you're okay," Farrah said and wiped her swollen eyes.

"Please, my Elle," Shane, her dad, started. "I got some of what happened, but we want to hear it from you."

"Shane, hun, we need to let her rest."

"Just tell me you're not part of some cult," he begged.

"No, Dad, I'm not part of a cult. It's just high school drama."

"That involves the teacher getting arrested?"

She wished she was in her temple room casting a spell to have her parents chill out, but in the meantime, she would have to endure the barrage of questions.

"It's a long story. I'm okay, I'm not doing anything wrong, and I'm not responsible for what the teacher does. We were victims here, Dad, so please just give me time."

Her parents nodded in understanding.

"How's everyone else doing?" Elle asked.

Farrah sat at the end of her bed. Elle knew the look that

emerged on her mom's face. She was about to deliver bad news. "We ran into all the parents in the waiting room. Rikki's parents and Quinn's dad said they would be just fine. They are tending to Rikki's burns and lacerations. Quinn is getting a few stitches as well. But …" She sighed. "It seems that Caden is still unconscious, and they have him in ICU."

"Oh no! Is he going to be okay?"

"They don't know yet."

"I need to go see him," she said and threw off her sheets to do just that.

A police officer stepped in. "Elle Windsor?"

"Yes," Elle replied and covered herself back up.

"We need to get your statement."

"Um, sure," Elle said.

<hr>

THE POLICE TOOK QUINN, Rikki, and Elle's statements. They explained in detail how Lyndsey had kidnapped Rikki and tortured her but left out the things that were too fantastic to be believed. For those details, each came up with believable explanations – Quinn got stuck on the fence on the way in but was able to disengage himself and stop Lyndsey from torturing Rikki any further. Caden had slipped and fallen down the embankment. They claimed not to know Lyndsey's motive.

<hr>

QUINN AND RIKKI were in bays next to each other, just as they had been when they got sprayed with pepper spray. Quinn chuckled in amazement at how much had happened in such a short amount of time, and yet that incident seemed like a long time ago.

As soon as Mason left Quinn to grab some coffee, Quinn

wanted to see if he could still reach Rikki telepathically, especially because he could hear her parents were still with her. He placed his hand over his birthmark.

"Rikki? Can you hear me?"

He waited in anticipation for a response.

"I can hear you," she said but sounded exhausted.

"How are you doing?"

"I'm okay. They have me on pain meds. I think they know me by name now." She chuckled out loud.

"What's so funny?" Quinn heard James ask Rikki, and couldn't help but laugh a bit with her.

"Nothing. I was just remembering something funny I said to Quinn."

"I'm glad that Quinn was there to save you," he whispered, but Quinn could still hear him and smiled.

"He's a good guy, Dad," she said to him. *I love you so much,* she said to Quinn.

"Do the stitches on your chest hurt? Why are you putting your hand there?" James asked.

"It doesn't hurt at all, Dad," she said.

Quinn exhaled in relief. *I love you too. Can't wait to be with you!*

Lyndsey sat in the interrogation room for an hour before a detective showed up. *This can't be good. Getting interrogated twice in the same day. Except this time, even though I can see that I didn't have a choice, they'll never see it that way. I am going to lawyer up to buy me time. At least I still have the ability to cast spells that don't involve my wand. Silly, Elle, thinking she completely took away my ability to use magic. I have one more* fuck you *before I disappear.*

The detective came in and gently placed a tablet of yellow, lined paper down on the table she was sitting at. He slid the chair out, took a seat across from her, and then leaned across the table, clasping his hands. He sighed as if wishing they hadn't had to meet under those circumstances. "Ms. Morgan, I'm Detective Sanders," he opened. "You're not having a great night, are you?"

"I guess not," she admitted, leaning back in her seat in defeat.

"Well, before we start, have you had anything to eat or drink? Can I offer you some water or coffee?"

She just shook her head.

"Very well. Before we begin, I need to read you this." He paused to reach into the pocket of his white dress shirt and put on his glasses to read her her rights verbatim.

She raised her hand and leaned in. "I'm going to stop you right there. I don't want to talk to you. I want to have an attorney present before any questioning."

He picked up his pad of paper like he respected the rules of the game. "Okay. That's your right," he said, then stood up and walked out the door.

Shortly after he left, one of the officers who had brought her there came in and took her to jail, where she spent the rest of the night.

EARLY THAT MORNING, a nurse came in to remove Elle's IV in preparation for getting discharged.

"I really want to see Caden," she said to her parents. "But I need you to do a few things for me. First, can you bring me a change of clothes, and second, I left my car parked in front of the Morgan House Ruins. Can you go pick it up for me? It has to be moved by seven, or it'll get towed."

"Elle, it's almost seven now," her dad pointed out. "And by the time we get out of here, it'll be well past seven."

"Shit. Okay, whatever. If it's there, great, but if not, I guess I'll have to get it from the tow yard."

"We'll head out once we can sign the papers," Farrah said. "Keep your phone nearby."

Once her parents left, she hurried over to see how Caden was doing. She walked into the waiting room, where she found Caden's parents sitting on a couch drinking coffee.

His mom, Raylene, stood up and gave Elle a warm hug. "Oh, Elle, I'm so glad you're okay."

"Thank you. I'm getting there," she assured his mom. "How's he doing? I would really like to see him."

"He's not getting worse, so that's good news," she said, tearing up. "So for now, it's a waiting game," she whispered to hide the wavering in her voice.

"Can I go in to see him?"

"Of course you can. We were just taking a coffee break. His sister, India, is with him right now, but you should still be able to see him. I think they're allowing two visitors at a time."

Her mom walked her to the front nurse and had her sign in before she was directed to the room that Caden was in.

She feared what she might see. As she neared the entrance to his area, which was partially covered by a curtain, India was sitting in a chair with her head back, quietly sleeping. Elle slowly moved the curtain aside. Her hand flew to her mouth, and tears burst out of her eyes. Long, thick tubes snaked around his body, through a neck brace, and down his throat as a machine breathed for him. She could see flecks of blood by his ear, just under the thick bandage that circled his head. His black and blue eyes were swollen shut.

India woke. "I'm sorry. I guess I fell asleep," she said, straightening herself up as if to prove she was not as wiped out as she acted. "He looks really bad, doesn't he?"

"Uh-huh," Elle said, her hand still covering her mouth.

"He'll pull through. I know it," India said, then stood up. "I'll give you time alone with him."

She sat in the chair closest to him. Her hand trembled as she picked up his hand and brought it to her cheek. "I'm so sorry," she said. Tears dropped off her chin onto his bed. "Please wake up so you can yell at me. I need you, Caden. What is taking you so long to wake up? I choose you, Caden. I choose *you*." Her chin quivered, and she lowered her head as she wept.

HER PHONE RANG, waking her up. She looked around, confused, not knowing how long she'd been out.

"Looks like your car was towed," Shane said. "We'll bring over your clothes, but then we both need to get to work, so we can't pick your car up for you. Not today anyway."

She sighed in resignation. "Okay. I'll have to deal with it later," Elle said.

Once she ended the call, she grabbed Caden's hand and held it to her cheek as she stared at him, willing him to wake up.

THAT SAME MORNING, Lyndsey secured a bail bondsman and posted bail. She was defeated and wanted to flee to Brazil to give August a proper send-off. Once she returned home, she was able to access the dark web, where she secured a ticket to Manaus, along with a fake identity, passport, and driver's license that would be ready for her within twenty-four hours. But there was no way she was going to leave with her tail between her legs.

She parked a block away from a gas station, then created a glamour to reduce her recognizability on any security cameras. She needed to act quickly before the glamour wore off. She told the clerk that she was out of gas and purchased a one-gallon can and an equal amount of gasoline to go in it. She hailed a taxi and gave the driver an address, claiming that her car had run out of gas near there.

The address was to Java and Book. She paid the taxi driver and pretended to walk to a car. As soon as the taxi was out of sight, she walked through the alleyway and into the corridor that separated Java and Book from the other shops. She poured the gasoline on the front door and front steps, then lit a match and dropped it, immediately setting the fuel ablaze.

She escaped using the illusion of a homeless person fleeing the scene.

Shortly after, she met up with a guy who went by the name of Abigor in the parking lot of the marina. Lyndsey paid cash for her plane ticket and her new assumed name, Cynthia Thomas, and fled without a trace.

ELLE WAS resistant to leave Caden's side, but she needed to give his family a chance to be with him, and she needed to take care of her car.

She took an Uber to the tow yard, where she was greeted by a man, who, according to what was sewn on his shirt, was named Sawyer. He was tall with squinty eyes, thin lips, and acne scars. His dark hair was stick-straight, and proper hygiene didn't seem to be high on his list.

"I'm here to pick up my white Kia Soul," Elle said.

"The white Kia Soul?" he asked, wide-eyed. There was something off in his voice.

"Is there a problem?"

"No. Um, no problem. Let me get the key to unlock the boot," he said, turning to a locker full of keys. When he reached for them, she could see his fingernails were painted black, and he had a pentagram tattooed on the back of his neck.

Elle raised her eyebrows. A knot twisted in her stomach as she began to pick up on his malevolent vibe. Her gut told her something was up with her car.

He began punching numbers into his old-fashioned cash register. "That'll be $537.69, and it needs to be in cash."

Elle's mouth dropped. "What the hell? It was just picked up yesterday. How did you get those numbers?"

"You have to pay the initial tow, mileage fee, then there's the daily fee, the hourly fee, and the release fee. And being that it's been here for two days … Yada yada yada," he droned.

Damn it! I don't have that cash hanging around. "How long do I have to come up with the cash?"

"You have sixty days before it goes to auction. But it's at a rate of fifty dollars per day until you come up with that cash."

"Wow. That doesn't seem right. Whatever. I left some, um, medication in the car, and I was wondering if I could go get it."

"You know, I just started working here, and I have to ask my boss if that's okay. Normally people just pay the fine, and we give them access to their cars, but if you're not taking the car now, I'm just not sure how that works. I mean, you could drive off with your car."

"But you just said there was a boot on it. How would I be able to drive away?"

"Oh, right, the boot," he said like he had forgotten it was there. He anxiously rubbed the back of his neck. "Well, I still have to ask."

"Come on. I need my medication."

He raised his eyebrow. "Why don't you tell me where the medication is, and I'll get it for you?"

"I don't want you handling my medication," Elle said. *I can't figure out what his deal is.* "Let me make a few phone calls."

She called her mom, who answered the phone frantically.

"Mom?"

"Oh, Elle, I was just going to call you," Farrah cried.

"What's going on, Mom?"

"Java and Book is on fire," she sobbed. "It's totally engulfed!" She could hear her dad comforting her mom in the background.

"What the hell?" She was in shock. "How?"

"They won't know until they put the fire out. This has been the worst twenty-four hours of my life."

Elle rubbed her forehead. "Okay. Shit. I'm at the tow yard, and they want all this money in cash to get my car. I guess I'm just going to have to come back. I'll head over there right now," she promised and hung up the phone.

She turned to Sawyer, who stood there with his arms crossed, one hand covering his chin. "I have an emergency. What's the daily charge again?"

Sawyer exhaled and lowered his arms as if relieved that she wasn't taking her car that day. "It's fifty dollars a day, and it's prorated at an hourly rate after that."

"Whatever," she said. "I need to call an Uber."

ELLE REMAINED AT HER PARENTS' sides for a couple days while they dealt with the devastation of losing Java and Book. She moved about in a daze, Ubering everywhere, too afraid to ask for help to get her car back. The only place that gave her any sense of comfort was at Caden's side. After being stabilized, he had been moved to a specialized unit for coma patients. There, he shared a room with another coma patient.

She ensured the curtain between him and the other patient was closed, then took a seat, thankful that the move out of ICU meant fewer machines, tubes, and wires, so she was able to sit closer to him. "Oh, Caden, how I wish you could hear me," she said, rubbing his hand. "There's so much going on. Lyndsey made bail, then Java and Book burned down. The police said they suspect she started the fire, but there's not a lot of evidence, and the worst part is that she is nowhere to be found. There's even rumors that she left the country," she said, then looked him in the eye to see if that shocking news would get him to react.

He didn't react.

She sighed. "Anyway, I'm just so glad that we have the support of our patrons and the community. They'll help us rebuild it." She grabbed and kissed his hand. "But what hurts the most, besides you not hearing me, is losing my sanctuary. I mean, I'm glad that I moved my journals and comp books after having that vision at August's, but that room is where I felt closest to my inner Mozelle. It's where I connected the most with my memories of my past life. My memories of being a person full of passion, love, and the desire to help people," she expressed, fearing that all those thoughts, recollections, and connections would blow away along with the ashes.

Her emotions exhausted her. She rested her head on the bed and closed her eyes. Horrifying images of cockroaches swarming at her feet entered her dream state. When she leapt away from them, they scattered, creating a pentagon and revealing her wand, which they had polluted. She covered her mouth to stifle her scream, instead coughed like she was dying of some lung disease. She turned around and left the dark, musty room she was in and found herself traipsing through the forest until she came to a precipice. The vision of Lyndsey clawing her way up the cliff, calling out August's name, reappeared just as it had in her previous life. Compelled to save her, she reached her hand out. Lyndsey's blackened eyes shot over to Elle's before she opened her mouth, allowing a scorpion to escape from the blackness inside. Before Elle could shoo it away, it crawled up her arm, up her neck, and into her mouth.

Elle jolted awake. Breathless, her eyes darted around the

moonlit room to reorient herself. The flashing green and yellow lights on a nearby machine were the beacons that evoked her bearings. She leaned over and pressed the heels of her hands against her eyes. *Damn it, that wasn't a dream. It was a warning.* "I need to get my car and wand back." She stood up, reached over the railing of his bed, and kissed Caden on his forehead. "I'm sorry to have to leave your side again. I'll be back."

———

She persuaded her mom to take a break from all the drama surrounding the fire and take her to the tow yard.

Sawyer was there again, which struck Elle as odd. He was the one who had towed her car. He had been there the morning she'd tried to pick up her car the first time, and now he was there again in the evening. Come to think of it, both times she had been there, no one else had seemed to be on the premises, which carried with it an eeriness she couldn't escape.

After settling the exorbitant bill, they followed Sawyer to her car, but at a distance.

"Oof," Farrah said. "There is something very off about this place and that guy."

"You feel it too?"

"I do," she admitted. "At least this will be our only dealing with him."

As Sawyer worked the boot, Elle looked around and noticed that her car was the only one with a boot.

"Why does my car have a boot on it, but the others don't?" she asked, crossing her arms.

"Oh, yeah, um, those cars are …" He paused. "Going to auction."

She and her mom both snorted. "So you're telling me that every car here, except for mine, is going to auction?" she asked, waving her arm around to demonstrate the vastness of his absurd claim.

He shrugged his shoulders. "I don't know what to tell you," he dismissed, then stood up after removing the boot.

"There is something very wrong about all of this," Elle huffed, then turned and approached the car. "What the—?" Her eyes grew wide at the sight of a dead cockroach on the driver's side window. *That vision.* "Jesus!" She flicked it off the window, then covered her nose and mouth over the strong smell of vinegar left behind. She looked back at Sawyer, who just stared back at her as if he was challenging her.

"Elle?" her mom said with suspicion in her voice, but it wasn't directed at Elle—it was directed toward Sawyer, who remained standing there.

Elle rubbed her forehead, uncertain what to do. She pressed the button to unlock the car, but it locked instead. "Wait, was my car unlocked?" Her heart pounded. *Holy shit, this is very bad.*

She threw opened the door and yanked open the glove box. The wand was gone. "Fuck!" She slammed it shut and shot out of the car.

"What the hell, Sawyer? Things have been stolen from my car!" Elle yelled, pointing toward the glove box.

His face turned dark. "We aren't responsible for items lost or stolen from the vehicle while in our custody. That's standard practice. File a police report," he said smugly, then took a step closer to her. "You have what you came for, Elle," he said, emphasizing her name. "You both need to leave now."

"Fine," Farrah surrendered. "Take me to my car, Elle," she directed and sat in the passenger seat.

Defeated, Elle got into her car and drove off.

"What was stolen, Elle?" Farrah demanded.

"Please, Mom. It's nothing. I mean, it's something, but please let me work this out on my own."

Her mom sighed in resignation. "Listen, Elle, I know that I

came down on you about using magic, and I'm sorry about that. I tried to stop you from going down the same path my aunt did, but I can't stop destiny. All I'm saying is that I don't want you to be afraid of telling me things. I promise not only will I not judge, but if you need my help, and I think you know what I mean, I'll be there for you."

"Thanks, Mom. That really means a lot to me."

"Are you going home or back to the hospital?"

"I'm going back to the hospital."

And with that, they went their separate ways.

<hr>

QUINN WAS LYING on his back, with Rikki in his arms as they floated in a raft along Stow Lake. Watching the clouds slowly drift, Quinn turned his head toward Rikki and gave her a lingering kiss on her forehead.

"This feels amazing," he whispered in her ear. "I could hold you in my arms like this for an eternity," he said, squeezing her. "These past few weeks, Rikki, have been so peaceful. I mean, after everything we've been through. From the moment our eyes met as Wade and Robin and having to fight our true feelings, to finally giving in, only it was too late. And just when we get to the place we're supposed to be in this life, Ms. Morgan, a.k.a., your daughter, decides to exact her revenge on us. Now we've finally reached this incredible point that some people reach in a matter of days. It's taken us two lifetimes, several curses, and the defeat of a dark witch to get us where we were meant to be."

"I'm sorry I was so impatient. I'm so grateful that you didn't give up on me even after I gave up on you." She caressed his cheek and turned his face toward her. "I love you, Quinn. With every vibration that flows through me, I love you!"

He leaned in and gently kissed her on her lips. "I love you too."

After a moment of slow and gentle kisses, they settled back into each other.

"I love it when the clouds look like waves," Rikki pointed out.

"I love your love for anything water. It's what got me to fall in love with you the first time. You know, standing in that garden, overlooking the bay," Quinn said. He let out a small groan, then planted a kiss on her forehead.

Rikki snuggled further into him, then hooked her leg around his.

"Rikki," he said, feigning a warning. "Please unhook your leg or else." His voice was low and seductive.

"Oooh! Or else what?" she teased.

Quinn flipped around and straddled her, locking in her wrists.

Rikki let out a playful scream and pushed against his hold.

When he saw her inflamed scars, he shot right up. "Shit! I'm sorry," he said, scooting to the back of the raft.

Rikki snorted. "They don't hurt anymore," she said, crawling up to him to regain their connection. The raft listed. Rikki's breath caught.

"Hold still," Quinn ordered, reaching out to her. She was just out of his grasp when she rolled in the opposite direction and the raft listed. Overcompensating, the raft flipped over.

They both came up for air laughing. The bottom of the lake was just within Quinn's tiptoe reach. They swirled around each other until they were in an embrace, staring into each other's eyes.

Rikki wrapped her legs around Quinn's waist. "Are you okay?" she asked, her lips barely touching his.

He swallowed reflexively. "Yes," he whispered, then closed the gap between their mouths.

Everything around them disappeared as the kiss grew unyieldingly in passion and depth. That was until the raft floated back, hitting Rikki in the head. They released each other with laughter.

Quinn helped Rikki back into the raft by pushing her rear up to hoist her in. He tried to hop in, but his belly got caught on the lip of the raft. He kicked to get him over the hump, but it was in vain. Stuck, he burst out in laughter, rendering him breathless and unable to speak. Rikki joined in the laughter and pulled him in by the belt loops of his soaking jeans. They rolled into each other, wiping their tears.

They rowed back to the dock. This time, they had come prepared and brought a change of clothes.

"Let stop by the hospital to see how Caden's doing," Rikki suggested.

"Sounds good."

When they arrived, there was a lot of movement in and out of Caden's room. They tried to get a glimpse of what was happening but were pushed back. Eventually, Elle emerged from the room with tears in her eyes.

"What?" Rikki's voice was full of anxiety.

"Caden's starting to wake from his coma."

"What do you mean?" Rikki asked.

"He opened his eyes," Elle said, giddy. "I mean, I know he only opened his eyes, but it's a sign of progress."

"Elle, that's great news," Rikki said and hugged Elle.

Quinn hugged her too. "I'm so glad to hear it. It's a big deal," he said. "I think he's going to pull through this."

"I think so too," Elle said, bringing prayer hands to her lips in excitement. "You're going to stick around, right?"

"Of course. We wouldn't want to miss this," Quinn said.

It didn't take long before all four were in the same room again.

By Thanksgiving, Caden's progression slowed. Elle recalled being told he was at the stage in his recovery they referred to as agitation, and she began to feel discouraged. He spent a lot of his days confused and even combative. But the doctors remained cautiously optimistic because even though his progression had slowed, it hadn't stopped. One thing was for sure—she wanted to be there with him every step of the way.

One day after she left the hospital, she sat in bed, remembering the details of their confrontation with Lyndsey. *You know what you've done to that wand of yours, don't you?* Lyndsey's words circulated her brain. She resisted looking at her journals. That would only give Lyndsey control over her, even after she'd supposedly left the country. *I can't tell if she was trying to mess with my head or what she was trying to do. But what if what I've done is really bad?*

She took out the blue journal that spoke of ethics and thumbed through it until she came across a section titled Wand Siphoning

Purpose: *To combine and elevate the power of a wand.*

Indications: This remains an egregious abuse of magic, and one needs to show extraordinary caution in the few circumstances it does not impose on an oracle's code of conduct.

It is commonly performed to strip another wand of its powers, but the consequences are great due to conflicting anointments the spirits have left behind. This is especially true if siphoning from a dark witch. The implications are enormous, as it invites severe and often unforgiving misfortunes, not only to the one who performed the siphoning but to those who were in contact with either wand leading up to the act of siphoning. Anecdotally, some report that it is further reaching than that in which it causes misfortunes to those close to the violators of this act. Some have claimed that if the wand isn't destroyed in a timely fashion, that misfortune will compound and can lead to the death of the soul itself.

Conclusion: Regardless of intention, due to the massive power the wand will possess after siphoning, the wand will need to be destroyed. See Wand Termination for instructions on effectively destroying wands.

"WHAT HAVE I DONE?" Elle cried, slamming the book down beside her. She reached for her phone and called Rikki.

"Hey! What's going on? Is Caden okay?"

"Rikki, I've made a huge mistake."

"Oh no, Elle," Rikki said lightly, as if not understanding the gravity of Elle's confession.

"No, Rikki. I really, really screwed up."

"What did you do?"

"I read what it meant to absorb the power and anointments of another wand. Rikki, we need to get my wand back—and fast, or—" Elle's eyes welled up.

"Or what?"

"Or it might be the death of all of us. And when I say death, I don't mean dying, reincarnating, and getting another chance. I mean, it'll be the death of our souls."

ACKNOWLEDGMENTS

I have to thank anyone who has crossed my path and allowed me to talk endlessly about my book and my writing process. I'm sorry if I bored you to death and didn't let you get a word in edgewise. But perhaps you nodded and grinned because you appreciated how I shined with enthusiasm. But for the ones that really were listening, I'm hoping my passion and excitement inspired you to do the things you love.

My deepest thank you goes to my husband, Dwain. I will never be able to thank you enough for working as hard as you do, so I can do what I love. I feel blessed every day because of it. I hope one day I can do the same for you. To my kids: Noah, Mariah, and Anyah - I love you, you're young, but know that you can never get too old to discover something new about yourself. You've helped me when I asked for it and even when I didn't. To my sister, Kasi, who has been here every step of the way, cheering me on, advising me, and inspiring me. And my brother, Brian, who has helped in other ways, like helping me with my website and my merch stores. To my mom, Jean, and dad, Leon, along with their significant others, Frank and Sara Jane - each of you have expressed pride in what I have done, and that makes me cry a happy cry. I'm crying now just thinking about it.

Thank you to my best friends: Tami, who has helped me when I needed an opinion on how something sounded and is the leader of my street team. And Lorrie who has been an amazing cheerleader and street team member as well.

Thank you to my editor, Jessica McKelden, who worked her magic *again* and made my book come alive.